THE HEARTS OF DRAGONS

Book Two of the Dragoon Saga

Josh VanBrakle

 Arboreal Press

Arboreal Press
Sidney, NY 13838
www.arborealpress.com

Library of Congress Preassigned Control Number: 2015933850
ISBN-13: 978-0-9891957-2-0
First Edition: 2015
Dragon image copyright Kuma/Fotolia.com

Find out more about the author and upcoming books by following Josh VanBrakle on Twitter @joshvanbrakle or by visiting www.joshvanbrakle.com.

ACKNOWLEDGMENTS

I want to first thank Shannon Delany, author of the YA series *13 to Life* and *Weather Witch*. In 2011, I attended a set of workshops Shannon hosted. Those classes changed my life. I'd long wanted to be an author, and Shannon's classes gave me the tools to fulfill my dream. You would not be reading these words were it not for her gifts as a writer, teacher, friend, and all-around fantastic person.

I also want to thank all those who reviewed drafts of this book: Jenny Lay, Tom Pavlesich, Tom Foulkrod, and of course my lovely wife Christine. Your edits, comments, and encouragement not only improved this book, they inspired me to keep going even when writing was hard.

I owe huge thanks to Heather Hilson, who once again showed her talents with an amazing cover design. Heather, your work, dedication, and friendship continue to impress.

Finally, Christine, thanks for embracing my weirdness. It isn't going away any time soon.

TABLE OF CONTENTS

CHAPTER ONE
Storm and Stone

A thousand years ago, Rondel Thara had made herself two promises. First, she would never forgive her husband. Second, she would never return here.

The old woman's steps reverberated across the abandoned entrance hall of Edasuko Tower. In spite of her five-foot height, the room's polished stone walls and distant ceiling made each footfall boom like a war drum.

The last time Rondel had walked through this room, nowhere on Raa could match it. Hundreds of the highest ranking Maantecs from the strongest clans had filled it. They had all come with the same purpose: to pay homage to their exalted emperor and his beautiful wife. Now, thanks to Rondel, they were gone and—unlike her—could never return.

But while its people had vanished, Edasuko's opulence remained. Despite a thousand years of neglect, the filigreed columns, priceless urns, masterwork paintings, and gold leaf inlaid into the floor showed no sign of damage or decay.

The tower's well-preserved state didn't surprise Rondel. No life, not even the most stubborn mold, survived long in Serona.

Rondel reached into her trousers pocket and pulled out the reason she'd broken her second promise: a palm-sized, flawless ruby. To anyone else, it would be a magnificent gem, one worthy of the finest queen.

Rondel hated it.

The only reason she'd kept the ruby these past seven months was because she hadn't known what else to do with it. Part of her believed the safest idea was to keep carrying it. After all, who could hurt the Storm Dragon Knight?

She scoffed. Plenty of people could hurt her.

Besides, even if someone didn't kill her over the ruby, she would eventually make a mistake. She would leave it in a cloak and forget it at a tavern. A thief would break into her room at an inn and steal it as she slept.

No, she had to hide it. That was the conclusion she'd come to, and that was why she'd come back here. Edasuko was the perfect location. No one but her could reach it alive. In the heart of the scorched land of Serona, the Burning Ruby and its foul dragon spirit Feng would be unable to threaten the world again.

Rondel ran a hand across her wrinkled brow. She couldn't linger. It was only a few degrees cooler in here than it was outside where geysers of white flame crisscrossed Serona's landscape.

Despite the sweltering conditions, though, Rondel found herself drawn to the rear of the entrance hall. There, in a room full of treasures, hung the room's most dominating aspect—four portraits, each more than fifty feet high.

As Rondel gazed at the paintings, she read the plaques aloud. "Belias Kui, Sky Dragon Knight." The giant figure had shoulder-length blonde hair that blew about him as he soared among the clouds.

"Nadav Moyasu, Fire Dragon Knight." Rondel clenched her fists. It was the actions of Nadav's power-mad subordinate Amroth that had forced her to hide the Burning Ruby here.

"Rondel Thara, Storm Dragon Knight." The old woman laughed at the absurd picture of her younger self, ten times her actual height. Her artist had rendered her in full steel lamellar armor, the battle attire of the Maantec nobility.

Eleven hundred years ago, the painting's unveiling had left Rondel breathless. Now she thought it looked amateurish, a caricature by someone who didn't know a thing about the subject of his work.

But then, how could he have? Back then, neither had she.

Then Rondel came to the final portrait. "Exalted Emperor Iren Saito, Holy Dragon Knight."

The sparks of Lightning Sight arced across Rondel's green eyes. She could still recall Saito's overjoyed look at their wedding and the soft touch of his lips on hers. Today, though, seeing his face only made Rondel hate him more. She might have Amroth and Feng to blame for bringing her here, but it was Saito who had allowed their evil to spread.

Rondel opened her palm and showed the Burning Ruby to the portraits. "You'd better not let this go anywhere," she said.

She looked around for a spot to conceal the gem, and that was when she noticed something wrong. At the corner of her vision, close to the hall's main doors, she caught a subtle movement. Lightning Sight made every detail plain to her, and what she had seen couldn't have been natural. She should be the only living thing for a hundred miles.

Rondel spun to face the new arrival. She stepped back in surprise. The newcomer looked like a person, but stone covered him from the bottoms of his feet to the top of his head. Only his mouth and eyes remained uncovered. In his left hand he carried a six-foot maul as though it weighed nothing.

The old woman grimaced. She knew that weapon, though she'd thought it lost after its Kodaman owner died a thousand years ago. It was the Enryokiri, the Stone Dragon Hammer.

Rondel slid the Burning Ruby back into her pocket. As she did, the Stone Dragon Knight's eyes followed the jewel's path. "Who are you?" Rondel asked.

The Stone Dragon Knight made no reply. Instead, he raised a rock-covered hand and launched three pebbles from it at Rondel's face.

Before the stones had covered half the distance to their target, Rondel had dodged them. Sending lightning magic to her muscles, she accelerated until her body blurred. She crossed the room in less than a second and landed in a crouch on her opponent's shoulders.

Rondel's dominant left hand drew the Liryometa, the Storm Dragon Dagger. "Evil must be annihilated," she hissed. She stabbed the nine-inch blade at her armored foe's head.

The hall rang with the clash of steel against stone, but the rock helm refused to crack. Rondel backflipped off her assailant, landed behind him, and swung her dagger up into his armpit. She figured the armor would be weaker at a joint, but the stone didn't yield there either.

Rondel leapt away, her back now to the room's massive doors. A glance at her dagger told her it was undamaged. Although she'd expected that, she still breathed a sigh of relief. Ryokaiten had greater durability than normal weapons, but they weren't invincible.

Her momentary lapse in concentration was all the opening her opponent needed. One second the ground shuddered, and the next Rondel was flying through the entrance hall doors. She landed outside on the baking earth. Dust surrounded her, and she coughed as she regained her footing.

When the air cleared, Rondel beheld her opponent. He still looked like a statue, but he had moved. No longer inside Edasuko, he had somehow gotten past Rondel and now stood between the old woman and escape. She could retreat back inside the tower, but it had no other exits. Her opponent had trapped her.

At least, he thought he had trapped her. Rondel fell into a run, her body a flash.

She was behind her foe and confident of escape when a wall rose in front of her. Rondel slammed into it. Her eyes teared, and she struggled to clear them. When she did, she saw that her opponent had enclosed them both inside a twenty-foot-tall circular stone barricade.

Rondel panted. Not since the Kodama-Maantec War had she faced an opponent this tough. Few earth mages could raise a wall this large, let alone do it quickly enough to outclass the Storm Dragon Knight's speed.

She needed a new strategy. Switching her dagger to her off hand, Rondel charged her attacker. As she did, she channeled magic into her now unarmed left fist. The Liryometa couldn't pierce the Stone Dragon Knight's armor, but maybe a point-blank lightning shot could. She punched at her foe's chest.

The moment Rondel's fist connected, she knew she had made the wrong move. Her lightning dissipated across the rock, and the impact shattered her hand.

The Stone Dragon Knight raised a boulder and launched it toward Rondel. It struck the silver-haired woman in the side. She rolled along the ground, wheezing.

Rondel cursed. She only had her off hand to wield her dagger now.

She couldn't breach her foe's defenses with that.

She looked around for another option. Above her Serona's eternal thunderstorm unleashed its fury. Though its rain evaporated before it reached the ground, the tempest released dozens of lightning bolts each second. No matter how strong the Stone Dragon Knight's armor was, it couldn't withstand one of those blasts.

Unfortunately, the lightning did Rondel no good. She had created that storm a thousand years ago, but it had long since surpassed her ability to control. If she tried to manipulate it, she was more likely to scorch herself than her opponent.

Across the hemmed-in space, a geyser of white flame erupted from a crevasse. When Rondel saw it, she knew what she had to do.

Rondel forced herself to her feet, sheathed her dagger, and pulled out the Burning Ruby. Lightning Sight told her that she had her foe's full attention. With all the strength her magic allowed her, Rondel hurled the ruby at the crevasse.

She had considered condemning the jewel to Serona's flames before, but she had rejected the idea. As much as she hated Feng, there could come a time when Raa would need his power. This Stone Dragon Knight, though, had left her no choice.

As expected, the Stone Dragon Knight's eyes followed the airborne ruby. Taking advantage of the distraction, Rondel drew her dagger and lunged. Her foe might have impenetrable armor, but that armor was incomplete. Rondel channeled lightning magic into her blade and thrust at her attacker's exposed mouth.

The blow never landed. As Rondel closed, the Stone Dragon Knight cast two spells at once. First, he created a hand of soil beside the crevasse to catch the Burning Ruby. Second, he extended his rock helm so that it covered his mouth. Rondel's thrust crashed into the armor. Sparks flew from the impact as stone and steel clashed, neither willing to give way.

Then, with a sharp *twap*, Rondel's dagger snapped two inches from the hilt.

The Stone Dragon Knight retaliated with crushing force. A hammerblow struck Rondel on the collarbone and dropped the old woman to her knees.

Her pain meant nothing. She was too busy staring at the broken dagger in her hand. The blade had survived more than thirteen hundred years. It had protected her family. It had even inspired her name. The weapon's round hilt, pommel, and crossguard made the dagger a rondel.

The earthen hand the Stone Dragon Knight had created approached. He retracted the armor from his left palm and picked up the Burning Ruby.

With the gem secured, the Stone Dragon Knight raised the soil around Rondel's feet to bind her in place. He then created a circle of stone around her. Slowly, torturously slowly, it started to rise.

Desperate now, Rondel cried for the second time, "Who are you?"

The rock walls stopped. The armor around the Stone Dragon Knight's face fell away. Rondel gasped. Her opponent wasn't a man, but a young-looking woman with long black hair. She looked vaguely familiar, but Rondel couldn't place her.

"Don't remember me?" the woman asked. "That's all right. I know you didn't help me out of charity, and had you known I was a Maantec, you wouldn't have helped me at all. After all, you hate Maantecs. You hate all of them."

Rondel strained to remember who the woman could be or how she knew her, but nothing came. The walls resumed their climb. "Well," the Stone Dragon Knight said, "tell Emperor Saito I send my regards."

Despite her position, Rondel managed to spit. It fizzed into steam the instant it hit the ground. "Never."

"I thought you might say that," the woman said with a shrug of her armored shoulders. "Fine, I'll make you a deal. Give my greetings to Iren Saito, and in exchange," she paused and grinned cruelly, "I'll give yours to Iren Saitosan."

Rondel's face turned ashen, and not from the fear of her imminent death. "What do you want with him?"

The Stone Dragon Knight laughed. "Can't you guess?"

Before Rondel could answer, the walls around her closed, sealing her in an airtight tomb.

CHAPTER TWO
Crippled

Iren Saitosan dug his toes into the sand as the gentle waves of the Yuushin Sea lapped against his shins. The cool water and briny scent invigorated him. All through the winter and now into spring, he'd spent every day of the past six months on this beach going through the same routine.

This time, he would succeed.

Iren put his hands together and held them in front of him. He pointed his left index finger across the water and focused on it until it was all he saw.

If he concentrated hard enough, maybe he could do it. Maybe he could breach the wall that his body had constructed inside itself, the wall that separated him from his magic and from his partner, the Holy Dragon, Divinion.

His body had created the barrier for its own protection. Iren knew that, but he didn't care. He couldn't go through life, a potentially eternal life, without magic.

Admittedly, he found his obsession with it strange. He'd grown up not knowing anything about magic. But Rondel had come along and revealed that his left-handedness marked him as a member of a magical species: Maantecs. At first he hadn't believed the old hag, but he'd since come to accept what he was.

Then his body had ripped that heritage away from him.

"Dammit!" Iren kicked at the surf.

"How long will you keep doing this to yourself?"

The female voice from behind him was melodious like the streams that filled Ziorsecth Forest. Iren turned and saw the speaker, a young-looking female Kodama in a long, green, silk dress. Her race's characteristic green hair cascaded from her head in tousled locks that reached midway down her back.

Iren let out a long breath. "As long as it takes, Minawë."

Minawë answered only with a concerned look. Iren frowned. Puffy rings encircled the Kodama's emerald eyes. She'd been crying again.

Iren had always considered Minawë a person of great strength. Though she looked twenty, her elegant face and lithe frame displayed a resolve few could match.

At least they had until seven months ago. That was when Amroth, overwhelmed by the Fire Dragon Feng, had attacked the Kodamas. The Fire Dragon had ripped Minawë's mother from the life-giving forest and let her succumb to the curse of her people.

Iren stepped past Minawë. He shook the salt water from his short tan hair, brown leather trousers, and white silk shirt. "It's sunset," he said. "Let's go back. It'll be dark before we reach the tree."

The pair climbed the hillside up from the beach. When they reached the top, they beheld the crater that had once contained the Heart of Ziorsecth, the largest tree in the world. The massive hole was more than five hundred feet across and two hundred feet deep. Just looking in it made Iren dizzy.

Only one thing grew within the crater. A single sapling, barely Iren's height, sprouted from the hollow's center: the new Heart of Ziorsecth.

Iren shook his head. The original Heart of Ziorsecth had towered thousands of feet in the air. It had been one more sacrifice to Feng's rampage. How many centuries would it take that new seedling to match its predecessor's splendor?

A flash of white beside the Heart caught Iren's eye. The Muryozaki, his old dragonscale katana and Divinion's resting place, gleamed in the evening sun. Six months ago he had left the sword in the crater to aid the tree in its recovery. If he couldn't use Divinion's magic, maybe the tree could.

Rather than cross the crater, Iren walked around it. He wanted to avoid the Kodamas' burial ground on the far side. Minawë spent more than enough time there. Just as Iren went to the beach daily, Minawë devoted every waking hour to kneeling at her parents' graves.

Iren understood her anguish. He was an orphan too. He knew what it was like to feel alone and abandoned. He'd lived that way his whole life.

Even so, he wished Minawë could find a way to overcome that grief. She was supposed to be the Kodamas' queen now, and her people needed a leader after the terrors of Lodia's invasion and Feng's attack. Yet Minawë hadn't once returned to Yuushingaral since Iren had recovered. The dead were keeping her from the living.

After hiking around the crater, Iren and Minawë entered Ziorsecth Forest. Darkness engulfed them as the thick canopy cut off the light of dusk. They walked another mile before stopping at a maple tree thirty feet in diameter.

No matter how many times Iren walked in these woods, the trees amazed him. More accurately, the tree amazed him. The entire forest—thousands of square miles—was in reality a single tree with many stems linked by a shared root system.

Tonight, though, Iren scowled at this stem's immense trunk. His fists tightened with frustration. Minawë raised a hand, and a large section of the trunk opened. Rotating on invisible hinges, it swung inward and revealed the hollowed-out space of the first floor greeting room.

Minawë gestured again, and this time a ball of light appeared in her palm. The orb floated into the tree and settled near the ceiling. Though tiny, it lit the chamber well. It cast its radiance over the organically carved wooden table and chairs designed for comfort and entertaining. In the back, it shone on the spiral staircase that led to the higher rooms within the tree.

Iren suppressed his anger, fearing Minawë would see. He needn't have bothered. She'd been too distracted lately to notice his moods. They hadn't even said a word to each other since meeting up on the beach.

It wouldn't have been like that seven months ago. They would have joked and teased one another. The briefest flicker of a grin crossed Iren's face as he thought about how Minawë used to call him "moron." He'd grown up taunted by everyone, so he knew she didn't mean it.

But Minawë hadn't called Iren "moron" for six months, not since the day he'd discovered he couldn't use magic. In a perverse way, he wished she'd say it to him, just once. He longed for proof that her mother's death hadn't turned Minawë into the shell Iren feared she had become.

Minawë created more orbs as the pair entered the tree and climbed the stairs. They passed the second floor, devoted to cooking, and the third floor, where the sleeping areas began. Minawë should have turned away there and left Iren alone to go to the guest room on the fourth floor. Instead, like every night, she went with him to light the way.

By the time they'd reached Iren's room, he couldn't take it anymore. "It's all right, Minawë," he said. "I can handle it from here."

The Kodama ran an uncertain hand through her green hair. "It will be total darkness. Can you manage?"

She meant well. She really did. That didn't make it better. "I can manage just fine!"

Minawë jumped back and covered her mouth. Iren sighed. "I'm sorry," he said. "Please go to bed. I'll see you in the morning."

Tears were in the queen's eyes as she left the room.

With Minawë and her magical light gone, the windowless room became utterly black. Iren felt his way to the dresser and pulled out a long Kodaman nightshirt. He changed into it and headed for bed.

But switching clothes had disoriented him. He smacked into a wall. It took two more minutes of fumbling to find the bed and crawl into it.

Iren lay awake a long time. He wondered how many more days he could put up with this. In Lodia, he would be one of the most powerful men. Even without magic, Maantecs had greater strength, speed, and resistance to injury than humans. Among the magic-dependent Kodamas, though, he couldn't even light his way to bed or open a door. He needed Minawë's help for the most basic tasks.

It wasn't fair. He had become the Dragoon. He had saved the world from Feng. Why was he being punished for that?

By the time exhaustion forced him to sleep, the answer still eluded him.

 CB

The dream came again.

It had started after his battle with Feng. At first Iren had dismissed it as delirium while he recovered from his injuries, but it had persisted. Now he had it at least twice a week. Tonight's was the most vivid yet.

He was inside a small house, sitting in a simple yet comfortable rocking chair. The rough, blocky wood under his fingers told him the piece was nothing of merit. Even so, its subtle motion and quiet creaking soothed him.

A fire burned in the hearth across from him, and above it hung the Muryozaki in its sheath. A layer of dust had settled on it. Iren had no use for it anymore.

He was more concerned with the woman in her upper twenties rocking in the chair next to him. Her head rested against his arm, her raven hair soft on his skin. Though she wore only basic homespun clothes, when Iren looked at her, he knew she was the most beautiful person on Raa.

She was all the more beautiful for the bundle she held to her chest, the child they had made together. As she rocked, she hummed a tune, soft and lilting. It rang at once of joy and sorrow, of love and loneliness, of boundless hope and endless despair.

Iren remembered the first time she'd hummed that song for him, though he couldn't place where or when it had happened. Back then it had made him smile. Tonight it nearly made him weep.

Choking back tears, Iren said, "He will be hated, just as I am hated."

The woman stopped humming. She looked at him with bold, deep brown eyes. "He will be loved," she declared, "just as you are loved."

Iren knew better, but he dared not disagree with her. Instead he smiled, leaned down, and kissed her on the forehead. "I don't deserve you."

She smiled back at him, and as happened every time she did, all his pain melted away, just for a few seconds. "You're tired, Iren," she said. "Go and lie down. I'll be in shortly. Our little man's almost asleep."

Iren rose and headed for the bedroom, but before he'd gone two steps, a knock came at the door. Iren's head whipped to face it. No one should be around this late at night.

The woman looked at Iren, concerned. He gulped as he walked to the door. He couldn't place why, but he knew this was no ordinary traveler. Reluctantly, he opened the door.

No one was there.

At that moment, as it happened every time he had the dream, Iren woke up.

CHAPTER THREE
Return to Lodia

This was it. Life or death depended on one shot.

Rondel stood inside her stone prison, now so hot from Serona's flames that she felt kiln-dried. Her teeth clenched the hilt of her snapped dagger. With her left hand smashed, she needed her right hand free to act as a conduit.

She concentrated for several minutes as she let all of both her own magic and what energy she could draw from Okthora flow into her right hand. For the purpose of escaping her cell, it didn't matter that she had broken her rondel. Its hilt remained intact, and more important, so did the three rings of kanji symbols stained into the red wood. Those rings connected her to the Storm Dragon's magic.

The old Maantec pressed her palm against the ceiling. Her hand glowed blue from the lightning coursing through it.

It had to be enough. She couldn't risk drawing more magic from Okthora, or he would rip control of her body away from her. That would admittedly release her from this prison, but it would cast her into one far worse.

At last she heard the detonating *crack* she'd been waiting for. Her cell shone white. The lightning bolt descending from the sky shattered the stone into dust as it connected with the opposite charge Rondel had built up on her hand to attract it.

Rondel didn't get a chance to enjoy her freedom. The bolt's energy overwhelmed the feeble magic in her hand. A shock ripped through her, and everything went dark.

CR

Iren stood again in the Yuushin Sea's surf, but everything felt different from yesterday. For one, the waves were higher this afternoon. Most broke against his chest, and the occasional one topped his head.

It was easy to see why. Thunderheads gathered over the Yuushin and filled the southwest sky with black. The waves would only increase in size as that storm blew in.

None of that bothered Iren. The tumultuous water suited his mood.

If he focused on his anger, maybe today he would get a result. During his training with Rondel, he had learned that strong emotions could make his magic act on its own. His feelings had killed the leader of the Quodivar bandit gang, and they had cured Minawë of her race's curse. Both spells had happened without conscious thought.

Iren stretched his arms in front of him. Concentrating on his left finger, he recalled his fury at bumbling around last night in the tree.

Five minutes went by, then ten, then thirty. Every wave crashed over his head now, and twice the current almost took him out to sea.

After an hour, he couldn't stand the punishing sea any longer. Iren stomped off the beach. He climbed the lip of the crater and sat down.

On the crater's opposite side, Minawë hunched over her parents' graves. Even at this distance, Iren could tell she was crying.

In his mind Iren heard the woman from his dream humming her lullaby. Her voice was strong yet soothing. She didn't use magic, and neither did he. When he was with her, he didn't need magic. He was a normal person, and she loved him for it.

Iren shivered. He cared for Minawë. He should be dreaming of her, but he didn't. He couldn't. Every day he stayed in Ziorsecth, he died a little more.

He made up his mind. He supposed he'd known it for a long time, but last night had settled the matter.

Iren slid into the crater and walked to the tiny Heart of Ziorsecth. Next to it lay the Forest Dragon Bow, the Chloryoblaka. Iren ignored it and instead picked up his katana. He slid the sheathed weapon into his belt.

Rocks tumbled in front of him. Iren looked up; Minawë was heading in his direction. "What are you doing?" she asked when she reached him.

The worry in her voice was so great that Iren doubted himself. But he'd made his decision. "I'm sorry, Minawë," he said. "I have to go."

"What?" She grabbed hold of his shoulders. "What are you saying? Why?"

Anger flashed in Iren's sky blue eyes. "Don't you understand? The Kodaman way of life relies on magic. I can't live like that."

"You don't need magic," Minawë replied. "You have me. Let me help you."

"You mean let you do everything for me. I can't even walk through the house alone. Without magic I'll be dependent on you the rest of my life. That's why I have to leave."

Minawë looked at him with despair. "Where will you go?"

Iren hadn't seen that expression on Minawë's face since her mother had died. He hated that he made her look that way, yet there was no escaping it. "Lodia," he said. "I won't need magic there. I'll be like everyone else."

"No, you won't," Minawë said. "You'll be an outcast, a traitor, and a Left. All the humans in Lodia are right-handed. They'll find out you're not human, and when they realize you're a criminal on top of that, they'll kill you."

"They won't recognize me. If they even remember Iren Saitosan, they'll recall a teenager, not a thirty-year-old man. Besides, I have to go to Lodia. There's a place I need to visit."

"Where's that?"

"My parents' farm."

Minawë's sad face turned to shock. "Your parents' farm? Why do you want to go there? I thought you didn't care about their murders anymore. I thought you'd given up on revenge."

"I did," Iren said. "That's not why I want to go. My father was the Holy Dragon Knight, even if he didn't realize it. If I go there, maybe I can find a clue about how to restore my magic."

"That seems like a long shot."

Iren shrugged. "It's the only lead I have."

Minawë hugged Iren so hard he could barely breathe. "If you regain your magic, will you come back?" Her voice was pleading.

He didn't answer right away. The black-haired woman from his dream appeared in his mind's eye, smiling in that way that could make all his pain vanish.

Iren pushed the thought away. She wasn't real. Minawë was. "I will," he promised. "I don't know how I'll regain my magic, or how long it will take, but when I do, I'll see you again."

Minawë reluctantly let go of him. Iren turned and headed up the crater away from her.

The moment he reached the tree line, Iren broke into a run east toward Lodia. He followed the empty swath of forest created by the old Heart of Ziorsecth's own eastward trek.

Even with the lack of undergrowth, though, his pace frustrated him. It was a tenth of what he could have managed using Divinion's magic.

Still, his Maantec muscles would let him go faster and take fewer breaks than a human. He would only need a few days to reach the border.

Once he crossed it, he feared he might never do so again.

CHAPTER FOUR
Traitors Reunited

Four days after parting with Minawë, Iren Saitosan stepped across the threshold of Ziorsecth and into western Lodia. He was used to the forest's dim light, so the morning sun on Lodia's open fields all but blinded him. He stumbled forward, shielding his eyes from the glare.

He'd only walked a few steps when he tripped and fell in a hole. Iren took in a mouthful of dirt and came up spluttering.

"Who on Raa put this here?" he demanded, though no one was around to answer. He waited until his vision adjusted, and then he climbed out and surveyed what he'd fallen into.

Iren took two steps back in amazement. The hole was thirty feet across and at least a dozen feet deep in the center. It didn't compare to the devastation where the Heart of Ziorsecth had ripped free of its roots, but whatever had landed here must have hit with a lot of force.

Dusting himself off, Iren headed southeast. He had no desire to travel on foot any longer than necessary, so he headed for the closest city, Orcsthia. He didn't have money for a horse or even food, but that didn't worry him. He'd figure something out when he arrived.

He'd hiked for several hours when he heard the telltale pounding of horse hooves. Iren paused to face the noise, and he spotted a pair of riders galloping toward him. Both wore thick leather armor and crude helms. One had a bow with an arrow already nocked, while the other cradled a spear across his lap.

When the horsemen reached Iren, they leveled their weapons. "Who are you?" the one with the bow asked.

Iren put his right hand on the back of his head. "Just a wanderer," he said. "Do you know how far it is to Orcsthia?"

"What do you want to do in Orcsthia?" the spearman demanded.

"An inn would be great. Can you recommend one?"

The spearman eyed Iren up and down. "You don't look like an ordinary traveler."

Iren had to give the guy that. His Kodaman silk shirt and leather trousers were definitely not Lodian style. He opened his mouth to explain, but then the bowman said, "Hey, what's that on his belt?"

With a silent curse, Iren realized his mistake. People might overlook his clothes as some odd fashion, but there was no mistaking his katana. No one in Lodia carried a sword like it, and even if they did, they'd never keep it on their right side.

"You . . ." the spearman gasped, "you're a Left!"

The bowman drew back his arrow. Iren threw up his arms and shouted, "Wait, it's a mistake!" He tried to think. "I'm not a Left," he said, improvising. "Actually, you just proved why I carry my sword this way. Bandits would love to attack a lone traveler on foot, but if they think I'm a Left, they'll leave me alone. Everyone knows Lefts are undefeatable in battle."

It wasn't much of a ruse, but Iren didn't need it to be. If the men believed him, they'd probably let him go. If they didn't, well, he'd reminded them how dangerous messing with a Left could be.

The riders exchanged glances, and at last the bowman lowered his weapon. "You shouldn't travel alone," he said. "People are going to think you're a spy."

"Yeah, we already nabbed one traitor yesterday," the spearman put in. "Don't make our job harder."

"Sorry about that," Iren said. "So would it be all right if I went to Orcsthia?"

The bowman scowled. "That's a different matter. The city's under martial law. If you want to go there, you'll have to come with us. Hand over your sword. If the mayor clears you, you can have it back."

"I guess I don't have a choice," Iren said. He pulled the Muryozaki, sheath and all, from his belt and gave it to the soldier. Part of him wanted to knock out the men and be done with this nonsense, but they were just doing their jobs.

Besides, hurting them wouldn't make him any friends in Orcsthia. He wouldn't get far in Lodia without a horse or provisions, and he should try to change clothes. The city was the only settlement within a day of here.

All the same, Iren felt ill at ease. Last year, he'd traveled Lodia's entire length without being stopped. Nobody back then would have questioned the business of a lone wanderer, bizarre sword or not.

It took the trio until early afternoon to reach Orcsthia's outskirts, and by then Iren was starving. He'd supported himself on food and water from the forest during his journey, but now he didn't even have a pack for supplies. That was one more item to add to his shopping list.

As he approached Orcsthia, Iren noted a system of earthworks surrounding the city. Workers had gouged a deep ring in the ground and then piled the fill in a wall close to the outermost buildings.

Iren scrunched up his face. The crude fortification looked new and hastily done. Its height varied, and the dirt hadn't settled. Iren had never been to Orcsthia, but he doubted the wall had been here a year ago.

At the city entrance, armed guards wearing chainmail stopped them and demanded identification. Iren's escorts each revealed a sheet of parchment with a wax seal. The guards nodded gruffly and then turned to Iren.

"He's with us," the spearman said. "We're taking him to the mayor for clearance." The guards didn't look pleased, but they ushered the trio through.

What Iren noticed first upon entering Orcsthia was the noise. People crowded the streets, far more than should be here given the city's size. Orcsthia was among the smaller of Lodia's cities, and it was more a hub for the surrounding farmers, mostly sheepherders, to bring their products to market.

Today must have been an active market day. It seemed like all the farmers for miles had brought not only their wares, but their flocks as well. Before long Iren and his guards were wading their way through a three-foot sea of bleating fluff balls.

Worse than the noise was the smell. Between the overcrowded conditions and all the animals, Iren couldn't help but pinch his nose. Contrasted with the meticulous clean of his childhood home in Haldessa Castle, this place better resembled a neglected latrine than a city. Garbage and waste, both animal and human, coated so much of the street that Iren couldn't avoid it.

Iren's escorts wound their way through the mass of humans and livestock until they reached the city square. The spearman smirked. "Looks like the mayor isn't wasting any time with that traitor," he said. He looked down at Iren. "It's your lucky day, traveler. I think we're just in time for a beheading. It'll be good for you to see it. If the mayor doesn't approve of you, that's where you'll end up."

Iren was in no mood to watch an execution; he'd come close enough to one himself last year. He thought he should be friendly, though, so he asked, "Who's the traitor? You said you caught him."

The spearman beamed with pride. "You bet I caught him, and what a catch! Once his head rolls and I get my reward, I'll never have to work again."

Looking across the body-to-body expanse of the city square, Iren observed the criminal. The condemned man stood on a platform above the crowd alongside an executioner and several soldiers. He wore ragged clothes, and he had a hood covering his head. He didn't seem like someone who would have a price so high a captor could retire after catching him. "What's his name?" Iren asked.

"B-something, I think," the spearman replied. "I don't remember exactly, but I do know that during Amroth's regime, he was the king's general! At least he was until he turned traitor and went to those cursed Kodamas. I wish I could kill the straw-haired filth myself. I lost my brother in that battle. I told him to ignore the draft like I did, but he never could do anything the least bit shady."

It was good the spearman was busy with his diatribe, because Iren had lost all color in his face. The executioner ripped the hood off the criminal's head, and that removed any doubt about the man's identity. Unable to control his panic, Iren whispered, "Balear!"

"Huh?" the spearman looked down from his horse. "Yeah, that's it. That's the guy's name. You a draft-dodger like me, Mr. Not-a-Left?"

"Something like that," Iren said as he worked to calm his hammering pulse. He couldn't let Balear die, not after all they'd gone through together. But a hundred yards, and the dragons knew how many people, separated them. He'd never reach his friend before the axe fell.

Unless . . .

Iren eyed the bowman, who had his full attention on the execution stand. The Muryozaki hung loosely from his saddle on the same side as Iren.

The young Maantec frowned. More than likely, this plan would kill him. If he didn't try, though, he'd regret it forever.

His strike came in a fluid burst of motion. Using his Maantec strength, Iren vaulted onto the bowman's horse behind the rider. He kicked the man in the head. The soldier fell from his horse, unconscious.

Iren freed the Muryozaki and drew it. The spearman's focus had drifted back to Balear, but the noise of his collapsing partner put him on alert. He had just enough time to shout a curse before Iren knocked him out with a blow to the head from the Muryozaki's dull side.

With his guards out of the way, Iren swung his katana and hit the spearman's horse on the rump with the blade's flat. The startled beast shrieked and charged into the square. Bedlam ensued as people screamed and fled from the crashing hooves.

Taking advantage of the break in the crowd, Iren rode the bowman's horse closer to Balear. The former general was already on his knees. Two men pushed on his back to force his head onto the chopping block.

Iren still couldn't reach the platform, but that was all right. The chaos in the square had distracted the executioner from his duty. The axeman ran to the guards surrounding the platform and jabbed a finger at Iren. The soldiers stormed through the crowd toward him.

He couldn't have asked them to do him a better favor. The guards' unsheathed weapons made all the residents between them and Iren flee the square. Iren now had a clear path to the execution stand.

Leaping from his horse, he charged the first soldier. The man wore an iron skullcap and heavy leather, but his face was unprotected. Iren swung the Muryozaki's back into the soldier's nose. Blood spurted, and the soldier fell to the ground, clutching his wound.

Iren raised the dragonscale katana high in his left hand to let the other guards know his heritage. "Left!" one of them cried. All of them backed away. Iren scaled the platform, ducked a blow from the axeman, and sent the would-be executioner tumbling to the ground with a shoulder charge. The unarmed men holding Balear released their prisoner and ran away without a fight.

Iren hauled Balear to his feet. The usually meticulous soldier looked like a beggar. His blonde hair hung long and scraggly, and he had a beard to match. His face was drawn and gaunt. When he saw Iren, though, his eyes lit up with mingled joy and astonishment.

"What on Raa are you doing here?" he asked.

Iren cut the bonds that tied Balear's hands behind his back. "Let's get out of here first. Can you fight?"

Balear rubbed his wrists. They were bloody and raw from the thick cords. "I would prefer not to."

"Believe me, so would I."

Whistles sounded across the courtyard. Dozens of soldiers poured into the square.

Iren surveyed the terrible odds. "We make for the west exit," he said. He didn't know if it was the fastest way out of the city, but at least he was familiar with that route thanks to his former escorts.

With a shout, Iren jumped off the execution stand. There was no other choice. The Muryozaki flashed, and a guard stopped breathing. Balear grabbed the man's sword and followed Iren.

As they dashed through the square, Iren's vision faded into the haze of combat. The battle for their lives became like a dance. Step, parry, thrust. Step, parry, thrust. One, two, three . . . one, two, three . . .

The rhythm stopped. Fifty guards surrounded them. Even Iren's Maantec abilities couldn't overcome those odds.

Balear put his back against Iren's. "I don't suppose you'd care to show them any of those moves you used against Feng, would you?"

The man was right. Iren needed magic, and he needed it now. He extended his right arm. Focusing his effort on his open palm, he called for Divinion to help him.

Nothing happened. No beam of white light knocked his enemies unconscious; no shield of energy surrounded him.

"Are you kidding?" he shouted. "It still doesn't work!"

The guards knew they had won. "Lay down your weapons," one of them called, "or die!"

Balear dropped his sword. "That's it, Iren. Thanks for trying, but we're not walking away from this one."

Iren sheathed the Muryozaki and put his hands on his head.

As the soldiers closed to capture them, a pebble bounced off a guard's helm and skittered to the ground. Several of the men turned to look, and at that moment, a black blur rushed in.

Two guards collapsed as a fist and a foot simultaneously connected with their faces. Three more dropped before the soldiers realized they had a new threat to confront.

The newcomer paused a second. Iren's jaw fell as he got his first good look at his rescuer.

It was a young woman with long black hair.

"Stop standing there and come on!" the girl cried. Then she was gone, leaving an opening in the guards' line where she had struck.

Iren pulled himself from his daze. Grabbing Balear, he shouted, "Hurry!" and chased after the woman.

"Who are you?" he asked when he and Balear caught up to her. Her straight hair had a red ribbon tied in it and whipped behind her as she ran. "Why are you helping us?"

"Questions later," she yelled, "if we're not all dead!"

The trio raced through the streets of Orcsthia, forcing their way through flocks of sheep as they headed back the way Iren had been escorted in.

But Iren knew what was waiting for them this way. "The exit on this side of the city is guarded," he said.

Their rescuer's pace didn't falter. "They're all guarded," she replied. "I hope you're decent with that katana."

Iren stumbled and nearly fell on his face. Humans didn't use katanas; they were Maantec weapons. "How do you—"

"I said 'questions later!'"

That ended the conversation. Up ahead, the gate guards stood at the opening of the earthen wall. Instead of the original two, though, fifteen men now blocked the exit.

Iren drew the Muryozaki. He slashed out and caught a soldier in the throat before the poor man could swing his weapon. The woman took the guard's blade before joining the battle herself. Balear collapsed on his knees, exhausted from his near execution and brutal rescue.

Iren ran to his friend's side to shield him from blows. Their new ally looked over her shoulder at them and scowled. Spinning in a circle, she disemboweled the three men attacking her with a single attack. She then sprinted to Iren and heaved Balear onto her shoulders. "Let's go!" she commanded. "I'll take him. You hold them off."

They rushed the gate together. Four men tried to body-block the exit, but the sight of Iren's katana in his left hand made them panic. Iren, Balear, and the woman passed the gate. Iren spun around, expecting pursuit, but the soldiers withdrew.

Relieved, Iren ran to catch up with Balear and their surprise savior. Both had blood on them, but Iren couldn't tell if it was theirs or some-one else's. Balear had lost consciousness, so Iren and the woman took turns carrying him as they fled the city.

An hour later, a farm appeared in the distance. "There's our desti-nation," the woman said. Iren still didn't have a clue what was going on, but this woman's sudden appearance and willingness to help him peaked his curiosity. He would see this through until he got some answers.

After another fifteen minutes, they reached the nearest structure on the farm, a barn, and ducked inside. Iren laid Balear on a pile of straw. After checking to make sure his friend wasn't injured, he faced their res-cuer. "I appreciate your help," he said, "but now an explanation would be nice."

The woman pointed at the Muryozaki. "You already know the answer. I'm a Maantec too."

CHAPTER FIVE
Lodia's Downfall

In retrospect the woman's heritage was obvious. No human could move with the fluidity she possessed. More telling, she held the sword she'd stolen from the gate guard in her left fist.

"I didn't think there were other Maantecs in Lodia," Iren said.

"There are more than you might think," the woman replied. "It isn't hard to pose as human. You move around now and then so people don't wonder why you aren't aging. Or, like my parents, you farm in the middle of nowhere. And of course, you have to do everything with your right hand." She raised her right palm and eyed it with disdain. "By the way, my name's Hana, Hana Akiyama. Nice to meet you."

"Likewise," Iren said with a smile. "I'm Iren Saitosan."

Hana started. "Seriously? The Iren Saitosan?"

"I didn't know I was famous."

"There are wanted posters all over Orcsthia advertising a huge reward for your capture. But they describe a teenager, not a grown man."

"I've had some interesting times," Iren said with a grimace. Maantecs aged only when they used their biological magic, the energy that gave them their immortal lives. Divinion had forced Iren to use some during the battle with Feng. It had saved Iren's life, but it had aged him ten years. It was one more punishment for saving the world.

Iren pushed away the memory. To distract himself, he focused on the woman in front of him. By all appearances, Hana was twenty, but that only meant she hadn't used any biological magic. She could have been born centuries ago. Iren wondered how old she was.

Remembering a similar situation with Minawë, he decided not to bring it up. "Why did you rescue us?" he asked instead. "And what is this place?"

"This was my family's sheep farm," Hana replied. "We should be safe here, at least for a while. No place in Lodia is truly safe these days. I was in Orcsthia selling the last of our flock when I heard the commotion in the square. When I saw you fighting alone against those guards, I decided to intervene. Lucky for you, eh?"

"I guess so," Iren said. He paused a moment, and a thought came to him. "You said 'we' a moment ago. Do you have relatives here, other Maantecs?"

Hana's expression darkened, and she turned away from him. "No," she said. Her voice caught. "My parents lived happily on this farm for years, until six months ago."

Iren frowned. Six months ago wasn't that long after Amroth's defeat at Ziorsecth. "What happened?"

Hana started to answer, but at that moment, Balear stirred. Iren and Hana ran to him. "Are you all right?" Iren asked.

Balear groaned. "Where am I?" He blinked twice and tried to sit up, but he fell back in the straw. He clutched his head with his hand. "Everything's spinning," he said. "You didn't make me drink Kodaman brandy by any chance, did you?"

Iren recalled the pungent odor of the maple-based liquor. "Sorry, old friend," he said, "no such luck."

The soldier's eyes struggled to focus. "So we survived?" he asked. "I was sure I would die back there. What happened?"

"An angel dropped out of the heavens and rescued us," Iren said with a flourish. "A left-handed angel by the name of Hana."

Hana blushed as Balear looked at her. "It was nothing," she stammered.

Now it was Balear's turn to blush. "It's an honor," he said, "to make the acquaintance of a woman at once so beautiful and capable in battle."

Iren rolled his eyes. "If you're well enough to flirt, you're well enough to tell me what's going on. Why was Orcsthia's mayor going to execute you?"

Balear shifted himself into a more comfortable position on the straw. "I left Ziorsecth six months ago to help restore peace in Lodia. You know that much."

Iren nodded. He remembered all too well the sad day two of his closest friends—Balear and Rondel—had departed the forest. He'd probably made Minawë feel the same way he'd felt back then.

He forced down a wave of guilt. "I trust it didn't go as planned."

"No, it didn't," Balear said. "I expected instability after Amroth's death, but I never thought a civil war would break out."

"A civil war?" That would explain why Orcsthia had constructed its earthen defense. Still, Iren had a hard time believing Lodia would fall apart because of the death of its lunatic king, Amroth.

"What did you expect?" Hana asked. "If you're General Balear Platarch, former head of the First Army of Lodia, you must have known what would happen when the Succession Law went into effect."

"Succession Law?" Iren felt like a Tacumsahen parrot, spitting back whatever someone else said. Yet he couldn't help but be confused. None of what Balear and Hana were saying made sense.

"Do you know how succession works in Lodia?" Balear asked him. "How the next king is chosen when one dies?"

Iren knew it all right. Last year Amroth had used that process to rise to power. "When the king dies, his first legitimate son replaces him," Iren said. "If the king has no legitimate son, then his chief advisor becomes the king."

"Right," Balear replied. "That's how Amroth became king even though he wasn't of royal birth. King Azuluu made him his chief advisor. But what would happen if a king died without either a legitimate son or a chief advisor?"

Iren stiffened. Amroth hadn't sired any children, and he never would have suffered an advisor. "I assume there's some process for choosing a new king."

"There is," Balear said. "It's called the Succession Law. If a king dies without a legitimate son or a chief advisor, the mayors of Lodia's large towns and cities gather in a council. They then choose who among them should become the next king."

"That sounds like a good idea," Iren said. "I don't understand why a rule like that would lead to civil war. After all, Lodia isn't that big. It only has a handful of cities."

"Actually, it doesn't," Hana interjected. "The Succession Law was written eight hundred years ago, less than two centuries after the Kodama-Maantec War. That war wiped out most of Lodia's population, and the country had yet to recover. Because the kingdom had so few people, the Succession Law's definition of a 'large town' was a lot smaller than what we would consider it today."

"And that definition was?"

"A hundred residents or more."

Iren whistled. There were unnamed farming villages that could meet that threshold.

"The law states that all the mayors of all these towns have a right to attend the council and potentially become king," Balear said. "Unfortunately, the law's creator never thought there would be so many towns with more than a hundred people. He didn't bother laying out a framework for when, where, or how the council would take place. He assumed the list of towns would be more like four or five, so the few mayors could easily communicate and come to a decision. With hundreds of towns involved, it's become total anarchy."

"Why wasn't the law changed as the population rose to keep this from happening?" Iren asked.

"Because the law's never been necessary until now. Most kings appoint advisors right after their coronation. King Azuluu was an exception in that he waited twenty years before choosing Amroth. As a result, no one ever saw a reason to change the law, even as it became outdated."

"Without a clear rule," Hana put in, "the towns turned against each other. A few have formed alliances, but it's pretty much every community for itself. The rural areas have suffered the most. Raiding parties attack farms to secure food and money. They capture anyone they think will be useful, and they kill those who put up a fight. It's chaos. The Succession Law has become Lodia's downfall."

Iren thought back to the pair of Orcsthians who had accosted him outside Ziorsecth. They probably didn't see many strong young men roaming alone these days. That's why they'd let him come to the city. They'd known all along that once he entered, he wouldn't be allowed to leave unless he joined them.

This wasn't the Lodia Iren remembered. This wasn't even the Lodia of Amroth. The nation had gone mad.

He wanted to help. If he could use magic, he could side with one of the towns and give them an advantage.

But that was pointless speculation. He didn't have magic. Even if he did, the last thing the people of Lodia would want was another Dragon Knight dictating to them.

"I did what I could," Balear said. He sounded like he wanted to convince himself more than Iren or Hana. "Over the past six months, I've traveled the country trying to get the mayors to hold their council. No one listened. Most threw me out. A few tried to kill me. I always escaped, but Orcsthia was too much. They're one of the strongest cities right now. Being so far from Haldessa, they were among the last to receive Amroth's conscription decree. A lot of the men ignored it. I thought that if I could convince Orcsthia to seek a peaceful solution, the other towns would recognize its strength and agree. Instead, the mayor declared me a traitor and planned to execute me. He even told the soldiers who captured me that he'd pay the bounty Amroth put on my head to show the country he was still a loyal Lodian."

"Strictly speaking, he wasn't wrong," Iren pointed out. "You are a traitor to Lodia."

"Not to Lodia!" Balear retorted. "And not a traitor! Amroth betrayed Lodia, not me. When I left him and joined the Kodamas against his army, I didn't do it to betray Lodia. I did it to save this kingdom from the demon that was Amroth."

"In so doing," Hana said, "you released an even worse devil."

"I know that," Balear spat. "That's why I haven't given up. I'll keep going to towns until someone listens. Someone besides me must hate this useless bloodshed." He paused and looked at Iren. "You'll help me, won't you? With the Holy Dragon, we can end this war in a month."

Iren's eyes went to the floor. "You saw what happened when the guards cornered us. Six months have passed since we parted, and I still can't use magic. I'm sorry, but I can't help you."

Balear looked taken aback. "If you didn't come because of the civil war, why did you leave Ziorsecth?"

"I want to visit my parents' farm. If I go there, I might find a clue about how to regain my magic."

Balear was silent for a minute. He scratched his chin. "Suppose you could use magic again," he said at last. "Would you be willing to help me then?"

In truth, Iren had hoped to return to Ziorsecth and Minawë. After seeing Orcsthia and hearing Balear's and Hana's tales, though, he couldn't refuse. "Yes," he said, "I can't stand by and let this country rip itself apart."

"In that case, I'll go with you to your parents' farm and help you however I can," Balear said. "I could use a break from getting thrown in dungeons anyway. Do you know where the farm is?"

Iren nodded. "When Amroth told me about the night my parents died, he mentioned Tropos Village. I think the farm is near there."

"Tropos?" There was a waver in Balear's voice. "You're sure that's what he said?"

"Absolutely. Lies or not, every word of that conversation is burned into my brain."

Balear's tongue flicked in and out. "I'm not sure that's a good idea. Tropos is close to Haldessa, and that's on the other side of the country. Crossing Lodia these days is dangerous. We could be set upon by raiders, or outlaws, or even a city's army."

Iren folded his arms. "Don't come then. Go back to Orcsthia and let me know how they welcome you. I'm going to Tropos. If you want me to help you restore peace in Lodia, you'll have to come with me."

"When you put it that way, I guess I can't dissuade you," Balear said. "So be it. As it happens, my mother lives in Tropos, so I know where it is."

Iren couldn't believe his good fortune. Helping Balear had almost killed him, but now he had a path to his parents' farm, even if it was hazardous. "It's settled," he said.

Hana threw up her hands. "What do you mean, 'settled?' You think you'll just wander on over to Tropos without any horses or supplies? Maantec or not, you can't cross Lodia that way."

"She has a point," Balear said. "Maybe we should go somewhere closer, like Caardit."

"No!" Iren shouted. "Nowhere else matters to me right now. I have to reach Tropos."

Hana grinned. "I might be able to help with that."

Iren and Balear looked at her in surprise. "What do you mean?" Iren asked.

She gave them a sly expression. "You've already made one scene today. What's the bother in causing another?"

Iren groaned. "You aren't suggesting we go back to Orcsthia, are you? Every soldier there will be looking for us."

Hana's mysterious look didn't change. "We don't have to go to Orcsthia. If I'm right, they'll come to us."

CHAPTER SIX
The Warm Hearth

The decades-old memory floated unbidden into Rondel's consciousness. She had forgotten it years ago, but now it resurfaced as clearly as the night it had happened.

She'd been walking the nighttime streets of Orcsthia, a grimy city filled with grimy humans. She had gone there with a purpose, but the journey had proven a waste of time. The object of her search was no longer there.

She would have left that night had it not been for the rain. It had been pouring, and Rondel's woolen cloak had clung to her.

The nearest inn had been a place called the Warm Hearth. The owners called it that because that was the best anyone could say about it.

Rondel had just spotted the inn's sign when she saw the struggle. Under the building's overhang, three men surrounded a young woman with long black hair. The girl lashed at her attackers, but she was no fighter. Two of the men held her against the wall, and the third had his hands on her chest.

Rondel scowled. She didn't need this. She was already in a bad mood. Her left hand brushed her dagger to check its position. Then she stepped under the overhang.

"Excuse me!" she said, adopting a wide grin and staring stupidly at the men. "What are you all doing there?"

When they ignored her, Rondel flapped her cloak and made a loud show of brushing off the rain. "Some storm," she said. "I'd hate to be traveling unprotected in it. You never know what you might run into."

The man in front of the girl shifted to face Rondel. His trousers were open. "Beat it," he spat. "We're busy here."

Rondel flicked her eyes to the trapped woman. "It seems you are. Run along, little girl. These three deserve a real woman like me."

One of the men restraining the girl laughed. "Like we'd want a shriveled old witch like you!"

"That was rude," Rondel said. Her grin vanished, and her voice dropped in pitch. "I'll have to teach you some manners. Let's start with something even your simple brains can understand: evil must be annihilated."

The three men never had time to scream.

Rondel wiped her blade clean and stepped back into the rain. She would stay somewhere else.

She was almost out of sight of the inn when a voice called, "Wait!"

Rondel turned. The young woman was running through the downpour toward her.

"I wanted to thank you," the girl said when she caught up.

"It was coincidence," Rondel replied. "I didn't do it for charity. Those men got what they deserved. Even so, in the future, you shouldn't wander alone."

"In that case," the girl said, "can I come with you? Will you teach me to defend myself?"

That wasn't what Rondel had meant. She frowned and asked, "Why?"

"Because sometimes Lefts like us need to wander alone."

Rondel put her back to the girl. "Not interested."

She stormed off, but she'd only gone four steps when she heard the words that froze her. "You're Rondel Thara, aren't you?"

Rondel whipped around. "How could you know that?"

"A strong, elderly woman with a dagger she holds in her left hand? There's no one else you could be. My parents told me stories about you."

"If your parents told you stories about me," Rondel said, "then you know what I did. I betrayed the Maantecs. Your people are almost extinct thanks to me. Doesn't that matter to you?"

"Not really," the girl said with a shrug. "I'm only twenty. I don't care about some war that happened a thousand years ago. The way I see it, you're the person who helped me. That's all."

Rondel didn't answer for a long time. She stood in the rain, staring at the girl. At length she asked, "What's your name?"

The girl told her.

"Let me share a secret with you," Rondel said. "I hate Maantecs. I hate all of them. This world nearly died because of our species, and you admit that you don't care. That's why I hate Maantecs. You're so arrogant that you think the only thing that matters in this world is you. With that attitude, if you became stronger, you'd only repeat the past. You'd only repeat the Kodama-Maantec War. So get lost."

⚃

Rondel groaned as she awoke. All of that had happened twenty-five years ago. Her eyes burned, and not just because being in Serona had dehydrated her.

Her snapped dagger lay beside her on the scorched earth. Rondel picked it up with her good hand and looked it over. It was like cradling a dead friend. A broken hand she could live with, but a broken Liryometa was a different matter. Not just any smith could repair it. A true Ryokaiten had spells cast on it to keep the weapon from rusting or dulling and to make it more durable in magic-enhanced combat.

The dagger was likely a lost cause. All the Kodamas skilled in forging magical weapons had gone off to war a thousand years ago and succumbed to Iren Saito's curse. As for Maantecs, assuming any of their smiths remained from back then, they would never help a traitor like her.

Rondel sighed and returned the broken blade to its sheath on her hip. For now, she would just have to hold on to the weapon and hope that a solution came to her.

Of course, even if she could repair the rondel, it wouldn't solve her problem. The Stone Dragon Knight's words rang in her head: "Give my greetings to Iren Saito, and in exchange, I'll give yours to Iren Saitosan."

Rondel shook her head. She had hoped that she'd seen the last of Iren. He had a way of making her life miserable, as he was proving at this moment. Rondel had no idea what connected her attacker, Iren, and the Burning Ruby, but she doubted it was anything pleasant.

She might as well get moving then. Rondel leapt to her feet and dashed across the hot expanse of Serona, heading east for Ziorsecth.

As she ran, the name of the girl she'd met outside the Warm Hearth—the same woman who had attacked her here in Serona—filled her mind. Rondel knitted her brow and muttered, "What are you planning, Hana?"

CHAPTER SEVEN
Violent Beauty

Iren's brow lowered. "You don't really expect this to work, do you?"

"Of course," Hana said. "Men are so predictable it's embarrassing."

"You don't even have armor. They'll gut you in a second."

"They couldn't hurt me if they tried."

Iren put up his hands. It was useless to argue with her. Besides, it was her idea.

Still, he was nervous about using Hana as bait. Something about her made his skin tingle. He'd seen those brown eyes and that long, straight, black hair before. Her bubbly enthusiasm and confidence matched as well. It was possible. Hana could be the woman Iren kept seeing in his recurring dream—the one holding his child.

"Here they come," Hana said, pulling Iren from his thoughts. "Go inside the barn and get into position."

Balear looked ill at leaving Hana unprotected, but Iren grabbed him by the arm and dragged him back to the barn. If Hana's crazy scheme was to have a chance of working, they had to play their parts too.

Iren and Balear climbed to the lofts on opposite sides of the barn doors. A triangular ventilation hole provided a small window, but the angle was wrong for Iren to see what was happening outside. He held his breath and hoped Hana was all right.

The minutes passed, and there was no sound. Iren glanced across at Balear. The soldier dripped with sweat. His grip on the sword Hana had stolen was so tight Iren doubted the man could wield it.

Just as Iren had given up and decided to go see what was happening outside, the barn doors swung open. Hana stumbled in backward, giggling like a child. She looked unhurt, though one sleeve of her top had fallen from her shoulder and now hung around her upper arm.

"Please, boys, there's no need to rush," she said. "There's plenty of me for all three of you."

Hana fell into the straw and spread her legs. "One at a time, please."

The three Orcsthian soldiers strode into the barn, and Balear's sword hand gripped even harder. A trickle of blood flowed down the hilt and dripped onto the wooden slats below him.

One of the soldiers loosened his trousers. When he was within a yard of Hana, he let them drop.

Hana winked at the ceiling. That was the signal. Iren and Balear struck.

With a yell they leapt down, each taking one of the men behind the fool in front. Iren knocked out his foe with the back of the Muryozaki. Balear, his sword arm too tense, used his left hand to punch his enemy in the face. The Orcsthian crumpled to the ground.

The half-naked soldier looked around in a panic as he realized the trap he and his fellows had fallen into. Hana stood and smiled. She struck the soldier in the gut with her forearm. The man folded in half, then flew backward under the force of the blow. He smashed through the wall of the barn.

Iren and Balear gaped. "How did you do that?" Iren asked. Even with his Maantec abilities, he doubted he could have sent a man flying.

"If you want to survive in this world," Hana said, "you need to be strong."

Iren blinked twice. Hana's words reminded him of someone. With a sideways glance at Balear, he could tell the Lodian had the same feeling.

They sounded like something Amroth would say.

Hana stepped over to the man Balear had knocked out. The Orcsthian's breath came with a sound like bubbles; Balear had broken the man's nose. Hana hefted the soldier to his feet and held him up with her right hand.

"What are you doing?" Balear asked. "He's defeated. Let's take their horses and supplies and go, like we planned."

Hana ignored him and cocked her left fist. "No!" Iren cried.

He was too late. Hana plowed her hand into the Orcsthian's chest. A horrendous popping followed as her blow snapped ribs. Then, like the other soldier Hana had attacked, the man shot out of the barn.

Balear scowled. "That was unnecessary."

Hana returned his look with a fiercer one. "He was the one who did this to me," she said, pointing at her shifted top. "Humans don't deserve to touch me."

The Lodian took two steps back and raised his palms before him.

Iren stepped between them. "Well, let's get out of here before anyone realizes these three are missing," he said. "Hana, are their horses outside?" When she nodded, he continued, "Then come on. We have a long road to Tropos, and the sun's already setting."

The trio left the barn without another word. As they mounted their stolen horses, Iren couldn't help but notice that his companions' faces were different from before the battle. A grim look replaced Hana's exuberant smile, and Balear's infatuated eyes had changed into ones filled with worry.

Iren sympathized with Balear. Granted, Hana's fighting abilities would help them cross the dangerous landscape that Lodia had become. Even so, as they rode, Iren wondered what they'd found in this strange Maantec woman.

CHAPTER EIGHT
Minawë's Resolve

Rondel charged through the twilight of Ziorsecth Forest's understory. The news she'd received was bad. She'd gone to the Kodaman capital of Yuushingaral, but the Kodamas had said that neither Iren nor Minawë had visited for six months. At last report, Minawë was still at the Heart of Ziorsecth.

That by itself was distressing enough. More disturbing was the rumor about Iren. Scouts had spotted him heading east toward Lodia—alone.

The old Maantec arrived at the Heart of Ziorsecth. Minawë knelt amid the graves, wearing the green silk dress that marked her status as the Kodaman queen. It looked big on Minawë, or perhaps more accurately, Minawë looked small in it.

Rondel took a few tentative steps. Minawë didn't look like she wanted to be disturbed, yet Rondel knew she had to speak with her.

A twig ended Rondel's preparations. Not paying attention to where she walked, the old Maantec stepped on it, and it snapped beneath her boot.

Minawë turned. Rondel inhaled sharply at the sight of the Kodama's tear-filled emerald eyes.

"Rondel?" Minawë called.

Rondel did her best to create her false grin. "You look surprised, Minawë. Is it so shocking that I would pay you a visit?"

"I thought you'd gone to wander Raa. I didn't expect to see you again. I don't think Iren did ei—" she broke off.

The Kodama's agonized expression told Rondel everything she needed to know. "So it's true," she said. Her smile faded. "Iren left."

Minawë nodded. "Several days ago."

Rondel cursed. She needed to find Iren before Hana did! "Where did he go?" she demanded. "Why would he leave?"

The way Minawë reacted made Rondel regret how she'd spoken. The Kodaman queen put a hand on her forehead. "It's because of me," she moaned. "He left because of me."

"That's silly," Rondel said, uncertain how to take Minawë's outpouring of emotion. "Iren cares for you. He wouldn't abandon you like that."

The look that Minawë shot Rondel made the old Maantec again wish she'd kept her mouth shut. Rondel raised her unbroken right palm in a placating gesture. "All right, all right. Tell me what happened."

Minawë recounted Iren's departure. When she finished, Rondel sighed and put a hand on Minawë's shoulder in a vain effort to comfort her. "I feared this would happen," the old woman admitted. "When I left six months ago, I wanted to believe Iren could be happy living here with you. Deep down, though, I knew it wouldn't be enough for him."

"He said it was like being crippled," Minawë said. "He couldn't live in a world of magic when he couldn't use it, so he went searching for a way to heal himself."

"That's why he went to Lodia?" Rondel asked. "That makes no sense. There's nothing in Lodia that can help him."

"He wanted to visit his parents' farm. He thought he might find something there."

Rondel stiffened. Iren wouldn't find anything there but grief.

Minawë shifted back to the pair of wooden grave markers before her. She grasped the one bearing the name "Aletas" with both hands. "Mother," she whimpered, "why did you leave me alone?"

A sad nostalgia filled Rondel. Six months ago, she had stood behind this same woman, who had knelt before these same graves. It was as though nothing had happened, as though no time had passed.

But time had passed. Rondel glanced past Minawë to the crater where the Heart of Ziorsecth had once towered. Its replacement had grown a lot in half a year, even though much of that time had been during the winter. The seedling drew strength from all the stems of Ziorsecth, so it far outpaced an ordinary tree.

As Rondel looked at the Heart, she caught a glimmer of something green next to it. She activated Lightning Sight. The moment it began, Rondel could pierce the distance without difficulty. She took a step back and ended her spell.

"Is that the Chloryoblaka down there?" she asked.

The queen craned her head around to look at Rondel. "Yes, why do you ask?"

"That isn't a secure place to leave your Ryokaiten."

Minawë shrugged. "No one knows it's here. Besides, we stopped Amroth. Mother didn't want that power, and I want to respect her wishes. Since Ziorsecth is no longer under threat, I left the bow there to help the Heart recover."

Rondel tried to clench her fists. Her broken hand sent pain through her as punishment for the attempt. Doing her best to keep calm, she asked, "Then do I have it right that you never touched the bow? You aren't the Forest Dragon Knight?"

"That's correct."

Rondel's eyes flared. "Do you think Amroth was Ziorsecth's only threat?" she shouted. "Do you have any clue why I came to see you and Iren today?" She pulled back her cloak to reveal her broken left hand. It was pressed against her chest in a crude sling she had fashioned after entering Ziorsecth.

Minawë gasped. "How? What happened to you?"

"Not what," Rondel said, "who. The Stone Dragon Knight did this to me. She took the Burning Ruby and nearly killed me in the process. Worse still, well . . ."

She used her good hand to draw the Liryometa from its sheath. When the rondel's broken edge came free, all the color vanished from Minawë's face. "That's why you came here," she breathed. "You wanted Iren's help against the Stone Dragon Knight."

Rondel shook her head. "I did want to find Iren, but not to get his help. Without magic he wouldn't stand a chance against this foe. I needed another Dragon Knight, one with magic better suited to fighting against rock than my lightning abilities are."

She gestured with her chin to the crater. "I wanted the Forest Dragon Knight. I wanted you."

At that final word, Minawë trembled. Still on her knees, she collapsed forward. Her fists clutched at the dirt. "I . . ." she began, but she didn't seem able to say more.

"Minawë," Rondel meant to say the name gently, but it came out harsher than she expected, "when the Stone Dragon Knight thought I was going to die, she told me she was looking for Iren. I don't know why, but I'm sure she wishes him harm. I can't protect him alone. We need to find him before she does."

The queen shook her head. "I can't," she said. "Mother tried to use the Chloryoblaka. Father did too. Look what happened to them! I can't. I'm not strong enough. I'm all alone. Oh, Mother, why did you leave me alone? I can't be the Forest Dragon Knight. I can't be the Queen of the Kodamas. I can't do anything!"

Rondel vibrated with rage. "What are you saying?" she yelled. "How can you just kneel there paralyzed? You aren't the Minawë I remember. What happened to your strong will? What happened to the woman who risked her life to help her people? Will you now hide in this forest and ignore your friend when his life is in danger?"

In a single lithe motion, Minawë swung around and rose to her feet. As she did, she punched Rondel across the face. The old woman sprawled in the dirt.

"What makes you think you know anything about it?" Minawë cried. "You have no right to speak to me that way!"

"You deny it so quickly," Rondel said as she wiped a trail of blood from her lip. "That proves I'm right. You may not think you're ready to face it, but you know what you have to do."

"You . . ." Minawë tensed her body. "Get out of Ziorsecth!" she screamed. "As Queen of the Kodamas, I command it. I never want to see your face again!" She ran away.

But escaping Rondel wasn't that easy. The old woman pushed to her feet with her good hand, then used magic to accelerate herself. She got in front of Minawë in a flash.

The queen was running so hard and had her eyes so tightly shut that she collided with Rondel at full speed. Unlike with Minawë's punch, though, this time Rondel didn't budge. Instead it was Minawë who fell. She landed hard on her back.

Rondel cast Lightning Sight and stared down at Minawë. "When I came here," the old woman said, "I felt as if time had stopped. Now I know why. You did let time stop. You let it stop seven months ago when Aletas died. Let it start again! You've been asleep for half a year, dreaming so you wouldn't have to confront the real world. Well, now you must confront it. Minawë, before it's too late, you need to wake up!"

The woman on the ground cried. Rondel felt a stab of pity. She continued more gently, "Do you know why Aletas took up the Chloryoblaka, even though she didn't want to?"

Minawë nodded. "To protect Ziorsecth and the Kodamas."

"No, they were a bonus. The real reason," Rondel pointed at Minawë, "was to protect you, the person she cared about most. She knew she might die in that battle. She fought anyway, because she wanted you to live."

Minawë clutched at her heart.

"So the only question now," Rondel pressed on, "is how best to honor her sacrifice."

For a long time Minawë didn't move. She didn't speak. Her eyes grew so distant that Rondel was certain the woman was reliving those last terrible moments of the Battle of Ziorsecth.

At length Minawë stood and returned to the burial ground. She knelt at Aletas's grave, then stepped past it and into the crater. When she reached the Chloryoblaka, she hesitated only a second before she grasped the bow.

The ground shuddered. A barrage of vines, each thicker than Rondel's forearm, burst from the soil. With incredible speed one wrapped itself around each of Minawë's arms and legs. The four vines lifted her into the air in a spread-eagle position. She screamed. The vines were wrenching away from her body.

Seeing that Minawë was about to be drawn and quartered, Rondel drew her broken dagger and slashed at the nearest vine. Her efforts were futile. The edge by the hilt wasn't nearly as sharp as the one at the tip had been.

Then Rondel felt a pressure against her legs. Two vines had

ensnared her and rooted her to the ground. A third wrapped itself around Rondel's unbroken hand. The plants didn't tug on her, but whenever she tried to move, they resisted with such strength that it was clear they could rip her apart.

Restrained and helpless, Rondel watched as the vines raised Minawë higher. "Fight it!" Rondel called. She hoped her shout would reach Minawë over the queen's screams. "This is Dendryl's test."

Rondel's vision grayed as fear brought her to the brink of passing out. The price of failing a dragon's test was death.

"Don't give up, Minawë! I believe—" Rondel's words were cut off as a new vine wrapped itself over her mouth.

Minawë's screaming stopped. She spoke, but the voice, while female, was not Minawë's. "Is this it?" it mocked. "Is this all the resolve you have?"

Minawë screamed again, this time in her own voice. The other speaker, whom Rondel guessed was Dendryl, the Forest Dragon, cut in, "Are you so afraid of death? My knight commands life and death. Can a spirit as feeble as yours be trusted with such power? You must not fear! To become my Dragon Knight, you must be willing to die. So tell me: will you die to become the Forest Dragon Knight?"

Rondel cursed through the vine sealing her mouth. She knew the game Dendryl was playing. The Forest Dragon could see Minawë's memories. It knew exactly how to hurt her.

"No answer?" Dendryl asked. "I expected more of you. Your father Otunë was willing to die as the Forest Dragon Knight. Aletas was too. I thought you would have their strength, but you're nothing but a remnant, a failure."

The vines tugged on Minawë's limbs again. This time she didn't scream. Her head hung limply. It was over.

Then Rondel heard a voice, low and quiet, yet firm.

"Dendryl," Minawë said, "I'm not willing to die to become your Dragon Knight."

"Because you're weak!"

"No. I'm not willing to die, because I can't let myself die. I have you and Rondel to thank for reminding me of that. You were right when you said Mother and Father were willing to die, but you don't understand the reason. They did it so I would survive. Do you understand? I have to live, because they died for me!"

The vines tugged on Minawë again, but she resisted. With a roar she pulled in her arms and legs, straining against the plants. Finally the tension was too great. The vines snapped.

Minawë landed hard, but she climbed to her feet. Her face contorted into a smile, and Dendryl spoke one last time, "You answered correctly. As I said, the Forest Dragon Knight commands life and death. Only those who can hold life sacred deserve to be my knight. I yield to you."

The vines retracted into the earth. Rondel raced to where Minawë stood.

"You did it," the old Maantec said.

Minawë stood there, still smiling, but she didn't respond. She teetered as though she were drunk. Then she fell sideways. She landed on the dirt and sent up a cloud of dust.

"Minawë!" Rondel shouted. She leaned down and felt for a pulse. It was there, albeit faint. Bruises covered Minawë's arms and legs.

The sight of those wounds broke Rondel. "Minawë," she murmured, "I'm sorry."

CHAPTER NINE
Tit-for-Tat

Three days after escaping Orcsthia, Balear Platarch sat with Iren and Hana on the edge of a thicket. He poked their campfire with a stick. He hadn't wanted a fire; it attracted attention. With the brisk spring night, though, they'd needed to risk it.

Balear threw his stick into the flames. He'd never imagined crossing Lodia would be like this. Three days, and three attacks. Travel wasn't this dangerous even when the Quodivar were at their height. Lodia was falling apart, and so far, he'd managed to do nothing about it.

Things would have been different if his father had been here. Dad would have known what to do. At the least, raiders would have thought twice about attacking them. Mom always said all Dad ever needed to do was brandish his sword and enemies would flee.

But Dad was dead, at the bottom of the ocean. Now Balear's only hope for peace lay with Iren.

Across from Balear, the Maantec stared into the fire as though lost in it. He'd been asking Balear questions about Tropos ever since they'd left the farm outside Orcsthia. The man was obsessed with the village and what he might find there.

Of all the places for Iren to want to go. What did he think he would learn there, anyway? His parents were dead, just like Dad.

"It won't be enough firewood," Hana said, interrupting Balear's thoughts with her confident tone that left no room for argument. "Unless we want to freeze tonight, I'd better get more." She rose from the fire ring and headed into the thicket.

Balear watched Hana leave. He couldn't figure her out. She'd rescued them in Orcsthia, but then she'd murdered those soldiers for no other reason than spite. It had been wrong. Their deaths hadn't been necessary. Too many Lodians were already dying these days.

He had to know more about her. Otherwise, she was too dangerous to have with them. Balear stood. "Will you be all right by yourself for a while?" he asked Iren. "Hana might need help carrying all that wood."

Iren looked up, his eyes unfocused. "What?" he asked. "Oh, sure." He went back to staring at the flames.

Balear sighed, hoping Iren wouldn't get killed while he was gone. He headed into the thicket. It took him a few minutes, but he caught up to Hana. She had already gathered a decent amount of wood, but she was piling it in one location to make it easier to bring back.

"I'm not a little girl, you know," Hana said when Balear reached her. "I don't need an escort."

"All the same," Balear replied, "it sets my mind at ease to know that someone is protecting you."

Hana laughed. "I recall protecting you more often than the other way around."

The former general reddened. "Yes, well, this way at least I know I'll be safe."

"If you want to protect someone," Hana said with a frown, "you should have stayed with Iren. That man doesn't know which end is up."

Balear was taken aback. "Are you serious? Iren's the reason I'm alive today. He defended Ziorsecth from Lodia's army, and he defeated Feng singlehandedly."

"By becoming the Dragoon," Hana pointed out, "and as a consequence, he can't use magic. Without that, he's more useless on the battlefield than you are. That's saying something since he's a Maantec and you're a human."

"He's faster than I am. He's stronger too."

"Those things don't matter. At least, they don't matter much. Skill matters. You've trained in swordsmanship for years. Iren clearly hasn't. Did horses raise him or something?"

Balear scowled. "You shouldn't mock him. He probably wishes

horses raised him. At least then something would have cared for him. He had to live alone his entire childhood. It was only last year that he found a home in Ziorsecth." Balear paused and shook his head. "I'm still shocked that he would leave that behind to return to a country where he has so many bad memories."

Hana added the armload of firewood she was carrying to her pile. She dusted off her hands and said, "I suppose I can't fault a human for not understanding, since you don't have magic. Iren is the Holy Dragon Knight. Any Maantec would recognize that sword of his. Not only that, he became the Dragoon, the first person ever to do so. He knows what he could do with that power. He could end this war in a stroke. What town would stand against one that had a Dragon Knight?"

Balear eyed her shrewdly. "If what you say is true, then you could end the war as easily as Iren could. All you'd have to do is kill him and take the Muryozaki. He can't use magic, and you say he's useless with a blade."

He'd meant to unbalance her, to trick her into revealing her true personality. But Hana took his suggestion in stride. "You're crueler than I would have thought," she said. "I thought Iren was your friend."

The former general shrugged. "He is, but I'm a knight of Lodia first. If Iren's death meant peace for this country . . ."

Hana smirked. "You wonder if I might kill him, but it sounds like you're the more likely suspect."

"Not at all!" Balear stammered. This wasn't going the way he'd intended. "Even if I became the Holy Dragon Knight, it would be wasted on me. Iren has a better chance of regaining his magic than I do of getting some in the first place. That's why I'm helping him. Iren is Lodia's best hope to end this civil war."

"I get it. You help him, and he'll owe you a debt. Tit-for-tat."

"That's how you see it? Iren would aid Lodia regardless. But if I help him, he might get his magic back sooner. I might save him from death at the hands of raiders. It's not about owing people favors. It's about doing what's right."

Hana folded her arms. "That's a fine sentiment," she said, "but it isn't true. There's no such thing as altruism in this world. Everyone has something they want out of it. Iren wants his magic back because of the power and freedom it offers. You're helping him because you want him to end the war for you, and you want the war to end so you can rest your conscience about betraying your fellow Lodians."

"If that's how you feel, then that's a sad way to look at the world," Balear said. "Still, I don't think you believe what you just said. After all, even if Iren and I have something to gain from helping each other, what about you? Why did you rescue us in Orcsthia? Why are you helping us now? What are you gaining?"

The corners of Hana's mouth crinkled upward. "Honestly? I'm not sure yet. But I'm traveling with the former general of the First Army of Lodia and the first person to become the Dragoon. Whatever I get, I'm sure it will be good."

She reached down and loaded her arms with wood. "This should be enough. Grab as much as you can carry."

By the time Balear picked up his load, Hana had already left. He'd hoped to learn more about why the girl had come with them, but he'd ended up with more questions than answers. He wondered if she truly believed that people only looked out for themselves. If so, what could have happened to her to make her feel that way?

It made him pity her. She was so beautiful, so strong, so intelligent, yet so distant and jaded.

Balear made up his mind. He couldn't change whatever had happened to Hana in the past, but he could influence the present. He could show her that there was such a thing as altruism.

Hana had said she didn't know what she would gain from helping them. If it could be up to Balear, he knew what he would give her. He would give her faith.

CHAPTER TEN
Voices

Minawë couldn't see or move, but she could hear voices. They spoke in her mind, their language like nothing she'd ever heard. It wasn't Kodaman, or Lodian, or even Maantec, what little she knew of that.

Since she couldn't do anything else, Minawë listened. At first she could only hear a few voices, but the more she relaxed, the more she heard. Soon they surrounded her until she feared she would drown in the cacophony. She panicked, and at once the voices disappeared.

After an eternity of silence, Minawë calmed herself. The voices slowly came back. Focusing now, she tried to isolate one of them, to understand it and why it was inside her head.

The best she could manage was a pair of voices that seemed intertwined. Their languages weren't made of words or even thoughts. They were more like emotions, and not all of them were pleasant. There was joy and celebration, yet there was also fear and pain.

Then, with a cry of agony, one of the voices stopped. The shock sent Minawë sitting bolt upright.

The rapid motion nauseated her. Minawë fell backward and lay for a moment with her eyes shut as she waited for the world to stop spinning.

"Welcome back, lazy," a voice said from somewhere nearby.

Minawë smiled. "Thanks, Iren."

There was a hesitant sigh, then, "Not exactly."

Minawë opened her eyes. Rondel sat in a chair next to her. "Sorry about that," Minawë said. The old woman brushed it off, but on closer inspection, Minawë could tell Rondel had been crying.

When Rondel caught Minawë staring at her, she stood and walked to the door. "How do you feel?" she asked, her back turned.

Minawë sat up carefully. She and Rondel were in a bedroom of a Kodaman tree home. "Dizzy," she said. "What happened to me?"

"You passed Dendryl's test," Rondel replied. She gestured to her right. The Chloryoblaka leaned against the wall. "I have to admit that I didn't know if you would survive it. You've been asleep for four days."

"You should have more confidence in your friends," Minawë said with a smile. "Iren slept for a week after he helped me get to Ziorsecth, and I never gave up believing that he would come back to me."

Rondel faced Minawë, and though the old woman's eyes still looked puffy, her grin was genuine. "It cheers me to hear you say that," she said. "I'm sure Iren will come back this time too. But just to be safe, why don't we go to him?"

A flash of memory came to Minawë. Rondel's injured hand was in a fresh sling, a reminder that the Stone Dragon Knight was searching for Iren. They had to reach him first! Minawë leapt to her feet, but she felt so wobbly she had to sit back down.

"We'll go after him soon enough," Rondel said. "Give yourself a minute to recover."

While Minawë waited for her head to clear, she asked, "Where are we?"

"In Yuushingaral, in your room in the queen's tree. I carried you here after you passed out at the crater. Are you hungry?"

"Now that you mention it, I'm starving."

"I made some food. Can you manage, or should I bring it to you?"

Minawë's brow furrowed. There was no way Rondel could have known when Minawë would wake. Had the old Maantec been cooking all this time just so some food would be ready when Minawë revived?

At this point Minawë was too hungry to think about it. She stood again, and this time she kept her feet. "I'm all right now," she said. "I'll come with you."

They left the room and headed to the tree house's second floor, which contained the kitchen and eating area. Rondel had assembled a forest feast: smoked trout, shiitake mushrooms, and an assortment of roots and tubers. She'd even located a wooden bottle of the Kodamas' maple brandy that Mother had liked to hide for special occasions. It didn't surprise Minawë that Rondel would know where to find it.

Minawë attacked the food. She devoured her trout fillet and didn't hesitate when Rondel offered up her portion. The old Maantec smiled. "I was going to ask how my cooking is," she said, "but I think I know the answer."

A sheepish grin sprouted on Minawë's face. She had crumbs and grease all over her. She wiped her mouth, doing a poor job of playing the regal queen she was supposed to be. "It's delicious," she said. "Thank you."

When they'd both finished, Minawë rose. "We should head out. Iren isn't getting any closer."

Rondel pursed her lips. "Are you sure you feel all right? You just woke up. Dendryl's test is no simple task. You can rest another day if you need to."

Minawë's eyes narrowed. Ever since she'd awoken, she'd felt something odd from Rondel. The mysterious timing of the food, the warm smiles, and the kind words were nothing like the sarcastic, slave-driving Rondel that Iren had told her horror stories about.

Now Minawë had figured it out. "You're coddling me," she said. "Why?"

Rondel looked insulted. "I'm watching out for your safety."

"I'm fine," Minawë said. "You were in such a hurry at the Heart of Ziorsecth. Now you're dilly-dallying like a worrisome doe with her fawn. If you want to look out for my safety, then do it the way you did for Iren. Toughen me up. I'm the one you're counting on to defeat the Stone Dragon Knight, remember?"

Rondel licked her lips. Finally, she rose. "All right, we'll do it your way," she said. "Let's gather some supplies and leave. But unfortunately, I can't train you the way I trained Iren. With him, we had time to stop and work as we traveled. You and I don't have that luxury."

"Then how will I learn?"

"You'll have to pick things up as we go. Pay attention when I speak, and practice on the road."

Minawë tried to look more confident than she felt. Still, she wouldn't run away now.

The pair spent most of the day filling packs with food, rope, and other supplies they might need for the journey. Minawë cast aside her queen's dress for the sturdy leather boots, leggings, and jerkin she'd worn on her previous trek to Lodia. Last of all, she donned a long leather cap so she could conceal her green hair.

Evening had arrived by the time they finished preparations. Rondel recommended they set off the next morning, but Minawë gave her such a firm expression that she relented immediately. Even so, the old woman showed a bit of the Rondel that Minawë remembered when she grumbled, "You can barely see in this accursed forest in the daytime. You're as bad as Iren. I'm going to trip on a root and twist my ankle, if not worse. If I break my other hand out here, I swear . . ."

Minawë laughed, clear and pure. The sound itself made her happy; it was the first time she'd laughed in months. Despite the weight of her pack, quiver, and Chloryoblaka, she felt lighter than she had since Mother's death.

They'd barely left Yuushingaral when they came across the corpse. It was a deer, and it couldn't have been dead more than a day. Minawë guessed from the layer of branches partially covering the body that a cougar had killed it and then stashed it here to eat more later.

Rondel wrinkled her nose at the smell, but Minawë stopped and looked at the carcass. Though the Kodamas ate venison, something about this deer unsettled her.

"What's the matter?" Rondel asked.

Minawë shook her head. "No, it's nothing."

Yet as they continued their journey, Minawë couldn't help but look over her shoulder at the corpse. In her heart she grieved for it, and for its voice forever silenced.

CHAPTER ELEVEN
The Farm

"We should be close," Balear called over his shoulder as he, Iren, and Hana headed down a worn dirt road.

Iren's heart fluttered. After weeks of travel, after years of not knowing about his parents, he was finally on the cusp. Soon he would see their home blossom on the landscape. There would be something there, some clue to his magic and how to get it back. There had to be.

"I thought you said your parents lived on a farm," Hana said. "No farm I know looks like this."

She had a point. The fields around them might once have produced crops, but now weeds choked them. Even the packed dirt of the road was washing away. The horses had to tread carefully to avoid the ruts where water had eroded the path's surface.

"Growing up, Mom told me never to come here," Balear said. "She called it a haunted place."

"Because a Left lived here?" Iren asked.

Balear's expression darkened. "Because one died here."

Iren frowned. He'd tried to avoid thinking about that. Although this farm was where his parents had lived, it was also the place where Amroth had murdered them.

"Lodian stories declare Lefts invincible," Balear reminded them. "One dying here was enough for the village to declare the site cursed. No one will resettle these lands as long as memory of him remains." Balear paused and worked his reins. "Iren, I don't know what you expect to find, but eighteen years is a long time. Don't hope for much."

Iren couldn't bring himself to respond. This place was all he had. He could do nothing but hope.

At last the trio topped a small rise and saw the farm. Rather, they saw what was left of it. A single ivy-covered building stood before them. A pile of rubble next to it indicated the vestiges of another structure, demolished by the same plants that had used it to climb.

Racing ahead of the others, Iren leapt off his horse and ran to the remaining building. He felt along the vines and found a trace of stone underneath them. A fervor took him, and he ripped at the ivy with all his strength.

The task was brutal, and before long, sweat cascaded off him. He stepped back to check his progress. He'd only cleared a few square feet. Snarling, he drew the Muryozaki and readied to slash at the ivy, but Balear rushed forward and grabbed him.

"Calm down!" Balear shouted.

Iren spun around in Balear's grip, brandishing the Muryozaki. His expression was savage.

"Those vines are all that's holding up this relic," Hana said. "If you collapse the place, what good will your long journey have been?"

Iren fumed, but he knew she was right. He stared at the ivy with futility. "I have to get in there."

"And we will," Hana continued, "but let's do it carefully. Come over here." She gestured to another side of the house. "You're tearing at the wrong spot. You've been ripping at a side wall. If you want to get in without destroying the place, then I think there's what used to be a porch over here. Where there's a porch, there's a door. Sheathe your sword. We'll help you pull down enough vines to get inside."

Balear nodded so frantically that Iren relented. Putting away the Muryozaki, he joined the others at what Hana claimed was a former porch. It was hard to tell that it used to be anything, but the vines did stick out farther here than anywhere else on the structure.

The sun crossed more than half the sky by the time the trio cleared enough ivy to expose the home's door. Iren grabbed the rusted handle. It refused to unlatch. He pulled on it, and it ripped apart in his hand.

"I've come so far!" Iren yelled. "I won't be stopped by a half-rotten door!" Stepping back to gain momentum, he slammed into the door with a shoulder charge.

The punky wood gave way immediately. Caught by surprise, Iren fell into the house. His landing sent a cloud of dust into the air.

Hana and Balear each grabbed one of Iren's legs and dragged him back outside. He coughed and spluttered as he wiped off his clothes. "Well, that worked," he said. He looked through the open doorway, but the dust was so thick it was like peering into fog.

They waited several minutes for the air to clear, and then they entered the house. They moved cautiously, trying to avoid stirring up another cloud.

With each step, Iren's eyes grew wider. "This is where they lived," he murmured. It was a simple structure with just two rooms. The floor was dirt, and the only furniture in this room was a pair of rocking chairs. When Iren touched one, he put his hand through the armrest without trying.

The most striking feature was the stone fireplace against one wall. It alone seemed in good shape. The vines hadn't grown inside the building, so the mantle's stone and mortar remained intact. Metal pots and pans hung around it, long since rusted.

It was so familiar, yet so foreign. Iren passed through the living area into the home's other room. There he found a dresser, a double bed, and a sight that made tears well in his eyes.

Next to the bed was a rough-hewn crib. Iren placed his hand on it, more gingerly than he had with the chair. He rubbed his palm along its simple contours. "This was mine," he said.

"Come on, Balear," Hana said. "Let's give him a minute."

The pair of them left, and Iren examined the rest of the bedroom. The tattered remnants of blankets, long since moth-eaten, draped over the bed. The dresser held a few pieces of clothing, but they were so damaged Iren couldn't tell whose they were.

Iren put his head in his hands. He would find no answers here. Anything that could have helped him was long gone, if it had ever existed. After all, this wasn't the home of a Dragon Knight. It was the home of a farmer, his wife, and their helpless baby boy.

Retreating from the dresser, Iren loosed a long breath. He threw himself backward on the bed.

He was so lost in his emotions that he forgot about the sorry state of the wood. The moment his body hit the decaying mattress, the bed collapsed. Dust flew up and blinded him as he fell to the ground.

Off in the distance Balear cried, "Iren? Iren! Are you all right?" Iren started to answer, but dust choked him.

He lay there several minutes, afraid to move and churn up more dirt. When he could breathe without gagging, he opened his eyes. He was staring at the ceiling. Splinters of rotten wood filled the room. The straw mattress had all but dissolved.

Groaning, Iren rolled over and pushed himself to his feet. His back ached. He went through a series of stretches. Bruised, he concluded, but not broken.

"Iren!" Balear's voice was closer now. Seconds later the soldier burst into the room, Hana close behind him.

"I'm fine," Iren assured them, but then he shook his head. "Let's go. There's nothing left. I'm sorry I dragged you both here."

"What will you do now?" Hana asked.

Iren shrugged. "I don't know. I guess I was counting on there being something here, so I didn't come up with a back-up plan."

"Well, there's no need to decide right away," Balear said. He put a hand on Iren's shoulder. "It's getting dark. We shouldn't go anywhere else today. Let's stay here tonight."

Stay here? Iren's throat tightened. Just standing in this room was overpowering. He tried to speak, to counter Balear's suggestion, but no words would come.

"We can't stay here," Hana said, her eyes on Iren. "This place could fall apart at any time. I don't want to die because some old roofing timber crushes me."

Iren thanked her silently, but Balear didn't look pleased. "Where should we go then?" he asked. "It's too late to head to another town, and there aren't any inns around here. We could camp out again, but all those briars in the overgrown fields will make for an uncomfortable night."

Hana grinned. "Why don't we stay with your mom? You mentioned that she lives in Tropos Village. That's barely a mile from here."

Now it was Balear's turn to look tight in the chest. "I . . . well, yes, I did say that, but we can't just drop in on her uninvited."

"Nonsense!" Hana laughed. "She'll be happy to see her son. Now let's get going!" Without waiting for the others, she left the room.

Balear pressed his fingers into his temple. "What did we get ourselves into with her?"

Iren smiled in spite of himself. "I've wondered that ever since we met her. She does make life interesting though."

"Hurry up, Balear!" Hana called from outside. "I don't know which house is your mom's. You don't want me to knock on every door in town, do you?"

Balear groaned. "Guess she isn't giving me a choice."

"Guess not," Iren agreed. "Come on; we'd better catch up with her."

Balear left, and Iren followed. As he exited the bedroom, he took a final glance back. The power of time was amazing. Even if he'd wanted to, he could never restore this place.

"Goodbye, Mom," he whispered. "Goodbye, Dad. I don't think I'll ever come back again." He sniffed and wiped his eyes. "Even so, I'm glad I got to see our home."

He turned to leave, and that was when he saw it. In the ruined pile of the bed, Iren caught the briefest glimpse of a color that didn't belong—a rich brown. Everything else in the room bore the muted colors of dust and decay.

Iren reached down and peeled back a layer of shattered bed. A triangle of leather poked out, all but buried in the rotten wood and straw. Iren pulled it free, and when he held it up for inspection, he gasped.

It was a book, and thanks to its position hidden in the bed frame, it had escaped the ravages of time. Iren leafed through it, wondering what it could be about. He could read and write, so he expected to quickly determine the book's contents.

As he paged through it, though, consternation replaced curiosity. The text wasn't Lodian. In contrast to the Lodian alphabet's rounded letters, the book's characters had sharp lines. They also weren't divided into words, at least not words Iren recognized. Except for a small group of markings at the top of each page, there simply seemed to be columns of symbols filling the book.

Rather, filling some of it. The first fifty or so pages had no writing whatsoever.

"Hey, Balear!" Iren called, but there was no answer. The others had gone on ahead of him. Iren left the house, mounted his horse, and galloped to catch up to them.

"You look better," Balear said when Iren reached them. "Did you find something?"

"I did," Iren said. He handed Balear the book.

"I can't believe this is in such good shape," Balear said as he opened it. "What kind of writing is this?"

Hana led her horse over to them and asked to see the book. She'd only had it a few seconds before she said, "It's Maantec kanji, like the writing engraved on the Muryozaki."

Iren grinned. This was the clue he'd come searching for! It was a Maantec book, and he had a Maantec right here who could tell him what it meant. He knew it must contain information about magic and how to heal his wounded body. "What does it say?" he asked.

Hana flipped to the book's back page, opened her mouth, and then shut them both. She handed the book to Iren. "I won't read this to you," she said. "How would you know what I read would be truthful? I could make up anything I wanted, and you would have no way of knowing."

Iren shrugged. "I trust you."

She blushed, the red in her cheeks making her even more attractive. Iren had a brief flash of the black-haired woman in his dream. She really could be Hana.

"I'll make you a deal," Hana said. "Rather than read that book for you, I'll teach you the Maantec language. That way, you can read what it says for yourself."

Iren's heart sunk. He'd found the clue he needed. He was certain of it. But instead of Hana simply telling him what was in it, now he had to learn a whole new language to find out. It was crazy.

"I will tell you one thing about that book, though," Hana said.

The excitement came back, just a flicker. "What's that?"

"See those symbols separated from the rest at the top of every page? They're dates."

Iren felt like he might pass out. His hands trembled as he realized what he'd found: his father's diary.

CHAPTER TWELVE
Tropos Village

When Iren, Balear, and Hana reached Tropos around sundown, Iren barely noticed they'd arrived. Had Balear not been there to confirm it, Iren wouldn't have believed he had entered a village. A few wattle-and-daub houses with thatched roofs dotted the area, along with a well and a one-room church. That was it.

Dismounting, Iren and the others walked among the homes. An empty breath of wind passed through the village. No one was around, which Iren found strange. Though it was dusk, it was too early for everyone to have gone to bed. Now that he thought about it, they hadn't seen any animals out to pasture either.

A chill ran up Iren's spine. This scene felt eerily familiar. "It's like Veliaf," he whispered.

Balear shuddered. "Don't say that," he replied, but Iren knew the same worry must be going through the soldier's mind. The last time they'd entered an unnaturally quiet village, it was because Quodivar bandits and Yokai had wiped out the town.

"This can't be a Yokai attack," Balear said. "Amroth defeated them last year in Haldessa."

He was right of course, but it didn't make Iren feel better. Humans could butcher a town just like Yokai could.

"This village is too small to be included in the civil war," Hana put in. "Conquering it would be a waste of resources."

"Then where is everyone?" Iren asked.

Hana shrugged. "If I had to guess, I'd say they're hiding."

"From what?"

"Isn't it obvious? From us."

Both Balear and Iren gave her shocked looks. "Why would they hide from us?" Balear asked.

"Because farmers aren't stupid," Hana said. "They know a war's going on, and they know we're not residents. They're assuming we're enemies." She glanced around. "Balear, you said your mother lives here. Our best bet is to try her house."

Balear squirmed. "Um, actually, I think there has to be somewhere else we can stay. I'm sure the church pastor would take pity on us."

"What's wrong?" Iren asked. "You don't want to see your mother?"

The young man threw up both hands. "No, no it isn't that! It's just . . ."

Hana smirked. "Haven't been home since becoming a traitor?"

Balear stared at the ground.

"They might not even know here," Iren pointed out. "A place this small—"

"Still receives wanted notices," Balear finished.

"So which house is your mom's?" Hana asked brightly, ignoring Balear's discomfort.

Balear gestured to one of the homes. "That one, but don't just go over there—hey, wait!"

Hana was already bounding across the open space toward the building. She banged on the door. When no one answered, she shouted, "Mrs. Platarch! We're here to see you! We brought your son, Balear! He's a friend of ours!"

Balear dropped his head and groaned.

The door opened a crack. "Balear?" a female voice asked. "Is it really you?"

Balear raised his hand and waved half-heartedly. The person in the doorway gasped. "Balear!"

The door flung open, and a middle-aged woman ran from the house. She wore a homespun dress covered with an apron, and her hair looked grayer than her appearance suggested it should be. Iren half-smiled. He wondered if Balear had caused it.

Balear's mother wrapped her arms around her son and pulled him against her. "You're home!" she cried. "When I saw that poster, I feared the worst. What has this country come to when it calls a sweet boy like you a traitor?" She smothered him with kisses, prompting a snort from Hana.

Iren looked away. Images of a rotting home in an unkempt field flooded his vision.

"Come on, Mom," Balear said, "you're embarrassing me in front of my friends!" His mother's thick embrace muffled the words.

The woman let go of him. "Your friends?" She looked at Iren and Hana. "Well, I'm pleased to meet you both. I'm Arianna, but everyone calls me Ari."

Iren and Hana introduced themselves, and then Ari asked, "What brings my boy home for a visit, and with guests? Oh, I'll have to throw some more vegetables in the soup. Come on in everyone. I was about to have supper! How exciting!" She took off for the house at a jog.

Iren cocked an eyebrow. "Is your mom always this enthusiastic?"

"I haven't been home in seven years," Balear admitted, "not since I left to join the Castle Guard."

"Oh," Iren said, suddenly reserved. Even after seven years, Ari had recognized her son immediately. It didn't matter that he never bothered to visit her, nor that his name was synonymous with treason. She'd run out and grabbed him like he was more precious than the finest diamond. Iren clenched a fist.

The trio followed Ari to her house, tied up their horses in the front yard, and set their swords inside by the door. Ari's home had an identical floor plan to Iren's parents'. The building had two rooms: an entryway that served as a combination of kitchen, dining, and living areas, and a single bedroom behind it.

Ari bustled over a pot above the fire, adding chopped onions and carrots to the soup. Simple though it was, Iren had never smelled a better scent.

"You've caught me unprepared," Ari said. "The merchants don't come like they used to, and, well, I can only do so much."

"Here, Mom," Balear said, "let me help."

Ari smiled. "I'm quite all right, dear, but if you want something to do, you can cut up those potatoes."

Uncomfortable yet again, Iren searched for a distraction. A painting hung on the far side of the room, and he walked over for a closer look.

The subject was a man about ten years older than Balear with wind-swept blonde hair. He stood on the deck of a ship and grinned like he'd just caught the biggest fish of his life.

Strapped to his back was a gigantic sword. If the proportions were true to life, the weapon would have been longer than the man was tall and weighed more than he could carry.

Exaggerated weapon aside, the painting's realism was stunning. Iren examined it for a signature. When he saw the artist's name in the bottom right, he read it three times to make sure he hadn't made a mistake.

Hana noticed him staring at the painting and came over. She had the same reaction as Iren. "A Feidl?" she asked. "Here?"

Ari must have heard her, because the woman wiped her hands on her apron and said, "That's my husband, Balio."

"Shi. . .oot!" Balear cried. He let go of the knife and potato he'd been peeling and put his thumb in his mouth. Drops of blood spattered the counter.

"Honestly," Ari said, "put a man in the kitchen and look what happens. I have some rags in the bedroom, dear. Top dresser drawer."

While Balear went to wrap his wound, Ari cut up the remaining vegetables. Iren cringed. They were the last bits of food in the house.

Hana walked to Ari and offered to stir the soup. The woman smiled and handed over a ladle.

As Hana worked, without looking up, she asked, "How long ago did they come?"

Iren didn't understand what Hana meant, but Ari must have. She stepped back and looked at the floor.

"It's all right," Hana said, "My parents died not long after the war started. Soldiers from Orcsthia came to our farm demanding food, and when my parents refused, well . . ."

Iren recalled the empty barn and farmhouse where they'd recovered after fleeing Orcsthia. Hana was another one, an orphan like him. In a perverse way, it almost made him happy.

"Men from Terkou came about a month ago," Ari murmured. "We thought we were safe, too small to be noticed. But after King Angustion lost his army, all the towns were desperate for soldiers and supplies. Even a place like this can't escape. Five or ten more men and a few more pounds of beef might make the difference between victory and defeat. At least, that was their opinion. I was lucky to escape with what I did."

When Balear returned with his thumb wrapped, Ari dished up the soup. They all sat down for dinner. For a long time they ate in silence, until it became unbearable for Iren. "So," he asked, "how does a woman in a tiny place like this get a Feidl portrait of her husband?"

Balear choked on his bite of potato, and Hana shot Iren a withering look. He flushed; apparently he'd made yet another social misstep. Growing up alone in a tower didn't allow for training in the finer points of manners.

Fortunately, Ari took it in stride. "It was a gift," she said. "Balio was a guard-for-hire in Kataile, though we could never afford to live there. Merchants paid him to protect their ships. Feidl was going to Tacumsah to paint a portrait of an island chieftain when pirates attacked. Balio fended them off all by himself. Feidl was so gracious he demanded that Balio let him paint his picture."

Iren eyed the portrait over Balear's shoulder. "So that painting is true to life?"

Ari laughed. "Feidl never exaggerated, even if it meant angering his patron by making an ugly subject look ugly."

"But there's no way it can be accurate," Iren insisted. "No one could lift that huge sword."

Balear stood. "I'm finished, Mom. If you don't mind, I need to take a walk." Without waiting for a reply, he stepped out the door and into the dark.

Ari smiled after her son. "Forgive Balear. I don't think he ever got over his father's death. He was such a small child then." She shook her head, clearing away tears. "They say the man who bested Balio was a giant more than seven feet tall. He took Balio's sword as his prize."

Now it was Iren's turn to gag on his soup. In a flash, he knew who had murdered Balear's father, and he knew that Feidl had indeed been accurate when he'd painted that sword.

Leaping from his chair, Iren ran to the portrait. "Hey," Hana called after him, "you could at least ask to be excused!"

Iren ignored her and reexamined the painting. The sword was in a harness on Balio's back, so Iren could only see a little of it. The parts that stuck out, though, looked exactly as he remembered them.

Suddenly he leapt back as though from a poisonous snake. "Impossible!" he cried. From the table, the two women gave him odd glances.

"Mrs. Platarch, did you ever see Balio's sword?" Iren asked.

Ari nodded. "He spent most of his time at sea, but he always carried it with him when he came home for visits. I thought it looked terribly heavy, but he was so strong that it never bothered him at all. He was Lodia's finest."

"Do you recall what the hilt looked like?"

"Well, now, let me think. It was wrapped in leather, and the leather had strange symbols burned into it. I asked Balio what they meant once, but he said they were meaningless decoration."

Iren swore, oblivious to Ari's and Hana's stern looks when the word passed his lips. He ran to the door, grabbed the Muryozaki, and rushed outside.

Balear stood beside the village well, staring at the stars. He faced the door at the sound of it shutting. "Iren?" he asked. "I'd rather be alone at the—"

"I know where your father's sword is."

The former general rocked back on his heels. "What are you talking about? A pirate took that sword a long time ago. If it still exists, it's off on some ship."

"No," Iren said, "it's in Veliaf. Or at least it's near there. Last year, Zuberi almost killed me with it."

"Zuberi," Balear said. His brow furrowed for a moment. "Oh, the Quodivar's leader?"

Iren nodded. He would never forget that battle. The giant Tacumsahen had swung his massive sword like it was no heavier than a dirk. Each time he slashed, a gust of wind had accompanied the blow.

Back then, Iren had thought it was the man's insane strength combining with the weapon's size to push the air away from it. Now he thought differently.

Iren held up the Muryozaki and pointed to the concentric rings of Maantec kanji carved around the hilt. "Your mom said Feidl's art is always realistic," he said. "The sword in that painting had writing on the hilt. I couldn't see it clearly, but what your mother said confirmed it for me. I think your father's sword was a Ryokaiten."

Balear turned ashen. "That can't be," he murmured. "That would mean that . . ."

"Yeah. Your father was a Dragon Knight."

The soldier put his back to Iren. He gazed down into the well. For a long time he stood there in silence. Then he said, "The only memory I have of my father is when I was four. He came home for a surprise visit. I was excited to see him, but not long after he arrived, he and Mom got into a terrible fight. I was too young to remember the details, but I know I've never heard two people yell like that. Afterward, Dad stormed out of the village. He didn't even spend the night; he just picked up his sword and gear and vanished into the dark. We never saw him again. We received word a year later that pirates had killed him."

He paused and released a long breath. "I never blamed Dad for leaving. He fought to protect Lodia, to protect Mom and me. You heard what Mom said. He was the best. After he died, all I wanted was to follow in his footsteps."

Balear's hands gripped the stone. "But I couldn't do it. I get seasick, so I can't serve on a ship. I joined the Castle Guard instead, yet rather than protect my fellow citizens, I murdered them."

Iren wondered what he would do if Balear started crying. It wasn't a scene he looked forward to.

He was about to speak when Balear faced him. "I want to go to Veliaf," the Lodian said. "Please come with me. You know where you fought Zuberi, and you'll be able to tell whether his sword is a Ryokaiten."

"And then what?" Iren asked. "If it is a Ryokaiten, when you touch it, it will test you. If you fail, you'll die. Are you prepared for that?"

"I don't know. That's why I need to go. All my life I've chased my father. This is my chance to find out if I can catch him."

Iren considered. It had nothing to do with recovering his magic. Still, it wasn't like he had a plan for how to do that.

"All right," he said, "I'll go with you to Veliaf, as long as Hana's willing to come too. I need to stick with her so she can teach me to read Maantec."

"Thanks, Iren," Balear said.

Iren thought Balear would smile then, but if anything, he looked more troubled than before.

CHAPTER THIRTEEN
Changing Leaves

Minawë would have enjoyed her journey through Ziorsecth, except that whenever she and Rondel rested, the voices came. She didn't know whether they were real or not. Either way, they both fascinated and terrified her.

She had to be careful when she listened to them. Sudden changes in her thoughts or emotions would scare them away and leave her in silence. Only when her mind settled would they return. The boldest ones came back first, but sometimes it took minutes and even hours before she could hear the smallest ones again.

Minawë wanted to ask Rondel about them, but she didn't relish admitting that she was hearing voices in her head. She also doubted Rondel could help much. The Maantec knew a lot about magic, but she wasn't a Kodama.

Not that Rondel didn't teach Minawë. The old woman emphasized that here in Ziorsecth, Minawë had little to worry about in using magic. The vast single tree that surrounded them provided an almost unlimited supply of energy. Once they reached Lodia, though, Minawë would have to restrain her spells.

That limitation worried Minawë. Based on Rondel's account, the Stone Dragon Knight was a Maantec. They drew magic from the air, so they had access to it wherever they went. By contrast, Kodamas like Minawë drew magic from being near other life forms, especially plants. That gave her an advantage in the forest, but not on Lodia's more open terrain.

It didn't help that she lacked any spells that she could use in battle. She could open the doors of the Kodaman tree homes, and she could create the glowing orbs that lit them. She knew how to draw water from the soil through the tree's vascular system so that she always had enough for cooking and cleaning.

But those practical skills wouldn't be much use in a fight. If she and the Stone Dragon Knight met now, Minawë knew she would die.

It was that realization that made her confess hearing the voices.

To Minawë's surprise, her revelation didn't startle Rondel. On the contrary, the old Maantec said, "I wondered how long it would take. It's said that Otunë heard the voices with his waking ears from the moment he became the Forest Dragon Knight."

"What are they?" Minawë asked.

"You already know, or at least, you've guessed. The way you stared at that deer carcass outside Yuushingaral, it was like you recognized it. You heard its voice, and then you heard that voice stop. Am I correct?"

Minawë nodded.

"The voices are those of other living things," Rondel said. "They're the path to your Forest Dragon Knight abilities. They are speaking to you; in turn, you must speak to them. As the Forest Dragon Knight, you are their general. They will follow your orders and defeat your enemies."

"How can I speak to them? Animals can understand Kodaman, but plants can't. Besides, I don't know what they're saying."

"Is the only way you communicate through words?" Rondel asked. "Frankly, I find words the least useful way to communicate. They're too easy to fake. Emotions and body language tell more. If you can decipher them, you can see truth through deception. And if you can control them, you can make anyone, and anything, believe what you tell it."

Minawë's brow lowered at that. Ever since Rondel's odd behavior in the tree at Yuushingaral, a suspicion had grown in Minawë's mind. The old Maantec was hiding something from her.

Whatever it was, getting it out of Rondel would be no small task. After all, the old woman was gifted at exactly the type of deception she had just described.

Still, Minawë wasn't sure what any of that had to do with

manipulating plants, and her creased forehead must have signaled as much. Rondel looked around them for a moment. Then she said, "Let's try an experiment. Put your hand on that maple trunk." She pointed to the one closest to them. Small by Ziorsecth's standards, it was still more than three feet wide.

Minawë did as instructed. The bark's deep furrows and scaly ridges felt coarse beneath her open palm.

"Relax your mind," Rondel said. "Focus on the tree. Hear its voice. Hear Ziorsecth's voice."

For several minutes Minawë stood there, feeling foolish. Then, as she was about to pull away, she felt it, like a tickle in her brain. It was less a voice than a vibration, low in pitch and so steady that it was no wonder she had missed it earlier.

The forest lacked the emotion of the other voices. It neither feared nor celebrated. It simply was. Like the wind, it was a force of nature, always changing yet ever-present.

Minawë didn't know the tree's language, so she couldn't talk to it with words. She focused on an image instead. It was spring, and the maple's leaves had just regrown. Minawë pictured those leaves, focusing on their bright green color. Then she imagined Ziorsecth in autumn, when the leaves cascaded in gold.

A chill ran through her, and she collapsed to her knees. She released the tree, sweat pooling on the nape of her neck. Her vision grayed. She laid on the ground to wait out the dizzy spell.

"I probably should have started you with something smaller," Rondel said. "Still, that was good for a first try."

It took Minawë fifteen minutes before she could move again. When she did, she looked at the maple. A smile blossomed on her face. Every leaf was shining gold.

CHAPTER FOURTEEN
An Old Acquaintance

The ride to Veliaf was even more dismal than the one to Tropos had been. Balear hated every minute of it. This part of the country was closest to where Amroth had marshaled his army, and the thousands of new mouths had been more than the region's farms could support.

Worse still, between Amroth's conscription order and the civil war, large stretches of the region had been depopulated. Balear, Iren, and Hana traveled through more than one village where all the residents had vanished.

The scarred landscape made Balear wish his mother had accepted his offer to bring her to Veliaf with them. It was strange. She'd been cheerful throughout dinner, but when Balear and Iren had come back inside, she'd treated them with reservation. She had let them stay the night, but at daybreak she'd quickly sent them on their way.

She would be all right. Balear kept telling himself that. The growing season had started, and she had a garden going. Assuming Tropos had decent weather and no more raids, she would make it through the year.

Balear sighed. If nothing else, having Mom along would have given him someone to talk to. He wanted to spend some time alone with Hana, but she was absorbed with teaching Iren Maantec.

After six days of blessedly safe travel, they reached Veliaf. The thirty-foot-high stone wall surrounding the town looked as imposing as Balear remembered it. Its lone gate, an impressive metal fortification, was shut.

The trio dismounted. "So do we knock or what?" Hana asked.

Balear looked up. Sentries paced the wall, but none of them stopped their patrols to hail the new arrivals. Three people weren't a threat to the town. "I don't know," Balear said. "Last year, we could walk right in."

Hana cracked her knuckles. "Well, in that case . . ."

"Please don't charge them," Balear pleaded. "That won't make a great first impression."

Hana looked disappointed, but she relented and instead pounded on the gate. "Hello?" she shouted. "Anybody there? We'd like to be let in!"

"Yes, I'm sure that'll work," Balear said, rolling his eyes.

A few seconds later, though, the gate creaked open. Hana grinned and stepped forward.

She stopped in mid-stride. Twenty soldiers barred their way. "General Balear Platarch," the one in front said, "you and your companions are under arrest."

Hana dropped into a fighting stance, but behind her, Balear placed his sword on the ground and held up his hands. "I won't fight them," he declared. "These people are my friends."

Iren pulled the Muryozaki off his belt and laid it beside Balear's blade. "A man from Veliaf saved my life," he said. "I won't kill them needlessly."

Hana looked murderous at their decisions. For a moment Balear thought she might attack anyway, but then she tossed down her sword and raised her arms as well.

"Bind their hands and take them to the jail," the soldier who had spoken before said. "I'll inform the mayor."

While the other guards tied up Iren, Balear, and Hana, the lead soldier retrieved the prisoners' discarded weapons and carried them away. Iren blanched when the man disappeared with the Muryozaki.

Balear understood Iren's worry. Depending on what happened, Iren might never see that sword again.

As the soldiers marched the captive trio through the streets, Balear scanned the village with disbelief. Veliaf had been a wreck last year, all its homes with broken windows and doors. No trace of that damage remained, though the town was as austere and foreboding as ever. The two-story row homes that lined both sides of all the streets seemed to glower down at Balear. It was late morning, yet the tight structures and perimeter wall cast everything on ground level into shadow.

When they entered the town square, Balear closed his eyes as he tried to shut out the memories. The effort was wasted. He could still see them: the pile of militia corpses, the Quodivar laughing as they beat a man to death, and the brutal justice Rondel had exacted on the criminals.

The soldiers took them to a plain stone structure. It had only the tiniest of windows, and they were far out of reach. The men directed their captives into the building and shoved them into prison cells separated by iron bars. They put Balear and Iren in the same one, but they gave Hana one to herself. The soldiers stripped the trio of their packs and other supplies and stored them in a corner of the jail. Then they left without another word.

"This is homey," Hana spat. "What did you think you were doing back there? Honestly, you men and your honor. What good is it if it gets us killed? I assume you both know the penalty for treason, or even for consorting with traitors."

Neither Iren nor Balear bothered to reply.

"I'm not waiting around to die," Hana said. She rolled her arms.

"Do what you like," Iren said. "I'm staying here."

"What?"

"Even if we escaped, we'd have to fight our way back through the town. That gate we came through is the only way in or out. I said it before. I don't want to hurt these people."

Balear nodded his agreement. "We risked our lives to rescue Veliaf from the Quodivar and Yokai. Starting a fight like we did in Orcsthia would make that effort meaningless."

"Fine," Hana pouted, "but remind me to ask how noble you feel when our heads are mounted on spikes." She put her back to them and sat down, leaning against the bars.

They waited in the cages for hours. Balear couldn't mark the passage of time precisely, but his grumbling stomach told him they'd missed the noon meal.

He'd just decided to take a nap on the cold stone to pass the time when a man came in carrying the Muryozaki. Iren and Balear both leapt to their feet. The newcomer, black-haired and middle-aged, looked at them with a nostalgic smile. "So I was right," he said. "It is you two."

Balear grinned and exclaimed, "Dirio!"

"I never expected to see you again," Dirio said with a laugh, "particularly after King Angustion sent these around." He held up a wanted poster showing a fairly accurate drawing of Balear. "As for you," he continued, turning to Iren, "you're a far cry from the teenage boy I remember, but there's no way anyone else has a sword like this."

Dirio tossed aside the wanted poster and pulled a set of keys from his pocket. "This is a poor place to catch up," he said as he unlocked the cage. When he handed Iren the Muryozaki, the young Maantec's relief was palpable.

"That woman over there is our friend too," Balear said with a gesture toward Hana.

"Yes, the guards told me what happened at the gate," Dirio said. He looked over Hana with disapproval. "It seems you're more spirited than your companions. I'm sorry, my lady, but for now, I'd prefer to keep you locked up."

Hana stretched like a cat as she stood. Then, without any effort, she grabbed hold of a pair of bars and pulled them until they bent enough that she could step through them. "I'm sorry, my gentleman," she said, mimicking his tone, "but I'd prefer to be free."

Dirio's jaw dropped, so Iren explained, "She's a Left, like me. You're lucky we convinced her to stay in there this long."

The black-haired man frowned. "It seems I have no choice," he said. "Very well, follow me."

He led them from the jail and back into town, weaving through several side streets. Eventually they reached a building twice the width of a normal row house but otherwise with identical architecture.

"Welcome to my home," Dirio said.

Balear looked up and down the street. "Don't you live on the other side of town?"

"Sorry," Dirio said, blushing, "I forgot to mention. I'm the mayor now."

Iren gaped. "You're the mayor?"

Dirio ushered them inside and into a plush office. A pair of guards stood in the room, but Dirio asked them to leave. He sat down in a high-backed chair behind a heavy wooden desk and said, "I have you two, as well as Rondel and King Angustion, to thank for it. The Quodivar killed the previous mayor when they took over the town last year. When you helped me rescue my fellow villagers, they were so grateful they unanimously asked me to lead them."

Balear smiled. "You're doing a good job of it," he said. "Unlike the other towns I've visited, Veliaf looks better than it did a year ago."

"It's more luck than leadership," Dirio replied. "We're too small to be a serious contender in the civil war, yet our wall gives us a defense few cities can match. An enemy could besiege us, but that would leave their city vulnerable in the interim. Combine that with our remote location, and we simply aren't worth the effort of attacking."

It was an enviable position, Balear thought. With the rest of the country imploding, Veliaf was probably the safest place in Lodia.

All the same, geography alone couldn't explain Veliaf's recovery. Dirio could brush it off as luck, but it took more than good fortune to go from conquered ruin to prosperous community in one year.

Dirio leaned back in his chair and pressed his fingertips together. He frowned. "So," he said, "what brings you here after all this time? Given the state of things, I'm sure it isn't a social call."

The mayor's change of demeanor surprised Balear. Dirio was their friend. He'd fought alongside them against the Quodivar and Yokai, and he'd released them from jail just now. Why had he so abruptly become distant and cold?

Iren must have felt the same as Balear, because he had a note of hesitancy in his voice as he said, "We came to see Akaku Forest. We want to visit the fort where Zuberi and Hezna died."

Dirio's scowl deepened. "I thought as much. You're interested in the sword."

Iren rocked on his heels. "How did you know?"

"After King Angustion defeated the Yokai and Quodivar at Haldessa, some of the villagers and I braved their cavern again. We visited the ruined Yokai stronghold too. When we did, we found the giant blade."

The mayor paused and chewed his lip. Then he continued, "Iren, we saved each other's lives. I've never forgotten what you, Balear, and everyone else did for Veliaf. That said, I can't take you to that sword. It is altogether evil."

"What do you mean?" Iren asked.

"We wanted to rebuild our strength after losing the town watch to the Quodivar. That sword was one more weapon to wield against any who might attack us."

"No," Iren cried, "surely you didn't touch it!"

"I didn't," Dirio said, "but one of the men with me did. He vanished the second his fingers brushed against it. We looked around but found no sign of him. A few minutes later, we heard a terrible crash deeper in the woods. We went to investigate, and we found his body broken almost beyond recognition. A tree was smashed to kindling beneath him. Since then, I've forbidden anyone to visit the fort. A few fools have defied that order, and none have returned."

Iren folded his arms. "Everything adds up," he said, though he seemed to be talking to himself. "The sword's wind pressure when Zuberi swung it, the Feidl painting, and the fact that those who touch the weapon die. That sword is a Ryokaiten. Worse, it's a Ryokaiten without an owner."

Listening to Iren, Balear knew Dirio had been wise to order his fellow villagers to leave the blade alone. But Balear hadn't come all this way for nothing. "You will take us to the sword," he commanded, feeling a bit of his old officer self come back, "or I will go to it alone."

Dirio looked back and forth between the two men. "I can't dissuade you?" He paused, then sighed. "All right. You aren't Veliafans, so I can't order you to stay away from it. It's too late to go today, though. A group of villagers is heading to Akaku tomorrow morning to hunt game and cut firewood. We'll go with them. You can stay the night here; the mayor's house has plenty of guest beds. In the meantime, I'll find you each a change of clothes. Those rags look like they're about to fall to nothing. I'll also arrange for baths for you. And Balear? There's a barber in town who can get rid of that matting of hair and beard. He'll get you looking like a soldier again."

The trio thanked him, and the meeting ended. Hours later, after dark, Balear lay in the first bed he'd been in since leaving Ziorsecth last year. His hair was trimmed, and he felt cleaner than he had in months.

Yet sleep wouldn't come. His mind wouldn't stop buzzing. He wondered about the sword and what he would do when he saw it. If he touched it, he might become a Dragon Knight like his father. He didn't have magic, but the sword's power would still help him end the war.

Then again, he knew the price of failure. He'd promised himself he would see peace in Lodia restored. Maybe it would be better if he left the sword alone rather than risk death. As long as he was alive, he could at least try to make a difference. He could help Iren regain his magic.

Balear sighed and rolled over. He closed his eyes. As he did, the Feidl painting of his father washed up in his vision. Dad had passed the dragon's test, but he had also been the greatest human fighter Lodia had ever known. Could Balear match his level?

He'd find out the answer tomorrow.

CHAPTER FIFTEEN
Another Visitor

A week after Balear and his companions had left, Arianna Platarch was still scrubbing away the stink.

Oh yes, her son's friend had hidden it well, but Ari was observant when it came to dinner. She'd noticed the way the man called Iren held his spoon. Why her good boy was consorting with a Left, though, she couldn't begin to guess.

Whatever the reason, she hoped Iren wasn't rubbing off on Balear. When Ari had first seen her son's wanted poster, she hadn't believed it. But another poster advertised a Left named Iren who was also wanted for treason. Admittedly, that poster described a much younger person. With Lefts, though, who knew? There couldn't be that many left-handed "Iren's" running around the country.

Ari scrubbed the table harder. This was the second time a Left had taken away someone important to her. While most Lodians only knew Lefts as creatures in bedtime stories, Ari seemed to have a knack for running into the devils. Like Iren, the Left who had come to Tropos twenty-five years ago had seemed decent at first. Yet Ari had known even before she learned he was a Left that he couldn't be trusted—especially when he started spending time with her sister-in-law.

Throwing her scrub brush in the bucket, Ari cursed, something she almost never did. If she could have, she would have replaced everything in the house, but the civil war had made everyone too poor.

Lefts had probably caused that too. They were at the root of everyone's problems. If it weren't for that Left, Balio would still be alive.

Ari had warned her husband not to let a Left around his sister, but the stubborn man had refused to listen. Even when the girl wound up dead, Balio wouldn't accept the truth. In his grief he'd blamed not the Left but the people of Tropos.

"For anyone else, you would have stood united against the killer," he had screamed at Ari the night she'd told him what had happened. "But for a Left and his wife? Of course not."

After that Balio had stormed out of the village. No one in Tropos ever heard from him again.

Ari stared into the water of her bucket. It needed to be changed, to have the filth dumped away. She carried the bucket outside and emptied it in some weeds far from her home. Then she headed to the village well to refill for another round of scrubbing.

An old woman was already there, hunched over the crank and trying with all her strength to turn it. She wasn't making any progress, though, because she could only use one arm. Her left one was tied against her body in a sling.

Ari rushed to her. "Here, let me help you," she said. Together they pulled up the well's laden bucket.

The elder, barely five feet tall, looked at Ari with grateful green eyes. "Thank you. Getting by with a broken hand is hard for a woman my age." She dipped her good hand in the bucket and took a long drink. "That's the nicest water I've had in years. They don't know what they're missing in Terkou."

"Terkou?" Ari asked. She forced herself to keep her voice level. It was Terkouan marauders who had attacked Tropos and conscripted the men. This old woman didn't seem dangerous, but the big cities could be scheming something. They loved to stomp on the little folk.

"Yeah," the woman replied, "I've wanted to get away from there ever since the war started. They don't know which end is up. Comes from living all on top of each other, I say."

Ari nodded as she filled her bucket. "I couldn't agree with you more. Well, I'm glad you escaped. Can I offer you a place to stay while you're in town? I'm afraid you won't find any inns around here."

"That would be kind of you," the woman said. "These old bones of mine aren't meant for sleeping outside. No, my camping days should be long behind me, if only those city fools would leave well enough alone instead of starting wars."

Ari led the way back to the house. Inside, she offered the elder a seat by the fire and then started a kettle boiling. "So," she said, "what brings you to Tropos, of all places?"

The old woman smiled sadly. "To be honest, I can't say I wanted to end up here at all. I just did. Wars don't care much for plans."

"No, they don't," Ari reflected, her eyes drifting to Balio's painting.

The elder followed her gaze. "That's a beautiful portrait," she said. "Did you paint it?"

Ari shook her head. "It was a gift to my husband a long time ago."

The kettle whistled, and Ari filled two clay mugs. She handed one to the woman and kept one for herself. "I'm afraid I don't have anything to put in it," she admitted.

Her guest cradled the hot water like it was Katailan wine. "It's warm," she said. "That's what matters."

Ari smiled. She liked this woman.

Sipping her water, the elder stood and walked to Balio's portrait. "Feidl," she said. "Seems to me I've heard that name before."

Ari opened her mouth to answer, but then the old woman stepped back and spluttered. "Are you all right?" Ari cried.

The elder coughed again, but then she recovered. "It went down the wrong way," she said. "Say, do you know if this picture is true to life? That sword seems much too large."

"You know, my son came home last week, and one of his friends asked me the same question." Ari hoped the bitterness stayed out of her voice.

"Did they now?" The old woman looked thoughtful. She paced the room twice. Then she flashed a grin so wide it took up more than half her face. "Well, this has been a splendid visit," she said, "but I'm afraid I must be off."

"Are you sure?" Ari asked. "You've only just arrived. I hope I haven't offended you."

"No, no, it's just that at my age you never know how much time you have left." She handed over her mug and walked to the door. As she opened it, she asked, "By the way, what's your son's name?"

It seemed like an odd question, but Ari said, "Balear."

The woman nodded. "Interesting." Then she was gone.

೮ঃ

Minawë approached Tropos on foot. She strained to hear the voices of the plants and animals around her, but she couldn't focus. She was too distracted by what she'd found at the farm. No one had been there, but inside the one building still standing, Minawë had seen bare spots in the dust where several pairs of feet had recently walked. She'd only missed Iren by a few days.

Those days might as well be years. Minawë kicked a stone on the path and sent it into the brush. Iren's plan to come here had been their only clue. There was no way of knowing where he would have gone next.

Minawë took a deep breath and listened for the voices again. Ever since Rondel had explained what they were, Minawë had spent every available minute observing them and trying to communicate with them. She couldn't speak their language, but her control with images had improved.

At last she heard them, just a whisper. Minawë concentrated on the weeds closest to the path. Under her direction they flowered, even though it was a few weeks early for most of them.

Her magic fueled their unnatural growth. It wasn't hard now that she'd figured out how. Kodaman magic derived from plants, so all she was doing was giving it back to them.

The flower-lined path cheered Minawë. She managed a smile as she entered the village and caught Rondel lounging by a well.

"How'd it go?" the old Maantec asked. She sounded tense.

"Someone definitely visited the farm," Minawë said, "but they're gone now. I have no idea where."

Rondel nodded. "In that case, my time here has been much more profitable. It's good I suggested we split up. I know where Iren went."

Minawë grabbed Rondel by the shoulders. "You do? Where?"

The old woman smirked. "An appropriate place for a reunion."

CHAPTER SIXTEEN
Dropped

Balear wrinkled his nose as he walked through Akaku Forest with Iren, Hana, and Dirio. Dismembered corpses were strewn among the dense spruces, and broken trees lay beneath the bodies. Most of the dead were human, but Balear noticed a few Yokai corpses as well.

"I thought Amroth killed them all in Haldessa," he said, gesturing at one.

"Most of them," Dirio replied, "but they didn't empty their lands. A few remain."

Iren nodded. "Yokai ambushed Minawë and me when we fled their stronghold last year. There were dozens of them."

Balear looked into the trees, uneasy. Yokai could leap great distances and climb like spiders. He wondered if they were out there now. A high-pitched cackling would be the only warning, and screams would follow it within seconds.

Fortunately, no Yokai or anything else disturbed them as they entered the clearing that had once been the creatures' fort. Last year, the Yokai leader had ignited a forest fire to trap Iren and Rondel, so Balear expected to find a charred, lifeless husk.

What he saw instead shocked him. The former battle scene was alive with new growth. Grass grew tall in the open sunlight, and a few tree seedlings pushed through the soil.

Then Balear forgot everything else in the clearing, because at that moment he spotted the sword lying in the grass. He raced to it. There was no mistaking his father's weapon. The double-edged blade portion alone measured seven feet, and at its base the steel was more than a foot wide and six inches thick. The hilt was so long Balear couldn't have covered it even if he'd had four hands.

Balear's breath caught. Sure enough, that hilt bore the same circular markings that adorned Iren's katana.

Iren caught up to Balear and looked over the gigantic sword. "So it is a Ryokaiten," he murmured.

Balear stretched an arm toward it, but Iren grabbed his wrist. "Don't do that," he said, "unless you want to die."

Hana and Dirio had arrived by now. "I warned you yesterday," Dirio said. "That sword made all the corpses we saw on our way here. It is evil."

"Not evil," Iren replied, "the dragons simply are. That said, it is dangerous. We should take it to Veliaf and hide it so people can't touch it. I'll carry it. I'm already a Dragon Knight, so it can't test me."

"If it won't harm you, that sounds like a good plan," Dirio said. "There's a vault in my house. We can store it there."

Balear's eyes flicked from the sword to Dirio, then to Iren, and finally back to the sword. He'd come all this way. This was Dad's weapon! He had wielded it, and so had Zuberi. Neither of them were Kodamas or Maantecs. They didn't have magic. They were humans like he was.

Of course, that didn't mean he was their equal. Balear had never met Zuberi, but he knew the man surpassed him. The giant Tacumsahen had murdered Dad, and he'd almost killed Iren.

While Balear warred with himself, Iren grasped the sword with both hands and pulled. His face reddened. His muscles bulged.

Iren fell backward on his rump. "I can't," he heaved. "That sword must be solid steel. It won't budge."

"We could bury it," Hana suggested. "It can lie underground for all eternity."

Dirio and Iren nodded, but at Hana's words, Balear shouted, "Wait!" He didn't know why, but he couldn't let them entomb this weapon. It deserved better. It deserved to breathe the air.

Balear reached for the blade. Iren rushed to restrain him, but the

Maantec was off balance from his fall. Balear's hand closed around the weapon's hilt.

Everything went black. A presence brushed against Balear's mind. In a snarling voice it said, "What, another worthless human?" Stabbing pain shot through his head, like an eagle's talons were ripping out his brain piece by piece.

The pain vanished as quickly as it had arrived. "So you're a Platarch," the voice said. "I thought I was rid of your family. I won't have it said of Ariok that I have a weakness for some misbegotten lineage. I'll test you like all the rest."

The darkness fled Balear's eyes, and he gazed around in awe. Surrounding him was the brightest, bluest sky he'd ever seen. A few clouds drifted beneath him.

At first he thought he was just disoriented. Surely the clouds must be above him. Then he saw the tiny green needles—the spire-like conifers of Akaku Forest—far, far below him.

"Where on Raa am I?" he shouted, but the wind ripped the words from his mouth. His pulse quickened, and he became lightheaded. Breathing up here seemed to do no good.

"The other dragons have complicated tests," Ariok said. "Mine is simple."

Balear gulped. He had a good idea what that test was, but he couldn't stop himself from asking, "What must I do?"

Inside his brain, Balear could sense the dragon smile. "Live."

Like a puppeteer cutting his doll's strings, the force holding Balear in midair vanished. He fell.

End over end he tumbled. Soon he couldn't tell which way was up. Mist soaked him as he passed through a cloud. Balear screamed, but he couldn't hear himself over the rushing air.

He was going to die. There was no question about it. Once as a child he'd fallen climbing a tree and broken his leg. It had healed well and never given him any trouble, but that was a fall from just a few feet. He recalled the bodies strewn across the forest. Now he knew how they'd ended up that way.

Even as his terror grew, though, his soldier's mind ordered him to focus. "Concentrate!" he yelled to himself. "Slow yourself down!" He shifted his body in different positions and found that spreading out as much as possible helped.

But it wasn't enough. At this speed the impact would shred him.

Balear pulled off his shirt and stretched it between his arms. He hoped the extra area would catch the wind and slow his fall. The force was too great, though, and the shirt ripped from his arms.

He was running out of time. The packed spruces of Akaku had gone from looking like a verdant field to a spiked pit.

There had to be a way to survive. There had to be! He needed to think. Dad had survived this. How had he done it?

Maybe that was the problem. Dad could survive it because he was the best. Balear was no Balio.

Not that he hadn't tried. He'd left his mother's side a boy and joined the Castle Guard to become a man. There were other recruits with more talent, but he'd overcome them with effort. He'd trained three times harder than anyone else. When someone beat him in a sparring match, he'd practiced all the more so he could win the next time.

Had all that work been for this? To perish falling from the sky?

No! He wouldn't allow it. The Castle Guard was gone. He was the only one left. Lodia was still at war. He had a duty to protect it and restore it to peace.

There was no way he would let some dragon and its devil magic interfere with that!

Although Balear had no idea what he was doing, he faced the ground. He was no longer screaming. Instead, his face scrunched with determination. He clapped his hands together, then pushed them away from his body, palms down.

The air responded to his gesture. He slowed a fraction, but he continued to plummet.

Balear put all his focus into his hands. To his amazement, the air bent around them. It swirled in a vortex, growing stronger until the only wind he felt came from his palms.

Just before he reached the trees, the air surged down. It shot toward the forest with such ferocity that the spruces beneath him cracked.

He had almost landed when his strength ebbed. His concentration faltered, and in that second, the wind around his hands ceased. He dropped to the ground with a crash.

ↂ

Iren rushed through the claustrophobic Akaku Forest, heedless of the branches that whipped at him. Seconds ago he'd heard the snapping of trees, and he knew what must have caused it.

As feared, Iren reached an area of woods that had been smashed to tinder by an impact from above. At least an acre was flattened, and in its center lay Balear.

"Balear!" Iren shouted. He climbed through the mess of broken logs to his friend.

The Lodian groaned, "Oh, hell."

Iren's jaw dropped. "You survived?"

Balear pushed against the logs with his arms. Slowly, he got to his knees, then to his feet. "Seems that way," he said. He did a few stretches. "I don't think anything's broken. All the same, I wouldn't want to go through that again."

"Does this mean you passed the dragon's test?"

"I guess so. He called himself Ariok."

"That's the Sky Dragon," Hana said from behind them. "His sword is the Auryozaki. He tests would-be knights on bravery."

Iren eyed her as she crossed the devastation. "You're well informed."

"Any Maantec could tell you that," she said with a shrug before facing Balear. "Not bad. It takes guts even for a Maantec to touch a Ryokaiten. Speaking of which, let's go get it. Now that it's yours, you'll need to practice your push-ups if you want to lift that monster, let alone wield it in battle."

They clambered out of the log pile and met up with Dirio before returning to the Auryozaki's resting place. When they arrived, Balear knelt before the enormous blade, clearly hesitant to touch it after what had happened the last time.

Iren frowned. Whether or not Balear had passed Ariok's test made little difference. Iren knew how heavy that weapon was. If he couldn't lift it, there was no way Balear could.

Balear grasped the hilt with both hands. The muscles on his arms tensed. Then, with casual ease, he picked up the sword.

Everyone around Balear gaped, and the Lodian looked at the giant sword with disbelief. "It's so light," he said. "It's like it's weightless." As though to confirm his suspicions, he let go of the sword with his left hand and swung it several times using only his right arm.

"How can that be?" Iren demanded. "That sword is gigantic! Here, let me try holding it again." He reached out, and Balear reluctantly handed over the Auryozaki. For a moment Iren held it there, but when Balear let go of the hilt, the sword plummeted. It dragged Iren with it, and his face bounced off the ground.

Iren spat out dirt and spruce needles. He shook his head and pulled on the sword with all his might. He couldn't raise it an inch. "You keep it," he said. "I'll stick to my katana."

He stalked away from the others. Behind him, he heard Hana and Dirio exclaim as Balear picked up the Auryozaki again and swung it. Iren could feel the wind off the slash. He cursed. Now even a human like Balear could become a Dragon Knight and use magic.

But not him.

CHAPTER SEVENTEEN
Cured?

Four days later, Iren stood once more in Akaku Forest. He held the Muryozaki vertically before him.

"Remember," he muttered. "Remember how it felt."

He focused on a tree thirty feet away. He couldn't use magic on his own, but the Muryozaki itself was magical. That might make the difference.

Iren pulled the katana back over his right shoulder. Last year, he had channeled magic through the sword to lengthen it so it could cut through Feng's leg. If he did the same here, an arc of light would reach out and slice the tree in half.

He took a deep breath and swung.

No magic came. The sword didn't extend. It didn't even glow.

"You should try getting closer," a female voice said from behind him. "Your sword isn't as long as Balear's."

Iren turned and saw Hana approaching. He glowered at her.

"Whoa, testy!" Hana said, raising her hands in front of her. "I didn't mean to upset you."

Her smirk gave away the lie. Iren sheathed the Muryozaki and stalked away from her. He hoped she'd leave him alone, but she bounded after him.

Iren headed in Balear's direction. The former general was practicing in the forest too, and with much greater success. As his giant Auryozaki sliced through the air, it dropped three-foot-wide trees like twigs.

"Tired of wrecking the forest yet?" Iren called.

Balear stopped in midswing. Sweat dripped off him. He had come to Akaku to train every day since he'd become the Sky Dragon Knight. "I didn't expect to see you out here," he said. He paused a moment, then grinned. He pointed his sword at Iren. "Hey, how about a match?"

Iren hesitated. He knew the Auryozaki's capabilities from his fight with Zuberi. Its length would keep him out of reach, and its weightlessness would let Balear swing it so quickly that Iren would have few chances to counterattack.

The situation would be different if he had magic. The spells he'd learned training with Rondel far surpassed what Balear could do.

Of course, if he could use those abilities, the match wouldn't be a contest. He returned Balear's smile. "Bring it on." He drew the Muryozaki.

Hana looked from one young man to the next and then, rolling her eyes, stepped between them. "Boys, those aren't wooden sticks. If you spar with sharpened blades, you'll kill each other."

Iren didn't listen. Hana had just provided the perfect distraction; Balear couldn't swing his long sword without hitting her. Iren ducked low, ran past Hana, and was under Balear's guard in a second. He slashed up, intending to stop his blade just beneath Balear's jaw.

He was almost there when Balear noticed what was about to happen and leapt backward. At the same time, he swung the Auryozaki down. It plowed into the earth and disrupted Iren's attack with a burst of debris.

The dirt momentarily blinded Iren, and that was all Balear needed. His sword *whooshed* as it carved a horizontal arc through the air. Iren raised his katana to block, but the force of Balear's blow sent him sprawling nonetheless. Apparently the Auryozaki was only weightless to its owner.

Iren staggered to his feet and readied for Balear's next strike. Hana shouted at them to stop, that they were both being stupid, but she might as well have disappeared.

Balear lunged, his arm and blade together giving him a ten-foot reach. Iren barely sidestepped the blow.

Then he saw his opening. Weightless sword or not, Balear was no

Zuberi. He couldn't attack as fast as the Quodivar leader had, and because of his shorter height, he could only swing his weapon in a couple directions. Iren deflected the Auryozaki with his katana and forced the giant sword sideways. He charged and penetrated Balear's defense again. This time, he knew the soldier was too unsteady to jump away. Iren thrust. He would send the Muryozaki past Balear's face and leave a harmless scratch along the Lodian's left cheek.

Iren was so intent on victory that he almost missed seeing Balear whirl the Auryozaki back around. With the sword weightless, the Lodian could swing it even while off balance. Iren cursed and converted his own strike into a vertical guard. Unlike his last block, though, he was close enough to Balear that only the base of the Auryozaki connected with his katana. Balear's leverage was less there, so Iren kept his feet.

The two pushed with all their strength as each tried to break his opponent's guard. Their eyes met, and Iren saw joy in Balear's face.

Something about that expression broke through to Iren, and he realized that he wore an identical look. He heard his own laughter, though he hadn't known he was making the sound until just then.

At once, as if they'd prearranged the spectacle, Iren and Balear separated. Iren sheathed the Muryozaki. He was panting and sweating, but he'd never felt so alive.

That was when it occurred to him. Magic didn't matter. He wasn't helpless without it. He could stand his own against a Dragon Knight. Maybe he couldn't live with the Kodamas, but he wasn't crippled.

"That was good," he wheezed. "You learned how to handle that thing quickly."

Balear hefted the Auryozaki over his shoulder. "Keep practicing with me," he said, just as winded, "and I'll be better than Dad and Zuberi in no time."

"Fine by me. I'll just get that much stronger too. I refuse to lose to you."

"Well, I'm not going to lose to you either."

Iren and Balear stared at each other across the expanse of forest for a few seconds, laughing as they caught their breath. Finally, Hana ran up and stood between them again. She folded her arms and glared. "If you boys are done screwing around, we should get back to Veliaf. Something's wrong here."

"You mean besides the fact that even though Balear's sword is twice as long as mine, he still couldn't win?" Iren asked with a smirk.

Hana's expression didn't relent. "No, this is something else. Don't you feel it? It's getting colder."

In truth, Iren felt warmer now than he had for a long time. As his sweat cooled, though, he realized Hana was right. The temperature had dropped significantly since he and Balear had started fighting.

Then he noticed something that made him step back in surprise. A snowflake had fluttered by his face.

"What on Raa?" he asked. "It's nearly summer. Even this far north, there's no way it can be snowing."

Yet snow it did, and it grew stronger by the second. Soon the flakes accelerated into a squall, and a white layer covered the ground and spruce branches.

"Let's get out of here," Iren said. He had no idea what was going on, but it stank of magic. These woods were still the Yokai's domain. Even if their numbers were reduced, they might have something to do with this.

The trio had only taken a few steps toward Veliaf when over the wind came a long, low, terrifying roar. The sound froze Iren in place. He craned his neck to look in the direction of the call. The others stared back too.

"What was that?" Balear asked.

Iren gulped. He had fought both Yokai and their larger cousins, the Oni. Though monstrous, neither could have made that sound. It was primal, more animal than anything sentient.

Heavy footfalls and a sloughing sound confirmed Iren's suspicions. Not even the ten-foot-tall Oni would be this loud moving through the woods.

At last, through the snow, the creature came into view. The moment it did, Iren's hands fell to his sides, quivering.

The monster towered fifteen feet high, and its girth was so great Iren doubted he could reach his arms around it. It wore no clothes, but white fur covered it. Its hands sported claws the length of Iren's forearm. On each foot, instead of toes, the monster had a single pointed nail as long and sharp as a dagger. Most horrifying of all, though, were its burning eyes the color of blood and its needle-like teeth protruding from its oversized maw.

Balear stood beside Iren, his body rigid. "That's a Fubuki," he breathed.

The Fubuki had no need of a weapon, but it nevertheless carried the most brutal creation Iren had ever seen. One end was a long, jagged bone spear, while the other bore a hammer larger than Iren's torso.

As Iren studied the weapon, his panic increased tenfold. Along the edges of the Fubuki's hand, familiar writing poked out. "Impossible," he said. "That weapon is a Ryokaiten. That thing is a Dragon Knight!"

CHAPTER EIGHTEEN
Frozen Wind

"We should run," Iren said.

Balear stepped toward the Fubuki and raised his Sky Dragon Sword. "We can't," he replied, the waver in his voice barely concealed. "If we do, and this thing follows us to Veliaf, people will die. We have to stop it here."

Iren had no idea how they could fight such a monster, even had it not been a Dragon Knight. Yet something in Balear's stance made Iren hold his ground. He drew the Muryozaki.

If he fought, he would die. Even so, Balear was willing to face this thing. Iren wouldn't let him do it alone.

"Hana," Balear called without turning around. "Go to Veliaf and warn them. Whatever happens, you have to live." The man had never sounded so intense.

Iren couldn't tell if Hana was happy to have the chance for escape. She looked at Balear, her expression one of genuine astonishment that Iren had never seen from her. Finally, though, she fled south.

At the sight of its quarry escaping, the Fubuki bellowed in challenge. Its cry sent shivers through Iren, and he almost dropped the Muryozaki.

"I wanted to bring peace to Lodia," Balear said. "It might not turn out that way. But if I have to die here, at least I can give Hana enough time to raise the alarm!"

Balear's resolve amazed Iren. If Ariok chose his knights according to bravery as Hana had claimed, then the Sky Dragon had chosen well in Balear.

With another horrible roar, the Fubuki charged. Balear stood firm, but Iren couldn't stop himself from retreating a step. It was a small movement, yet it was enough to expose his weakness. The Fubuki focused on him. Its spear thrust at Iren's face. Iren managed to sweep the weapon aside and countered with a slash to the monster's wrist, hoping to disarm it.

He had to abort his strike, though, as the Fubuki's Ryokaiten spun around. Iren leapt back as the hammer end swung at him. The bizarre weapon missed him by an inch, yet the force of its passing threw Iren to the snow.

Iren swore. If that hammer landed a direct hit, his corpse would be less recognizable than those Ariok had dropped from the sky. Worse, he couldn't block it. The hammer would smash through any guard he could manage.

"Lodia!" Balear cried as he struck at the monster's exposed left side. Iren smiled; it was a good plan. The Fubuki's Ryokaiten was in its right hand, so it had to cross its own body to bring the weapon to bear. Even if it did, the spear would do little against Balear's gigantic sword.

Unfortunately, the hammer could do plenty. Faster than Iren thought possible, the Fubuki used the heavy weapon's momentum to spin it into Balear's sword.

The crash of the two massive Ryokaiten rang across the forest. Iren nearly bit off his tongue as his teeth clapped together. Balear went sprawling, and clouds of snow flew into the air as he tumbled along the ground. The Fubuki was unfazed.

Iren struggled to his feet. The Fubuki had its back to him as it focused on Balear. Rather than shout and reveal his presence like Balear had, Iren snuck up behind the creature and slashed silently at its arm.

The monster couldn't see him, but whether through scent or some other means, it must have known he was there. Its spear lunged backward. Iren's shirt ripped as the weapon sliced through his right side.

It missed his flesh, though, and the Fubuki's mistake was made. In failing to impale Iren, it had let him get too close. Iren stabbed up into where he hoped one of the monster's kidneys was.

Iren had thrown his full strength into the thrust, yet his sword only penetrated a couple inches into the monster's thick hide. Undaunted, the Fubuki backhanded Iren in the shoulder. The force of the blow made Iren drop the Muryozaki and sent him flying. He landed with a crash next to Balear.

The Fubuki reached down with its left hand and grabbed the Muryozaki. The katana looked like a toy in the beast's enormous paw. With a howl that shook the forest, the Fubuki hurled the sword in the opposite direction from Iren. The blade speared a tree forty feet up all the way to the hilt.

Iren's eyes flicked from the Fubuki to the Muryozaki with despair. Even if he could climb that high, he'd never be able to pull the weapon out of three feet of wood.

"It doesn't look good for us," he said.

"No, it doesn't," Balear admitted, "but that doesn't mean I'm giving up."

The soldier stood and pointed the Auryozaki at the Fubuki. Iren couldn't help but be impressed.

"Don't charge him," Iren advised. "He wants you to get in close so he can hit you with that hammer. Take advantage of your sword's length and attack from far away. Aim for his right hand or arm. If you can make him drop his Ryokaiten, you might have a chance."

Balear nodded but didn't speak. He circled the Fubuki warily.

Then the monster did something that made Iren's blood chill more than it already had. It smiled.

The tip of the Fubuki's spear glowed a light blue, and a spike of ice lanced from it. Balear saw it at the last second and raised his sword to block. The ice shattered against the blade.

When he lowered his weapon, the once-implacable Balear was shaking. The fifteen-foot-tall Fubuki was impossibly tough on its own, but it could use magic as well.

Again the spear illuminated, but instead of a single shard, this time a barrage of them launched from it. Balear stabbed the Auryozaki into the ground and hid behind it. The spikes bounced off it without harm.

The rain of shards stopped, and Iren saw the Fubuki's plan. "Balear, move!" he shouted, but he was too late. Balear's sword protected him, but it also blinded him to what his enemy was doing. The Fubuki surged around Balear's defense.

With a victorious howl the Fubuki thrust its spear. Balear flung himself away, but surprise slowed his reaction time. The spear pierced his right arm at the elbow.

Balear's wound wasn't fatal, but then it turned blue. Iren watched in horror as the flesh around the spear froze. The ice radiated out, creeping over Balear's arm.

It had just reached his shoulder when the ground shook. The Fubuki backed its weapon out of Balear and whipped its body around in search of the disturbance's source.

The monster's blood-red eyes settled on Iren. He gulped. The Fubuki must have decided he was causing the tremors.

Iren was sure the Fubuki would slay him, but then he realized he'd misinterpreted the beast's gaze. It wasn't looking at him, but past him.

Hoping the Fubuki wouldn't pounce on him the second he turned his back, Iren looked over his shoulder. The moment he did, he gasped.

Hana stood fifty feet away. In her hands she clutched a long-hafted brown war hammer.

The Fubuki bellowed in challenge, but Hana stood firm and unafraid. When the Fubuki pointed its spear at her, Iren called, "Look out for the ice shards!"

Hana didn't move. The spear glowed blue, and a barrage of bolts shot toward her. Iren slammed a fist into the snow, unable to do anything to stop the slaughter.

As the shots landed, though, they bounced off Hana as if she wore heavy armor. She cocked an eyebrow. "Is that all?" she asked. "I guess I shouldn't expect anything more from someone who isn't a Maantec."

The forest shook again, and dozens of rocks of various sizes burst from the ground. They floated in the air around Hana. She smiled. "Let me show you how it's done."

The stones shot forward with such speed that Iren could barely track them. They pummeled the Fubuki, but its hide prevented any serious damage. Even so, several red splotches appeared on the monster's fur.

For the first time, the creature stepped back. Iren had no idea how intelligent Fubuki were, but this one was smart enough to know that it had lost. With a final roar, it swung its Ryokaiten in a broad arc. Snow whipped around it, and it vanished.

The temperature warmed back to what it had been before the Fubuki's arrival. Iren let out a breath he hadn't realized he'd been holding. The monster had retreated. They were alive.

But not for long. Iren ran to Balear and cradled him in his arms. The man's eyes were blank.

"We have to get him to Veliaf," Hana said. The ground rumbled, and the dirt under Balear lifted up, levitating him.

Hana next raised the chunk of earth beneath herself. Like a leaf on a breeze, she floated to Iren's katana and withdrew it effortlessly from the tree it had impaled.

"H. . .How?" Iren stammered once Hana returned to the ground and handed over the sword.

"Later," she said, "after Balear is stable. Come on." She walked south toward Veliaf. The floating mound with Balear trailed behind her.

For a long time Iren stood transfixed. He watched Hana as she became smaller and smaller. It wasn't the shock of learning that she was a Dragon Knight. It was that she could save them, and he could not.

CHAPTER NINETEEN
Decisions

"You can come in now," Doctor Raebeld said, "but only for a few minutes. He's still weak."

Veliaf's doctor ushered Iren, Hana, and Dirio from the hallway of the town hospital into the stark sick room. As Iren crossed the threshold, his heart caught in his throat. Balear lay on a bed with bandages wrapped around his torso. Nothing remained of his right arm; it was gone all the way to the shoulder.

"I did everything I could," Raebeld said, running a hand through his thinning gray hair, "but I couldn't save it. The tissue was dead before you brought him here."

Iren's body felt tight. "This is terrible."

Raebeld shook his head. "Actually, he was lucky. The ice had only spread through his arm, so nothing vital was damaged. If it had gone into his torso, you wouldn't be seeing him, unless it was at his funeral."

Iren tried to appreciate the optimism, but he couldn't. This was his fault. If he could have used magic, the Fubuki wouldn't have posed a threat. Intimidating as it had been, its abilities didn't match the Fire Dragon's. A single beam of light would have killed it, and if it had somehow still managed to wound Balear, Iren could have healed him.

Hana put a hand on Balear's forehead. "He doesn't have a fever," she said. "That's good."

"When you brought him back two days ago, I wasn't sure I could save him," Doctor Raebeld admitted. "All things considered, he's making a remarkable recovery. He has a strong will to live."

As if in answer, Balear groaned and tried to sit up, but without his right arm, he couldn't do it. Raebeld frowned. "Yes, a strong will to live, and a stronger will in general. Do I have to tie you down? I told you to rest."

Balear glared at the doctor, but Iren ignored the exchange. He was busy eyeing Hana. His fists clenched. In truth, it wasn't entirely his fault that Balear was in this condition. The blame fell on Hana too. She was the Stone Dragon Knight! When the Fubuki appeared, she could have defeated it easily, yet she'd played the part of a damsel in distress and fled. Only when Iren and Balear were on the verge of death had she intervened.

"All right now, that's enough," Raebeld said in a tone that forbade argument. "Let the man sleep. Balear, I'll check back later, and I swear, if you've budged an inch, I'll haul blocks of stone from the mine and set them on your chest."

Hana gave the doctor an innocent smile. "Sir, if you want to make sure he doesn't move, I can stay with him. I promise to let him rest."

Raebeld didn't look happy about it, but he said, "Very well. Balear defies all my orders anyway. At least this way there's someone to yell at him when he does." He shooed Iren and Dirio out of the room, then hustled down the hospital hall. Dirio followed him.

When they'd gone, Iren stole back into the room and shut the door. Inside, Hana stroked Balear's nose with her thumb. "I'm sorry," she whispered. "I'm so sorry." A tear dripped from her cheek and landed on the bed next to him. Balear reached up with his left hand and wiped away the trail it left on her face.

Iren's cheeks flushed, but he had come too far to leave. "So what happened out there?" he demanded.

Hana sniffed. She kept her gaze on Balear as she said, "My master taught me that advertising yourself as a Dragon Knight attracts those who want the power for themselves. I wanted to tell you, but I couldn't. Now I realize that was a mistake. If I'd attacked right away, none of this would have happened."

Though Iren scowled, he understood Hana's reason. Rondel had once given him the same advice.

Balear stirred. "I don't blame you, Hana," he said. "You came back. That's what matters. We would have died without your help."

Another tear fell from her face.

Balear shook his head. "No more of that. What concerns me now isn't what happened, but why. The Fubuki only live in the frozen lands of Charda, farther north even than Akaku. What was this one doing so close to Veliaf?"

The door opened a crack. A voice from the other side of it said, "I might be able to shed light on that subject."

Dirio entered the room. "I had a feeling everyone would be in here, despite Doctor Raebeld's orders."

He sat on the floor against a wall. He looked old. "I'm beginning to think removing the Yokai from Akaku Forest was the worst decision Amroth made for Lodia's security," he said. "Well, maybe not the worst, but it ranks right up there."

"What do you mean?" Iren asked. He and Dirio knew firsthand how brutal the Yokai could be.

"I suspect the Yokai created a balance of power in the north. They lacked the numbers to invade Lodia, yet neither was Lodia in a position to attack them. At the same time, they had enough strength to keep out the Fubuki."

"So what you're saying," Hana cut in, "is that without the Yokai, the Fubuki are moving south and taking Akaku for themselves."

Dirio nodded. "We've lost a few patrols in the woods, but I always thought it was remnant Yokai. The events of two days ago changed my mind. There may be a few Yokai left, but I think they're being overrun. The Fubuki saw their chance and seized it."

"Forgive me for saying it, but that sounds speculative," Balear said from his bed. "We saw one Fubuki. That doesn't prove they're invading."

"True, and had you run into any other Fubuki, I'd dismiss it as a random event. But because you fought a Dragon Knight, I believe that changes the situation."

"Why?" Iren asked.

"Children in Veliaf grow up hearing stories about Fubuki," Dirio explained. "According to those tales, they can't survive warm temperatures. Normally that would mean we'd have nothing to fear from them. Based on your account, though, this Ice Dragon Knight can change the weather. Do you see where I'm going?"

Iren put a hand to his forehead. "With that Dragon Knight as their vanguard, the Fubuki aren't limited to cold climates. They can invade not only Akaku, but Lodia at any time of year. With the civil war going on, Lodia's in no shape to stop them. There's no way they wouldn't take advantage of a situation like that."

"My thoughts exactly."

A knock at the door interrupted their conversation. "Mayor Dirio? Sir, are you in there?"

Dirio stood, care-heavy wrinkles on his not yet fifty-year-old face. "Yes, what is it?" he asked as he opened the door.

A guard stood on the other side. "We've apprehended two new-comers at the gate," he said. "One of them claims to know you. I thought you'd want to know."

"I'll be right there," Dirio replied. He looked around the room. "You three show up, and within days I have a Fubuki Dragon Knight breathing down my town's neck. I wonder what these guests will bring." With that, he left.

Iren leaned against the wall. "Insane," he said. "It's insane. What are we supposed to do?" He wanted to help Veliaf, to help Lodia, to help Balear, yet he could do none of those things. Without magic, he couldn't defeat even a normal Fubuki. If they did invade, he would be useless against them.

He slammed his fist into the wall. "If only I could use magic!"

Hana eyed him for a long moment. Then her face lit up. "Iren, I may have thought of a way to help you."

He started. "How?"

"It occurred to me just now as I was thinking about my teacher. He's one of the oldest Maantecs alive, and he knows more about magic than anyone I've ever met. If you talk to him, maybe he'll be familiar with your affliction. He might even know a way to cure it."

It wasn't much to go on. Seeing Balear on that bed, though, with flat bandages where his arm should be, convinced him. "Where does your teacher live?"

"In Shikari," Hana said, "far away at the southernmost tip of Raa. You could travel on foot for months and still not reach it."

Iren's head dropped to his chest. He didn't have months to cross the continent on a "maybe," and he let Hana know it.

Instead of looking upset or even surprised by Iren's reaction, Hana smiled. "It would take months if we had to travel on foot, but who said we had to go that way?"

Placing her hand on the floor, Hana slowly raised her palm. As she did, the war hammer she'd held when she'd defeated the Fubuki appeared and rose up with it. Grasping the hammer, Hana sunk halfway into the floor.

"This is the Stone Dragon Hammer, the Enryokiri," she said as Iren gazed in astonishment at the half-woman before him. "It follows me underground no matter where I go. With its magic, we can travel through the rock faster than we can run. If we leave now, we can reach Shikari in two days."

Iren leapt to the door. "I'll get my things."

੪

Balear lay alone, forgotten by everyone. The room where Doctor Raebeld had put him was utilitarian, like all of Veliaf. His bed was a straw mattress laid over intertwined ropes tied to a wooden frame. A single chair gave the doctor a place to sit. That was it for furniture.

The only other object in the room leaned upright on the far wall. Balear couldn't stop looking at it, yet he desperately wished it would go away.

It was the Sky Dragon Sword.

According to Raebeld, Hana had brought it for him on a floating bed of earth. He could still feel the touch of her thumb on his nose. His remaining hand was wet with her tears. They made him furious. How could she come in here and give such an emotional display, and then dash off with Iren to the other side of the continent?

It was because they were Maantecs, and because they were Dragon Knights. Balear was neither. Ariok had given him a chance to be a Dragon Knight, but the Fubuki had taken that away. He would never fight again.

Footsteps approached Balear's room. Outside the door Doctor Raebeld yelled, "No! My patient needs to rest. I was lenient with you before, but I will not exhaust him with all these people!"

"I understand how you feel," Dirio's voice replied, "but these two have come a long way."

Balear wondered who would bother to visit a disgraced former general like him. He got his answer when a familiar high-pitched female voice said, "That's right, doc. Do you know how many times I nearly broke a hip walking here? And look what happened to my hand along the way! Honestly, if you want to stop me from seeing him, it's going to take more than you've got."

Balear smiled despite himself. The speaker had to be that crazy old Maantec, Rondel. Only she could pretend to be so frail yet finish with an undertone of threat.

"Please, I must insist—" the doctor began, but then Rondel opened the door and strode inside.

"Well look, doc!" she called. "Balear's wide awake and looking fine to me. I think we'll be all right without you for a few minutes."

She was the same as Balear remembered her, five feet tall and with a broad, stupid grin that he knew was false. Behind that expression, Rondel's emerald eyes scanned the room with poorly veiled wrath.

Those eyes concerned Balear, but more disconcerting was seeing Rondel's left arm in a sling. He couldn't imagine anyone wounding her that badly.

The most surprising part of the old woman's arrival, though, was not Rondel herself. It was the person who walked in behind her. Dressed in leather with a long cap that covered her hair, the woman might have passed for a young Beranian. Her rich tan complexion, green eyebrows, and longbow covered in living vines, however, all gave her away.

"Minawë," Balear said, doing his best to sound cheerful, "I never expected to see you in Lodia. Welcome."

Rondel looked hurt. "Oh sure, ignore me. Typical male, notice the outwardly attractive lady while missing the real beauty in the room."

Balear couldn't help but smile a second time. The cagey old woman usually grated on his nerves, but something about seeing her again made him happy.

"Now," Rondel said, an edge in her voice, "I think you two should leave us alone. We've come far, and we'd like to catch up with our old comrade."

Doctor Raebeld opened his mouth to protest, but Dirio silenced him with a look. "You don't want to argue with that one," the mayor said. "They won't stay long."

Raebeld huffed and complained, but Dirio shoved the doctor out of the room. He then left as well, shutting the door behind him.

"Well, Balear," Rondel said, "it looks like you've seen better days."

Balear touched the bandaged empty socket of his right shoulder. "How much did Dirio tell you?"

Rondel's grin vanished. "Enough. I wish we'd been faster catching up to you. I didn't expect you to fight the Ice Dragon Knight, and I never thought that if you did, that it would be a Fubuki on top of it. You're lucky you survived." She glanced at the gigantic sword leaning against the wall. "I see you have the Auryozaki to thank for that. I should have realized last year that Zuberi had it. It didn't seem possible to me, though, so I assumed it was another big sword. Zuberi was a giant himself, after all. I'm impressed it chose you."

Balear shrugged as best he could considering he only had one arm and was lying on a bed. "It once belonged to my father," he said.

"I see." Rondel walked to the blade and stroked it with her wrinkled hand.

Balear shifted his attention to Minawë. She seemed tense. "Iren's not here," he said, "if that's what you're wondering."

Rondel's hand continued to probe the Auryozaki as though Balear had never spoken. Minawë, however, dropped her eyes to the floor. Her shoulders slumped. "Dirio told us we'd find him talking to you," she said. "Did he step out to let you rest?"

"I wish," Balear said. "I don't think he's in Veliaf anymore. He left after you two arrived." He told them about his journey across Lodia with Iren and Hana.

Minawë looked distraught throughout Balear's explanation, and she peppered him with questions. Rondel, though, listened in silence. Only when Balear finished did she turn away from his sword and eye him with fury. "Do you know how I broke my hand?" she asked. "The Stone Dragon Knight attacked me in Serona. She almost killed me."

Balear paled. That was impossible!

Lightning Sight sparked in Rondel's eyes, turning her expression murderous. "I never thought she would dare do something like this."

Balear's confusion increased tenfold. "Wait, you know Hana?"

"Only a little," Rondel said. "I rescued her from some thugs about twenty-five years ago, but she was just a regular Maantec back then. She couldn't even fight. I never figured she would become the Stone Dragon Knight, let alone attack me or kidnap Iren."

"She didn't kidnap him," Balear protested. He trusted Rondel more than he did almost anyone, but this was absurd. "If she'd wanted to do that, she had plenty of opportunities while we traveled across Lodia. He went with her willingly. She said that her teacher might be able to help him regain his magic."

Rondel's brow furrowed. "There aren't many Maantecs who could teach a Dragon Knight. Did Hana say who they were meeting?"

"She didn't say his name," Balear replied, "but she said he lived at the southern end of the continent. Shikari, I think she called it."

Rondel spat. "So this is his doing."

Minawë spoke for the first time in a while. "His?" she asked. "Who do you mean?"

"Melwar."

"Who's Melwar?"

"Katashi Melwar is a Maantec lord about my age. His clan was second in power only to the emperor's. During the Kodama-Maantec War, he was Iren Saito's best friend and closest advisor."

Rondel paced the room twice. "This is bad. If Melwar's behind this, then Iren is in terrible danger. We have to follow him."

"That's crazy!" Balear shouted. "You'd have to cross all of Raa. Hana said that would take months."

"Which is why the sooner we start, the sooner we'll arrive. Whatever their purpose is with Iren, I doubt Hana and Melwar will let him go now that they have him."

Minawë nodded. "I'm ready."

Rondel cocked an eyebrow at Balear. "What about you?"

"What about me?" Balear shot back.

"Melwar isn't a Dragon Knight. At least, he wasn't the last time I saw him. Still, he has impressive magical abilities. If we have to fight him and Hana, we could use another Dragon Knight."

"In that case, look elsewhere," Balear said. "I'm no Dragon Knight, not anymore." He gestured at his missing arm. "I guess it's karma. I always mocked Iren for being a Left. Now I'm one too."

Rondel shrugged. "What's so bad about being a Left?"

"You were born a Left. I can't fight with just my left hand. Even if Ariok's sword is weightless for me, I would be clumsy with it."

"Amroth was the finest soldier in Lodia," Rondel pointed out. "He got there having to use his right hand, his off hand."

"Amroth was a Maantec. You're faster and stronger than humans. It was easy for him."

"Easy?" Rondel retorted. "You think it's easy to learn to use your off hand? It doesn't matter what race you are, Balear. It's no simple task."

"That's my point! Besides, Amroth was a monster. Don't you dare compare me to him!"

"As you wish," Rondel said. She shook her head. "I don't have time to argue with you. Minawë, let's go." She opened the door and let the Kodama exit first.

Rondel craned her neck to look back at Balear. "Amroth was a monster," she said, "but he was also a master of war. He knew what it took to be a great soldier. Of all the members of the Castle Guard, he chose you to be his companion and later his general. What made you stand out to him? Think about it." She shut the door and disappeared.

For hours afterward, Balear lay face-up on his bed. He stared at the ceiling with his hand tucked behind his head. Night fell, and the room darkened. Even then, he continued staring, and thinking.

CHAPTER TWENTY
The City of Maantecs

Hana Akiyama glanced with disgust at Iren Saitosan. He lay beside her feet, moaning. Hana sighed. At least he'd stopped puking.

She couldn't blame him for his discomfort. She had created a void in the earth large enough for both of them to stand and that held enough air for two hours. The space moved as one, so those inside it could be in any posture. It was a fast and convenient way to travel without all the nonsense of dealing with the hideous terrain between Lodia and Shikari. All the same, it was disorienting for the uninitiated.

Hana didn't care. She loved traveling this way. With the speed it gave her, she had delivered the Burning Ruby to Lord Melwar within two days of killing Rondel, and she'd had plenty of time to reach Lodia to intercept Iren.

She still couldn't believe how easy it had been to murder that crone. Twenty-five years ago, Rondel's power had awed her. Now that Hana had the Stone Dragon, though, no one could stop her.

Well, almost no one. But she was useful to Lord Melwar, and as long as that remained the case, he would keep her alive.

She had proven her capabilities to him too. Not only had she killed Rondel, someone even Lord Melwar had been unwilling to confront, but she had convinced Iren to trust her. He'd come with her by choice. With him in her possession, she and Lord Melwar finally had a chance at achieving their dream.

Iren forced himself into a sitting position. "How much farther?"

"Nearly there," Hana said. She knew the seemingly blind route by heart. "If you need to pass the time, practice your Maantec. You'll need it when we arrive."

The young man frowned, but he recited the vocabulary drills Hana had set up for him. He still couldn't read anything in the language, but he was doing better with spoken words. Every so often Hana would ask him a question in Maantec to see if he could answer her in kind. Most of the time he failed, but he managed one or two brief exchanges.

An hour past noon two days after leaving Veliaf, they surfaced in the broken land of Shikari. Hana shuddered as she took in the karst topography. Even though she'd spent years training here, she'd never gotten used to the place. Jagged white crags dotted the landscape, and most had entrances to at least one cave.

The ground was equally pockmarked. Now that she and Iren had returned to the surface, they had to watch every step to avoid the cracks. Most were just a tripping hazard, but some were wide enough that a person could fall through them.

Iren looked as stunned as Hana had been the first time she'd seen it. "Welcome to Shikari," she told him, her breath visible despite the bright sun overhead.

"Isn't it summer?" Iren asked. "Why is it so cold?"

"It's summer in Lodia, but we've crossed to the southern end of the continent. The seasons are switched here. Shikari doesn't get snow, but the rains this time of year are frigid and make travel by sea almost impossible." She paused. "Actually, we have that weather to thank for this land's safety. Armies can't invade by sea, and the broken terrain makes the region a natural fortress. Shikari was the only Maantec territory that never saw fighting during the war a thousand years ago. Because of that, it's become a haven for Maantecs. It's our last stronghold on Raa."

"If this is a Maantec stronghold, where are the Maantecs? How do they live? What do they eat in this wasteland?"

"There are patches suitable for farming vegetables, and there's so much water that the region is great for rice. Other than that, fish makes up most of the diet. The ocean surrounds Shikari on three sides."

That made Iren smile. "I love the ocean."

Hana kept her expression composed, but inside she was laughing. The boy was so innocent. It made him fun to play with.

"You'll love where we're going, then," she said. "Hiabi, the capital and only city in Shikari, sits at the southern tip of the continent. You can see the ocean in every direction but north."

They walked most of the afternoon, taking in the austere landscape. Just before they came within sight of Hiabi, though, Hana halted them. "Now pay attention," she said. "The Maantecs who live here aren't like me, someone adjusted to living among humans. They follow the old traditions. Their etiquette is more rigid than these peaks. If you don't conduct yourself with politeness, there's no guarantee of your safety."

Iren groaned, which made Hana scowl. "It's no joke," she said. "Maantecs value pride and respect. If you insult them, even in ignorance, tradition might call for them to defend their honor."

"Grand."

Hana smiled and touched him on the shoulder. "If it's any consolation, all you have to do is mimic me. We're both Dragon Knights, so we're considered equals in Maantec culture."

"Sounds good," Iren said. He took a few steps, but then Hana grabbed him.

"One more thing," she said, "let me do the talking. For now, you should speak as little as possible, and only when spoken to. That will reduce the chances of you insulting someone."

Iren shrugged. "I'll do my best." He resumed walking, but Hana snagged him again.

"One more thing."

"What is it?" he asked, rolling his eyes.

"Other than Lord Melwar, don't let anyone know you can't use magic. Act like the all-powerful Holy Dragon Knight. You can't hide that katana from onlookers, and if word gets out about your affliction, you'll have countless challengers seeking Divinion's power."

Iren's hand leapt to the Muryozaki. He clutched it to his side. "I'll never let anyone take him," he declared.

He stepped forward, but before his foot even reached the ground, Hana had hold of him. "One more thing."

Iren threw up his hands. "How many 'one more things' are there going to be?"

"Unless you want to start a fight, don't touch that thing's hilt like you did just now. Everyone who can see you will take it as a sign that you intend to draw it, or worse, to unleash Divinion's magic."

Iren smacked himself on the forehead. "I hope I made the right decision coming here."

Hana crossed her arms. "Do you want to use magic again or not?"

"Of course I do!"

"Then come on. There's no other way."

With a long sigh, Iren took a step. This time, Hana let him go. They walked side by side until they rounded a corner. When they did, Iren stopped in midstride, his jaw slack.

The reaction was justified. Standing before them was the largest city on Raa since the fall of Serona. Its stone outer wall stood twice as high as Haldessa's, and its footprint was five times as large as that city's had been before its fall.

The wall hid most of Hiabi, but the most important part was prominently visible: the central castle. Instead of turrets and towers like a human castle, the elegant fortress rose in sweeping levels with upturned roofs of black ceramic tiles.

Hana marveled at it. Human architecture could never match the splendor of what Maantecs could build. The castle carried the eye up with it, as though daring someone to gaze upon its heights.

It was magnificent, yet it was practical too. Invisible from this distance were the hundreds of arrow slits, openings for dropping rocks or burning pitch, and archers patrolling the wall.

"This is Hiabi," Hana said, "home of Lord Melwar."

They neared the outer wall's gate, itself a massive steel structure. Two guards stood before it carrying wooden poles longer than the men were tall. The staves crossed in the center, and while the men might have looked imposing on their own, they were purely for the sake of tradition. If an enemy had the strength to breach the gate, these two men wouldn't make a difference.

Hana strode up to them, head raised. When they recognized her, the men separated their staves and bowed low.

"My lady," one of them said, his tone of utmost respect, "welcome back to Hiabi."

"I'm in a hurry," Hana said. She tossed back her hair with her hand. "Send a messenger to Lord Melwar that I've arrived with Iren Saitosan, the Holy Dragon Knight. Should Lord Melwar deign to grace us with his presence, I would be most appreciative."

Iren looked at Hana like she'd sprouted a third arm. She ignored him. He'd have to figure out the details of Maantec hierarchies later.

The guard who had spoken before bowed again and said, "At once, my lady." He banged three times on the gate. With a loud creaking, it split into two halves and opened outward.

The moment the gates widened enough for her to pass, Hana swept through them. She moved so quickly Iren had to jog to keep up.

Iren's head swiveled as they walked. The inside of Hiabi was like a much larger version of Veliaf. The buildings stood a story taller than Veliaf's, and the streets were narrow and twisting.

The confusing design was deliberate. If someone didn't live here, they would become lost within seconds of entering. For a force invading the city, it would mean certain death as arrows rained from the buildings around them.

But Iren wasn't looking at the buildings. He was looking at the people. Thousands of them walked the streets. It took him only a minute before his expression shifted from awe to shock. Hana knew what he'd just figured out. These weren't humans. They were Maantecs.

"Hana—" Iren began, but she waved him off with her hand.

"I thought I told you silence," she said.

Iren stopped in the road. "Hey, you said the Maantecs value respect and that I shouldn't insult them. What about you?"

Hana whirled around and grabbed Iren by the shirt. His hand reached for the Muryozaki, but before he could touch it, she tugged on him and hauled him into an alley.

"The Maantecs do value pride," she hissed, "and because of it, they have a rigid class system. The people here know I'm the Stone Dragon Knight, and Dragon Knights are among the highest classes. In Hiabi, only Lord Melwar outranks me. I'm expected to give orders, and so are you. Now listen. You're strolling around the city gawking at everything and following me like a lost pet. That isn't how a Dragon Knight acts. You need a commanding presence."

"I've never commanded anyone in my life," Iren said. "How am I supposed to act like something I've never done?"

"I don't know, but figure it out. Otherwise, any number of the countless Maantecs out there will interpret your humility as weakness and attack you. Do you want that? No? Then portray invincibility. Hold your head up and don't look at all surprised by the city, no matter how much it baffles you."

They reentered the street. Hana kept one eye on Iren as they walked. The young man tried to mimic her confident posture. Hana could only hope the pitiful attempt would fool the low-class simpletons around them.

Fortunately the throng of people separated before them. Hana suspected it was more because of her reputation than Iren's.

That said, the crowd's size increased the farther they walked, and that was because of Iren. Rather, it was because of his sword. Every Maantec knew that gleaming white katana. More important, they knew who and what it represented, even if its owner didn't.

The more people they passed, the more Iren's posture deteriorated. Hana knew he must feel out of place. Back in Veliaf, Dirio had given Iren a new tunic to replace the one the Fubuki had damaged. No one in Lodia would have looked twice at him for wearing it, but here it marked him, and Hana too for that matter, as outsiders.

Hana wanted to pull Iren aside again, but the crowd was too thick now. The Maantecs pressed in, their kimonos flowing in the city's cool ocean breezes. Hana couldn't wait to change out of this stifling Lodian outfit and into something proper again. It had been too long.

They reached Hiabi's castle keep without incident. Word of their arrival must have preceded them, because the guards admitted the pair at once.

"Take off your boots," Hana ordered when the doors closed and shut out the commoners. "No one may wear shoes inside."

Iren didn't look happy about wandering around a strange castle with only linen stockings on his feet, but he complied. Hana removed her own footwear, and they stood in the entryway a moment before a man dressed in a black kimono came up to them.

The servant greeted them with a bow. "My lady," he said, "we received your message from the gate. His lordship has set aside adjacent rooms in the south wing. I'll show you to them."

"Will Lord Melwar see us?" Hana asked.

The man sucked air through his teeth. "His lordship is very busy," he said, "but he states that if you will consent to dine with him this evening, he will entertain you."

Hana nodded curtly. "Take us to our rooms then. I want to look presentable."

The servant bowed and gestured to his left. "This way."

As they walked through Hiabi's keep, Hana took a long breath. It was wonderful to return to civilization. She took in the trappings of a proper home with joy. Tapestries and paintings on silk lined both sides of the hall, most of them nature scenes. Several depicted birds so lifelike they looked like they might fly out of their portraits.

They climbed three sets of stairs before pausing at a sliding door. The servant bowed again, then opened it. "This will be the Lord Holy Dragon Knight's room."

Hana took a glance inside and said, "It will do. I assume mine is the one to the right?" She pointed, and the servant nodded. "Good. You may leave us."

When they were alone in the hall, Hana told Iren, "I'll get ready and then come help you. You shouldn't meet Lord Melwar looking like a barbaric human. Don't leave your room."

Iren was so pale Hana wondered if the man would pass out. Without a word, he entered his chamber and shut the sliding door behind him.

As Hana walked to her own room, she couldn't help but worry. All their plans, all their hopes, depended on Iren. Right now, though, he didn't look like their savior. At the moment, he'd be lucky to survive.

CHAPTER TWENTY-ONE
Dinner Preparations

Iren surveyed his room and did his best to make sense of it. The place looked nothing like bedrooms in either Lodia or Ziorsecth. Straw mats covered most of the floor, and wooden planks made up the rest. There was no furniture. Several built-in closets and drawers lined the walls, but that was it. Iren wondered if he could even call the space a "bedroom," since there wasn't a bed anywhere in it.

The room's strangest features were the walls made of paper stretched over wood that crisscrossed the chamber. Like the sliding door, they attached to wooden tracks in both the ceiling and floor that allowed them to move.

Curious, Iren played with the walls. He discovered he could change the room's configuration in an almost infinite number of ways, hiding or exposing certain sections at will.

Shifting the walls revealed features of the room that had been blocked from the entrance. In one corner, Iren found a cedar basin more than large enough to sit in. A pair of metal pipes protruded above it with their ends cut off. At first he thought it might be some kind of washtub, but if those pipes brought water, he could find no way to turn it on.

Iren waited alone in the room for what felt like hours. To keep busy, he opened the drawers and examined their contents. Most had clothing, but in one closet, he came across a thick mattress and set of blankets that he guessed were for sleeping. He grimaced. He hoped it wasn't Maantec custom to sleep in a closet.

A knock at the door pulled him from his explorations. "Come in," he said.

The sliding door opened, and Hana entered. Iren inhaled sharply at the sight of her. During their travels, she had worn modest clothes, but now she looked every inch the high noble her Dragon Knight status made her. She wore an ankle-length dress of pink silk adorned with white cherry blossoms. Her black hair hung freely down her back and framed her oval face. Iren blushed; he couldn't keep from staring.

"If you're done gawking at my kimono, can we work on you?" Hana asked. "We don't have much time. Lord Melwar won't take kindly to the way you look, or smell for that matter. We'd better start you with a bath."

Iren craned his neck around. "So that is what that tub is for."

Hana ignored him and walked to the cedar basin. She placed a hand on each of the two pipes, and water began flowing from them.

Iren ran his fingers through the streams. One was hot, while the other was cold. The combination made the water in the basin perfect for soaking. "How did you do that?" he asked.

"The pipes connect to cisterns," Hana said, "one heated, the other unheated. Apply magic to the pipe, and you can open and close it."

Though he wanted to hide his chagrin, Iren knew he did a poor job of it. Maybe Hana could open and close them, but he couldn't. Like the Kodamas, the Maantecs were a magical race. Of course they used it for everyday conveniences.

When the tub filled, Hana touched the pipes again. The water stopped. "Go ahead and wash up," she said. "I'll see if I can find something for you to wear."

Iren shifted the sliding walls to give himself some privacy. Undressing, he slipped into the hot water. He sighed in contentment.

While he soaked, he could hear Hana rooting around in the room. "Say, Hana," he said, "I was wondering if you could tell me a little more about Hiabi. Walking through the city made me realize I don't know anything about this place."

"What would you like to know?" Hana asked. Her voice was muffled, like she had her head in a closet.

Iren thought for a moment. "What else can you tell me about this Melwar guy who's in charge here?"

Hana didn't respond, and a moment later it hit Iren why. "Right," he said, cringing. "What do you know about Lord Melwar?"

"Lord Melwar has overseen Hiabi for more than a thousand years. It and Shikari are the ancestral lands of his clan. His family has ruled here for millennia."

"They've done a good job," Iren said, "if the number of people in the city is any sign. I never would have guessed there were so many Maantecs left. Rondel told me our species was almost wiped out."

"Not everyone here was born in Shikari. After the war Lord Melwar opened his lands to all Maantecs. He wanted Shikari to be a place where we could live apart from the other races." Hana paused. "Aha! This will be perfect for you!"

Iren was a little concerned about what she had found, but the bath made him so relaxed it didn't bother him much. On a nearby shelf, he located a washcloth and soap. "How will I speak with Lord Melwar?" he asked as he scrubbed. He couldn't believe all the dirt that came off him. "You've taught me a little Maantec, but it's not enough to carry on a conversation."

"Don't worry about that," Hana said. "Lord Melwar's traveled all of Raa and knows every language spoken on it. I've heard you could blind-fold him and drop him anywhere on the continent, and he could find his way back to Hiabi unaided."

"He sounds like a great man," Iren said. "I'm looking forward to meeting him."

"I'm glad. Lord Melwar is looking forward to meeting you as well."

Iren was washing his leg, but he stopped midstroke. "What do you mean? How could he even know who I am?"

Hana didn't answer. Iren was about to press her to explain, but then without warning, she pulled open the sliding wall and exposed him. Iren flushed as Hana looked over his naked body. He thought he sensed appreciation from her.

She confirmed that suspicion a moment later when she offered him a white towel with a cocked eyebrow and a smirk. Iren's blush deepened. He climbed out of the tub, yanked away the towel, and hastily wrapped himself in it.

Without a word, Hana grabbed a second towel and began to dry him. As her hands rubbed against his chest, Iren's pulse quickened. This close, he was keenly aware of Hana's soft hair, the smooth lines of her face, and her full breasts that swelled even with her flowing kimono.

"You know, Iren, my room is right next to yours," Hana whispered. "I'm sure we'll be seeing a lot of each other during our time here."

Iren gulped. "Let's just focus on getting ready for dinner," he said. His voice sounded high and strained.

"As you wish," she replied, and just like that, the moment ended. Hana hung her towel on a rack next to the tub. She then handed Iren an armful of clothes. "These should be your size."

Iren shifted nervously. Hana rolled her eyes and turned away.

Watching Hana for any sign of peeping, Iren removed his towel and dressed himself. Maantec clothing would take some getting used to. The undergarment looked like a diaper, and he felt extremely awkward putting it on. The trousers—if they could even be called that—weren't much better. They were gray, pleated, and so baggy that Iren could have sworn he was wearing a skirt.

Hana had given him two shirts, the first a white undershirt and the second sky blue with a long v-shaped cut in the front. The blue shirt's back bore a white stylized image of a serpentine dragon that filled most of the space.

For Iren's feet, Hana had selected a pair of gray socks with a notch between his second and third toes. A broad white sash completed the ensemble. Iren tucked the Muryozaki into it.

"What do you think?" Hana asked without turning around.

Iren walked forward so she could see him. "I look like a girl," he grumbled, pulling at his trousers.

Hana laughed. "In Lodia, maybe," she replied. "Here you look like a true lord."

"'Look' does sound like the right way to put it," he said.

"Like I said before, just do what I do, and you probably won't die."

"Grand."

"Keep remarks like that to yourself in front of Lord Melwar," Hana cautioned as she headed for the door.

Iren followed her for a few steps. Then he stopped and looked behind him at the tub and his pile of Lodian clothes.

"Why are you dallying?" Hana asked. "Lord Melwar is not a man to keep waiting."

"Hana, I . . ." he paused, unsure what to say. "I want to thank you. I'm totally lost here. I don't know what will happen with Lord Melwar, but I hope you'll keep helping me while we're here."

A sly smile played across her lips. "Of course," she said, "anything you need."

CHAPTER TWENTY-TWO
Lord Melwar

The socks were the most irritating part of the outfit, Iren decided as he and Hana walked through the halls of Hiabi Castle. The material between his toes itched, and he fidgeted in a vain attempt to make the socks more comfortable.

He still wasn't used to them by the time he and Hana arrived at a door where she said, "Remember, mimic me and don't speak unless you're spoken to."

Iren rolled his eyes. He wondered how many times she was going to give him the same advice.

Hana slid open the door and entered. She took two steps inside and prostrated herself on the floor. Iren followed and copied her.

The prostrated position created two problems. First, it left Iren unable to know what was happening. Second, and more important, he couldn't see Hana, so he had no idea if he was mimicking her.

Fortunately, he had only lain on the floor a few seconds before a male voice said, "Enough of that. You two are guests, not servants. Rise."

Iren lifted his head a sliver, just enough to see Hana out of the corner of his eye. When she stood, he got up as well and took in the room. It was large, three times the size of the one provided to him. Candles on sconces lit the walls, while coal-filled braziers illuminated and heated the center. Like Iren's room, straw mats covered the floor, and there was almost no furniture.

The sole exception was a high-backed chair on a dais at the room's far end. Carvings of serpentine dragons wound around its dark wood.

A man sat on the chair, and Iren assumed that man was Melwar. He looked in his mid-thirties, making Iren wonder what spell he must have cast to use some of his biological magic. His hair was black, and like most of the other Maantecs Iren had seen while walking through Hiabi, he had it tied in a topknot. In dress he wore much the same as Iren, but his outer shirt was a deep purple. Two circular crests adorned its front, each below one shoulder and depicting a mountain.

"Hana," Melwar said, his voice formal and filling the space, "it has been too long. It is good to see you once more in Hiabi."

Hana bowed low. "Thank you, Lord Melwar."

Melwar then faced Iren. "And to you, Iren Saitosan, Holy Dragon Knight, I bid you welcome to my humble city and home."

Iren started at the direct address. He figured he should say something in return, but his mind blanked.

A bell rang in the distance, and Melwar clapped his hands. "Well, we shall have more time for conversation later. Let us eat."

The Maantec lord stepped off his dais and came down to meet them. As if on cue, the room's sliding door opened, and a virtual troop of servants entered with trays of food. Iren glanced around, confused. There were neither tables nor chairs. He wondered if Maantecs ate off the floor.

He wasn't far off. The servants set small wooden trays with foot-high legs in front of Iren, Hana, and Melwar. The other two Maantecs knelt and sat on their feet so that their knees stopped just shy of the trays. Hana gave Iren a sharp look when he remained standing, so he knelt as well.

The servants next placed on each tray a bowl filled with white rice and a plate of fish and vegetables cooked in brown sauce. The only utensils were a pair of sticks the length of Iren's forearm that sat on the far end of his tray.

Iren examined his food with a mix of longing and disgust. It looked delicious, and the smell coming off it was impressive. That said, he had no idea how he was supposed to eat with sticks.

He looked at Hana for guidance. She picked up her sticks and held them between the fingers of her left hand. She then deftly plucked a chunk of yam off her plate, dipped it in the rice, and popped the whole thing in her mouth. Melwar did the same.

The technique seemed simple enough. Keeping an eye on Hana, Iren picked up his sticks.

The piece of fish he grabbed lifted half an inch before it split and fell in two pieces back to the plate. He tried again with a radish slice, hoping it would be firmer, but it too dropped. The sticks clacked together.

Across from Iren, Melwar stopped eating. "You have never used chopsticks?" he asked.

Iren flushed. "No," he said, more curtly than he'd intended. He quickly followed up with, "Lord Melwar."

Melwar shrugged. "Well, you did grow up in Lodia. They are so uncivilized up there. We will have to teach you. It does take a little practice."

"I look forward to it," Iren said. He forced a smile.

"You are a poor liar," the Maantec lord replied.

With that, Melwar resumed eating. Iren resumed picking up and dropping his food with increasingly loud and frustrating *plops*.

Though the food was beyond him, drinking proved simpler. On each tray the servants set a tall, narrow, ceramic vessel along with a short, broad cup. Iren saw how Hana poured and drank hers, then followed her. The liquid was warm, and it burned going down. Iren wondered if it was alcoholic. It made him think of Rondel. She would know.

Concerned that he might make a fatal mistake of etiquette if he drank too much, Iren kept to sips. Meanwhile, he was improving with his chopsticks. After ten minutes, he got his first bite into his mouth. It had long since become cold, but he counted it a victory.

After that he managed better, though Melwar and Hana had to wait several minutes while he finished. The servants returned and cleared the trays with silent efficiency.

When it was just the three of them in the room again, Melwar said, "I must apologize to you, Iren. Neither Hana nor I have been honest with you."

Iren glanced at Hana, but her face revealed nothing. He turned back to Melwar. "I'm uncertain what you mean."

"Even in this remote place, we have our information sources. You are more famous than you know. After all, you became the Dragoon."

"You know about my fight with Amroth and Feng?"

"The release of a dragon and the coming of the Dragoon are rare events. The first has only happened a handful of times, and no Dragon Knight before you has ever succeeded in the Dragoon transformation. When I learned of those events, I sent Hana to find you, gain your trust, and bring you here."

Iren whipped to face Hana. "So it wasn't coincidence that you rescued Balear and me in Orcsthia. You were waiting for us."

"Not exactly," Hana said. "I knew from accounts of the Battle of Ziorsecth that you'd stayed in the forest, and I dared not enter that place to follow you. But I figured that if you ever left there, you would do so through Lodia. With the Yuushin Sea to the south, Serona to the west, and frozen Charda to the north, it was your only option. I did gamble that you would go south via Orcsthia rather than north via Caardit, but Caardit's pretty remote to be a logical stopping point."

Iren thought back to his first few hours with Hana. "I guess that means the story you told about your parents' farm was a lie."

Hana shook her head and sighed. "No. That farm did belong to my parents, and Lodian raiders did kill them as part of the civil war. What I kept hidden, though, was that I had left home a long time ago, years before you were born. I never saw my parents alive after that. Still, I knew the farm was there, and it made a convincing cover. That's why I used it."

"But why cover up your identity at all?" Iren asked. "If your goal was to bring me here, why did you travel across Lodia with Balear and me? As the Stone Dragon Knight, you could have kidnapped me the minute we left Orcsthia."

Hana opened her mouth, but Melwar interrupted, "It was vital for her to gain your trust, and for you to come with her willingly. Had we forced you to come here, you would never have listened to my proposal."

"Proposal?" Iren asked. "What kind of proposal is so important that you have to go through all this maneuvering?"

Melwar's face grew somber. "When you came to Hiabi, no doubt the number of Maantecs here surprised you. My ancestors' land has become a haven for our kind, but it is far from ideal. To reach us, Maantecs must either brave a journey through Aokigahara Rainforest, or they must sail along the coast through the worst storms our world experiences. I lack perfect information, but I would guess that more than half of all Maantecs who attempt to come here die along the way."

The color drained from Iren's face. For all the thousands of Maantecs he'd seen in the city, thousands more had died trying to get here.

"I have long hoped that someday, our people will not need to make such a trek," Melwar continued. "Right now they do so because they have no choice. If they are discovered in any other nation, they are considered demons. I wish to change that. I want to see a Maantec emperor restored. Such a man could speak for all of us, treat with other nations, and find a way for Maantecs and other races to live in peace."

"Hold on," Iren said, "you can't mean . . . me?"

"Traditionally, the Holy Dragon Knight is also the Maantec emperor. No one but you can do it. I am master of Shikari, but beyond it I have no authority. Besides, who better to lead us than the man who became the Dragoon?"

Iren felt like he might pass out. When he'd left Lodia with Hana, he'd never expected anything like this. He'd thought he was coming here to regain his magic. Emperor of the Maantecs? It was impossible. He was no leader. For most of his life, people had shunned and hated him. He couldn't do it.

And yet . . .

If the Maantecs united, he could leverage that strength to get other nations to work with him. He could end Lodia's civil war by backing whichever mayor seemed best. The Kodamas might even make peace with their ancient foes. After all, Minawë was their queen.

Iren stood and steeled himself. "I'm no politician," he said. "I'm certainly no diplomat. I'll need a lot of help."

Melwar smiled and rose as well. "I have led both Hiabi and Shikari in peace for a thousand years," he said. "What small experience I have, I am happy to share with you."

"Great," Iren said. "So how do I become the emperor? Is there some kind of ceremony?"

The Maantec lord scowled. "You think it will be that easy? Do you think the Maantecs will just accept you? I know you became the Dragoon, but others will not have heard that tale or will not believe it. They will demand proof of your abilities. They will expect you to heal the sick and battle enemies with magic."

Iren winced at Melwar's final word. There it was again. If only he could use magic, he could become the Maantec emperor. He could end Lodia's civil war. He could create peace between Kodamas and Maantecs.

"That's a problem," Iren admitted. "I can't use magic anymore."

"As I feared," Melwar replied. He put his thumb and index finger to his forehead. "When I heard you had become the Dragoon, I suspected that might happen."

"That's why I journeyed all this way," Iren said. "Hana told me you were her teacher, and that you were the most knowledgeable Maantec when it came to magic. Can you teach me how to use it again?"

"It is not a matter of education," Melwar said. "It is an anomaly in your body."

"Then can you heal it?"

The Maantec lord shook his head. "No one can heal you."

Iren's hands fell to his sides. His gaze dropped to the floor. "Then this trip was pointless. I'll never use magic again."

"No one can heal you," Melwar repeated, ignoring Iren's outburst, "because you are not injured."

"Of course I'm injured!" Iren cried. "Maantecs are magical beings. Everything here, even taking a bath, requires it. How can I not be injured?"

"Do you know why you cannot use magic?"

What did that have to do with anything? Iren opened his mouth to tell off the annoying man for not getting to the point when Hana jumped up and shot him a panicked look. Forcing down his frustration, he said, "The Dragoon's magic was too powerful. It could have killed me, so my body sealed off my magic to prevent me from doing it again."

Melwar nodded. "Correct, and that is why I cannot heal you. What you have is not an injury, but a magical wall constructed by your body."

"But if I'm not injured, is there any way to get my magic back?"

The Maantec lord smiled, but it wasn't a pleasant expression. "It is only a wall," he said. "You can knock it down."

Melwar's simple description made Iren's heart skip. If this barrier was all that stood between him and his magic, he'd have Divinion back, become the Maantec emperor, and return to Lodia in a matter of days.

Melwar must have seen his excitement, because the Maantec lord said, "Do not think it will be easy. Or safe. Your body created that barrier to protect you. It did not make it to be removed. You could die."

Iren set his jaw. "Just tell me what I need to do."

"Very well," Melwar said. "Defend yourself."

"Wha—" Iren began, but then Melwar's stance changed. Though he was unarmed, the Maantec lord's hand went to his sash as though grasping at a hilt. A shadow grew at the spot, and from it Melwar pulled a long, black blade. It shifted and twisted as he held it aloft, as though it were as insubstantial as smoke.

Iren had never seen a spell like that before, but something told him it was more dangerous than it appeared. He drew the Muryozaki. Whatever that bizarre sword was, Melwar's touching it meant that he intended to attack.

Hana's hands went to her mouth, and in that instant of distraction, Melwar struck. He slashed horizontally, but his attack was slow. Iren raised the Muryozaki to block with plenty of time to spare.

As their blades met, though, Melwar's sword passed through Iren's. Surprised, Iren panicked and ducked low to avoid Melwar's attack. Even so, the cut caught the tip of Iren's hair. Several strands fell to the floor.

Iren retreated from Melwar and eyed the Maantec lord in shock. That shadow blade had passed through the Muryozaki, yet it had somehow become solid enough to nearly slice off Iren's head.

Though Iren didn't know how such a technique could be possible, it was simple to counter. He couldn't block Melwar's sword, so he would have to avoid it. The next time the Maantec lord attacked, Iren sidestepped the vertical slice. As Melwar was still following through, Iren thrust. He didn't want to wound Melwar, but the narrow miss earlier had forced him to think otherwise. This might be a fight to the death.

Still, Iren didn't want to kill Melwar if he didn't have to. Rather than a lethal blow, he aimed for Melwar's sword hand.

The Maantec lord didn't even attempt to block or dodge. Iren's blade struck its target.

Iren half-smiled in victory, but almost instantly, he knew something was wrong. His blade hadn't met any resistance, and Melwar had neither cried in pain nor dropped his sword.

Thrown off balance, Iren took another step forward. His momentum drove his sword through Melwar's chest.

"No!" he shouted, dropping his katana. If he had killed Melwar, then all hope of regaining his magic was gone forever. He rushed to cradle the dying lord in his arms, but instead of holding Melwar, Iren passed right through him. It was as though the Maantec lord were as insubstantial as his sword.

Only then did Iren realize the Muryozaki had fallen to the floor. It had landed soundlessly on the straw mats. Melwar was unharmed.

The next second, Iren felt a breeze and the slightest pain as Melwar's blade cut a shallow line in Iren's right cheek.

The Maantec lord stepped away. His strange weapon vanished. He waited while Iren picked up the Muryozaki and sheathed it. Once he had, the Maantec lord said, "You are not ready yet. Hana, bring him to the garden tomorrow at dawn. We will begin his instruction."

Hana knelt and bowed so that her head touched the floor, and Iren recovered his wits enough to mimic her. The two of them left Melwar in his chamber and headed back to Iren's room.

"What on Raa just happened?" Iren demanded when they arrived.

Hana laughed. "I think you just got yourself a new teacher."

Iren groaned.

CHAPTER TWENTY-THREE
Mountain Fire

Rondel and Minawë galloped across southern Lodia. Ahead of them loomed the high peaks of the Eregos Mountains.

As they rode, Minawë silently thanked Dirio for giving them the horses Hana and Iren had ridden to Veliaf. Crossing Lodia on foot had been dangerous enough. Crossing all of Raa that way seemed impossible.

In spite of the improved travel conditions, Minawë despised every second. This journey shouldn't be necessary. They had been in the same village as Iren. Had they arrived a few minutes sooner, they might have caught up to him before Hana ensnared him.

It didn't help Minawë's mood that Rondel had ridden in brooding silence ever since they'd left Veliaf. Minawë had tried to engage her in conversation the first day out, but the old Maantec had worn such a frightening expression that Minawë had given up the effort.

She wanted to dismiss Rondel's sullenness as mere frustration at having missed Iren. Yet something told her there was more to it than that. She had suspected that Rondel had been keeping a secret ever since Ziorsecth. Now Minawë was certain of it. There was more to this mission than rescuing Iren. Whatever it was, Rondel knew it and didn't intend to share.

After four days of travel, though, the old woman's attitude eased a little. She still hadn't spoken, but she didn't seem furious at the world anymore.

Minawë decided to risk it. She couldn't handle the silent travel much longer. "How's your hand?" she asked.

Rondel shook her head and blinked several times. "I'm sorry, what?"

"I asked about your hand," Minawë laughed. She rolled her eyes. "Hey, are you daydreaming over there? That's more like Iren than you."

The old Maantec chuckled, and Minawë felt the tension between them drop. "I guess so," Rondel said. "As for my hand, I wish I had better news. It isn't infected; I can thank Serona's heat for that. Unfortunately, it didn't set right. I don't think I'll ever use it again."

Minawë recalled Balear lying on his bed in Veliaf, missing an arm. At the time, she had wondered why Rondel would go to such lengths to comfort him. Now she understood.

"Slow down," Rondel called, interrupting Minawë's thoughts. The terrain around them had changed. It sloped up and was littered with large rocks. Caught by surprise, Minawë swayed in her saddle.

"And here you were making fun of me for not focusing," Rondel said with a smirk.

Minawë shot the woman a dirty look, but secretly she was glad Rondel was making sarcastic comments again. It meant the old woman was back to normal.

"Does this mean we've crossed into Eregos?" Minawë asked.

Rondel's horse trotted up beside hers. "I'm not sure where the border is, but for all practical purposes, yes. There are only a few small Lodian towns at the base of the mountains, and we'll avoid them. We've gotten caught up enough in their war."

Minawë had to agree with her. They'd seen more devastation crossing Lodia than Minawë had witnessed in her life. It made the damage Feng had caused to Ziorsecth last year seem minor.

As they rode higher into the foothills, Minawë's pulse quickened. Despite her frustrations, a sense of adventure was growing on her. Eregos's peaks awed her. They seemed to stretch forever, and more than a few speared the clouds. "Will we have to climb them?" she asked, entranced and afraid at the same time.

"Thankfully, we won't," Rondel said. "There are a few passes between the mountains. It'll be rough going for the horses, but nothing they can't manage. I'm more concerned about the Tengu."

"Tengu?" Minawë had heard them mentioned a few times, but she knew nothing about them.

"Mountain men," Rondel explained. "They're mostly livestock herders, especially goats."

Minawë breathed a sigh of relief. "So they aren't dangerous."

"No! They're quite dangerous. They're the reason Yokai no longer live in these mountains. And during the Kodama-Maantec War, the Maantecs would have conquered Lodia had the Tengu not sided with the humans and Kodamas fighting there."

"What makes them so dangerous?" Minawë asked. "Are they strong?"

Rondel shook her head. "Compared with Kodamas and Maantecs, the Tengu have little magical talent. For the unwary, though, they can be the deadliest of opponents. They excel at illusion and trickery."

Minawë gulped. "I hope we don't see any."

"Even if we do, they're peaceful enough that as long as we don't threaten them, we should be safe. Still, I'd feel more comfortable if Lodia weren't in the middle of a civil war."

"What does that have to do with the Tengu?"

"Take a look around: scrubby pine trees, dry earth, steep slopes, and rocky soils. This isn't farmland. The Tengu rely on trade with Lodia to supplement the meat and dairy from their livestock. But Amroth's drafting of an army and the civil war will have vastly reduced Lodian agriculture. The Tengu may be growing desperate. They might fear an invasion, or worse," Rondel's expression turned grim, "they might be planning one."

After that, Rondel suggested they ride in silence to avoid attracting attention. They traveled through the afternoon, stopping only to refill their water skins at a spring.

Minawë had no idea how long the journey through the mountains would take, but she hoped it would be over quickly. Her earlier adventurousness was eroding at the reality of what they faced. The rocky trail didn't allow the horses to go faster than a walk, and each step echoed off the surrounding cliffs. Rondel's idea of riding quietly was impossible. They'd be better off sneaking through here with a troupe of drunken bards.

She was about to ask Rondel what they should do about the noise when they crested a ridge. The moment they did, all Minawë's thoughts of their journey fled as she beheld the valley below them.

Everything in it was scorched black. From the ridge where they stood to the far valley wall, no vegetation survived. A few husks of old pine trees remained, but they didn't have a single needle on them. An acrid smell filled the air, and smoke still rose from several areas.

Rondel dismounted and took a few steps into the charred valley. Kneeling, she picked up a clump of burned soil and rubbed it in her fingers.

Panic rose in Minawë's throat. This was why Hana had taken the Burning Ruby from Rondel. She had reforged the Karyozaki and created a new Fire Dragon Knight.

Minawë drew her bow and nocked an arrow. The flames that had destroyed this valley couldn't have gone out more than a couple days ago. If the Fire Dragon Knight was still here, they were dead. Rondel couldn't fight, and Minawë wasn't ready to face any Dragon Knight yet, certainly not one of the same ilk that had slain Mother.

Rondel paused in her examination of the soil. She cocked an eyebrow. "What has you so worried?"

Minawë couldn't believe the woman's nonchalance. "What has me so worried?" she cried. "The Fire Dragon Knight is here! He'll kill us!"

The old Maantec stared at Minawë for a long moment. Then the old woman burst out laughing. "You think the Fire Dragon Knight caused this?"

"Of course! Look at this destruction! This valley must be hundreds, maybe thousands of acres in size."

"You're right," Rondel said with a nod. "It is small, now that you mention it."

"Small?"

Rondel made her way back to the ridgeline. "Minawë, this is no dragon-caused disaster. We're coming into summer, and the mountains here get little rain. Combine the two, and this region is rife with wildfire."

Minawë was shocked. "You're saying this devastation is natural?"

"As natural as we are. It doesn't take much to set off a blaze like what caused this. A careless Tengu with a campfire or a bolt of heat lightning would be all that's required."

Minawë dismounted and entered the valley. She heard no voices here. "If what you say is true," she said, "then how can anything survive in these mountains?"

Rondel walked to the husk of a pine. "Take a close look at this tree," she said. "The plants here are adapted to fire. This one has extremely thick bark. It may look charred, but it's doing fine."

Minawë put a hand on the tree, and to her amazement discovered that Rondel was right. It was still alive. In fact, it felt more than alive. The tree's voice conveyed sheer delight.

"It doesn't make sense," Minawë said. "This tree is overjoyed about the fire. How can that be? What does it have to be happy about?"

Rondel grinned. "That's why I was checking the soil. Grab some yourself, and you'll see."

Minawë didn't know what Rondel was driving at, but she obliged. Picking up a handful of dirt, she sifted it through her fingers. At first she didn't sense anything. Then she heard tiny voices from the soil.

"These trees have serotinous cones," Rondel explained. "Your father taught me about them after I joined his side in the Kodama-Maantec War. The cones can withstand intense heat, and it's only after such heat that they open and release their seeds."

Sweeping her gaze over the blackened landscape, Minawë understood. "Of course," she said. "There are no other plants to compete with the seeds. If they're released only after a fire, then they can grow unrestrained."

"That's why the tree's so happy," Rondel said. "It knows that while it has suffered, its sacrifice has given its children the best chance for success."

Minawë thought back to the pair of graves at the Heart of Ziorsecth. Mother and Father had given their lives so she could survive. She wondered if they had felt the same elation as this tree at the moments of their deaths.

"We shouldn't linger," Rondel said. "Night's falling, and we don't want to be out and exposed either in this valley or on the ridge. We'll backtrack a little and find a place to camp."

Minawë walked a few steps toward the ridge, but then she halted. She placed both hands on the ground, her Chloryoblaka clutched between them. Closing her eyes, she reached out to the seeds around her. She could only touch those within about thirty feet, but it was enough. She let her magic flow into them and willed them to grow.

When Minawë opened her eyes again, a circle of seedlings had sprouted, their blackened parent at its center. "What do you think?" she asked.

For a long time Rondel didn't answer. Finally she smiled. "It's wonderful."

CHAPTER TWENTY-FOUR
Training Regimen

When Hana woke Iren at dawn, he had no desire to get up. The thick mattress—Hana called it a futon—and cylindrical pillow she'd pulled from the closet last night were by far the most comfortable bedding Iren had ever slept in. But Hana insisted, and after she lifted one side of the futon and rolled Iren onto the floor, he got the message.

A servant entered bearing a tray with a teapot and a pair of cups for them. Hana sipped hers, but Iren sucked his down, grateful for the heat and invigoration it provided.

Once Hana finished her tea, she helped Iren pick suitable clothes. She chose a less ostentatious outfit than she had the previous night, a simple tan shirt with the same baggy, pleated trousers.

The clothing matched Hana's. She had dressed like a Maantec man and tied her long black hair in a ponytail.

Still groggy, Iren let Hana guide him through the castle keep, down several flights of stairs, and outside into a large central garden. Ringed by the keep, the garden was simple yet elegant. Small trees, bare in winter's chill, lined a maze of stone walkways.

The garden's middle, however, had no plants at all. Instead, sand filled a square area about the size of Iren's bedroom.

Following Hana's lead, Iren removed his socks and stepped onto the sand. It was frigid, not far above freezing, and he shivered. Even so, he dug his toes into it, savoring its therapeutic crunch. He breathed deeply. Though plaster and stone ringed him, in the distance Iren could hear the ocean waves crash on the shores that surrounded Hiabi on three sides.

The morning breeze showed his breath, but it also brought the sea's salty tang. That air woke him more than any tea ever could.

"I thought you might like it," a male voice said from behind him. Iren turned and bowed. Hana did the same beside him.

"Lord Melwar," Iren said.

"Rise," Melwar replied. "We have work to do."

Iren lifted his head to look at Melwar. The Maantec lord dressed the same way he had the previous night. In each hand he held a wooden sword shaped like the Muryozaki. He tossed one to Iren. "We will start with these."

Iren fingered the wooden katana doubtfully. "How is this supposed to help me use magic again?"

"You think you can survive breaking your body's magic wall with your strength as pitiful as it is? Hit me first."

Setting the Muryozaki on the ground, Iren held out his new wooden sword in challenge. Melwar half-smiled. He snapped his fingers, and Hana stepped between them.

"Before you may face me," Melwar said, "you must prove that you can defeat someone of your own rank. Win against Hana, and then we will fight." He handed the Maantec woman his second wooden sword and stepped back.

"The rules are simple," Melwar continued as Hana squared off against Iren. "Do not leave the sand. You may use the wooden sword and your body, but magic is forbidden. The winner is the one who lands the first blow with his or her sword."

Iren gritted his teeth. The lord's exercise was a waste of time. Still, Melwar was in charge here. He'd just have to go along with this nonsense for now.

Fortunately, he wouldn't have to go along with it for long. After observing Hana's fights in Lodia, Iren knew he could win. Hana was an aggressive fighter. She never worried about blocking, because her Stone Dragon Knight abilities gave her armor that swords couldn't pierce. In a match where magic wasn't allowed, that inexperience with defense would make her vulnerable.

True to expectations, Hana made the first move, attacking with a vertical slash at Iren's head. It was fast and hard, with no thought to the stomach she'd left exposed in the process. Iren blocked her strike, redirected the force off to his right side, and countered with a thrust at Hana's abdomen.

He was certain his blow would land, but then Hana sidestepped to her left and avoided it. She cut horizontally, and Iren felt pain in his right arm as the wooden sword connected. Hana stepped back and made a show of pretending to sheathe her weapon.

"Hana wins," Melwar said.

Iren seethed at the mundane way the Maantec lord stated the obvious. "How?" he demanded of Hana. "I thought you didn't care about defense."

"Only a fool doesn't care about defense," she said. "If you're judging me by the fights we shared in Lodia, that's a poor decision. I didn't bother with defense back then because we never faced an opponent that warranted defending myself against."

"One more time then," Iren grunted. "I won't take you lightly again."

Hana shrugged. "If you want." She readied her wooden sword.

"No," Melwar interrupted, "one attempt per day. You both will meet me here at dawn each morning and duel. That is all we have time for. After all, Iren, this is only the first part of your training regimen."

The way Melwar said "regimen" made Iren gulp.

"Hana, that will be all for today," Melwar continued. "We will see you tomorrow." Hana bowed low and left the garden.

When Melwar and Iren were alone, the Maantec lord said, "Last night when I attacked you, you saw that I prefer shadow magic. You should consider my selection fortunate. Had I chosen any other, you would have no chance of using magic again."

"How so?" Iren asked.

Melwar folded his arms and scowled. At first Iren had no idea why the annoying Maantec was dallying, but then he realized his mistake. "Please explain, Lord Melwar," he said, cursing mentally. This etiquette stuff was going to be the end of him.

His apology appeared to satisfy Melwar. The Maantec lord answered, "There are nine types of magic, and each has its opposite: fire and ice, water and air, earth and life, light and shadow. Lightning is its own opposite; it has positive and negative charges. These energies are at constant war with each other as they strive for balance. For that reason, although they oppose, they also attract one another."

Melwar paused and pointed at Iren. "You are the Holy Dragon Knight. To break your barrier, we must build up enough shadow magic in your body so that the attraction between it and your trapped light magic is stronger than your body's wall. When that happens, your barrier will break as the magics collide with each other. Unfortunately, the pain of enduring all that energy inside you would kill you in a second. To have a hope of surviving a breach of your body's wall, you need to increase your pain threshold."

Iren blanched.

"The second part of your training regimen will be an endurance trial," Melwar pressed on, ignoring Iren's discomfort. "I will attack you with shadow magic, and you will try to stay conscious. Simple, right?"

"Yeah, real simple," Iren spat before he could stop himself.

"Under normal circumstances, I would be within my rights to attack you for showing me such a callous attitude," Melwar warned. "However," he added with a sly grin, "I think you are in for enough punishment as it is. Prepare yourself."

Iren retrieved the Muryozaki and held it before him. "I'm ready, Lord Melwar," he said, though he knew it was a lie.

Melwar raised a single hand. The shadows in the garden deepened, shifting much faster than they should to mark the passage of the sun. They enveloped Iren and grasped at him like hands.

Then as one they stabbed into him. It was like a hundred knives driving into his flesh from every direction. He screamed at the pain that seemed to last for all eternity, and he blacked out.

CB

Iren woke in his room. He was on his futon and looking at the ceiling. His body ached. He tried to stand, but he could only raise his head a few inches.

"Not bad," a female voice said. "Lord Melwar thought you'd sleep until dawn."

Hana appeared above Iren, still dressed like a man. She dabbed a wet cloth on his forehead. The water was cool and refreshing.

"What happened?" Iren asked. "What time is it?"

"About two hours until sunrise."

"That doesn't make sense," Iren said. "It was just after dawn."

"Yes, you've been asleep almost a day."

Iren recalled the agony of Melwar's attack. He felt over the parts of his body that he could reach. It took incredible effort to move his arm, but at least nothing was broken. He couldn't even find the slightest cut or wound. "Did you heal me?" he asked.

Hana shook her head. "You didn't have any wounds. Even if you did, I don't have any healing abilities."

"I see." Iren figured he should rest, but there was no way he could sleep after lying unconscious all day.

"Well, since you're awake," Hana said, rising and walking out of Iren's field of vision, "I guess we may as well put the time to good use."

Iren didn't know what she meant, and without intending it, the memory of the bath two days ago came to him. His heart raced. Part of him was terrified, but he was also curious. He'd never been romantically involved with a woman. In Lodia everyone had hated him, and when he'd lived with Minawë, they'd both been preoccupied. Now, with Hana having seemingly no other purpose but spending time with him, the idea filled his mind.

Hana returned with the diary Iren had found at his parents' house. "Let's keep up our practice of Maantec," she said. "You want to know what this book says, don't you? Besides, Melwar and I are exceptions in Hiabi. If you want to communicate with other Maantecs, you should learn our language."

Iren shook his head to clear his thoughts. Of course Hana just wanted to continue his lessons. She didn't feel anything for him.

He did his best to concentrate on Hana's instruction, but within a few minutes his head swam. He'd spent most of the day asleep, yet he still felt exhausted.

A "training regimen," Melwar had called it. A fresh wave of soreness washed over Iren. "Training death-march" sounded more accurate.

CHAPTER TWENTY-FIVE
The Tengu

After more than a week in the mountains, Minawë didn't feel like they were getting anywhere. The spires of Eregos rose as high as ever, and the horses had trouble negotiating the uneven paths. Minawë had taken to walking alongside hers to spare the beast her weight.

The trail narrowed as Rondel and Minawë approached the next mountain pass. Sheer stone walls towered on either side of them. Eventually the cliffs became so close together that the pair needed to go single-file. Rondel took the lead, still on her horse.

A crack of thunder echoed off the canyon walls. Minawë covered her ears at the reverberations. She wanted out of this place right away, but ahead of her, Rondel stopped.

"What's wrong?" Minawë asked.

Rondel dismounted without answering. Minawë slid past Rondel's horse so she could see what was going on.

Blocking their path was the oddest creature Minawë had ever seen. It stood no taller than Rondel, yet its girth surpassed its height. In one hand it held a large gourd, and in the other it clutched a shepherd's crook. Except for its chestnut face, the creature's body was covered in white, downy feathers that made it look like an oversized baby bird. That appearance was all the more realized by the creature's absurdly long nose, which measured the length of Minawë's forearm.

"What is that?" Minawë asked, though she had a good idea of the answer.

Rondel didn't shift her gaze from the creature. "It's a Tengu."

The Tengu must have heard them, because it cocked its head sideways. It stared at them with huge brown eyes.

Rondel hobbled forward, by all appearances a shuffling elder. "Please, Master Tengu, won't you let us pass?"

"Haruu hoo hoo," the Tengu grunted in what Minawë guessed was laughter. The throaty sound caused the Tengu to shake all over. "This is a good place to pass. That's why they call it a pass."

"Indeed," Rondel said, the patience in her voice forced, "so if you'll step to one side, we'll be on our way."

"And what way might that be?" The Tengu looked at Minawë. "Ah, I see. Little Kodama, have you brought your grandmother here to die? Will you leave her here with us?"

Minawë didn't know how to take that. She couldn't think of a response.

Rondel could. "I'm not her grandmother," the old woman retorted, "and I'm not ready to die either. We're on a journey."

"Granny is rude!" the Tengu laughed. "I wasn't talking to her."

Rondel seethed. She opened her mouth, but Minawë put a hand on her shoulder. "Let me," she said. "It seems interested in me."

She stepped around Rondel. "What the old hag says is true," she told the Tengu.

A grunt sounded from behind her. Minawë suppressed a smile. Iren used to call Rondel "old hag" to rile her. This Tengu delighted in teasing Rondel; maybe it would appreciate Minawë if she did the same.

"She can be forgetful," Minawë continued, shaking her head in mock exasperation, "but this time she was right. We're headed south to find a lost friend of ours. He's in Shikari."

The Tengu's feathers fluffed at that. "Nice going," Rondel grumbled, "the Tengu hate Maantecs, remember?"

"Haruu hoo hoo!" the Tengu laughed. "That was mean of you to deceive me. I can't let Maantecs through."

"You will let us through," Minawë said. She removed the Chloryoblaka from her back. "I'm no Maantec. I'm a Kodama, and I'm the Forest Dragon Knight."

"Forest Dragon Knight?" The Tengu cocked its head sideways

again. "If you're a Dragon Knight, why don't you just fly away? You don't need to bother with me at all."

"Master Tengu, please, I can't fly. That's why we're walking."

"Oh, you can't fly! What a pathetic Dragon Knight you are! Even sparrows can fly. If you can't do what a sparrow can, you must be a very stupid person!"

They were the last words the Tengu spoke. Rondel gave no warning; Minawë felt only a rush of air as the Maantec rushed past her. The Liryometa flashed, and Rondel drove its round pommel into the Tengu's skull. The creature dropped to the ground, breathing shallowly.

Minawë ran to Rondel. "What did you do that for?" she cried.

Rondel sheathed her broken weapon. "I got tired of waiting."

"That's no reason to knock him out!"

The old Maantec said nothing and returned to her horse. Minawë frowned. Something was wrong. Rondel wouldn't attack someone just for trying her patience. There must have been another reason.

Whatever it was, Rondel didn't want to discuss it. She rode up to Minawë, glared down at her, and barked, "Hurry and get back on your horse. We don't have much time. If there are other Tengu around, they'll never let us leave these mountains now."

Minawë started to argue that that was why Rondel shouldn't have struck the Tengu in the first place, but an unearthly shriek drowned out her words. She looked up and gasped. The cliff tops on either side of them swarmed with hundreds of Tengu, each armed with a horn bow.

Leaping onto her horse, Minawë galloped down the narrow mountain pass. Rondel rode just ahead of her. The Tengu screeched in challenge and then, as one, shot their bows.

There was no escape, and Minawë knew it. She and Rondel couldn't maneuver in the tight space, and the arrows were so plentiful they were like a collapsing roof.

Even so, Minawë and Rondel remained unharmed. The arrows rained down, but they passed through horses and riders alike without injury.

Minawë grasped the situation at once. All the Tengu had fired simultaneously. That was impossible even for a trained militia. The

Tengu were casting an illusion that made their bowmen and arrows appear far more numerous than they actually were.

There must have been at least a few real ones, though, because an arrow struck Rondel in the left shoulder, and another grazed Minawë's back. In the drowning barrage, Minawë couldn't tell which arrows were real and which were fake. She would have to ride at full speed and hope to outdistance them.

She thought she had escaped when she and Rondel reached the end of the mountain pass. The cliffs separated from each other and put space between them and the Tengu.

But as Minawë glanced back, her optimism died. The horde of Tengu, real or imagined, poured over the cliffs. The creatures flapped their arms to slow their descent, like gigantic chicks dropped from the nest. Minawë would have laughed had the swarm not been so menacing.

The arrows continued unabated. Then without warning, Minawë's horse pitched forward and threw her from the saddle.

As Minawë rolled to a stop, she saw that her steed had caught his foot in a hole and stumbled. She ran back toward him, but before she had covered half the distance, two real arrows pierced him. The horse cried a long, mournful neigh and then lay silent.

Minawë stared in shock at the dead animal, and it took an arrow scratching her arm to pull her back to reality. She turned and ran, putting everything she had into her legs.

Soon enough, though, she had to slow down. The ground was steeper here, and the many boulders and crevices threatened to snap her leg just as they had done to her horse.

Eventually she caught up to Rondel, who had abandoned her own steed and was also making her way on foot. The old woman still had an arrow protruding from her left shoulder. Blood ran down her arm.

"What do we do?" Minawë asked. "We can't run, and those Tengu aren't slowing down."

Rondel looked behind her at the apparent army of foes rushing toward them. "The Tengu are built to survive in these mountains," she said. "They know the safe paths. If we can't speed up, we'll have to slow them down."

"And your suggestion for that would be?"

"Well, I did come up with one idea," Rondel said with a grimace, "but it'll probably get us killed."

An arrow pinged off a rock at Minawë's feet. "Like we have a choice?"

"My thoughts exactly."

Rondel drew the Liryometa as they continued their flight. The dagger shone blue in the grayness of the overcast evening.

Thunder rumbled above them, and Minawë realized Rondel's plan. Dry mountain grasses and scrub pine surrounded them. The memory of the charred valley flashed back to her.

Minawë felt pressure on her right side, and she almost fell as Rondel shoved her. "Go that way!" the Maantec howled. "Don't look back!"

She obeyed, mostly. Minawë couldn't help but peek over her shoulder to see what Rondel was doing. The old woman threw down her dagger. Then she leapt behind a boulder several feet away and covered her ears as best she could with a broken hand.

The charge Rondel had built up inside the Liryometa was too much for the storm to resist. Even with Minawë's lead, the lightning strike threw her to the ground.

When she recovered, all Minawë could hear was ringing in her ears. Around the lightning's impact site, the forest was already aflame.

"Rondel!" Minawë shouted in vain as the fires obscured her vision. She couldn't believe how quickly the wind spread the flames. It carried embers across the landscape. Soon a burning line sprouted that separated her from the Tengu. For the first time since the mountain pass, all the arrows, real and imaginary, ceased.

But Rondel's plan hadn't saved Minawë. With the direction of the wind, the fire was coming straight for her.

She fled, hoping Rondel was all right. The lightning bolt itself might have killed the old Maantec, but even if it hadn't, she would have been in the middle of that blaze when it ignited.

Minawë picked her way through the woods. The flames behind her closed in. Sweat poured off her. The heat was more intense than even what Feng had thrown off.

She couldn't outrun the fires. They were too fast. She'd have to fly to escape them.

Fly? The thought struck her through the terror of the burning forest. She remembered the Tengu's words: "Oh, you can't fly! What a pathetic Dragon Knight you are!"

Maybe the creature was right. Mother or Father could have figured a way out of this mess, but not her.

She wouldn't let herself believe that. Rondel had said the Tengu were tricksters. The one in the pass had seemed to be insulting her, but maybe, in its own weird way, it had meant something good by it.

"Even sparrows can fly," it had said. "If you can't do what a sparrow can, you must be a very stupid person!"

He made it sound so simple. Want to fly? Just be a sparrow.

That was it. It was that simple. If she could change the form of plants using Dendryl's magic, perhaps she could do the same to herself.

Minawë channeled the Forest Dragon's energy. As she did, she focused on the shape of the sparrows in Ziorsecth. She pictured her body changing, shrinking, and sprouting wings.

The transformation was excruciating. Her bones crunched and popped as they rearranged themselves. Her muscles strained as parts of her changed at different speeds. All the while, the fires drew closer. They were behind and to either side of her now. Soon, even if her attempt worked, she would still die.

At last her body felt normal again. The transformation had succeeded. With a flap of her wings, Minawë took flight. She soared above the burning mountainside. Her keen bird eyes swept the ground as she searched for Rondel. It took her two large circles, but she finally spotted a tiny two-legged form moving south away from the flames.

As she swerved toward Rondel, Minawë saw the Tengu on the other side of the fire. They had given up the chase. They must have stopped their illusion too, because now there were only a dozen of them.

Minawë was glad the Tengu had let Rondel go rather than risk the forest fire. Although they had nearly killed her, Minawë felt terrible for what had happened. The Tengu had been guarding their home. It was no different from the way the Kodamas protected Ziorsecth.

Tweeting a song in the Tengu's honor, Minawë descended to reunite with Rondel.

CHAPTER TWENTY-SIX
Defender of Lodia

Dirio Cyneric, mayor of Veliaf, trudged through the narrow, windy streets of his village. He'd just left the office, head full and spirit leaden.

He'd thought being a mine foreman was tough. At least back then, he'd supervised at most a dozen men, and he could always pass the blame up or down the chain as necessary. Now if he failed, he couldn't fault anyone but himself.

And he had failed. Veliaf didn't have the manpower to defend itself. It was only a matter of time before one of the large cities arrived with an army. When they did, Dirio would have to surrender and join them. It wouldn't matter whether he agreed with them or thought they stood a chance of winning the throne. He would have no other option, except to see his town destroyed.

Again.

As he passed through the austere village, Dirio caught sight of a white uniform heading for the town hospital. He smiled and called, "Doctor Raebeld!"

The doctor stopped and looked at him. "Mayor Cyneric," he said. The doctor was the only person in town formal enough to use Dirio's last name. "To what do I owe the honor?"

Dirio walked over to Raebeld. "I was hoping to run into you. How's our boy?"

Raebeld didn't need to be told who "our boy" was. "Considering all that's happened, Balear's doing well," he said, "but he'll never heal if he doesn't rest."

The mayor shook his head. He still had a difficult time processing what had happened. He was used to injuries; Veliaf's mine was a dangerous place. Something about Balear's wound, though, struck him especially hard.

Maybe it was the sheer strangeness of it. Dirio unconsciously put his left hand on his right bicep. He couldn't avoid thinking about it, what it must feel like to have your arm pierced and then frozen from the inside out. He shuddered.

"Actually, I'm not concerned about his physical injury anymore," Raebeld said. He opened the hospital door and gestured to invite Dirio inside. "Thanks to whatever devil magic that Fubuki used, the wound is clean where he lost the arm. There's little danger of infection as long as he keeps it bandaged until the skin grows over it. Even so . . ." he trailed off, and his expression grew foul.

"What's the matter?" Dirio asked.

The doctor sighed. "I've seen miners who have lost limbs. It's different from most injuries. It affects the mind. Sometimes people think they still have their arm or leg, even though it's gone. I haven't seen that from Balear, but still, he worries me."

"What makes you say that?"

"He's a soldier. Has been his whole life. I don't know how he'll recover from losing his dominant arm. Maybe he never will. In any case, I don't think he'll fight again."

"That might be for the best," Dirio said. "Personally, I think Lodia could do with a little less fighting right now."

"You don't understand. Fighting is all that young man has. It's what he knows. It's what he does. If you take that away, what's left?"

Dirio didn't have an answer for that. He and the doctor walked in silence through a hallway with doors on both sides. When the mine was in full operation, the sick rooms on the other sides of those doors saw a lot of use. Fortunately, Balear was the only patient at the moment.

They reached Balear's door. Raebeld was about to open it when Dirio heard muffled words from the other side.

". . .ven, twenty-eight, twenty-nine . . ."

The mayor frowned. "What's he doing in there?"

Raebeld didn't hesitate. He flung open the door, and Dirio blinked several times in surprise. Balear was out of bed and lying face-down on the floor.

No, Dirio realized, not lying. Balear was doing one-armed push-ups. He was midway through one, his body at its lowest point. He shook, and his face resembled a ripe apple.

"Thir. . ." he groaned. "Thir. . ."

"What on Raa are you doing?" Raebeld cried.

The distraction was enough. Balear collapsed on the floor. His chest heaved, and sweat poured off his body. He gasped for every breath.

"I was . . . so close," he said.

Raebeld shot Dirio a commanding look. "Help me get him into bed. Grab his ankles; I'll take his shoulders."

When the pair finished manhandling Balear into bed, Raebeld turned his harsh expression on the former general. "Rest!" the doctor screamed. "Rest! How thick are you? It's only one word! It's only one syllable!"

Balear flushed a deeper red, something Dirio didn't think possible. "I have to get stronger," Balear wheezed. "Amroth trusted me."

"Amroth was a monster who put Lodia in the mess it's in," Raebeld shot back. "I couldn't care less what he thought of you."

"Raebeld . . ." Dirio began, but the doctor's gaze cowed him into silence.

"I'm your doctor," Raebeld pressed on. "Do you want to live? Then follow my orders. You're a soldier. You should be able to do that much."

Balear looked at the ceiling. His expression was distant, like he was seeing something other than the room.

"I am a soldier," he said after a long time. "I'm a member of the Castle Guard, the only one left."

"And unless you want them to disappear forever, you'll stop these ridiculous exercises," Raebeld said. "If I catch you one more time, I'll strap you to the bed."

Dirio expected Balear to back down, but the young man glared at the doctor in challenge. "Try it," he snarled, "and I swear I'll kill you."

Patient and doctor glowered for a moment before Dirio intervened.

"Balear, Doctor Raebeld wants to help you," he said. "He has a lot of experience treating wounds. I know it's hard, but—"

"You don't know," Balear interrupted. "You don't understand at all. I have to get better. I have to get stronger."

"Why?"

"Because Rondel opened my eyes to the truth. Amroth might have been a monster, but he still chose me as his second-in-command. When he and I came to Veliaf last year to defeat the Quodivar, everyone in our group was a Maantec except for me. I was the only human. Do you get it? There's a reason for that."

Balear sat up and swung his legs over the side of the bed, prompting immediate protestations from Raebeld. The soldier looked at him with cold certainty, and the doctor fell into silence.

Dirio was stunned. He'd never seen Raebeld intimidated by anyone.

"That Fubuki will come back," Balear said. It wasn't a guess. When Dirio heard it, he knew it was true.

"It could come back today," Balear continued. "It could be out there now. I don't have time to sit around."

Balear stood and walked to the corner of the room where his gigantic sword leaned against the wall. He picked it up. "Iren, Hana, and Rondel all left," he said. "We can't count on them to protect us. I'm Lodia's only Dragon Knight. No one else can stop that monster."

He brushed past Dirio and Raebeld on his way to the door. They both had to jump to get out of the way of the Auryozaki.

To Raebeld's credit, the doctor tried one last time to dissuade Balear. "Stop this," he said, though the strength and command had gone out of his voice. "You can't defeat that thing with just your left arm."

Balear didn't bother turning around. "I will," he declared, "because Amroth believed in me. He knew what I was before I realized it myself. I'm a defender of Lodia."

He left the room. A few seconds later, the door to the street slammed.

CHAPTER TWENTY-SEVEN
Suicide Forest

At sunset four weeks after escaping the Tengu, Rondel and Minawë at last reached the end of the Eregos Mountains. Below them, the ground sloped down, and a mile away, fog shrouded the landscape.

Rondel's left shoulder twinged. Her wound was bothering it again. She'd removed the Tengu's arrow and applied a rudimentary bandage made from a piece of her cloak, but it was no substitute for what a real healer could do.

She was lucky to have survived at all. That lightning bolt had almost knocked her out, and retrieving the Liryometa had resulted in burns on much of her body. Most had scabbed over by now, but a few of the heavier ones remained.

A shriek overhead interrupted her thoughts. A moment later a hawk smashed to the ground in front of her. Rondel rolled her eyes. "I thought Kodamas were supposed to be graceful."

The hawk stood and shook its head in a most un-birdlike fashion. Then it grew. Its feathers shrank into its skin, and its beak changed into a nose. Last of all, its wings changed into arms, and Minawë stood before Rondel, looking indignant.

"Flying is easy," the Kodama said. "Turns out landing is trickier."

Rondel smirked. "Naturally."

Minawë folded her arms. "Doubtless you didn't get Lightning Sight correct your first time around?"

"It took me thirty years to perfect," Rondel admitted, but then she added, "let's hope it doesn't take you that long."

Rondel didn't want to tell Minawë, but the Kodama's pace amazed her. Even Otunë had never used Dendryl's magic to change his shape.

"Are you daydreaming again?" Minawë asked. "Let's get going."

"Not tonight," Rondel said. "We'll camp here and head down in the morning."

"Down?"

"See where that mist starts? The Eregos Mountains don't end in foothills on their southern border like they do in Lodia. Instead, they come to an escarpment that plunges more than a thousand feet. We'll have to climb down it to proceed."

"You climb. I'll fly."

Rondel laughed. "You think you can? You have no idea what's in that fog. It's a vast jungle, more expansive than Eregos: Aokigahara. Maantecs have another name for it, though." Her tone darkened. "They call it Suicide Forest."

"You can drop the melodrama," Minawë said. "I grew up in a forest, remember? I'm not scared of them."

"Aokigahara is nothing like Ziorsecth," Rondel warned. "In Ziorsecth, the tree trunks are so wide and the canopy so dense that most places have little underbrush. Aokigahara is a green wall. It has plants at every layer from ground to canopy. If you flew down that cliff, you'd become tangled in the forest's branches and break a wing. You might even die."

"So how do we get down? We don't have any rope, and even if we did, it wouldn't reach a thousand feet."

"There are spots along the wall where a person can climb," Rondel said. "It won't be pleasant, but it's doable."

Rondel activated Lightning Sight and examined the cliff edge for any irregularities that might indicate a way down. Her shoulders slumped. "As best I can tell, there aren't any such paths near us. We'll sleep here tonight. Tomorrow, we can walk along the wall and search for a place to descend."

With that Rondel sat against a pine tree and settled in for an uncomfortable night. She wished they still had their supplies, but they'd lost everything with the horses in their flight from the Tengu. The food and camping gear would have eased the pain of Aokigahara a lot. They'd survived Eregos by having Minawë transform and hunt, but that might not work in the tangled rainforest.

While Rondel rested, Minawë stared at the cliff before them. "I have an idea," she said.

The Kodama shrunk and changed into a white owl. Rondel smiled despite herself. "So that's your plan."

Minawë cocked her head sideways, then went even further so that she was looking at Rondel upside down. Rondel laughed. "Would you get going? You're creeping me out."

Ignoring the comment, Minawë took flight. Rondel used Lightning Sight to track her at first, but then Minawë entered the mist and was lost even to the enhanced vision. Rondel closed her eyes to wait for Minawë's return.

A hoot jolted her awake. Rondel looked up in time to see an owl flop down hard and roll twice on the ground before settling to a stop.

Minawë changed back to her Kodaman form and rubbed her arms. "There's a way down not far west of here," she said. "If we hurry, I think there's enough light for us to scale the cliff this evening."

Rondel frowned. She had no desire to enter Aokigahara at all, let alone at night. Minawë looked so excited, though, that it was hard to refuse her.

Besides, every minute they delayed was another Hana and Melwar could spend with Iren. "Show me what you found," Rondel said.

Minawë led her to the cliff and turned right. The pair walked along the edge about fifteen minutes before Minawë stopped and indicated that they had arrived.

Rondel looked over the cliff with Lightning Sight. Sure enough, a steep natural stair led down the escarpment, though there was no way to tell if it went to the bottom.

"It's more like a ladder than a staircase," Rondel said. "You're sure you want to do this tonight?"

It had been easy for Minawë to be brave at the campsite, but faced with the actual descent, Rondel could tell the Kodama was nervous. The route was absurd, even in daylight.

Rondel expected Minawë to give in and allow for another night in Eregos, but instead the Kodama's face steeled. "Well," she said, "let's stop wasting time."

The old Maantec grated her teeth. It wasn't hard to see which parent Minawë took after.

Minawë slid a leg over the edge, but Rondel stopped her. "Let me go first," the old Maantec said. "Lightning Sight will let me see the hand-holds better. Follow my lead."

Rondel started down the cliff. Using Lightning Sight, she found the peculiarities in the rock face and then relayed the information to Minawë. It was rough going, but before long they'd covered a considerable distance. When Rondel looked past Minawë, she could no longer see the cliff's top.

The farther they descended, the more treacherous the wall became. The fog hindered Lightning Sight and made the rocks slippery.

The climb shouldn't have been a challenge for Rondel, but thanks to her wounded left arm, she had to make the descent one-handed. With lightning magic enhancing her strength, though, she was managing.

A scrabbling of rock was Rondel's only warning. Minawë screamed and fell. Rondel instinctively reached out with her broken left hand. It snapped its splint and shot toward Minawë. For a moment they touched, but Rondel couldn't get a grip.

"Minawë!" Rondel cried. She scanned below her with Lightning Sight, but it couldn't penetrate the mist. Cursing repeatedly, she scrabbled down the rock face as quickly as she dared.

"Minawë!" she called again, though she knew it was hopeless. No one could survive a fall like that.

After what felt like an eternity in her panicked state, Rondel felt solid ground beneath her. Her eyes swept the dark jungle, but she caught no sign of Minawë.

Her chest tightened. Minawë must have transformed and become hung up in the forest canopy. Rondel forced away the mental image of a broken bird corpse lying in those upper branches.

Rondel dropped to her knees. Suicide Forest had claimed yet another life, and it was her fault. She had gone along with Minawë's suggestion to descend tonight even though she had known they should have waited until morning.

There was a motion beside her. She drew her broken rondel. "Who's there?" she asked, doing her best to sound fierce despite her grief.

"Rondel?"

"Minawë!"

The Kodama forced her way through a tangle of shrubs. "I'm all right," she said. "I transformed as I fell. I wasn't thinking about it. I just knew I had to change if I wanted to survive."

"But what did you change into?" Rondel asked. "If you became a bird, there's no way you could have broken your fall in time, let alone stopped before slamming into the canopy."

Minawë blushed. "Well, it will sound weird, but I didn't know what else to do. I just knew I needed to fly, so that's what I became."

"A fly?"

She nodded. "Once I changed into something that small, it was easy to get down safely. Although since I was so tiny, you beat me here. It also didn't help that the fly's eyes are hard to use. I could see in every direction at once!"

Rondel fell back on her rump and whistled. Then, without intending to, she burst out laughing. Minawë looked at her oddly for a few seconds, and then she joined in. The pair cackled loud and long, and soon Rondel was crying and laughing at the same time.

"Please don't ever," Rondel gasped between sobs, "ever do that to me again. You're going to give this old woman a heart attack!"

"I'll do my best not to fall off any more cliffs," Minawë replied.

Rondel slowly regained control of herself. "All right, I've had more than enough excitement for today. Let's camp here. Aokigahara is no place to stumble around in the dark."

"No arguments this time," Minawë said. She leaned against a nearby tree and sat down. Rondel stood to join her, but then she stopped short.

Minawë's brow furrowed. "What's the matter?"

"Quiet," Rondel hissed as Lightning Sight flashed. She searched the jungle. One . . . two . . . three . . . damn.

Rondel raised her Liryometa, but then an arrow shot past her. It pinged off the escarpment and left a scratch on her right ear.

Minawë reached for the Chloryoblaka, but another arrow landed inches in front of her. "Don't move!" a voice called, and Rondel's mouth dropped open as she realized the language wasn't that of Lodia.

"Hands up!" another voice shouted in the same language. Rondel snarled, but she obeyed. Lightning Sight had already picked up a dozen of them, and there might be more hiding in the trees where it couldn't spot them.

Minawë looked around. "What's going on? Who's there?"

They came out of the trees like ghosts. Dressed in brown leather, they appeared—first ten, then twenty. Paint and tattoos covered their bodies. They all had drawn bows, and most of them carried long, broad knives as well.

But none of those features caused Rondel's surprise. Her shock came from the detail she noted as the new arrivals bound their prisoners' hands and took away their weapons.

They all had green hair.

CHAPTER TWENTY-EIGHT
"My Name Is . . ."

The past month had been without question the most brutal of Iren's life. Melwar's rigid schedule made last year's training under Rondel seem like a morning stroll. Each dawn, Iren ate a hasty breakfast in his room, then headed to the castle's central garden to battle Hana. He lasted longer with each match, but he never won. Hana was always a move ahead, countering the instant Iren committed to an attack.

His failures were all the more frustrating because he knew Hana was only the first step. As impressive as her abilities were, Melwar's would be far superior.

After each sparring match, Iren next had to contend with Melwar's pain test, which was even worse than the fights with Hana. Melwar had explained that the spell he was using didn't wound Iren. Instead, it activated all his nerves at the same time. Confronting such stress, the body's natural inclination was to pass out.

"The pain of breaking your magical barrier will surpass what I can inflict with this spell," Melwar had warned him. "If you want to survive, this technique must become nothing to you. When you can endure my spell for an hour and remain conscious, then we will be ready to attempt to remove your barrier. That assumes, of course, that you can land a blow on both Hana and me by then. Otherwise, we will keep up the pain training for as long as it takes."

After that explanation, Iren had understood the reasoning behind Melwar's dual training methods. Both motivated Iren to do better at the other. The sooner he defeated Hana and Melwar, the sooner the pain test would end, and the sooner he mastered his pain, the less drained he would feel when he fought them.

Both those outcomes seemed far off. He still lost consciousness for hours after Melwar's spell, and he lived in a constant haze of exhaustion and sore muscles.

Though the physical strain pushed Iren harder than he had ever worked before, the mental effort of learning the Maantecs' language and customs was tougher yet. During the trip to Veliaf, Hana had only taught him a handful of vocabulary. Now that she had him trapped in his room every day while he recovered from Melwar's spell, she became a diligent taskmaster. She drilled Iren in everything from etiquette to fashion to the use of chopsticks. She taught him more Maantec words, but she expanded beyond verbal pronunciations to the written kanji that represented them.

To speed his learning, Hana said everything to Iren twice, once in Maantec and again in Lodian. She then commanded him to respond in kind as much as possible.

Iren thought his language training had escaped Melwar's notice, but one day the lord addressed him in Maantec. Without thinking, Iren answered the same way. Melwar smiled slyly at him. From that moment on, Melwar only spoke to Iren in Maantec.

Of all Iren's tasks, writing in Maantec came easiest of all. That surprised him given how much he hated writing in Lodian. But as Hana showed him, his frustration with Lodian stemmed from that language's writing style. It assumed a right-handed author, so it went from left to right and top to bottom. As a result, a left-handed person rubbed what he had just written with the side of his hand and smudged the ink.

Maantec writing, by contrast, started on the top-right of the page and went down first, then moved from right to left in columns. Once Iren adjusted to the new format, his handwriting improved in both speed and legibility.

Unfortunately, all his progress did nothing for deciphering his father's diary. Unlike the simple constructs Iren wrote for lessons, his father used long, flowing sentences and kanji that gave even Hana trouble. She guessed that Iren's father had been old enough to have lived through the Kodama-Maantec War, because many of his kanji had gone out of use since then.

Though Iren couldn't translate the diary, he had at least figured out that all this time he'd been trying to read it backwards. Maantec books had their spines on the right, not the left, and they read in the opposite direction from Lodian books.

His first real break with the diary came when Hana taught him how to write his name in Maantec. For inspiration, he kept the scroll with the words "My name is Iren Saitosan" open at all times in his room.

Two nights later, he was leafing through his father's writing by candlelight. He was about to shut it when a column of kanji caught his attention.

Thinking he'd made a mistake, Iren stared at them closer. He tried to convince himself they weren't there, but no, they were the first words on the first page. The kanji matched. Iren was so astounded he read them aloud, though he could manage no more than a whisper.

"My name is Iren Saito."

CHAPTER TWENTY-NINE
Captured

In spite of the hostile Kodamas surrounding her, Minawë couldn't help but feel awed by Aokigahara. Every step through the rainforest brought something new. Even in the dark, she'd lost count of the number of different plant species she'd seen.

But it was more than the variety. This place had an energy to it, a force that surged through her. Rondel had been right, perhaps more than she'd realized. Aokigahara wasn't at all like Ziorsecth. Ziorsecth had immense magic, but its dominance by a single plant gave that magic structure. Aokigahara had no such order. Its magic was like a flood. The untamed power made Minawë dizzy, yet part of her longed to immerse herself in it.

Not that she would have a chance to do that. Her ability to hear the plants' voices had vanished when her captors had taken away the Chloryoblaka.

"Keep moving," the guard behind her barked. He shoved her.

Minawë winced. Just as Aokigahara differed from Ziorsecth, these Kodamas were unlike her northern kin. They seemed as wild as the forest around them, and it didn't matter whether they were male or female. The women were as battle-hardened as the men, and their bodies were equally adorned with tattoos, weapons, and scars.

Their violent demeanor aside, Minawë's captors peaked her interest. All her life, she had believed there were no other Kodamas besides those in Ziorsecth. The rest had died from Iren Saito's curse.

She wasn't surprised that Kodamas could live here. Aokigahara had at least as much magic as Ziorsecth, if not more.

Ahead of Minawë, Rondel slumped and nearly fell. Her trio of guards hauled her to her feet amid fresh punches and kicks.

Minawë grated her teeth. She wished she could do something. As much as the Kodamas had struck her, those beatings paled in comparison to what they'd done to Rondel. The Maantec was a bleeding mess.

They traveled all night. As dawn approached, Minawë stumbled more often. She'd been awake almost twenty-four hours now. All she wanted to do was sleep, but still they marched through the wet brush.

"Blindfolds from here," her guard snapped, and before she could protest, a strip of cloth covered her eyes. Minawë struggled for a moment, but a blow to her stomach convinced her to stop. Fierce hands gripped her arms and guided her forward.

After another hour of tough hiking, Minawë felt cold steel between her hands. It jerked, and her bonds fell away. "Up," her guard ordered.

Reaching out, Minawë found the rungs of a rope ladder and climbed. The ladder ended in a wooden floor, and she heaved herself onto it. Guards grabbed her again and held her arms. They stayed that way for several minutes before she heard grumping behind her.

"Tramp me through a soggy jungle in the dead of night, then make me climb this ridiculous ladder one-handed. What way is this to treat an old woman?"

Minawë smiled, but it died when a loud *smack* rang out. "Shut your mouth, Maantec spy!"

"Leave her alone!" Minawë shouted before she could stop herself. Just as quickly, a sharp pain slapped across her face.

"That's enough!" a male voice boomed. Even though Minawë was blind, she could sense everyone nearby freeze.

"Lord Narunë," a guard said, "we captured these spies at the cliff wall. They were carrying Ryokaiten. We thought you'd want to interrogate them."

"Thank you," the male voice replied. "Now leave us; I'd like a word with these spies in private."

There was a pause. It was as if no one could believe what the man called Narunë had said but couldn't work up the courage to contradict him. Finally, one of the Kodamas murmured, "Lord Narunë, to have

Ryokaiten, they must be exceptional mages. Are you sure it's wise to—"

"I said, 'Leave us!'"

That settled the matter. There was a scuffling as the guards around Minawë made their way back down the ladder.

Silence followed for a few moments. Then without warning, Minawë's blindfold was ripped away.

She blinked in the sudden brightness. The sun had risen, and the mist spread its light such that everything seemed aglow. She and Rondel stood on a wooden platform wedged high in a tree. The structure had no walls or ceiling; the tree's giant, waxy leaves formed a better roof than anything a person could make.

Minawë gazed about in wonder. The mist wasn't as thick as it had been when they'd descended the cliff, so she could see a good distance. Every tree in sight had at least one platform identical to this one, and on each platform sat at least one Kodama.

Their presence astounded her. There were hundreds of them, at least as many as lived in the entirety of Ziorsecth. In Minawë's wildest dreams, she'd never imagined there could be so many, let alone in a single community.

Unlike Minawë, Rondel didn't seem to care about the scenery. She glared at the Kodama before them, and in particular at the bow he held in one hand and the broken dagger clutched in the other.

Minawë had spent enough time with Rondel to know the old woman was searching for a way to retrieve their weapons and escape. But it was impossible. If Minawë got hers and flew away as a bird, the Kodamas in the other trees would shoot her from the sky. As for Rondel, she would have to descend via the rope ladder, making her a similarly easy target. This open platform imprisoned them as effectively as the finest dungeon.

While their prison lacked walls, it did have a jailer. He looked the part too. The man called Narunë stood a head taller than any Kodama Minawë had met in Ziorsecth, and his shoulders were twice as broad as Iren's. He wore no shirt, and tattoos of fierce animals Minawë had never seen covered his bronzed skin.

"So," Narunë said, "Maantec spy, is it?"

"We're not spies," Rondel spat.

Narunë looked her over. "You're a Maantec, and you were spying at the cliff base. I'd say that makes you a Maantec spy, wouldn't you?"

"We weren't spying. We're travelers."

"No one travels to Aokigahara." Narunë held up the broken rondel. "Besides, I know what this is, Rondel Thara."

Minawë tensed, and Narunë flicked his eyes to her. "That proves it. You are Rondel. You look different from the last time I saw you."

Rondel cocked an eyebrow. "Well, you look like the same wild man as before. No wonder Otunë chose you to lead this crazy expedition."

Narunë threw his head back and laughed, a deep bellow. His right eye closed while he did it. He wrapped his burly arms around Rondel and lifted her into the air. "You look like a dried up mango!" he cried. "Last I saw you, you were young and beautiful. What happened?"

"It's a long story," Rondel replied, a smile on her face despite her awkward position. "A thousand-year-long one, to be precise."

"I want to hear it," Narunë said. He released the old Maantec and stepped back. "First things first, though." He faced Minawë. "Who's this you've brought with you?"

"I would have thought the bow you're holding would be all the clue you needed. This is Minawë, daughter of Otunë."

Narunë's gray eyes looked Minawë up and down. "She is about the right height, I guess. There isn't much resemblance otherwise. Though in truth, little one, that's to your benefit. My brother never was much to look at." He paused, then put on a big grin. "Speaking of Otunë, how is he these days? Still the same stoic bastard?"

Rondel probably answered him, but Minawë didn't hear her. She was too busy absorbing what Narunë had just said.

He had called Otunë "my brother." This wild, tattooed man was her uncle.

CHAPTER THIRTY
No Mind

Iren read the diary's opening line again and again, wishing it would change. "My name is Iren Saito."

In a flash Iren understood why Hana had refused to read the book to him back in Tropos. He'd believed it was his father's diary, but it wasn't. It had been written by Iren Saito, former emperor of the Maantecs and dead for a thousand years.

Iren let the book slip from his hands. Since Melwar had offered to help him regain his magic, Iren had no longer cared about the book providing clues about that. Still, he'd hoped it would give him a link to his parents.

With a curse, Iren laid back on his futon, his hands behind his head. He couldn't care less about Iren Saito. The emperor was a madman. He'd led his race to near extinction trying to conquer Raa. Worse, when he realized he would lose, he had killed himself to curse the Kodamas. He'd committed suicide and doomed two species merely to avoid the shame of defeat.

It was just as well that the diary was worthless. The language lessons, while interesting, diverted Iren's attention from the real issue of breaching the wall that kept him from his magic. He could communicate in Maantec, at least enough to be understood. When he next saw Hana, he would tell her she didn't need to bother teaching him anymore.

His mind made up, Iren fell asleep easily, but his dream returned. He was back in the house, sitting with his wife and looking at his child. The knock at the door came. Like before, when he opened it, no one was there.

The next morning Iren arrived at the garden early and took the opportunity to stretch. By the time Melwar and Hana arrived, he had warmed up. He took his stance. Instead of attacking first, as he often did, Iren examined every inch of Hana for a sign of what her actions would be.

Hana made the first attack, and Iren blocked it with ease. He countered, but it was a feint. He wanted to feel her out and expose her right side. From their many duels, Iren had learned that Hana's defense was slower on that side. It wasn't by much, but it was enough to give him a chance of victory.

Hana sidestepped Iren's feint and attacked his head, but he saw the strike almost before she committed to it. Something about the way her body moved and the positioning of her arms told him she was going to use an overhead blow. He dodged and struck at her left side. He didn't want to give away that he knew about her weakness. Hana deflected his blow at the last second, but he came closer to striking her than he ever had before.

As their duel intensified, their speeds increased until the wooden swords blurred. Iren's eyes glazed over even as they studied Hana with utmost intensity. His thoughts drifted.

Then he heard a strange music. It swayed in a fast, uneven beat, and he couldn't help but time himself to it.

The pair fought evenly for a time, but then Iren caught a change in Hana. She breathed harder. Her sword dipped. Her face scrunched in frustration, and in that moment Iren knew he would win.

There it was! His last block had knocked Hana's sword hard to the left, and she had lost her balance. The right side of her body seemed to scream, "Hit me! I'm open!" Without any thought, Iren swung.

The wooden blade crashed into Hana just below her rib cage. She dropped to her knees in the cold sand and grasped the impact site with both hands.

Melwar stepped between them to end the contest. The moment he did, a veil fell away from Iren's eyes. He blinked several times. At some point during the fight, the sun had risen high enough to brighten the courtyard. They'd started their match at dawn; they must have fought for hours. To Iren it felt like seconds, and part of him wondered if the duel had happened at all. It felt less real than the dreams about his wife and child.

"Congratulations, Iren," Melwar said, "you win."

Iren bowed first to the Maantec lord and then to Hana. "Thank you for an excellent fight," he said.

Hana stood and returned Iren's bow, but she had a look in her eyes that unsettled him. Despite the sun overhead, her pupils were dilated. Her expression was one of hunger.

A moment later Hana collected herself. She asked to be excused and then left the garden. She stumbled the entire way.

"Did I hurt her that badly?" Iren asked.

"No," Melwar said, "if I had to guess, I would say you exhausted her. You gave her a fight the likes of which she has never experienced. You gave me the same thing, for that matter. I have never seen a duel last so long."

As if in response to Melwar's words, fatigue struck Iren. His vision grayed, and he had to sit down. "Wha. . .what's happening?" he panted.

"You were on the verge of falling too. I knew one of you would make a mistake soon and lose, but I could not tell who it would be."

"Then why didn't I feel tired until just now?"

Melwar looked down at him but didn't answer.

Iren's vision slowly returned to normal, though his lightheadedness remained. Hoping he wasn't being rude, he laid back in the sand and gulped air to calm his hammering pulse.

"Are you going to pass out?" Melwar asked.

Iren took a final deep breath. The worst seemed to have passed. "I don't think so."

"Good. I do not like repeating myself, and the answer to your question is important. I would not give it if you were going to faint partway through."

"I appreciate your concern," Iren said with only the mildest trace of sarcasm. "So now will you explain what happened to me?"

Melwar nodded. "You have a rare trait. You can use No Mind."

"No Mind?"

"The first masters of it gave it that name to describe what happened to them. Tell me, what do you remember about your fight with Hana?"

"Nothing," Iren said. "It was dawn a minute ago, or so it seems."

"That is No Mind: a state lacking conscious thought. Rather than waste time making decisions, the body combines keen observation with muscle memory to react instantly. At first I doubted you could use it, given how poorly you judge social situations. It seems you are more discerning in battle."

Iren thought back. "When I left Haldessa with Rondel last year, thieves ambushed us our first night out. I fought four of them at once. I didn't have combat training, yet I defeated them easily. The whole time, I heard music in my head, as though the fight were set to it."

"No Mind users often describe the rhythm of battle as musical," Melwar said. "You must have entered No Mind in that fight without realizing it. It is good that you did; No Mind is likely the reason you survived that night. Had you been thinking clearly, you no doubt would have felt confusion about how to move, reluctance about committing to an attack, and horror over your first murder. No Mind frees the brain from such emotions and lets the natural impulse to survive take control. It is a powerful technique, one few enemies can stop. That said, it is not something to use often."

"Why not?"

Melwar pointed down at him, still lying on his back. "That is why. When you are in No Mind, your body only thinks about survival. It does not concern itself with petty details like exhaustion. If the battle does not end, your body will keep fighting until it drops."

Iren recalled the way Hana had struggled away from the training ground. "Can Hana use No Mind?"

"Yes, though she has to fight a while before the trance hits. That is why she could never defeat me in a duel, and thus why fighting me is your next challenge."

"What do you mean?"

"Even with the pain training I have given you, I cannot truly prepare you for the intensity of breaking your body's magical barrier. If your mind is conscious, the agony will overwhelm and kill you. But if you are unconscious, your body will not be able to resist my shadow magic, and you will also die. For our attempt to succeed, you need to be awake and at full strength, yet you must also lack conscious thought."

"In other words, I can't rely on battle to enter No Mind," Iren said. "To regain my magic, I need to be able to enter it at any time."

"Exactly, and that is what you will need to do in order to hit me. I can also use No Mind, and I can enter it seconds after starting a fight. At the risk of boasting, no Maantec can enter No Mind faster than I can. If you want to hit me, you will need to surpass me. You must enter the trance before we start, so that whatever move I make, you can react to it and defeat me in one blow."

The Maantec lord put his back to Iren and stepped off the sand. "We will forgo your pain training today. Call it a reward for defeating Hana. Besides, you are not in any condition to face it. Continue to come here at dawn, and you and I will fight."

Iren raised his head. "Wait a second. If even you need to enter battle to use No Mind, how can I do it without fighting?"

"If I knew that, I would be able to do it too," Melwar said over his shoulder. "To be honest, I have my doubts that it is even possible. But if you ever want to use magic again, this is the only way."

CHAPTER THIRTY-ONE
Narunë's Game

Rondel could barely keep her feet. As usual, though, the bullheaded Narunë was oblivious to her plight. Well, maybe what she had to tell him next would get his attention.

"Otunë's dead," she said. "He has been for a thousand years."

The smile on Narunë's face faded, and a pensive look replaced it. "I guess that strange disease got him."

"Disease?"

"During the war, my brother ordered me to take my division and attack Shikari. We were supposed to be a rear guard assault to take out Saito's reserve supplies. Had we succeeded, the Maantecs wouldn't have been able to continue. We were set to invade, but when my first group of soldiers left the jungle, they died. I don't know why. After that day, though, the rest of us never dared to leave Aokigahara."

"So that's why no one's heard from you," Rondel said. "Narunë, what happened to you was no disease. When we invaded Serona, Iren Saito cast a curse. It killed all the Kodaman fighters, including your brother."

Narunë scowled. "So Saito won the war."

"No, he's dead too, and I can't say that anybody won that war. After the battle in Serona, the fighting stopped. There were no leaders on either side, and even had there been, there was almost no one left to fight."

The tattooed Kodama walked to the edge of the platform and sat down. His feet dangled over the edge. "I always figured I'd die first.

Otunë was so calm, and I've never met a more powerful Dragon Knight. I can't believe he's gone."

Rondel winced. She had meant to startle Narunë, not send him into a melancholy.

To change the subject, she looked at Minawë, who had a shocked expression. Rondel smiled. "I take it you've figured out who Narunë is."

Minawë shook her head back and forth as though clearing some mental fog. "You're my uncle, aren't you?"

Her voice had the effect Rondel had hoped for. Narunë leapt to his feet and grinned. He never could stay depressed for long. "That's right," he said. He studied his niece. "So you're Minawë. That's a good name. It's kingly. Though I guess that's weird, considering you're a girl!" He loosed his bellowing laugh.

"Kingly?" Minawë asked.

"Nawë was an ancestor of your father's," Rondel explained. "Narunë, he was, what, your great-grandfather?"

The big Kodama waved her off. "You think I can remember such things? Please, all I care about is that he's the most famous Kodaman leader ever, even better than my brother. If you're named after him, you have a lot to live up to."

Narunë laughed and closed his right eye again, and that was when Rondel caught it. She knew that grin from centuries of doing it herself. It was too broad. Narunë knew. He was playing the fool, but he had figured out Rondel's secret.

She had to get him away from Minawë before he let anything slip. If the girl ever found out the truth, she would hate Rondel forever.

Before Rondel could think of a plan, though, Narunë said, "I've been a terrible host. Rondel, you look like a jaguar mauled you. Our healer can put you back together. As for you, my niece, I offer you my own home, the best tree house in the city. The guard at the base of this tree can show you the way. Oh, and I suppose I'd better give this back to you." He handed her the Forest Dragon Bow.

Rondel suppressed a smile. Narunë was Otunë's brother, after all. It didn't surprise her that he had come up with a way to have a private conversation with Rondel before she had.

They all headed down the rope ladder, and Minawë left with the guard for Narunë's house. Narunë in turn led Rondel to a tree several hundred yards in the opposite direction.

Unlike the guard platform, this tree had a full building constructed within its canopy, as well as a pulley system to raise and lower visitors in a basket. "The trees here aren't thick enough to make homes inside them like in Ziorsecth," Narunë said, "so we adapted."

They climbed into the basket. Narunë tugged on a rope, and a few seconds later they lifted off the ground.

The tree house's construction was impressive; Rondel had to give it that. It was so organic that she had difficulty spotting the built parts through the curtain of wide jungle leaves. Though not as inconspicuous as a Ziorsecthan home, it came closer than she would have expected.

When the basket stopped, Rondel and Narunë were inside a large, open room made of wood. Curtains of leaves divided the space into sections. Pained moans echoed throughout it.

"Welcome to our hospital," Narunë said, his voice grim. "It isn't normally this crowded, but, well, we've had some unusual times lately."

A male Kodama dressed all in white came up to them. "Lord Narunë, how may I help you?"

"This woman needs treatment," Narunë said, "somewhere private."

The healer examined Rondel. "You're a Maantec," he spat.

"And a guest in this village," Narunë added before Rondel could loose the sarcastic comment on her tongue. "Treat her as one of us. No, treat her as a war hero."

That set the healer aback, but with a frown he said, "This way."

The healer escorted them to a separate room in the back of the tree house, walled off by thick wood on all sides. "We designed this room for high-ranking patients," the healer said. "We made it soundproof so they could discuss matters of state while in treatment. It hasn't seen much use for that, but—"

"It will serve," Narunë interrupted. "Now excuse us. I'll be along shortly. When I'm gone, I expect you to give this woman your utmost attention. I want her healed as quickly as possible."

To his credit, the man hesitated only briefly before saying, "Of course, Lord Narunë."

When they were alone, Narunë dropped his false smile in favor of a scowl. "Now," he said, "tell me what you're really doing here."

"We're going to Shikari," Rondel replied. "A friend of ours was kidnapped, and we think he's being held there."

Narunë twirled the broken Liryometa in his hand, but he wasn't paying attention to it. He was studying Rondel's face. "I see," he said at length. "That isn't the answer I was hoping for. Rondel, I can't let you go to Shikari."

Rondel blinked twice. "You what?" she asked. "I thought you were my friend. How can that be your answer?"

He held up a hand. "I am your friend, and under normal circumstances, I'd have no problem helping you. At the moment, though, I have a greater concern."

"And that would be?"

"This jungle has more than animals in it. There are Yokai here too."

Rondel frowned. Thousands of years ago, the Tengu had pushed the Yokai out of the Eregos Mountains, and most of the monsters had gone south. She hadn't realized they were still alive. That said, a few Yokai shouldn't pose a problem for battle-hardened Kodamas, and she told Narunë as much.

The burly Kodama huffed. "We've held them in check for a thousand years, despite their superior numbers. But in the past few months, the balance of power has changed. Out of nowhere, their Oni leader, Azar, somehow became the Fire Dragon Knight."

A wave of pain radiated from Rondel's left hand. For a moment she was back in the scorched fields of Serona, watching Hana take the Burning Ruby. "That can't be," she murmured.

"Tell that to the Kodamas lying wounded out there. Azar did that to them. They aren't the only ones, either. I've lost a hundred of my best fighters to him already. We can't compete with the Karyozaki, so I've ordered my patrols back to the village. The ones who brought you in last night were some of the last."

Rondel clenched her fist. Hana didn't have the knowledge to reforge the Fire Dragon Sword, but Melwar did. Hana must have taken the Burning Ruby to Melwar before she went to find Iren. Why Melwar had reforged the Karyozaki, though, and why he had given it to an Oni instead of one of his own men, were questions Rondel couldn't answer.

"So you see, it's simply too dangerous to cross Aokigahara at the moment," Narunë said. He smiled slyly. "Of course, if Azar were dealt with, that might change the situation."

Rondel had been trying to guess Narunë's game ever since the platform, and now she saw it. "You don't have to be so roundabout," she said. "I know a quid pro quo when I see one. I get rid of this Oni, and you'll help me and Minawë reach Shikari."

"Well put."

"And if I refuse?"

"You already know the answer to that." His smirk deepened as he leaned in and whispered, "It only took me a few seconds, you know. As soon as I saw her, I knew. She'll be staying in my home. We'll have days to talk. Who knows what we might discuss?"

So that was how it was. "Understood," Rondel said. "In exchange for your silence and your help getting to Shikari, I'll kill Azar for you. Now give me back my Liryometa."

Narunë held the broken dagger aloft. "What, this piece of garbage? It won't do you any good like this. I have a smith from the war days. I'll let him take a look at it. Who knows? Maybe he'll come up with something."

Rondel sighed in resignation. She wanted to believe the Kodamas could fix the rondel, but she doubted Narunë's smith would know what to do with it. And without the Liryometa, Rondel had little confidence she could win against the Fire Dragon Knight.

That settled it. She couldn't afford to die here, not with Iren still in Melwar's hands. Forget Narunë. Forget Azar. Forget even the Liryometa. She would look for an opportunity to escape the hospital, find Minawë, and get out of this settlement undetected. "Narunë, I'm a tired old woman," she said. "Please leave me. I need to rest."

The faintest dimples sprouted on Narunë's face. "Of course. Sleep well. I'll check in on you later." He walked to the door.

He was about to open it when he looked back at her. "A word of caution: don't leave the hospital," he said. "The healer and I know you aren't a threat, but the rest of the Kodamas, well . . ." Narunë smiled again, that fake yet cunning grin so much like Rondel's. "Let's just say I hope there won't be any unfortunate accidents."

Narunë left. Rondel lay on the bed, sleep failing her even though she needed it. She was irritated, as much with herself as with Narunë. The two of them might be old friends, but this time the man had outplayed her. She had no choice but to pursue Azar. If she tried to run, she'd be seen as an enemy and attacked. Even if she escaped, she couldn't complete her mission in Shikari without Minawë or the Liryometa, both of which she now had no idea where they were. Worst of all, if she showed any sign of becoming uncooperative, Narunë would tell Minawë the secret Rondel had kept from her for a thousand years.

Through her frustration, Rondel had to admit a begrudging admiration. Not only had Narunë trapped her perfectly with only a few minutes' preparation, he'd done it without Minawë ever suspecting and without Rondel being able to say anything against him. He really was Otunë's brother.

CHAPTER THIRTY-TWO
Hana's Final Lesson

It was after sundown by the time Iren recovered enough to leave the training garden. He headed to his room, his body still aching. He supposed he should order some food from the kitchens, but he wasn't hungry. All he wanted at the moment was a long, long rest.

When Iren entered his room, he found its candles lit and his futon set up. His lips pursed. He knew he'd packed up the futon before meeting Hana and Melwar this morning. It was another crazy Maantec rule. Beds were for sleeping. They weren't to be left out and create a messy appearance.

Considering how tired he was, though, Iren wasn't about to second-guess it. Melwar had probably ordered one of his servants to prepare the room in advance.

Iren removed his sweat-soaked kimono and stood naked in the room. He wished he could have bathed, but the cedar tub was useless to someone without magic. He walked over to it anyway to get a towel and wipe off the sweat that yet clung to him.

The tub was full. Iren dipped his hand in it; the water was hot.

Iren's eyes circled back on the room, now on alert. The futon he could understand, but the tub was too much. Not even Melwar could have the foresight to have a servant draw a bath with such precise timing. This water couldn't have entered the tub more than half an hour ago.

All the same, Iren doubted the tub was part of any unfriendly scheme. He slipped into the bath and sighed.

After a long soak and a scrubbing so harsh it left his body red, Iren reluctantly left the water, opened the tub's drain, and dried off. From a nearby closet he retrieved a loose-fitting white robe, traditional Maantec sleepwear. He put it on and walked to his futon to settle in.

He'd just pulled the blankets back when a voice from behind him said, "Did you like my surprise?"

Iren whipped around. Hana stepped out from behind a set of sliding walls. The dim candlelight reflected off her white sleeping gown and gave her a glowing complexion. Her black hair hung in loose tumbles over her shoulders.

"Hana!" Iren yelped. "What is all this? What are you doing here?"

She approached him. Her scent, a perfume made from cherry blossoms, filled Iren's nose. "What's the matter?" she asked with mock timidity. "Don't you want me here? Do you want me to leave?"

Iren's heart pounded. She was standing too close. It made him uncomfortable, and he wanted to ask her to return to her room. Instead, through rapid breathing, he said, "No, of course not. You just caught me off guard."

"It wouldn't be much of a surprise otherwise."

Everything about this felt wrong. Iren stepped back, but Hana followed him. He decided to try a distraction. "I read the first sentence of the diary," he said. "It isn't by my father after all. It's by Iren Saito."

"I know that," she said. Her lips were inches from his face. His head tingled when her breath brushed against his hair.

"So," he pressed on, struggling to keep his composure, "we don't need to continue our lessons. You can go and do whatever you'd like."

The wicked smile she flashed instantly made him regret what he'd said. "No, wait," he stammered, "I didn't mean—"

She put a finger to his lips. "It's all right," she said. "I understand. But my purpose here is to teach you about Maantec culture. I've helped you with the language, the food, and the dress. Even your manners have improved. If you don't want my instruction, that's fine. Before we part, though, there's one last part of Maantec life I want to teach you."

He gulped. "What part is that?"

Hana looked into his eyes. The same hunger from the garden earlier that day was back in her expression. "I think you already know."

Before Iren realized what Hana was doing, she had untied the sash holding her gown together. With a gentle shrug of her shoulders, the garment dropped to the floor. Iren opened his mouth to tell her to stop, to say that this had gone far enough.

Then she put her lips against his, and all thought of resistance vanished.

∞

The candles were out. Hana Akiyama lay awake in the darkness. Next to her, Iren Saitosan snored so loudly Hana would have had difficulty falling asleep even without old memories flooding her thoughts.

There had been no choice. She kept telling herself that. Lord Melwar had given her specific instructions. This was all to gain Iren's trust, and it had worked.

At first Hana had taken pleasure in the idea of controlling him. Even now, she smiled with the knowledge that after tonight, Iren would trust her implicitly.

Yet as she lay there, Hana couldn't help but feel doubt. It was supposed to be impersonal, but from the moment Iren had defeated her in the garden, she had looked forward to tonight. Something about the way he'd moved resonated with her. Their contest today had more resembled a dance than sparring. No one had ever matched her so perfectly.

Thus she doubted herself. She wondered if she could see her task through as Lord Melwar had intended. She hadn't needed to fake her pleasure tonight the way she'd planned to do. More revolting, she was starting to pity the naïve man next to her. After all, it was a scene not so unlike what had happened this evening that had set Hana on the path to becoming Lord Melwar's slave.

The memories flashed through her. For twenty-five years she'd worked to forget them, but they never went away. Those worthless humans in Orcsthia had almost raped her, and Rondel had slain them.

If only the old Maantec had taken Hana with her! How different her life would have been!

But no. Rondel had walked into the rain, and it was barely a day later when Lord Melwar had found Hana and recruited her. She recalled his words to her, the ones that had shaped her into who she was.

"You cannot blame Rondel for not taking you," he'd said. "After all, she did not rescue you. That happened as a result of her actions, but it was never her purpose. She came to deliver Okthora's Law to those fools. If she had arrived after they had finished with you, she would have killed them and moved on exactly as she did last night."

"How can someone be so heartless?" Hana had asked. Her innocence back then still sickened her.

"It is not about heart," Lord Melwar had explained. "People do not act out of charity. They are always looking out for themselves and their own benefit. Even when someone gives a gift to a friend or a coin to a beggar, it is because they are looking for something in return, some fleeting sense of rightness. If you want to be strong, stop looking for charity and start looking for those you can use to gain more power."

The way the man had looked at her then, Hana had known Lord Melwar was one of those people. She couldn't have explained how she knew, but she had. "And what would you want of me," she'd said, "if I came with you and used you for power?"

He'd smiled at that. "Revenge."

That was all he'd said, yet the word had pulsed through Hana's body like a wave. "Teach me then," she'd told him. "Give me power, and I'll give you vengeance."

CHAPTER THIRTY-THREE
False Left

Balear rose before dawn and headed for Veliaf's exit. The night guards no longer tried to stop him when he asked to leave the village. They just opened the gate and let him out.

Once he passed underneath Veliaf's wall, Balear took off at a jog to warm up. It felt good to work his body. As his muscles adjusted to the motion, he sped up until he was sprinting as fast as he could. He then slowed to a more manageable pace and held it for an hour, running east from Veliaf.

By the time he reached his destination, the first peaks of sun had appeared on the horizon. They cheered him. The past three days had been dreary with a maddening drizzle that couldn't be called rain yet had soaked Balear more than a thunderstorm.

As he had every day for the past month, Balear started with a long round of stretches. He'd performed these motions thousands of times during his tenure in the Castle Guard, yet each one felt different now. He unconsciously leaned to his right as a counter to the change in his center of weight. Several times he swayed like a raw recruit, and twice in a particularly deep stretch he lost his balance and fell.

Balear considered it an improvement. Yesterday he'd fallen four times during these exercises, and his first day out, he'd spent more time on the ground than in stretches.

When his body felt limber, he picked up the Auryozaki. Though the blade was weightless, Balear still found it cumbersome in his left hand. He swung a few times, but every cut was jerky and imprecise. He more closely resembled an apprentice butcher than a swordsman.

His stance was off. It felt backwards. No, it didn't feel backwards; it was backwards. He was used to holding a sword in his right hand and leading with his left foot. With the blade in his left hand, his feet were wrong. His hips were wrong. His torso was wrong. He tried to switch, to reverse everything, but his body fought him. After six years in the Castle Guard, every stance had become part of his muscle memory. He could drop into a flawless defensive posture in a heartbeat. At least, it would have been flawless had he a right hand to hold his sword.

With a frustrated shout, Balear whipped his arm in a wide arc. The Auryozaki *whooshed* as it slashed through the air.

Partway through the swing, the awkwardness of Balear's stance made him lose his footing. He tripped, spun in a half-circle, and wound up on his back looking at the sky.

Balear raised his head a few inches and then slammed it on the ground. He might be getting better at stretches, but his swordsmanship hadn't improved at all. He'd come out here every day for a month and trained until the sun set. It was a brutal routine: wake up before dawn, eat a hasty breakfast, run an hour, train all day, run back to Veliaf in the dark, eat supper, and fall asleep.

He shuddered as he realized he'd forgotten to include hygiene in that sequence. Back in Haldessa, Balear had always kept his uniform well-trimmed, his face clean-shaven, and his hair cropped short. Now he looked about as hairy as the Fubuki, and he smelled worse.

Thinking of the Fubuki made Balear struggle into a seated position. He had to get better. He had to find a way to defeat that thing. Hana had wounded it, but she hadn't killed it. It would recover. When it did, it would return.

"Dad," Balear whispered, "how would you have fought that beast?"

The trouble, of course, was that adjusting to his injury wasn't enough. He and Iren together couldn't stop the Fubuki last time. Somehow, he needed to be better than the two of them combined, and he'd have to do it with his off hand.

"Yo, Balear!" someone called from his right. Balear faced the voice and saw a man running toward him. It was Dirio.

The miner-turned-mayor jogged up to Balear. When he stopped, he put his hands on his knees and took several deep breaths. "I haven't run that much in years!" he panted. "I'm impressed you can do that twice every day."

Balear stood. "They're just my warm-up and cool-down," he said. "The real work happens out here, although it isn't going well."

Dirio straightened himself. "I guessed that from talking to the gate guards yesterday. I think their exact words were, 'He's like a mad dog. Don't get in the way of that one, sir.'" The mayor laughed. "Please don't tell them I told you that."

Despite himself, Balear chuckled. "No, they're probably right. But what brings you out here? It must be important if it couldn't wait until I returned tonight."

"Actually, it's related to what the guards said," Dirio replied. "I'm sorry, Balear, but I can't have a mad dog in my village. With the civil war going on, we're on a knife's edge as it is."

All the feeling drained from Balear's legs. "What are you saying?"

The mayor looked Balear in the eye. "I'm saying that I'm here to help you."

"Help me?" Balear spat. "How does booting me from Veliaf help me?"

Dirio lowered himself into a fighting stance. The position was unprofessional, but Balear recognized it from breaking up plenty of tavern fights over the years. "Prove to me that you can stay in Veliaf," Dirio said. "Prove it to me with your fist."

Balear scowled. He might only have one arm, but he could handle a politician twice his age. He set down his sword and rushed Dirio.

The fight ended before it started. Balear threw a kick, hoping to take advantage of Dirio's shorter reach, but his body was used to moving with a right arm. As his empty shoulder instinctively twisted to provide counter-balance, the lack of weight made him slip. He hit the ground without Dirio throwing a punch.

The mayor looked down at him. "I said 'with your fist.' Try again."

Balear climbed to his feet, his vision as red as his face. He wouldn't let some bureaucrat humiliate him! He charged and swung his left arm at full strength. A few missing teeth would teach Dirio to toss him out.

Dirio was ready. He shifted his head a few inches to his right, which put him outside Balear's attack. At the same time, he brought his own left hand up and swept Balear's arm across his body. The motion again put Balear off-balance, and Dirio took advantage to punch Balear's exposed kidney.

Balear dropped to his knees. Dirio thrust his right hand at Balear's nose. He stopped an inch short.

"I'm no soldier," the mayor said, "but Veliaf's not a soft town. If you want to lead here, you have to stand up to a few bullies. I've probably ended more brawls than you have, and I know that doing so sometimes requires more than force. Sometimes it requires restraint."

"Restraint?" Balear howled. "You want me to have restraint against that Fubuki? Do you think it will show restraint to you and your town when it comes back?"

Dirio cocked an eyebrow. "Are you telling me you want to become the Fubuki?"

Balear had his mouth open to rebuke the mayor. He shut it without a word.

"If you stay in the village, that would be as bad for Veliaf as having the Fubuki there," Dirio said. "It might not happen today. It might not happen a month from now. But I know that at some point, you would snap and lash out like you did just now. I asked you to prove your worth with your fist, and you did. You attacked with reckless abandon. I can't have someone like that in my village, especially when that someone has a seven-foot sword and a dragon at his beck and call. So stay out here. I'll have my men bring you a tent and some food. When you've put this madness behind you, you can come back. I hope that for all our sakes, that time comes soon."

Dirio spun on his heel and left.

CHAPTER THIRTY-FOUR
Spying Sparrow

Minawë rose with the dawn and stretched. She loved it here.

She'd spent three weeks in Aokigahara, and she now wondered if, once she rescued Iren, they might live here instead of Ziorsecth. The rainforest was so alive, and there were so many Kodamas. It was as if Saito's curse had never happened.

She walked to her wardrobe and rooted for something to wear. Her uncle had searched the village to find the best clothes to fit her. A month ago he hadn't known she existed, yet he'd dropped everything to see to her happiness.

At least, that's how he'd behaved the first week. Since then they'd barely spoken, and that was only during the evenings. He always left before she woke up, and he usually didn't come back until after dark.

He was of course always friendly when he saw her, and his loud, winking laugh cheered her spirits. Still, Minawë had the impression that her uncle was being evasive about something. He asked a lot of questions about Ziorsecth and her parents, but he refused to divulge much of his own past.

It wouldn't have bothered Minawë, but Narunë was the only person around to talk to. Rondel was still in the hospital, and her uncle refused to let Minawë wander the village. He'd even stationed guards at the base of the lift to his tree house. He'd claimed that Minawë's presence might provoke the other Kodamas.

Minawë had believed her uncle at first, but as she'd thought about it more, his explanation made no sense. Why would her presence upset the

Kodamas? She had been excited to learn that more of her race survived. Surely they would feel the same way.

Whatever the reason was, Minawë couldn't stay cooped up inside. The forest was too amazing. She had to see it.

That was why, for the past week, she had adopted a different approach. This morning, as she did each day, she grabbed the Chloryoblaka, transformed into a sparrow, and flew out her bedroom window.

Through her travels, Minawë had learned to spot her uncle from the air. No matter where she went, she kept an eye on him during her wanderings. That way, she knew he wouldn't discover her missing.

Minawë flew across the settlement toward the Kodamas' hospital. Narunë went there daily, so Minawë had quickly figured out where it was. She couldn't see inside it, but she would occasionally catch sight of Narunë and Rondel standing together out on the tree house's deck. Sure enough, that's where they were today.

It bothered Minawë to see them like that. Whenever she asked her uncle about Rondel, he insisted that she was healing but not well enough to receive visitors. Minawë knew Narunë and Rondel were old friends, but that was no excuse for her uncle to lie to her.

Something else was going on. Minawë was certain that Rondel hadn't told her everything about their mission to rescue Iren. Perhaps whatever the old Maantec's secret was, Narunë was in on it.

Minawë's curiosity got the better of her. She fluttered to a branch within earshot of the hospital's deck. Several leaves overhung where she stood, so it was easy to see what Rondel and Narunë were doing without them noticing her.

"—looking a lot better," Narunë was saying. "Is your hand back to normal?"

"Yes, I think so," Rondel replied. She flexed her fingers. "Remind me not to punch any more rocks."

"As if you'd take my advice!"

"Well, maybe just this once." Rondel smiled briefly, but then she became serious again. "By the way, thanks. I didn't think I'd ever use my left hand again."

"Not at all," Narunë said. "Now that you're healed, you're free to go after Azar whenever you like. He shouldn't be hard to find; Fire Dragon Knights tend to be conspicuous."

Minawë jumped on her branch. Fire Dragon Knight? So Hana and Melwar had reforged the Karyozaki after all. Minawë had no idea who this Azar was, but based on her uncle's tone, he wasn't anyone pleasant.

"How's the work on my Liryometa going?" Rondel asked. "I should have it before I hunt for Azar."

Narunë sighed. "I wish I had better news. My smith is one of the best, but so far your weapon's stumped him."

"In that case, you know there's a good chance I won't come back," Rondel said. "What will you do then?"

It took Narunë a long moment to respond. His fingers clutched the deck's railing. "I don't know," he said at last. "I had all but lost hope for my people when you showed up. If you can't defeat that monster, it will only be a matter of time before he kills us all."

Rondel frowned. "That's what I thought. In that case, can you promise me something? If Azar comes, make sure Minawë gets out of this forest alive."

Narunë set his jaw. "Even if I have to drag her to the cliff at Eregos, I'll make sure she escapes."

From her listening spot, Minawë felt her sparrow lungs breathing faster and faster. What were Rondel and her uncle talking about? Rondel sounded like she was going off to die. If there was a Fire Dragon Knight out there, why would the old Maantec face it alone? Minawë was the Forest Dragon Knight. She could help.

She was about to fly down there, transform, and tell them that when Rondel said, "By the way, whether I come back or not, it doesn't change our agreement. You still can't tell Minawë."

Minawë stopped, her wings open. Couldn't tell her what?

Narunë held up both hands in a placating gesture. "Please, Rondel, I have more tact than that. You've held up your end of the bargain; I'll keep mine too."

"That's good to hear," Rondel replied. Lightning Sight sparked in her eyes, and she pointed to them with her thumb. "If I do come back and find out that she knows, you'll have these to answer to. I won't show you any mercy."

"I wouldn't expect it!" Narunë said, bellowing his laugh.

Rondel glared at him for several more seconds. Finally, though, she ended her spell and headed for the door that led inside the hospital.

She had almost reached it when Narunë said, "By the way, while I won't reveal your secret, I do think you should tell Minawë. She deserves to know."

The old woman shook her head and smiled sadly. "She deserves to be happy."

Narunë cocked an eyebrow. "Aren't those the same?"

Rondel paused as though considering. For a moment she looked like she might respond, but then she opened the door and stepped inside.

Minawë was certain the strange conversation was over, but then Narunë said, "Actually, I'm surprised she hasn't figured it out. Even if I didn't know about you and Otunë, it was obvious when you two were standing together the morning you arrived. She has Outnë's height, but she has her mother's good looks, not to mention her eyes."

Minawë's heart skipped. No way. She looked at Rondel, who had stormed back onto the deck. With her keen bird sight, Minawë saw the Maantec's emerald eyes. Minawë didn't often look at her own face, but she'd seen it reflected in water enough times. Narunë was right. They were the same.

In her shock Minawë twittered a call. Rondel made no movement, but Narunë's brow furrowed. "That's odd," he said.

"What is?" Rondel asked.

"I heard a song sparrow just now, but they don't live this far south. There can't be one here."

Minawë swore inside her mind as Rondel swore aloud. The old woman shoved Narunë out of the way as she ran to the edge of the deck. "Where? Where is it?" she demanded. Lightning Sight flashed.

Minawë had to get away. She couldn't face it. She couldn't face her. She took flight, but she knew Lightning Sight would detect the motion. She had to fly far and fast, somewhere Rondel couldn't follow.

"Rondel, come back!" Minawë heard her uncle cry as she spun away from the hospital. "Azar is out there! He'll kill you! Stop, Rondel!"

Minawë ignored the shouts. She ignored everything except the pain in her wings as she pumped them as hard as she could. Pain was good.

When her mind focused on pain, it could fool itself into believing that it had never heard the terrible truth, the secret Rondel had kept from her all this time.

Aletas wasn't her mother. Rondel was.

CHAPTER THIRTY-FIVE
I Will Be Strong

Minawë flew until her wing muscles burned. The sun reached its peak and sailed on, yet still she raced. She had long ago left Rondel behind. As fast as the Maantec was, she couldn't keep pace with a tiny bird through the tangle of Aokigahara.

Even so, Minawë refused to slow down. She knew the old woman would never stop hunting her, and she needed time to think.

There was no point in going to Shikari now. Getting there wasn't the issue; the sparrow knew which direction was south. Without help, though, Minawë couldn't rescue Iren. Hana was guarding him, and she had defeated Rondel. Minawë couldn't win against her.

She could go home to Ziorsecth. It terrified her that she considered it, but the prospect made more and more sense the longer she thought about it. Why should she suffer like this for Iren? He had walked out on her and left her to her grief.

But no, she couldn't abandon Iren to whatever fate Hana had planned for him. Minawë could picture him, an awkward teenager helping her cross Lodia before Saito's curse could take her life. She was alive because of Iren. He had cured her of the curse, and he'd defended her and her people against Amroth and Feng.

While Minawë warred with herself, the air around her grew hotter. Aokigahara's ever-present fog thickened and darkened. It choked her lungs. Minawë kept flying, too preoccupied to care. Then she burst through a clearing in the trees, and her inner debate was forgotten.

Flames devoured the forest. Great teeth of red, yellow, and orange whipped from tree to tree, leaving nothing but char behind them.

In the center of the blaze walked creatures from a nightmare. Minawë remembered them from her imprisonment last year in Akaku Forest. They were Yokai.

A dozen of them stalked through the burning forest. They swaggered on reverse-jointed legs as their lanky arms provided counterbalance. In each hand they carried a two-foot sword adorned with hooks and flanges meant to torture enemies as the Yokai butchered them. Adding to their arsenal, three-inch bone spikes grew above each eye. Their hair matched the red of the flames around them, and their oversized yellow eyes glowed as if they too were on fire.

Most of the Yokai were no taller than Rondel, but one in the center towered above the rest. He stood three times their height, his gargantuan size marking him as the rarest of the Yokai—their mutant form, an Oni.

The Oni didn't carry a flanged sword like his kin. Instead his right hand clenched an impossibly long blade. In shape it matched the Muryozaki, but though it was no wider than Iren's katana, its length surpassed the Oni's height.

A smoldering tree blocked the Oni's way, but he didn't slow down. With an easy swing of his arm, the beast's sword sliced through the trunk. The Oni pushed down the tree with his other arm as he passed. When he did, Minawë caught a glimpse of the weapon's handle, and she saw the telltale kanji rings on its hilt that marked it as a Ryokaiten.

She had to get away. There was nothing she could do against a monster like that, let alone one that was a Dragon Knight. She banked in midair and fled the terrible scene. It was her only hope of living.

After a few seconds, though, Minawë stopped. She landed on a branch and watched the grim procession. The Oni was burning a line through the forest. With each step the monster took, Minawë heard the voices of the plants and animals in his way screaming and dying. They filled her mind first with panic, then with emptiness.

Minawë made her decision. She flew back toward the Oni and landed in front of him and his minions. Her sparrow eyes glared at him in challenge.

The Oni noticed her and loosed a cackling laugh. "Look at this, boys!" he jeered. "This one wants to stop us!" The other Yokai all howled in response, and the Oni continued, "Not much of a survival instinct. I guess it's for the best that we kill it."

"You will not," Minawë said, and though she was a sparrow, the words came through. Her body grew as she transformed. "I am the Forest Dragon Knight. I wield the powers of life and death. You have killed those living here before their time. I'll never forgive you for that!"

She rose to her full height, her Kodaman form restored. Her right hand grasped the Chloryoblaka.

The Oni laughed at her. "So one Kodama has the courage to confront Azar."

Minawë didn't hesitate. She drew back the Chloryoblaka. As she did, the bow curled and created its own arrow. Minawë loosed it at the Oni's throat, but the wood burned up inches away from him.

Azar didn't so much as blink. Instead he gestured with his open hand, and his Yokai minions leapt at Minawë.

She pulled back her bow again, but the Yokai were too fast. Minawë leapt sideways and barely avoided a fatal blow from one of the monsters' flanged swords. Cursing, she tried to think of a strategy. She didn't have enough time to shoot her bow. Even if she could, the Yokai maneuvered so quickly that Minawë doubted she could hit them. Their reverse-jointed legs and long arms made them remarkable climbers. They leapt from tree to tree at a dizzying speed, cackling all the while.

As Minawë watched one Yokai, another landed behind her and slashed at her head. She ducked and rolled, mud covering her.

Before she could regain her feet, a second Yokai leapt in front of her. It thrust its sword. This time, Minawë was off balance and couldn't maneuver. She was going to die.

"Help!" she cried. Minawë shut her eyes against the pain.

Then she heard a soft *thunk*. She opened her eyes and gasped. A tree had sprouted in front of her. Its trunk curled above her, protecting her life with its own.

Her opponent was as stunned as she was. Its flanged sword could rip apart flesh, but the weapon's odd construction meant that it could become lodged in tough material like wood.

The monster yanked on its blade, but the tree held firm. When the

Yokai swung its second sword to cut the first loose, that weapon became trapped as well. Minawë drew back her bow and shot an arrow into the creature's head.

The Yokai's death gave the others pause, just enough for Minawë to decipher what had happened. She recalled Mother's battle against the Lodians. Mother had used Dendryl's magic to control the plants, making them move and attack her enemies.

That gave Minawë an idea. She relaxed and slipped into the strange world of the forest. Its cacophony of voices—many still screaming in fear—threatened to overwhelm her, but she held firm. After months of hearing them, she'd finally spoken their language. Her cry for help had come out not in Lodian or Kodaman, but in the same voice as the life around her. She couldn't explain how, but with that one word, she knew the plants' speech had become part of her.

"Defend me!" Minawë cried in a language she didn't know, yet completely understood. "And defend yourselves! Stop the invaders!"

A Yokai descended, but a second tree sprouted even before the beast reached the ground. It blocked the monster's strike and then grew a new branch that it used to impale its foe. Elsewhere, vines wrapped around the Yokai and crushed them like vipers ensnaring their prey.

When the last Yokai fell, Minawë faced Azar. The Oni stared down at her with baleful eyes. He swung his blade in a broad arc, and a ring of fire leapt from it. The flames engulfed the plants around Minawë and cut off her escape. In moments she stood exposed on the charred earth.

"What now?" Azar laughed. "Your magic doesn't work outside the forest. Soon the curse will claim your life, and I'll take that bow back to my men. One of them can be the next Forest Dragon Knight and butcher the rest of your kind with it. That is, if any escape my trap."

At the word "trap," Minawë finally grasped Azar's strategy. Looking past him, she saw the line of blackened ground he'd created. It wasn't straight. Instead, it curved gradually to the left. She'd thought he was wantonly destroying the forest, but he was more cunning than that. Azar was burning a ring around the Kodaman settlement. If he finished it, he would cut off the Kodamas from the jungle. They would have nowhere to escape without falling victim to Saito's curse. Their choices would be simple and grim: die from the curse, or die from the Oni's flames.

Minawë had to stop him. Unfortunately, she had no idea how. The fight with Azar's minions had all but drained her magic. She could manage two or three more small spells, but that was it.

The Oni advanced. His long blade gleamed red as it reflected the fiery rainforest. Minawë drew her bow again and shot, this time at point-blank range. The arrow struck Azar in the stomach, but it clattered off his natural hide armor.

While Minawë wracked her brain for an idea of what to do next, the Oni raised his hand and loosed a torrent of fire at her. She cried out for defense. A tree sprouted before her and blocked the flames.

The spell left her exhausted. Worse, it would only delay the inevitable. The fire would burn through the trunk, and then it would do the same to her.

As the tree glowed, a voice shouted, "Minawë!"

A weight crashed into her at high speed. It knocked her from her position on the burned ground and sent her tumbling into the woods.

Before Minawë could regain her footing, she heard a gut-wrenching scream. She whipped her head around.

Rondel was engulfed in flames.

Azar halted his attack, revealing Rondel's charred body. The old woman faced Minawë. Then, to the Kodama's shock, Rondel smiled. "Remember the mountains, Daughter," she murmured, "and remember . . . your mother."

Minawë couldn't believe what she was seeing. It was happening again, just like Father, just like Mother.

She should run. Rondel had given her life to provide Minawë this one chance of escape. Yet Minawë couldn't make her body move. Her muscles refused the command to flee. Instead they made her stand and confront the Oni, even though she could do nothing against him.

"I'm tired," she said.

"Of course you are," Azar replied. "Let me help you rest."

"No," Minawë spat, "I'm tired of people dying for me. Never again, do you hear me? I will be strong! I will be strong so that no one else will have to die because of me!"

Minawë understood Rondel's last words. The old Maantec hadn't sacrificed herself so Minawë could escape. She'd done it so Minawë could stop Azar.

What's more, thanks to what Rondel had said, Minawë knew how. She only had enough magic for one more spell, but that was enough. She stretched out with her mind and called the roots of the nearby plants. They sprang from the ground and wrapped around her legs. She urged their energy into her, drawing from their lives to strengthen her own.

With the plants' magic, Minawë grew a hard, brown coating over her body. She then divided the shell until she was covered in thousands of round, tiny seeds.

The new armor didn't faze the Oni. He raised his palm again and unleashed a column of flame.

It was what Minawë had waited for. She didn't avoid the fire. It engulfed her, yet she felt no heat from it.

When the blaze subsided, Azar surveyed his work. "I'm impressed you're still standing," he said, "even if you're nothing but a husk."

He spun on his taloned foot to leave, and that was the last step he took. Minawë thrust out her arm, and the seeds on her body erupted. Vines burst from them, hundreds upon hundreds. They lanced out, smothered the Oni, and wrenched back his hand until he dropped the Karyozaki. They left only his face exposed, and though he struggled, he couldn't move.

Minawë walked forward, amused by Azar's surprised expression. "How?" he snarled. "I thought you were out of magic."

"I was," she said, "so I borrowed yours. Those were serotinous seeds. They can only sprout after absorbing incredible heat."

"Impossible!" Azar howled. "A Kodama using plants can't defeat an Oni wielding fire!"

"You're right about that," Minawë said. "I didn't defeat you. If you want someone to blame, then blame my mothers. Both of them." She picked up the Fire Dragon Sword and headed toward Rondel to check on her.

"What, you'll just leave me here?" Azar yelled at her. "You Kodamas always were too soft. Even if you take that sword, I'll eventually break free of these vines. When I do, I'll kill you and all your worthless race."

Minawë looked over her shoulder at him. "Too soft, you say? Well then, let me teach you something my mother taught me."

Her voice and face turned to iron. "Evil must be annihilated."

Nine inch thorns sprang from the vines holding Azar. The Oni's scream lasted less than a second.

CHAPTER THIRTY-SIX
Failure

Hana Akiyama woke to a tapping at Iren's door. She glanced at the young man lying next to her; he was still snoring.

It made sense that he was a heavy sleeper. Though the Lodians had treated Iren poorly, he had never known real danger growing up. Hana was different. Sleep was the only time she was vulnerable.

Still, she was surprised that someone would wake her this late at night, especially when she was with Iren. They had slept together several times the past three weeks, and she had instructed the servants not to bother them.

Hana waited in bed a few minutes, hoping the fool would go away. But the tapping continued, so at last she dressed and crept to the door.

"What is it?" she hissed.

The voice on the other side was shaking. "His lordship demands your presence, my lady."

Hana felt cold. Lord Melwar knew she was with Iren. What could be so important that he would call on her now?

When Lord Melwar demanded your presence, though, you didn't question it. You didn't dawdle either. Hana slid open the door as quietly as she could, and then she took off at a run for the lord's room.

When she arrived, she prostrated herself. "How may I serve?"

Unlike when Iren was with her, Lord Melwar didn't ask Hana to rise. She had to keep herself spread out on the floor as he said, "A runner arrived a few minutes ago. He bore a message from our scouts along the Aokigaharan border. The Yokai report that the Kodamas apprehended two spies: a woman of their own kind and a crone. The Kodama had a bow covered in living vines, and the crone had a broken dagger. Sound familiar?"

Hana couldn't believe it. "Rondel?"

"I was under the impression I ordered you to kill her in Serona. Explain your failure."

Hana trembled at the way Lord Melwar emphasized that last word. "I was sure I killed her," she said. "I covered her in an airtight coffin of rock. I thought either the heat or the lack of air would finish her."

Though Hana couldn't see him, Lord Melwar's anger was palpable. "You underestimated her. I warned you not to do that. Now Azar's mission will fail as well."

Hana needed to fix this. "My lord, let me go to Aokigahara," she said. "You're training Iren yourself now. You don't need me here. If Azar and I work together, I know we can kill Rondel."

"If you are begging for your life by trying to show your value, that is unnecessary. You must remain here to build Iren's trust. Besides, this news from the Yokai is now several weeks old. Azar is likely already dead. He was supposed to kill the Kodamas in Aokigahara, but he was never skilled enough to fight another Dragon Knight. Moreover, even if you did join Azar, your presence would make no difference. Now that Rondel has seen you fight, she will have a plan to defeat you. That must be why she brought the Kodama. The Yokai's description of her bow matches the Chloryoblaka. She must be the Forest Dragon Knight, and somehow she has become free of Saito's curse. Inside Aokigahara, you would have no chance against her."

Lord Melwar paused. Hana understood enough of the man to know he was thinking of a strategy.

When he spoke again, it was with casual certainty. "Rondel and the Forest Dragon Knight are coming here. They know we have Iren."

Hana suppressed a wince as she recalled her boast to Rondel in Serona. She had proclaimed that she would give the crone's greetings to Iren Saitosan. Had she not said that, Rondel wouldn't have known to follow her.

Lord Melwar had paused again, and Hana knew he had detected her increased nervousness. Nothing escaped the man's notice. "I have been going slowly with Iren," he said. "I thought we had plenty of time to convince him of the purity of our cause. Thanks to your failure, we will need to speed things up. No matter. He is ready to begin the meditation sessions anyway. By the time Rondel arrives, we will be ready for her."

"When she gets here," Hana dared to say, "may I have a chance at redemption, at killing Rondel?"

"No," Lord Melwar replied. Hana could picture the gleam in the Maantec lord's eyes as he said, "I have a different opponent in mind for her."

CHAPTER THIRTY-SEVEN
The Hearts of Dragons

"Picture the ocean."

Iren sat on his knees in his room with his eyes closed. He listened to Melwar's words, struggling to focus only on them.

"Can you see it?"

There was a rare urgency in Melwar's tone. In the past two days he'd begun pushing Iren harder. Out of nowhere, Melwar had added this meditation practice, and the lord already expected Iren to be proficient at it.

Iren had no idea what had changed to put the calm Melwar on edge. He hoped Hana didn't have anything to do with it. He had woken two nights ago and found her gone, and he'd seen almost nothing of her since then.

"Concentrate, Iren," Melwar interjected on his thoughts. "Answer my question."

Iren pulled himself back to the exercise at hand. "I see it," he said. His mental image of the Yuushin Sea in Ziorsecth sparkled in the late afternoon sun. He stood on the beach, and the water swept in and out over his ankles.

"Good," Melwar said. "Now remember, the waves are your thoughts. Each thought is its own wave, from the tiniest ripple to the mightiest tsunami."

Iren grimaced. If the waves were his thoughts, then his head was a jumbled mess.

"Make the waves disappear," Melwar intoned. "As your thoughts disappear, so will the waves. Make the sea flat, like glass."

Iren tried to calm the churning Yuushin. When he focused, he could remove most of the waves, but two thoughts remained. The first was Hana. Even though they hadn't spent much time together lately, her cherry-blossom scent filled him. He was convinced she was the woman in his dream.

That dream was the second thought. It came to him at least twice a night now, and sometimes in these sessions, he would lapse into it too.

The images flashed before him again, his black-haired wife and the baby they had made together. The beach dissolved into a farmhouse at night. A fire crackled in the hearth. His wife looked at him and said, "You are loved."

Iren snapped back to reality. He still couldn't do it. According to Melwar, these meditations would help him enter No Mind without fighting, but he was no closer to that goal than he'd been the first time he and Melwar had dueled in the garden.

Those sparring bouts weren't going much better. Melwar's swordsmanship was superb. In their first six matches, the Maantec lord had defeated Iren with a single blow every time. Iren had made his way to lasting through two or three strikes, but by that point Melwar could enter No Mind and defeat him easily. Iren would never win unless he could activate the trance before the battle started.

Unfortunately, that scenario was looking more unlikely every day. A month had passed since Iren had defeated Hana, and he now understood why Melwar thought entering No Mind outside a fight might be impossible. It was like looking in two directions at once. Iren needed absolute concentration to achieve No Mind, yet the technique was defined by the purging of concentration.

Despite the paradox, Iren wouldn't give up. He was on the cusp of regaining his magic. The pain training was progressing well. He could last almost an hour now, and his recovery time had dropped to less than an hour. Melwar figured that in another two weeks, Iren would be able to withstand the pain without losing consciousness at all. He wanted to be ready to break his barrier when that time came.

Melwar frowned at him from across the room. "A thought distracts you," the Maantec lord said.

Iren bowed to the floor. "Lord Melwar," he said, "in your experience with magic, have you ever had visions of the future?"

"I have heard stories of those who have vague dreams that later come to pass," Melwar replied. "I also recall a Maantec legend that claims the Dragon Knights are fated to be drawn to one another. At best, though, these prophecies are hazy and open to interpretation. A true vision of the future is impossible. The future is not fixed. Our actions determine its shape." He paused and stroked his chin. "That is your lingering thought, then. You have had a dream and are curious about it."

Iren told Melwar about the farmhouse vision. When he finished, he thought Melwar would berate him for letting it distract him. Instead the Maantec looked thoughtful.

"You are not seeing the future, but the past," Melwar said. "You are seeing the world through the eyes of a former Holy Dragon Knight."

"How can that be?"

"You know that when you use Divinion's magic, you also draw in some of his will, correct? His memories come along with it. But while the kanji circles draw the dragon's will back into the Holy Diamond, the memories linger. They are buried in your subconscious. It is not well known even among Dragon Knights, but if a knight concentrates, he can see the past through the eyes of his predecessors. If you focus hard enough, for example, you could experience what happened to Iren Saito a thousand years ago. Also, unlike an ordinary memory, which fades with time, the dragons' memories are perfect. You will experience what happened in every detail as though you were living it yourself."

Melwar's explanation struck Iren like a blow from a wooden katana. In seconds the Maantec lord had shattered Iren's perspective that his dream had been of him and Hana living together as husband and wife.

But then who was he seeing in those dreams? The memory could belong to any Holy Dragon Knight.

"Is it possible to control these visions?" Iren asked. "Can I choose a memory and enter it at will?"

"I do not encourage it," Melwar said. His frown deepened. "There is a reason few Dragon Knights know about this ability. Knights have died from using it."

"Died?"

"As I said, these visions go beyond normal memories. While you are in one, you become the person whose memory you examine. You see what they saw and feel what they felt. You will retain your own thoughts at first, but you can lose yourself if the memory stretches too long. Surrounded by the previous knight's experiences, particularly if they are traumatic, you forget that you are not that person. If that happens, you will never escape. You will be trapped in the memory until your real body dies of exhaustion."

Iren felt lightheaded. He'd thought his dreams were innocent, but if Melwar was right, Iren risked death every time they affected him.

That was all the more reason to end them. "How do I enter a memory?" he asked. "If I can learn what this dream is about, maybe I can get it to stop plaguing my thoughts."

Melwar sighed. "Under normal circumstances, I would not teach you how to do this. It seems, however, that until you resolve this memory, you will not achieve No Mind. Very well. You have learned the first step: meditation. Focus your mind as I have taught you these past two days. When the ocean becomes as still as possible, think back on the time you want to examine. The more precise you can be, the better. The memory will come to you."

Iren bowed once more. "Thank you, Lord Melwar."

The Maantec nodded. "You are welcome, but Iren, please take care. Only you can pull your mind from a memory. No one on the outside can help you. More important, never forget that while the past has triumphs, it has failures too. Be cautious in your search for truth. More often than not, it does not bring happiness. It only brings more pain."

With that Melwar left the room. Iren extinguished the candles and sat on the floor. He pictured the ocean. The sea appeared, and the waves calmed. He focused on the dream. The scene in his mind stayed the same. He concentrated harder, but he remained on the sand.

He was about to give up when a figure appeared down the beach and walked toward him. Iren wondered if he was lapsing into the dream again, but as the person came closer, he realized the newcomer was an old man with white robes and sandals flecked with blue.

Iren gasped. "Divinion!" he shouted. He raced across the sand and slammed into the old man, wrapping him in a hug. "What are you doing here? Aren't you trapped in the Holy Diamond? Did I use magic?"

"One question at a time!" the old man laughed as he disentangled himself. When he was free, he looked around the beach and said, "This is an interesting place to meet. It doesn't surprise me that the mental image you can conjure best is a seaside."

Iren looked at him blankly. "So then, are you just an image in my mind, something I made up like this ocean?"

Divinion shook his head. "Nope, I'm the real Holy Dragon. I'm afraid I must admit to being the one who's caused your recurring dreams this past year. I wanted to get your attention."

"Well, your plan worked," Iren said. "Those dreams, or memories, or whatever they are, have been driving me crazy!"

The old man smiled sheepishly and put his right hand behind his head. It was an odd gesture for the most powerful being on Raa. "Sorry about that," he said, "but I wanted to talk to you."

"About what? What could be so important that you would pester me for a year?"

Divinion flushed. "Nothing, really. When your body created its magical barrier, part of my will remained inside you from the Dragoon transformation. The wall prevented the Holy Diamond from pulling me back into it. I've been trapped in your subconscious ever since. I was lonely."

"Lonely?" Iren asked. He put a hand to his forehead. "You sent me those memories because you were lonely? I thought you were a god!"

"Gods get lonely too. We may have great power, but the hearts of dragons yearn for companionship just as those of other species do. When I was in the Holy Diamond, I could count on you using magic and releasing me from that prison on a regular basis. With your barrier in place, I thought I would never see the outside world again. I thought I would never see you again. It terrified me."

Iren had nothing to say. He couldn't believe Divinion, the Holy Dragon, could be terrified of anything. Then again, if their places were reversed, Iren knew he would find the dragon's situation unbearable.

Now that he thought about it, it didn't shock him that Divinion would go to such lengths to contact him.

That raised a question though. "Why use a memory?" Iren asked. "You could have just come yourself."

"I tried that at first, but even in your sleep, I couldn't touch your conscious mind enough to reach you. Instead, I took advantage of our shared memories of past Holy Dragon Knights. When I focused on an especially strong memory, one where you were present, I found I could connect with your dreams. I hoped the repeated vision would prompt you to come looking for me."

Iren thought about the memory Divinion had sent him. "You're not making sense," he said. "I'm not in that memory. I've never been married. I've never had a child. I've never lived in a farmhou—"

He stopped short. He had lived in a farmhouse, though never as an adult. "I am in it, aren't I?" he whispered. "I'm not the man whose eyes I'm looking through. I'm the baby in the woman's arms. That woman isn't Hana; she's my mother. The man is my father."

Divinion nodded.

"But that doesn't make sense either," Iren said. "The woman in the memory calls me 'Iren.' How would she know that's my name?"

The Holy Dragon had no answer for that. "Let's just enjoy that we can talk to each other again," he said. "Even if you never regain your magic, if you meditate, you can reach me here any time."

"I would like to talk to you more," Iren admitted, but even as he spoke, he knew Divinion had changed the subject. The dragon hadn't liked where Iren's question was leading.

That only made Iren want the answer more. Why would the woman call him Iren? Melwar had said he would see the memories exactly as they happened. How could that be unless . . .

His breath caught. "She's not addressing me," he murmured. "She's talking to my father. My father's name is Iren."

It couldn't be.

"Divinion," Iren said, his voice fast, "I need to see a memory. I need to see the first memory you have of the Holy Dragon Knight after the end of the Kodama-Maantec War."

The old man looked crestfallen. "I should have known this would happen. I thought you had moved past your parents. It seems I was wrong. So be it. I will let you see the memory if you wish, but I advise against it. It will only hurt you."

Divinion's words echoed Melwar's warning, but Iren didn't care. He needed to know. "Show me."

The dragon sighed, reached out, and touched Iren on the forehead. In an instant, the beach, ocean, and Divinion disappeared. Iren was left in darkness.

ℭ𝔰

Iren felt himself open his eyes. He had no control over his actions. He was in the memory.

He lay on a stone floor. The smooth black rock spread around him. He pressed his hands down and pushed onto his knees. "I'm alive?" he whispered.

Standing, he walked to the floor's edge. He stood atop a gigantic tower a thousand feet in the air. The landscape mortified him, and he panicked as he realized he wasn't dreaming. This was reality. This was what he had caused.

Storm clouds covered the sky. Lightning arced from cloud to cloud and struck the ground dozens of times every second. Rain gushed from the storm, but it evaporated before it struck the earth. On the ground, once a verdant country dotted with rice paddies, everything was scorched red and dry. White flames erupted from crevasses that crisscrossed the land. Some of those fires reached as high as the roof on which he stood.

He had seen all that before, during the battle. The scenery wasn't what sickened him. The corpses did.

They filled the land. Nearly all his Maantec forces had fallen; only a handful still moved amid the destruction. More terrifying, though, not a single Kodama remained alive. They all lay dead, their hair bone white in a sign that their biological magic had left them.

Iren vomited over the tower's edge. This wasn't supposed to happen. His spell wasn't supposed to do this. He remembered the biological magic flowing out of him. He'd intended to create shields around the combatants—Maantec and Kodama alike—so they couldn't harm each other. He'd wanted to stop the fighting while he went to King Otunë and negotiated a Maantec surrender. It would have been shameful, but at least it would have saved the rest of his people.

Instead, something had gone horribly wrong. His spell had somehow taken on a life of its own, knocking him unconscious while it wreaked its gruesome work.

The Muryozaki lay on the roof next to him. Iren trembled to look at it. Divinion had been his companion for more than two hundred years. What would the Holy Dragon say when he saw this massacre?

Iren couldn't face the dragon's judgment. He picked up the katana. His finger brushed against its blade. Blood flowed for a second before the wound healed itself. He would need to be fast. He pointed the sword at his abdomen.

"Stop!"

The command echoed in Iren's head. He froze. He recognized that voice.

"Divinion?" he asked. "How can you be here? You should be locked in the Holy Diamond."

"Your spell used enough magic to draw me forth. You cannot die here, Iren Saito."

"I must!" Iren cried. "Don't you see what I've done? I've wiped out my people and the Kodamas as well. I'm disgraced, more than any Maantec who has come before me. Death by seppuku is the only proper punishment. I name it as Maantec emperor."

"Fool," Divinion spat, "do you think death will bring back those butchered on your account? Can you save them by killing yourself?"

"Then what do I do?"

"Live," the dragon said. "That is your punishment, Iren Saito. Live with the pain of what you have done."

Iren felt like Divinion had stabbed him a thousand times. He fell on the roof of Edasuko Tower and wept until his eyes ran dry.

CHAPTER THIRTY-EIGHT
The Rest of the Dream

Iren Saitosan pulled himself from the ancient emperor's memory. His body shook. He'd returned to the seaside within his mind, but the waves were more disturbed than ever. The sky was black as the new moon and full of clouds.

A light approached from down the beach. It was Divinion, and he had shed his human form in favor of his true reptilian shape.

Iren gulped. The god was a gigantic white serpent with wings that seemed to extend to infinity. Blue hairs grew down his spine, and one blue whisker thirty feet long extended off either side of his muzzle.

"He survived," Iren said when the dragon reached him. "Iren Saito didn't die a thousand years ago."

"He lived in exile for a thousand years," Divinion growled, baring teeth that made the Muryozaki look dull. "No one knew he had escaped death, so history recorded that he died in that final battle, killed by his use of biological magic."

Iren recalled the diary he'd retrieved from his parents' farmhouse. He'd set it aside weeks ago, but now everything became clear. "My name is Iren Saito," the book had begun. Iren's first impression of it had been right after all. It was his father's diary, and his father was Iren Saito, the man responsible for genocide against both Kodamas and Maantecs.

Then a new realization made Iren gasp. "Divinion, not everyone believed Saito was dead. Rondel knew. She must have."

The dragon's eyes narrowed. "What makes you say that?"

"My name. Rondel gave it to me. Last year she said she named me 'Iren Saitosan' because I reminded her of Saito. In a way I suppose that's true, but as I think more about it, I don't think she meant to name me at all. She was surprised when Amroth showed me to her. She played off her mistake as naming me, but in reality she just said what I was: Iren Saito's son."

Divinion said nothing. He set his piercing gaze over the stormy Yuushin. That look, more than the memories Iren had seen, convinced him of the truth.

There was one problem though. Rondel wasn't there when his parents had died. Amroth had killed them. How had she known who Iren was? Had she known Saito was living in that farmhouse? They had been lovers before Rondel betrayed Saito during the Kodama-Maantec War. A thousand years was a long time. Maybe they had made amends.

There was one way to find out, but Iren didn't know if he could handle it. Melwar's caution about viewing traumatic moments rang in Iren's head. He could lose himself and become trapped. If that happened, he would die.

He had no choice. He had to put these questions about his past to rest. As long as they distracted him, he could never achieve the focus needed to reach No Mind. He would never regain his magic or become the Maantec emperor.

Iren stared up at Divinion, his expression set. "You told me you needed a strong memory to connect with me," he said. "You used the night my parents were murdered, didn't you? That's why you stopped it before I could see who their visitor was. I need to see the rest. I need you to show me how they died."

Divinion kept his huge eyes looking across the waves. "I do not want to show you that memory, but I know I can't dissuade you. Please remember this, though: your father's memories aren't the only ones that matter. That's all."

os

The world darkened a moment before it filled in with the warm glow of a nearby hearth. Iren Saito rocked in a simple chair, one he'd fashioned himself. His wife sat in its twin next to him. Her head rested on his bicep, and she cradled their child in her arms.

"He will be hated," Saito warned her, "just as I am hated."

His wife looked at him with bold determination. "He will be loved, just as you are loved."

Saito sighed. She didn't understand. There was no way his child could grow up to be loved.

But he couldn't tell her the truth of his past. Instead he smiled, kissed her on the forehead, and said, "I don't deserve you."

"You're tired, Iren," she said. "Go and lie down. I'll be in shortly. Our little man's almost asleep."

Saito rose, but as he walked to the bedroom, a knock came at the door. His head whipped to face it. It was hours past dark; no one should be here this late. He wondered if the townsfolk had come for them again, but no, it was too quiet for there to be a mob outside. With a glance toward the dusty Muryozaki above the fireplace, he approached the door and swung it open.

There was no one there.

Saito closed the door and faced his wife and son. They were so innocent. They didn't deserve to be wrapped up in this. They didn't deserve to die.

Maybe he could still save them. Saito smiled at his wife for the last time. He kissed her on the lips. He would never taste them again.

When they separated, he put a hand on his child's head. "Stay in the house."

His wife watched as Saito retrieved the Muryozaki and slid it into his belt. "What do you mean?" she asked. "What's going on?"

Saito rounded on her. "Just stay in the house!"

Her eyes bulged. In the five years they'd known each other, Saito had never raised his voice to her.

He walked to the door. "I'm sorry," he said.

He knew they were last words.

There was still no one at the door when Saito opened it a second time. He'd expected that. Far off in his field, though, he thought he could see them—the two orbs of blue light that marked tonight's visitor.

Saito stepped outside and shut the door. He drew a small amount of magic and directed it to his eyes. It changed them so they could detect more light.

The instant the spell began, he saw her. Trying to appear more confident than he felt, he strode into the long grass.

"I've finally found you," the woman said when he reached her.

"I knew you would, Rondel."

"Do you plan to run away from me again?" she asked.

Saito resisted the temptation to look back at the house. Rondel had confronted him like this more times than he cared to remember in the thousand years since the Kodama-Maantec War's end. He'd always fled, but now he had people to protect. He wouldn't let her hurt them. "No," he said, "it's time we finish this."

Rondel didn't smile, even though it was the answer Saito knew she wanted. She drew her Liryometa, cold in the night. The sparking blue of Lightning Sight was equally frosty.

Saito shivered. "Is there any way we could avoid this?" he asked. "It seems another life, yet I still—"

"Okthora's Law is absolute," Rondel interrupted. "You know that as well as I do. Evil must be annihilated. You sentenced yourself to this fate a thousand years ago."

With a sigh, Saito unsheathed his katana. It felt strange in his hands. He hadn't used it in combat since the war.

They started slowly, a dance meant to feel out each other's strengths and weaknesses. Saito mostly defended. Each time he swung his blade, he saw Rondel as he once knew her: vibrant, intelligent, and beautiful. She was everything he could have ever desired.

As their battle intensified, tears streamed down Saito's face. He didn't want this, but he knew that if he surrendered, if he gave himself to Rondel's blade, it wouldn't satisfy her. She had waited a thousand years for this revenge. She needed to feel like she'd earned it.

Then Saito heard a sound that made his blood curdle. The grasses behind him rustled. As the battle brought the sound's origin into view, Saito saw his wife standing there. She carried their son in her arms.

Saito fought with renewed fervor. Lightning Sight saw everything. Rondel must know they were there. If he didn't stop her, if he didn't kill her, she would kill them.

Rondel's abilities astounded him. Even though she'd lost almost all her biological magic, she was still as precise as she'd been during the war.

By contrast, Saito's arms felt like he'd strapped boulders to them. Even the Muryozaki felt clumsy. It was all he could do to defend himself. Two minutes had gone by since he'd last counterattacked.

He couldn't win. No matter his desire to protect his family, his old strength had abandoned him after a thousand years of inaction.

There was only one thing left to do. If he could hold out a little longer, maybe he would have enough time to cast one last spell.

Saito poured magic into the technique. He didn't know if it would work, if it was even possible, yet he had to try.

Seconds passed. The spell demanded more energy. He gave it some of his biological magic, and even that wasn't enough. Out of options, Saito slowed himself so he could add in the magic he was using to keep up with Rondel.

The moment he did that, though, Rondel caught him. Her blade pierced his arm. In a last desperate act, Saito flung the Muryozaki toward his wife. He hoped he'd had enough time and that she would pick up the sword.

Defeated, Saito knelt on the hard earth. He looked into Rondel's sparking eyes. "I love you," he said.

She stabbed him through the heart.

It hurt less than he'd expected. As he crumpled to the ground, the last sound he heard was his wife, his second wife, screaming in the night. His final sight was Rondel stalking toward his unarmed family, and as he died, he despaired.

Everything went black for a moment. Iren Saitosan had no idea what was happening. He thought he'd been kicked out of the memory, or perhaps that he'd died along with his father.

Then the blackness filled in. He was looking at a night sky from the ground. Beside him lay the unsheathed Muryozaki. He couldn't make sense of his thoughts. Whatever body he was in, the person couldn't think in words.

Then he realized what memory he was viewing. It was his own, as an infant, just after his parents' deaths.

Rondel appeared above him, her Liryometa still streaked with his parents' blood. Iren the baby didn't understand, so he didn't cry. He just stared at her, looking into those murderous eyes.

The old Maantec thrust her dagger toward him, but inches from his face, she stopped. Lightning Sight's sparks disappeared, replaced by the deep green of Rondel's true eyes. She snarled, her body tense. Then, with a violent shake of her head, she stalked away into the dark.

Iren lay in the grass for a long time, unable to pull himself from the memory. He had seen the truth, just as he'd wanted, but this was unbearable. In his mind he wailed, even as the baby version of him cried for his mother.

While Iren struggled to end the memory, a new person walked into the infant's field of vision. He was huge and barrel-chested. "Looks like whoever that was took care of our work," he said in a deep bass. "Could you get a good look at him, Amroth?"

A second man, by appearance barely twenty and with flame-red hair, stepped into view. "No, Captain Ortromp," he said, "but I'm glad they showed up. Judging from the sparks of their weapons, I'm not sure either of us could have killed that Left."

Iren stared in shock at the man who would, in time, become king of Lodia and the Fire Dragon Knight. As though Amroth could sense the baby gazing at him, he looked down at the infant and the sword resting against him. Amroth's eyes widened in recognition, and he murmured, "The Muryozaki?"

Amroth shifted his gaze to his companion. "Captain!" he shouted. "There's something here!"

Ortromp came over. "A Left child," he said. "We have to kill it."

"Kill it, sir?"

The captain walked out of Iren's line of sight. "See this man, Amroth?" he called. "See how his sheath is on the right side? He's a Left, a monster. If we let this kid grow, he'll become one too. Better to kill him now, while he's helpless."

Amroth looked down again, and Iren the adult could see the Maantec-in-hiding work out a plan. "I'm sorry, sir," Amroth said at last. "I can't. He's a baby. I can't kill an innocent baby."

Ortromp stormed back into view. "Do it, soldier!" he roared. "That's an order."

"I refuse."

"Then stay out of the way!" Ortromp shoved Amroth, who fell to the ground. The captain drew his blade and came for Iren.

As Ortromp raised his weapon, though, Amroth regained his feet. With an easy motion, he unsheathed his sword and stabbed his captain in the gut.

"You don't understand," Amroth said. "I need this child. Someday he's going to get me everything I desire. I won't allow a barbarous Right like you to interfere."

Ortromp gasped as he clutched at the blade piercing his abdomen. "You . . ." he breathed, "you're a Left!"

Amroth smiled as he swung his weapon up and carved his former superior in half. He wiped the blade clean, put it away, and hefted Iren onto his shoulder. "There, there, little Holy Dragon Knight," he sneered, "no harm will come to you. I need you to kill the Fire Dragon Knight for me so I can take his place. I'm going to take good care of you, my beautiful weapon."

ଓ

Iren shot from the memory like a bolt from a crossbow. He didn't return to the beach. Instead, he found himself back in his room in Hiabi. He stumbled his way to the latrine and threw up until nothing remained in his stomach but bile.

Amroth hadn't killed his parents. Rondel, his friend and former teacher, had.

Iren roamed the corridors of Hiabi in a daze. He had no idea where he was going or why he was going there.

At some point he ran into a soft wall. It was Melwar. The Maantec lord took one look at Iren, wrapped his arms around him, and said, "I am sorry, Iren. I am so sorry."

CHAPTER THIRTY-NINE
To Slay a Monster

Balear trained.

He trained through the summer, while the brutal sun beat on his head. He trained into fall, which he marked by the changing colors in a small forest to the south.

When the nights became frigid enough that he needed a fire, Balear headed for those woods and settled there. The guards from Veliaf had provided him a tent, camping gear, some food, and traps so he could catch game without using a bow. He lived like a wild man, staying far from the village. He was alone.

At least, he was physically alone. Every evening, after he'd spent all day working with the Auryozaki, he heard Ariok's voice in his head. It was never more than a whisper, but he knew the Sky Dragon was watching him.

There were also the dreams. They were the most vivid of his life. They showed Balear places he'd never been and people he'd never met. In one he flew above a wide, green plain speckled with thatched-roof farmhouses. In another he fought with the Auryozaki in his left hand— even though his right arm was intact—against a Kodama who could control water. A third had him sailing on a large ship, waiting for a pirate attack he knew would come yet had no idea when or where.

All the while, Balear practiced. He didn't fall down anymore. Ever since the dream with the Kodama, his stances no longer felt backward. He couldn't explain it, but after that night, all the left-handed movements made sense.

The harder he trained, though, the more dreams he had. Lately, almost every one was a battle. He always fought left-handed, even though in those dreams he still had his right hand. His opponent was never human; they were either Kodamas or Maantecs. He won every fight, but they were often narrow victories. His opponents would attack with magic, and he responded in kind.

The dreams were strange enough while Balear was in them, but when he awoke, they didn't fade. He remembered every detail of what he'd seen.

Balear shifted his training approach to mimic the fights in his dreams. In his mind's eye, he could see each opponent. As he copied the moves he saw at night, his control over the Auryozaki increased.

His left arm strengthened too. Back at the hospital, Balear had barely managed thirty push-ups. Now he could do more than a hundred and still have enough energy to leap up and continue training.

Balear didn't concern himself with Dirio or the comments the mayor had made back in the summer. If Balear was a "mad dog," then so be it. Sometimes it took a monster to slay a monster.

CHAPTER FORTY
What Are You Going to Do About It?

Melwar ushered Iren into the Maantec lord's chambers. Even at this late hour, there were servants at the ready. Melwar pointed to each in turn. "Light the brazier," he commanded. "Bring us hot rice wine. Wake Hana and have her come here at once."

Iren was in a haze as the servants rushed to follow Melwar's orders. When Melwar sat him down, Iren felt like he would pass out. The Maantec lord held him steady, and a few minutes later a servant arrived with a tall ceramic bottle of steaming rice wine. She offered a cup to Iren, but instead he grabbed the bottle and took a long swig.

"It's a lie," he said. "Rondel couldn't have killed my parents."

Melwar didn't answer. Instead, he looked past Iren's head. Iren turned and saw Hana come into the room, bow shoddily, and approach Melwar. Her hair was tousled, and her nightgown was crumpled.

Melwar and Hana sat next to each other opposite Iren. They each poured themselves a cup of wine. Melwar sipped his, but Hana threw hers back like she was in a tavern drinking contest.

When the Maantec lord finished his drink, he said, "You relived Emperor Saito's death."

"It's a lie," Iren repeated.

Melwar rubbed his forehead with his thumb and index finger. "I knew you would find out eventually, but I still do not know how best to explain it."

Iren clenched his fists. "So you knew? All along, you knew Saito was my father, and you knew Rondel killed him. Why didn't you tell me?"

"Because I had no proof," Melwar said, "and because it was more important for you to focus on regaining your magic so you could become the emperor."

"But Rondel can't have murdered my parents," Iren insisted. "Feng told me Amroth murdered them."

"He lied to you," Melwar said, "for the same reason Amroth lied to you."

"What do you mean?" Iren asked. "Amroth lied to manipulate me into helping him become the Fire Dragon Knight. But why would Feng lie? What did he have to gain?"

"He hoped to keep you from becoming the Dragoon. As the Fire Dragon, he must have known you had the potential to do it. No one had ever become a Dragoon before, so he did not know what to expect. Rather than risk defeat, he decided it would be best to keep you from transforming in the first place. He thought his lie about Amroth would do that."

Iren's brow furrowed. "How could a lie stop me from becoming the Dragoon?"

"Because becoming the Dragoon requires a will so focused that your dragon cannot break it. If you are distracted, if the smallest doubt is in your head, you will not retain control. Feng counted on his lie unsettling you enough to prevent you from changing. He underestimated you."

Iren folded his arms. He was still coming to grips with what he'd seen, but the finality of Melwar's tone left little room for argument.

That begged a question of its own. "How do you know all this?" Iren asked. "You live so far from Lodia. Knowing about my father is strange enough, but you even know details about Amroth's and Feng's conversations with me. How could you have so much information?"

For a few seconds Melwar didn't answer, but then he said, "Iren, forgive me for not telling you sooner. The truth is that Hana and I have watched you almost your entire life."

Iren's head whipped from Melwar to Hana and back again. "You've what?"

"I have long known that Emperor Saito survived the Battle of Serona," Melwar said. "He wanted to live in hiding, and since he was my emperor, I respected his wishes and kept his secret. Even so, I kept an eye on him. I clung to the hope that he would come back and reunite the Maantecs."

Melwar sighed. "But centuries passed, and he did not return. I grew impatient. When I heard a rumor that he was in Lodia, I went to seek him out. Unfortunately, Rondel found him first. I was dismayed, but then I learned that the new captain of Haldessa's Castle Guard had brought home a boy whose parents a Left had slain. I knew that child had to be Saito's son. I resolved to take you away from Haldessa and raise you to become the Maantec emperor.

"When I reached the castle, though, I discovered Rondel was there too. If I tried to take you, she would attack me. I could not match her, so I had no choice but to leave you, my emperor's only son, in the care of humans."

The Maantec lord looked into Iren's eyes. "Ever since that day, I have waited for a chance to separate you from humans and teach you of your Maantec heritage. Because I needed to be here most of the time to govern Shikari, I asked Hana to observe you and, if Rondel left, convince you to come here."

Iren cradled his head in his hand as reality sunk in. Rondel had hidden the truth from him all along. She'd claimed to hate Iren because he was a Maantec, but it was more than that. He was a constant reminder of the murders she'd committed and of how she'd orphaned a child just like her parents' killers had done to her.

"There is something else you should know," Melwar said. "A while back, we received a scout report from Aokigahara. Rondel is headed for Shikari. She was waylaid in the rainforest, but I have no doubt she will overcome any difficulties. She could arrive in a few weeks."

Iren clutched his knees and stared wide-eyed at Melwar. Rondel was on her way! His parents' murderer was coming here!

Melwar frowned at Iren's reaction. "Wish all you want that your parents still lived, or that someone else had killed them. Know, however, that such wishes cannot come to pass. I do not believe in 'should have' or 'could have.' To me only one question matters: what are you going to do about it?"

The question struck Iren like the flat of a blade. What was he going to do about it? About Rondel killing his parents? About her coming here?

A strange calmness overtook him. His heart rate slowed. In his mind's eye he pictured his friend's wrinkled face—her emerald eyes, her silver hair. He whispered his father's final words, "I love you."

He had his answer.

"You have to break my barrier," Iren said. "Now."

Melwar looked at him with shock. "You have not yet mastered No Mind outside of battle. You will never survive the attempt."

"I don't care. I have to see Rondel, and I can't meet her without magic."

"The pain will overwhelm you."

"Pain can't reach me," Iren murmured. "I am already numb."

Melwar looked him over, the lord's eyes searching for something Iren couldn't see. Finally, he released a long breath and said, "Draw the Muryozaki. If this works, you will need its healing power to restore any other parts of your body damaged by my spell."

Iren unsheathed his father's katana. "I'm ready," he said.

"No, you are not," Melwar replied. "You are just stubborn."

Melwar placed both hands on Iren's chest. The Maantec lord's arms darkened until they looked like they'd been charred. Then he spoke a single word in Maantec, and Iren drowned in pain.

It was like his body was being ripped into pieces and set on fire. He screamed, but he hardly knew it. His eyes rolled back in his head, and he flirted with unconsciousness. The pain training had been nothing compared with this.

He was going to die. He had no idea how long it would take for the barrier to give, but his body couldn't last another second.

Then an image floated before him. Rondel leered at him with cold, sparking eyes. For a moment he was back in his own memory. He was a baby looking up at her. His parents' blood stained her dagger.

Through the pain, Iren fixated on that image. The agony came worse than ever, but Iren endured. He couldn't afford to die here, not before he saw Rondel again.

A tremendous tearing sound filled Melwar's room. White energy surged through Iren like a wave. It smashed apart his body's defenses, drawn toward the shadow that opposed it. The two magics clashed inside him, and as they touched, they detonated.

The pain of breaking the magic barrier had been the worst Iren had ever experienced, but the explosion afterward surpassed it tenfold. He never even had time to cry out before his heart stopped.

CHAPTER FORTY-ONE
Gifts of War

Rondel groaned as she came to and struggled to sit up. She was in a large room, surrounded by wood. It made up the floor, walls, ceiling, and every piece of furniture. She sat on a bed with a soft mattress and silk sheets. Her clothes were also silk, and when she rubbed the fabric between her fingers, she recognized the weave as Kodaman.

She'd spent enough time in this room to know where she was—the Kodamas' hospital. She couldn't believe it. The last thing she remembered was Azar cooking her alive. Now she didn't have a mark on her.

Narunë's face popped around the doorway. "Sitting up already!" he shouted, which prompted hushing sounds from the main room of the hospital. "It's only been three weeks. I expected you to be out for a month. Our healer had a time keeping you hydrated, but he's the best for a reason."

Rondel rubbed her face to clear some of the confusion. It didn't help.

Narunë handed her a wooden cup. "Here, drink this."

She sniffed it. "Water? I could use something a little stronger."

"That's like you," Narunë said. He stepped inside the room and shut the door. "Stick to water for now. Maybe if you behave and don't cause me too much grief, I'll sneak in something for you. We don't have any maple brandy, but several of the local fruits make excellent wine."

Rondel sipped the water. To her chagrin she had to admit that it did help clear her head. "What happened to me?" she asked between swallows. "What happened to that Oni?"

Narunë smirked. "Minawë happened. She killed Azar. Our sentinels saw the line of smoke and went to investigate. They brought you back to the village."

Rondel barely heard what Narunë was saying. She was hung up on Minawë killing Azar. "Is Minawë hurt?" she asked. "Is she in the hospital too?"

"No, no, calm down!" Narunë couldn't seem to stop grinning today. "She's watched over you all this time. She hadn't eaten in two days, so I made her promise to find some lunch. She's been worried about you, and so have I." His smile became, if possible, even wider. "If you died, what on Raa was I going to do with this?"

Narunë reached behind his back and pulled from his belt the sheathed Liryometa.

Rondel accepted it from him and drew it. She gasped. It was repaired. "How?" she asked. "You said your smith couldn't fix it."

"You have your daughter to thank for that, too," Narunë said. "She brought the Karyozaki back with her. From examining it, my smith Palentos was able to repair your rondel. It was delicate work, since he couldn't touch the Karyozaki. Still, I never lost faith in him."

Rondel's restored dagger awed her, but she frowned all the same. "I appreciate your smith's work, but bringing the Fire Dragon Sword here was a mistake. Some of your Kodamas might try to control it."

Narunë shrugged. "Not likely. After we finished with your rondel, I had Minawë hide the Karyozaki. Only she and Palentos know where it is now. Even I couldn't tell you where they put it."

The door to the room opened a crack, and a familiar voice asked, "How's she doing, Uncle?"

Narunë laughed. "Come see for yourself!"

Minawë stepped inside. She smiled when she saw Rondel sitting up.

"I hear you've been taking care of me," Rondel said. "Thank you."

The Kodama blushed. "It was nothing," she said. "I'm glad to see you awake." She paused a moment before adding, almost inaudibly, "Mother."

Narunë stood. "I'll take my leave," he said. "Minawë, Rondel is still recovering, so don't keep her too long." He left the room and shut the door behind him.

For a long time Rondel and Minawë sat in silence, neither able to meet the other's eye. Finally, Rondel said, "I hear you killed Azar."

"Only because you saved me."

Rondel looked at the ceiling and whistled. "That was a hell of a gamble."

"What do you mean 'gamble?'" Minawë asked. "I thought you saved me because you knew I could kill him."

"Sure, let's go with that." In truth, Rondel had hoped Minawë would take advantage of her sacrifice and escape. She had never imagined that Minawë could defeat that monster.

Rondel looked on her daughter with new respect. She had always admired her, but since Minawë had become the Forest Dragon Knight, the woman had far surpassed Rondel's expectations.

Minawë creased her eyebrows. "Why are you staring at me?"

Rondel shook her head. "Oh, nothing. I just had a strange thought. The Maantecs nicknamed Aokigahara 'Suicide Forest.' Who could have suspected it would become a place of healing for me?"

To Rondel's surprise Minawë said, "I can understand why they call it that. I feel like I died here. The Minawë who left Ziorsecth and the Minawë sitting here now can't be the same person."

The room felt stuffy. Rondel wanted to blame the tropical climate, but she knew there was more to it than that. "Minawë, I never wanted you to learn the truth, but now that you have, I'll keep no more secrets from you. Ask me what you will."

Minawë thought for a moment. Then she said, "How did you seduce my father?"

Rondel cringed. She suspected it wouldn't be the last time in this conversation she reacted that way. Even so, she said, "During the Kodama-Maantec War, our races fought to a standstill. Iren Saito knew that to defeat the Kodamas, he would have to take Ziorsecth Forest. He invaded it twice, but both times your father, Otunë, repelled him.

"Those defeats taught Saito that he couldn't conquer Ziorsecth without some kind of an edge. He needed a spy, and I was the only one who could do it. I was faster than any other Maantec, and I was small and clever enough to avoid detection. I could also enhance my senses, so I could learn secrets from a distance."

Minawë waved her hand dismissively. "I'm familiar with the history of the war. You said you would answer my questions."

Rondel shivered despite the room's heat. "I'm not telling you this to dodge your question," she said, "I'm saying it because it matters. My role as a spy is how I first came to know your father. I spied on him and the other Kodamas for years. What do you think I saw?"

When Minawë shrugged her shoulders, Rondel continued, "I saw people. I saw women and children. I saw families. I saw that our terrible enemies, the Kodamas, were no different from us. They weren't evil. They weren't inferior. They just wanted the war to end.

"As I traveled from Ziorsecth to Serona and back again, the disparity between Otunë and Saito magnified. Saito sought conquest; Otunë sought peace. Saito wanted to rule; Otunë wanted to serve. In the end, it was Saito's fault that I defected. Had he not sent me to spy on the Kodamas, I never would have learned enough about them to make me join their side. As it was, I finally approached Otunë and offered him my rondel."

"Why didn't the Kodamas kill you?" Minawë asked. "They would have had no reason to trust anything you said."

"Did you already forget that I was a spy? When I confronted Otunë, he was alone in a Kodaman tree home. I slipped in without his guards noticing. When I woke him, I saw his fear. The Chloryoblaka was out of reach, and he knew he couldn't best me when he'd been startled from sleep. The fact that I didn't kill him then convinced him to accept me.

"After I joined him, I wanted to march against Serona and wipe out the Maantecs. But Otunë argued that even with my help, it would cost many lives to invade Serona. To give the invasion the best chance of success, he needed information about the Maantecs. So instead of using me to support his military, he gave me a different job."

Minawë interjected, "Double-agent."

Rondel nodded. "Saito was my husband. He shared all his strategies with me, never suspecting that I relayed everything to his foe. That's all it was for the first year.

"Over time, though, something changed. I found myself not just caring about Otunë's people, or Otunë's cause, but Otunë himself.

He was so strong, yet he was also vulnerable. When you saw him in public, rallying his soldiers, he defined resolve. But I saw a side of him he didn't show anyone else, not even his wife. When I brought him information, it was always one-on-one. Narunë was the only other person who knew we were meeting. It had to be a secret, otherwise a captured Kodama might reveal the truth under torture. As a result, Otunë didn't have any masks around me. I saw his face contort in agony whenever I informed him of some Maantec victory or of Saito's latest plot. I saw him cower on beds with his head in his hands, wondering if the war would ever end. I wanted to lessen his pain, or at least to share in it."

Rondel wiped her eyes. "I never meant to pull your father away from Aletas, but in the end, that's what happened. For all her qualities, Aletas never took part in the war. She could whisper words of comfort to Otunë, but she didn't understand what he was going through. I did. In me he found a kindred spirit, someone who had seen the horrors of war and was as disgusted as he was."

"And that was when you started sleeping together." Minawë's voice was cold. It made Rondel cringe again.

"No," she said, "it was innocent enough at first. We would meet ostensibly for me to relay information, but in reality it was so we could comfort each other. Things gradually escalated, but we only shared a bed once—the night before we stormed Serona's capital of Edasuko. That night, both of us were terrified, not for ourselves, but for the Kodamas we led and for each other. We both feared that it was the last night we would be alive."

Rondel sighed. "It isn't an excuse, but take comfort in this. Otunë never stopped loving Aletas. Our night together was born of passion, fear, and desperation. It never would have lasted. Had Otunë survived the war, I have no doubt he would have gone back to Aletas. He was not the type to abandon those who cared about him."

Minawë sat so still Rondel wondered if her daughter had turned to stone. Finally, the Kodama said, "So I was conceived that night. You were pregnant with me during the final battle."

"That's right," Rondel said, "although I didn't know it. At the time, I didn't think it could happen. Otunë was Kodaman after all, and I was

Maantec. Even if it was possible, the thought of becoming pregnant never entered my mind. You probably already know this, but because of our immortality, it's difficult for Maantecs and Kodamas to conceive. A couple can sleep together hundreds of times without becoming pregnant. That's why our populations never recovered from the war, even though it happened a thousand years ago. Conception takes extreme emotion from both partners, because the child is created from tiny amounts of biological magic from each parent. Those energies combine in the mother's womb and create the child. In our case, Otunë and I were so anxious about the upcoming battle that we met the conditions for pregnancy without realizing it."

Minawë folded her arms. Her expression was still flat and cold, but she didn't look angry. On the contrary, she looked like she was working out a puzzle. "If what you've said is true," she said, "then I was conceived before Saito's curse took effect. Shouldn't I have died in your womb, an unborn victim of his spell?"

"The mother's body protects the child," Rondel said. "As long as you were within me, the curse couldn't harm you. It also affected you less than a typical Kodama, because you're half Maantec. That's why you were able to survive in Lodia during your mission last year. Your Maantec blood slowed the curse's effects and prolonged your life."

"I always wondered about that," Minawë said. "Mother died in seconds after Feng pulled her from Ziorsecth, but I lived outside the forest for weeks. Even so, I would have died eventually. That's why you left me in Ziorsecth as a child."

Rondel didn't answer right away. It would be so much easier to let Minawë go on thinking that the curse was why Rondel had abandoned her. She had promised her daughter no more secrets, though, so she said, "Leaving you in Ziorsecth did keep you safe, but that wasn't why I left you there. The truth is that where I was going, I couldn't have you with me. I went in search of Iren Saito, in order to kill him."

"Iren Saito?" Minawë looked shocked. "But he died during the final battle! All the histories say he did!"

"All the histories are wrong, or at least they misrepresent the truth. In a way, Saito did die in that fight. The emperor was gone, his army defeated, but the Maantec who was Iren Saito survived. He renounced his title and became a wanderer. I think he wanted to forget what he'd done.

"But I couldn't forget. I hunted him across the continent. By the time I brought him the justice of Okthora's Law, you were an adult who believed Aletas was your mother. I couldn't face you, so I went into hiding. I thought I'd never see you again, but then Iren Saitosan and I rescued you in Akaku Forest."

Rondel leaned back against her bed's headboard. For a thousand years she'd kept these secrets. A small part of her felt relieved not to have them locked inside anymore, but the greater part felt ashamed that she had them at all.

Minawë, meanwhile, had become contemplative. She had a hand on her chin, and her gaze looked at something far away. "When I was a child," she said, "Mother warned me once about seeking revenge. She said it couldn't make me happy. I had no desire for revenge, so I didn't understand why she spoke to me so passionately. Now I do. She knew you were my mother, and she knew the pain you must have felt abandoning your child to pursue Saito. That brings me to my final question. Even if it was for one night, I was still born of Father's affair. Why would Mother take me in? Every moment with me would remind her of it."

"True," Rondel said, "but you also reminded her of something far more important. You see, when I returned from the war, I brought Aletas two gifts. One was the Chloryoblaka. The other was you. Do you understand? Aletas's husband went away to war, and only his weapon and child came back. Aletas protected you because you are Otunë's legacy. As long as you live, part of him lives on as well."

Rondel took a deep breath. Tears soaked her cheeks. She looked at Minawë, and she was crying too. "Minawë," Rondel said, "my daughter, I never meant to burden you with all this. I wanted only for you to be happy. The Kodamas have suffered so much. I didn't want to hurt you more than I already had."

"No," Minawë replied. She reached in and embraced Rondel. "I'm grateful, truly. All of you—Father, Mother, and you—fought to protect me. All of you sacrificed yourselves for me. The least I can do is love you in return."

Rondel pulled back from the hug. She'd expected Minawë to rage at her mother's deceit. Instead, her daughter's words stole Rondel's breath. "You . . ." she whispered, "you lo. . ."

Minawë smiled and kissed Rondel on the cheek. Then she walked to the door. "I don't see any reason why someone can't have two mothers," she said. "If anything, it makes me more fortunate than most, including Iren Saitosan. So, Mother, that only makes it all the more important that we help him. You'd better recover your strength soon, because I won't stop until we rescue him." She left before Rondel could reply.

For several minutes Rondel sat in her bed and stared at the door. At last she laid down to rest. When she fell asleep, she dreamed, and for the first time that she could remember, the dreams were good.

CHAPTER FORTY-TWO
Winter Comes

Five weeks later, Minawë, Rondel, Narunë, and a troop of Kodamas stood on Aokigahara's southern edge. Minawë was at once elated and dismayed. After so many months, she had reached Shikari, the place where Iren was. That said, they still had to journey through this harsh land of jutting peaks and deep crevasses. All the while, they would be exposed to attack. Shikari was Maantec territory after all.

Minawë ran a nervous hand through her long green hair. In Lodia it just stood out; here, it marked her as an enemy.

"I wish we could go with you," Narunë said.

Minawë fought back tears. She'd only known him for a few months, but she would miss her uncle.

"You've already done more for us than we could have hoped for," Rondel said.

"I suppose," Narunë admitted, "but I wish my niece had better protection than a decrepit Maantec."

Rondel laughed. "Your niece doesn't need protecting. It's the other way around. She's protecting me. If you have any doubts, ask Azar!"

Narunë joined the old woman in her laughter, but Minawë kept silent. Sometimes even the strongest person needed a little protection.

"You'd best be on your way then," Narunë said after he'd calmed down. "You might have reached Shikari, but it's a hike to reach Hiabi on the other end."

Minawë threw her arms around Narunë, heedless of everyone watching. "Goodbye, Uncle."

He stroked her hair. "Journey well, Minawë."

Rondel smiled. "Narunë, my best to all of you. With luck we'll see you shortly, and with a Maantec in tow."

"Not another one!" Narunë cried. "One of you causes enough trouble!"

They all laughed, and then Rondel and Minawë left the forest. Minawë shuddered when she stepped beyond the tree line. Compared to the vibrancy of Aokigahara, Shikari was desolate. Minawë reached out to the plants, but they were scraggly and poor. She frowned. She had needed the forest's energy to defeat the Fire Dragon Knight. That wasn't an option out here.

If Rondel had any worries about traipsing through enemy territory, she didn't show them. Instead, she talked amiably, like she was giving a tour. She pointed out the various mountains, caverns, and distant terraced farms.

They camped that night in one of the innumerable caves that filled this broken country. After they'd eaten, Rondel looked seriously at Minawë. "Make sure to sleep enough tonight," the old Maantec said. "We don't know what we'll face tomorrow."

Minawë gulped. "Will we reach Hiabi tomorrow? Is Shikari that small?"

Rondel shook her head. "It would take weeks to traverse on foot at regular speed. We don't have that long. I wanted to go slowly today so you could get a feel for the landscape. Starting tomorrow, though, you will fly, and I will run. I've been to Hiabi before, so I know the way. We'll meet up outside the city. Assuming I'm recalling the distance correctly, we should arrive by midafternoon."

"How will I know which city is Hiabi?"

"It's hard to miss. It's the only city in the territory. Apart from the farmers who work the terraces, few Shikarians live outside it."

With that, the old woman curled up on the cave floor and made herself as comfortable as possible. She was snoring within minutes.

Minawë knew she should rest too, yet she lay wide awake. Six months had passed since she'd seen Iren. Compared with her thousand-year life, it was nothing. Even so, she wondered about him, and how much he might have changed.

❀

Balear Platarch woke to three inches of snow outside his tent. It caught him by surprise. He'd noticed the weather growing colder, but he hadn't realized he'd spent so much time in the wild.

Fear took him. Maybe it hadn't been as long as it appeared. The Fubuki could change the weather and make it snow.

Balear reached for the Auryozaki and held it aloft. His eyes surveyed the woods. The Fubuki had white fur; in the snow-covered forest, the beast would be almost invisible. His pulse hammered, and his breathing came so fast it made him dizzy. If the monster snuck up on him, he would die before he could swing his sword. He recalled the piercing pain of the Fubuki's Ryokaiten as it stabbed him, and the cold numbness that spread through his body as the weapon worked its terrible magic. That had just been his arm. What if it thrust through his chest?

He needed to calm down. Back in the summer, the Fubuki hadn't bothered with stealth. It had announced its presence with a roar so terrifying it locked its enemy in place. That hadn't happened here.

Balear took a deep breath, visible in the frigid morning air. The Fubuki hadn't come. This snow was natural. With a shiver as much from relief as from cold, Balear set to work on a larger fire and breakfast.

The meat had just finished cooking when the realization hit him. The Fubuki had used magic to make its summertime blizzard. Balear didn't know a lot about magic, but he imagined it must require a huge amount of it to manipulate the weather. That meant the Fubuki had been holding back during their fight, yet it had still proven an overwhelming foe. In the winter, when it didn't have to waste magic chilling the air, its power would become incredible.

Balear didn't bother packing up his campsite. He threw some snow on the fire to quench it, and then he took off at a run toward Veliaf.

He prayed he wasn't too late.

CHAPTER FORTY-THREE
The Storm Dragon Knight's Duty

From the air, Hiabi was even more imposing than the rest of Shikari. The buildings seemed endless, a mass of ceramic tile roofs that concealed thousands of Maantecs.

The realization made Minawë's eagle form tremble. The Kodamas were all but extinct, and Amroth's war had decimated Lodia. If the Maantecs ever united, no nation on Raa could withstand them.

A high wall encircled the city, and Minawë scanned it for sentries. She wanted to know the city's defenses. According to Rondel, the plan was straightforward. The old Maantec would scale the wall, sneak inside, and make for the castle keep. That was where Iren would likely be held. Minawë would meet Rondel there, changing from bird to Kodama inside so Hiabi's citizens wouldn't see her green hair and raise the alarm.

Minawë was about to head for the castle to wait for Rondel when she noticed something odd. Two people stood outside the city several hundred yards from the main gate. At this height, Minawë couldn't make them out even with the eagle's keen vision, so she descended in hopes of a better look.

The first person was a woman with long black hair. Her posture indicated absolute confidence. She was unarmed, which Minawë thought odd for a guard.

Next to the woman stood a man. He had tan hair shorter than the woman's, yet it was long enough that he had tied it back in a ponytail. His clothing looked like nothing Minawë had ever seen: a long-sleeved, sky-blue top above what appeared to be a pleated gray skirt.

Minawë maneuvered so she could see the man's face. The moment she did, she shrieked. Her cry echoed off the mountains north of the city. She plummeted as she briefly forgot she was in midair, but at the last moment she regained her wings and sped back to Rondel.

"I saw Iren!" she said after returning to her Kodaman form.

"Where?" Rondel asked. "In one of the castle courtyards?"

"No, he's outside the city! He's with a woman with black hair."

Minawë thought this was the best news they'd received in a long time, but Rondel didn't look happy about it. "You're certain it was him?" she demanded. "Was he restrained?"

"No," Minawë said, "he was just standing there." She thought for a second, and then she snapped her fingers. "Hey, maybe that woman helped him escape. We can rescue him without entering the city!"

Rondel didn't answer for a long time. At length she said, "Minawë, as your mother, I want you to promise me something. Whatever happens, please don't interfere."

"What's that supposed to mean? I thought you brought me along to defeat the Stone Dragon Knight."

"I wasn't referring to the Stone Dragon Knight. This is something else. Something . . . well, let's not jump to conclusions. Iren's waiting for us. Let's go."

All pretext of stealth gone, the pair walked around a corner and into view of Hiabi. Minawë gasped at the city's size. It had looked large from the air, but from the ground, it was enormous.

"Stay focused," Rondel spat. "From here on, there's no time for sightseeing."

Minawë swallowed the rebuke that came to mind. Rondel was right. They didn't have to linger here. They could grab Iren and leave.

Several hundred feet away, Iren and the woman with him moved toward Minawë and Rondel. Minawë's pulse quickened. Iren was right there! They could be back in Aokigahara tonight if they hurried.

As the pairs closed, Minawë readied to shout Iren's name. Before she could, though, Iren said, "I've been waiting for you, Rondel."

Minawë's excitement died in her throat. Iren didn't sound like himself. His voice was low and angry.

Rondel stopped walking. "Yes, I imagine you have. Tell me, what amusing stories about me have you and Hana been swapping?" She glanced at the young woman next to Iren.

Minawë took a step back as she realized the woman must be Hana, the Stone Dragon Knight and the person who had kidnapped Iren.

Only the two of them didn't look like kidnapper and victim. If anything, they stood a little too close together.

"Actually, just one," Iren said. He paused, and when he continued his voice had all the venom of the most poisonous snake in Aokigahara, "The one where you murdered my parents."

"It's a l—" Minawë started to yell, expecting to hear Rondel reject it too. Instead, the old woman kept quiet.

"Will you deny it?" Iren asked.

"If it's true," Rondel replied, "what will you do?"

"The same thing I should have done to Amroth. I'll kill you."

"Revenge?" Rondel said with a scowl. "I thought you'd moved past that. I seem to recall you saying you didn't care who murdered your parents. You only cared about protecting your friends."

Iren hesitated, but it lasted a mere second. "I do care about my friends," he said. "For a long time, I thought you were one of them. But all that time you lied and pretended you didn't know about my parents or what happened to them. Well, now I know the truth!"

Minawë couldn't believe the accusations she was hearing. She was about to intervene on Rondel's behalf when the old woman retorted, "The truth? How arrogant! What makes you think you know anything about it?"

"I saw it," Iren said. "I used Divinion to relive my father's memories—Iren Saito's memories."

Minawë had thought the conversation couldn't get any weirder, but she'd been wrong. No matter how much these Maantecs had manipulated Iren, he couldn't believe Emperor Saito was his father.

To Minawë's further surprise, though, Rondel nodded and said, "Then you know why I had to kill him."

Rondel put it so matter-of-factly. There was no guilt. There was no regret. She'd admitted to murdering Iren's father as easily as if she'd told them it was sunny today.

"Okthora's Law," Iren said.

"You know what Saito did. I didn't lie to you, except to repeat the official version of events that says he died a thousand years ago. I didn't want to ruin the image you had of your father as a simple farmer. The reality was that he was a madman obsessed with power and Maantec dominance."

Minawë couldn't listen anymore. "This is impossible!" she cried. "Iren Saito can't be your father!"

Iren looked at Minawë as though noticing her for the first time. "Rondel, you dragged her along?" he asked. "Why? Was it to soften my heart against killing you?"

"Don't be so self-centered," Rondel said. "Minawë's here because of Hana."

Hana smirked. "You needn't have bothered. I have orders. This is between you and Iren. I'm not to interfere."

"Not to interfere?" Rondel mimicked Hana's smile. "Is that what you call attacking me, stealing the Burning Ruby, reforging the Karyozaki, and giving it to an Oni to wipe out the Kodamas in Aokigahara?"

Iren's resolute expression wavered. He looked at Hana. "What's she talking about?" he asked. "You reforged the Karyozaki?"

The formerly implacable Hana shifted on her feet. "Not me," she said, speaking faster than before, "Lord Melwar. He wanted to buy time to make sure you could regain your magic before Rondel arrived. Azar was supposed to delay them."

"A lie," Rondel said, "and a poor one. Hana took the Burning Ruby from me before you even left Ziorsecth. She thought she'd killed me, so there's no way she could have known we were following you."

Iren's eyes flicked from Hana to Rondel and back again. "Then why, Hana? I almost died to stop Feng. It took the Dragoon to defeat him! Why would you and Melwar risk that again?"

Hana gulped, but then her face hardened. She tossed back her hair. "For conquest," she said. "We didn't want to waste Maantecs fighting veteran Kodamas in Suicide Forest. Azar and his Yokai know the jungle better. They were supposed to kill the Kodamas so they'd be out of the way once you became Maantec emperor. You could have led our armies north without interference. Besides, there was no risk in it. Melwar knows all about the Ryokaiten. He reforged the Karyozaki correctly. There was no danger of Feng taking over Azar's mind like he did to Amroth."

Iren eyed her with wrath. "I can't believe this. I can't believe you. I trusted you. All this time I thought you were helping me, but you were just using me. I thought you and Melwar wanted me to become emperor so we could bring about peace. That wasn't it at all, was it? You wanted me to unite the Maantecs so you could conquer Raa!"

"Are those goals so different?" Hana asked. "Your father believed they were the same. The other races need to be ruled. Look at Lodia! They're falling apart because they lack the steady hand of a powerful, immortal Maantec leader. If you brought the Maantecs together, the humans would surrender without a fight. Under your rule, Lodia would have peace forever!"

He should have rebuked her right away. Minawë clutched at her chest. The old Iren never would have entertained such nonsense. Instead, it took him nearly a minute before he said, "You're right, Hana. For a time Iren Saito did believe that. Yet in the end he changed. He realized the Maantecs don't deserve to rule any more than any race does. He came to respect the other races. He even loved and married a human. If I'm going to follow him, then I have to refuse you." He met Hana's gaze. "I'm sorry. I can't be your Maantec emperor."

For the first time since Iren had made his accusation against Rondel, Minawë dared to hope. They had almost been too late, but they had arrived in time after all. Iren had seen through Melwar's deceptions, and he would return home. If Hana or Melwar attacked, Iren would stand alongside Rondel and Minawë to stop them.

Then Iren turned back to Rondel. "Don't think this changes anything between us," he said. "I haven't forgotten you, or what you did. You say you follow Okthora's Law, but that's an excuse. Even if it did apply to Saito, which I'm not sure I believe, it doesn't explain your other murder." He clenched his fists and growled, "It doesn't explain why you killed my mother."

Up until that point, Minawë had thought Rondel composed in the face of Iren's accusations. Now the old woman's jaw hung slack. She stepped back as if Iren had slapped her. Her eyes fell to the ground.

"Why did you do it?" Iren demanded. "Why did you kill her? She didn't know who he was. She didn't know about Maantecs. She thought he was a farmer. You claim evil must be annihilated? Then explain why she was evil!"

Rondel collapsed to the dirt. "I never meant to kill her," she said. "I went to that farmhouse intending only to kill Saito. Had she stayed in the house, she would have lived. But when I heard her wailing for Saito's worthless soul, I couldn't stand it. He didn't deserve to have someone cry over him. He didn't deserve to have a wife. He had that chance with me, and he wasted it."

The Muryozaki sang as Iren drew it from its sheath. "I've heard enough," he hissed. "I thought you were a good person, fighting against evil. I was wrong. You're nothing but a jealous hag who couldn't stand that someone else might be happy with the man you tossed aside!"

Rondel laughed then, but it was unlike any laugh Minawë had ever heard from her. It was too high-pitched even for Rondel's sarcastic front. It was shrill, almost manic. "I knew," she said, "that I made the wrong choice that night."

Iren wasn't laughing. "You thought killing an innocent woman could be the right choice?"

The old Maantec stopped her bizarre cackling and regained her feet. Her eyes sparked as Lightning Sight activated. "I wasn't talking about your mother," she said. "I was talking about you. I could have killed you that night too. I almost did. You were lying in the grass, your shoulder against the Muryozaki's hilt. I knew then that you were the Holy Dragon Knight. It was unthinkable. I couldn't let another Saito become the Holy Dragon Knight. I thrust my blade down to end your life, but then I saw your eyes—Iren Saito's sky blue eyes. And not the eyes of the man I'd killed, but the eyes of the kind-hearted boy who healed me after my parents died, the eyes of the man I married. When I saw those eyes, I couldn't bring myself to kill you, so I left you there.

"I thought I could forget the whole thing, but the next day the dreams started. Everywhere I went, I saw your eyes. I saw you suffering. I realized I'd killed you, even if I hadn't stabbed you. You were an infant. If you didn't starve, you'd freeze. Either way, you'd die. So I went back to find you at the farmhouse, but of course you were already gone."

Minawë listened in stunned silence. She knew some of this tale. Amroth had found Iren and taken him for his own by that time. He must have been on his way to Haldessa when Rondel reached the farmhouse.

"When I arrived and found three fresh graves, I despaired," Rondel continued. "I thought you had died, and I knew I would never survive the guilt. I went to Haldessa, and that was when fortune came to me. Amroth arrived with you in his arms. When I saw you alive, I couldn't help but exclaim in surprise. Not because I wanted you around, but because your survival meant I didn't have to die."

Iren raised his sword. White light swirled around him like a tempest. His magic had returned. "Stop talking, Rondel," he said. "I'm not interested in your guilt, or how much you suffered. I care about avenging my parents. I care about avenging my mother." He stepped forward.

Minawë leapt between them. "Stop!" she shouted. "I won't let you two do this!"

"You're going to defend this murderous witch?" Iren asked. "After all you've heard, you'll still protect her?"

"I have to protect her," Minawë said. "She's my mother."

The light circling Iren stopped. "She's your . . ."

"And like you," Minawë said, hoping she sounded bolder than she felt, "I'll fight to protect her. If you want to kill her, then you'll have to kill me too."

Iren eyed her uncertainly. Minawë thought she'd managed to avoid the coming tragedy.

A pressure touched her shoulder. She looked to her right. Rondel had a hand on her. "Minawë," her mother said, "you're in the way."

"What are you saying?" Minawë screamed. "You can't mean to go through with this!"

"I have to," Rondel replied. "It's why I came here."

"What? No, we came to rescue Iren!"

"Does Iren look like he needs rescuing? Open your eyes. If Hana or Melwar had wanted to kill him, they had plenty of chances long before we arrived. No, ever since Balear told us about Hana bringing Iren here, I've known Melwar's plan. He meant to corrupt Iren by exposing his past. Even if Iren doesn't become the Maantec emperor, Melwar has still turned him from the Holy Dragon Knight he once was into a demon obsessed with revenge. I knew Melwar would succeed in doing that, and I knew that because he would succeed, I would have no choice but to fulfill the Storm Dragon Knight's duty."

Minawë's brow furrowed. "The Storm Dragon Knight's duty?"

"Okthora's Law says that evil must be annihilated. It's meant in a broad sense, but it has another meaning as well. The dragons can only test potential knights at the moment they first make contact. After that, the knight can change in any way, and the dragon is powerless to break their bond. Divinion is the Holy Dragon. He chooses knights based on purity of heart. Once he chooses, though, his knight can become twisted, as Saito did. When that happens, the Holy Dragon can be corrupted."

"Corrupted? How?"

"When a Dragon Knight uses magic, his will mixes with that of the dragon," Rondel said. "If the Holy Dragon Knight is wicked, his will can corrupt Divinion's. If that process isn't stopped, Divinion himself could become evil. The Holy Dragon holds all the good in the world in balance. If he became corrupted, that balance would break, and Raa would fall into chaos."

"That's why you weren't upset when you found out I couldn't use magic," Iren interjected. "If I couldn't reach Divinion, then I couldn't corrupt him. I thought you had more faith in me than that. You told me last year that I didn't remind you of Iren Saito anymore."

"Yes, and look how wrong I was. You turned out just like him in the end. I didn't want to believe that you could. For a while I fooled myself into thinking you could avoid his fate. In a corner of my mind, though, I knew it was only a matter of time before you became corrupted. But if you couldn't use magic, then I would never have to worry about it. I would never have to fulfill my duty as Storm Dragon Knight. Now it seems you have your magic back, and that means I have no choice." Rondel drew her dagger.

"Then the duty of the Storm Dragon Knight," Minawë gasped, "is to kill the Holy Dragon Knight!"

Rondel kept her eyes on Iren. "Before the Holy Dragon Knight can corrupt Divinion, that person must die," she said. "The Storm Dragon Knight bears that responsibility. Evil must be annihilated, and a new

Holy Dragon Knight, one pure of heart, must be chosen. When that person inevitably becomes corrupt, they must die as well. For the sake of the world, this cycle must continue."

Iren raised his Muryozaki. Minawë's eyes filled with tears as her mother and best friend squared off against each other. "Please," Minawë begged, "please don't do this."

Neither Iren nor Rondel responded to her. They locked eyes, each waiting for the other to make the first strike.

"Don't do this," Minawë repeated. When they continued to ignore her, she drew her Forest Dragon Bow. "In that case, I'll stop you myself!"

Magic welled within her. She would summon vines like she had in Aokigahara and ensnare them. Then they wouldn't be able to kill each other. They would have to listen to her.

A gray blur flashed by Minawë's head. Pain arced across her cheek. She wiped her face, and blood smeared her hand. Neither Rondel nor Iren had moved, which meant only one person could have attacked her.

Hana stood not a dozen feet away. She had kicked off her sandals so that she was barefoot. Three pebbles, each no larger than Minawë's fingernail, floated in midair in front of the Maantec.

Minawë eyed the woman with loathing. "I thought you were ordered not to interfere."

"I was," Hana said, "but I have a second order. This battle is between Iren and Rondel. No one may get in their way. I'm here to ensure that." She smirked. "If you want to stop them, you'll have to go through me."

Against Azar, Minawë had been terrified. Now she felt only cold fury. All of this was Hana and Melwar's fault. She raised her bow. "Fine, bitch," she said, "let's go."

CHAPTER FORTY-FOUR
Yukionna's Servants

When Veliaf appeared on the horizon, Balear stopped a moment to stare in disbelief. The landscape had transformed from what he remembered. A foot of snow blanketed the area around the village, and its wall had changed from slate gray to a glimmering blue-white. Looking closer, Balear realized ice had covered it.

He charged forward, heedless of the cold. The heavy snow slowed his progress to a crawl. Balear cursed. At this rate the Fubuki would ransack Veliaf and move on before he could get there.

As he trudged, flickers of movement by the town gate caught his eye. At first Balear mistook them for tricks of the windblown snow, but then he realized what they were.

Fubuki. Four of them.

Balear denounced himself as a fool. Of course there was more than one! Granted, the number was small, but based on what the Ice Dragon Knight had demonstrated in the summer, four were more than enough.

The fifteen-foot-tall Fubuki smashed against Veliaf's gate with hammers larger than Balear's body. Their strength was unreal. Balear doubted Iren or any other Maantec could match it. Every hammerblow dented the gate.

Balear wracked his brain for a way to distract them. He didn't have any ranged weapons and couldn't have used them with one arm anyway. Still, he had one tool that might work over a distance.

"Hey!" he shouted. "Fubuki! Do you want to fight a Dragon Knight?"

He had no idea if the Fubuki could hear him over their pounding hammers, but whether by coincidence or not, one of them looked up. It roared and bounded toward Balear.

Although the snow slowed Balear, it didn't affect the Fubuki. The beast plowed through the drifts with brute force.

Balear raised his Auryozaki. Memories of his only previous fight with a Fubuki surged through him. The Ice Dragon Knight had defeated him effortlessly. It hadn't even used much magic. If this monster charging him had the same combat skill as the Ice Dragon Knight, Balear might die before he could meet his previous foe again.

Then the Fubuki was on him. He leapt to the side as the creature's hammer smashed into the ground and flattened the snow into slush. Balear noted the back end of the hammer had no spear, unlike the Ice Dragon Knight's weapon.

Using the Auryozaki's weightless advantage, Balear swung from an otherwise impossible stance. The Fubuki raised its hammer, but it was too slow. The Sky Dragon Sword cut off the monster's arm at the elbow.

As the blade swung, Balear felt a strange tugging at his mind. He recalled one of the dreams from his training. In it he had used magic to launch a cutting arc of wind off his sword and attack a foe at range. He'd never bothered attempting the move in real life. He knew he didn't have magic like Maantecs or Kodamas.

So when the air current off his sword sliced the Fubuki in half, Balear nearly fell over at the sight of it.

"I," he stammered, "I used magic?"

He didn't have time to consider it. The other three Fubuki had seen Balear kill their ally, and now they charged him together.

Balear set his jaw and thought back on the dreams from his time in the wild. He'd considered magic impossible before, but now he felt like he'd used it a hundred times. He remembered every spell he'd seen in his dreams, and he knew exactly what to do.

One Fubuki was faster than the others. As the beast approached, Balear swung his sword. The air current leapt off it and beheaded the monster while it was twenty feet away.

Balear flicked back the Auryozaki and fired another shot. In his haste for a second kill, though, he aimed poorly. The attack went low and grazed a Fubuki's shin, slowing but not stopping it.

Fortunately, the injury meant the two beasts arrived separately instead of together. Balear deflected the first's hammer off his sword and countered by driving the massive blade up into the monster's abdomen.

By the time the Fubuki with the wounded leg arrived, Balear had freed his sword and felt confident enough to make the first move. Before the monster could swing its hammer, it lost both legs. Its head followed a second later.

Balear took a moment to catch his breath, then pressed on to Veliaf. When he reached the gate, he banged on it twice with the butt of his sword. "Open up!" he shouted. "It's Balear. I'm here to help!"

No response came. What that meant Balear didn't know, but he wasn't getting in the village this way.

Then again, neither were the Fubuki. If any remained, they must be on the far side of Veliaf attacking the northern part of the wall.

Balear plodded through the snow around the town's perimeter. Veliaf wasn't large, but it still took him half an hour to reach the far side. Now that he knew there was more than one Fubuki, he feared he would come upon an army of them. As a result, when he reached them, he stopped in surprise.

There were only five of them. Four stood against Veliaf's wall and pummeled it with their hammers. The fifth hung back, and Balear could identify that one by its weapon alone.

The Ice Dragon Knight raised the spear end of its Ryokaiten, and a layer of ice sprouted on a bare patch of Veliaf's wall near his subordinates. The other Fubuki then hammered the frigid stone. After they'd chipped off the ice, the Dragon Knight cast its spell again, and the process repeated.

Balear watched in confusion through three cycles of hammering. The strategy made no sense. Granted, flecks of stone came off each time a blow landed, but even with four Fubuki pummeling the wall, they would need hours to breach it. All the while, the defenders could rain arrows on them.

But then, no arrows were falling. Balear looked up at the wall and saw why. Atop it stood a dozen human bodies encased in ice. They had bows in their hands.

A cry went up from the Ice Dragon Knight. The other Fubuki stopped their attacks and faced their leader.

The Dragon Knight shifted to look at Balear. "Sky Dragon Knight!" it called, its voice a gravelly roar, "I thought you would have flown away by now. Or can't you do that with only one wing?"

Balear scowled; he hadn't known the Fubuki were capable of speech. He forced himself to stay calm. "Mock me if you want," he said, "but your team at the gate is dead. I killed them."

"Did you now?" the Fubuki asked, cocking its head sideways. "A human can't kill four Fubuki. Here, I'll prove it." It gestured to its allies, and they strode over to Balear.

The Lodian let them surround him. Then, as the monsters raised their hammers, Balear smiled. He spun and let magic flow into the Auryozaki. He'd seen this technique in one of his dreams, one where he'd been caught in the middle of an enemy army. As he whirled around, wind sliced out from the Auryozaki in a circle. It cut down all four Fubuki at once.

Balear stopped his motion and leveled his sword at the Ice Dragon Knight. "Your turn next."

"You have new tricks since we last met," the creature said with a smile that showed its needle-like teeth. "Good. I hate boring fights. That's why there were only nine of us. Any more, and I might as well attack this town while hopping on one leg."

The Fubuki wanted to goad him. Balear knew that. If he rushed in, as he and Iren had in the summer, he would die.

He needed to focus. Every enemy had a weakness. That was a fundamental rule of battle, one Amroth had drilled into him in the Castle Guard. He had to find it.

Balear took a step forward. "You won't conquer Veliaf," he said.

"Conquer?" the Fubuki looked incredulous. "I don't want to conquer it."

"What?" Balear asked, taken aback. "You're attacking the wall, and your other Fubuki were trying to get through the gate. What are you doing here if not conquering?"

For a few seconds the Fubuki considered Balear. Then it threw back its head and laughed. "You thought those four were supposed to get through the gate? They were just to keep the humans from running away. I needed them penned up so I could kill them all."

The color drained from Balear's face. "You didn't come to raid?"

"Fubuki do not raid. We are servants of the Ice Dragon Yukionna, and she has only one wish: the death of all things."

Balear felt cold, colder than the snowy conditions warranted. No one defended the walls. No one had answered at the gate. It wasn't because they were afraid.

It was because they were already dead.

The one-armed man looked at Veliaf's frozen wall and comprehended. "This ice extends all the way through the village, doesn't it? The other Fubuki were diversions while you froze everyone."

The Ice Dragon Knight bared its hideous smile again.

Balear clenched the Auryozaki. He was too late. He'd come to save Veliaf, but there was no one left to save.

There was one thing, though, that he could do. He pointed his sword at the Ice Dragon Knight. As he did, a great wind whipped around him. If he couldn't protect the people of Veliaf, at least he could avenge them.

CHAPTER FORTY-FIVE
No Mind's Flaw

A year ago, Iren Saitosan had trained under Rondel. They'd spent four months practicing together. In all that time, Iren had only once landed a blow on her.

Those experiences flooded Iren's mind as he stared across the distance between him and Rondel. Back then, not only had Rondel held back on her attacks, but she'd also been unarmed. Now she had her Liryometa. More important, their fight today was no sparring contest. Only one of them would walk away.

The pair circled each other. Iren couldn't help but wonder what the old hag was thinking. She'd trained him in both magic and swordsmanship. She'd saved his life more than once. All the while, she had known this day would come. Did she feel any sorrow? Any fear? Any doubt?

If so, she hid them well. Rondel's face looked as intense as during any other battle Iren had seen her fight.

Despite her grim expression, though, Rondel didn't attack. She watched Iren and mirrored his movements as he slowly stepped in a long circle.

Melwar had warned Iren about that tactic. "Rondel will not make the first strike unless she sees a sign of weakness," the Maantec lord had told him yesterday after Hana, scouting along the Aokigaharan border, saw the old woman enter Shikari. "She depends on Lightning Sight to give her an edge. She will combine it with her high speed to react to your movements and get inside your guard before you can counter."

Iren knew Melwar was right. Last year, Rondel had used the same strategy against Amroth. The Lodian king had countered by using magic without moving, but in the end, Rondel had still won.

Only one living person had defeated Rondel: Hana. Yet Melwar had insisted that Iren—not Hana—fight Rondel. At first Iren had thought Melwar made that decision to give him a chance for revenge, but now he realized that wasn't the case. Hana must have seen both Rondel and Minawë on her scouting mission. If Hana fought Rondel, then Iren would have had to fight Minawë. Even if she was Rondel's daughter, Iren couldn't bring himself to attack her.

Iren wondered whether Minawë or Hana would win their fight. He'd gone three-quarters of the way around the circle, so his back was to them. Their battle sounded more exciting than his and Rondel's. The area shook every few seconds as plants and rocks clashed.

A particularly nasty explosion sent dust and shrapnel flying past Iren. Rondel ducked and shielded her eyes from the storm.

Iren saw his opportunity. He used magic to accelerate himself and raced toward Rondel, stabbing the Muryozaki at her chest.

He thought he had connected, but then Rondel's body blurred and disappeared. With a curse, Iren swiveled his head around to look for her. Now that he had moved, Rondel's strategy would begin.

A rush of air moving toward him caught his attention. Iren leapt aside as the Liryometa thrust through the space where his head had been not a second earlier. He swore again. The strike proved what he had hoped might not be true. Rondel wasn't holding back. She intended to kill him, just as he intended to kill her.

Before Iren could think of a counter, Rondel disappeared again. Unwilling to stand still and wait to be attacked, Iren took off at random.

He ran flat out. As he did, his eyes swept the battlefield in search of Rondel. The effort was futile. Without Lightning Sight, he couldn't track her rapid movements.

Rondel appeared in front of him. Iren barely managed to slow down enough to avoid impaling himself on her blade. He swung the Muryo-zaki in a horizontal arc, but Rondel blocked it. The vibration of the clashing weapons rippled through Iren's arms.

Flicking her wrist, Rondel turned Iren's katana and stabbed at his gut. He backpedaled, but he couldn't get away. Rondel's dagger pierced him. A jolt of lightning went with the blow and launched Iren backward.

When he skidded to a stop, he couldn't move. Iren knew what Rondel had done. She had used a similar technique last year to paralyze him, though she hadn't stabbed him that time. The attack had ended that match. Had Rondel wanted to kill him back then, she would have had plenty of time to do so.

Unfortunately for Rondel, Iren had improved since that training match. He had used Divinion's magic to heal himself while he flew through the air. Before Rondel could reach him to deliver the killing blow, Iren was back on his feet and uninjured.

Rather than rejoin the fight, though, Iren took advantage of the distance between him and Rondel to retreat. He didn't intend to escape; he knew he couldn't. He just needed a few seconds to think.

Rondel wasn't any faster than he was. They should be fighting evenly, but they weren't. Rondel was dominating.

Her advantage came down to Lightning Sight. With it, Rondel could track Iren no matter how quickly he moved. By contrast, Iren could barely see the old hag.

But his eyes weren't the problem. They were capable of keeping up with her. The problem was Iren himself. He couldn't interpret what his eyes saw fast enough to judge which way to block, let alone to counter.

Then like the igniting of a flame on a moonless night, the answer shone in Iren's thoughts. He kept on running, but he forced himself to calm down. His breathing slowed. His muscles relaxed even as they worked at full power. His mind went blank, and he settled into the technique Melwar had forced him to master: No Mind.

The blurring of Iren's surroundings stopped. When his brain no longer had to worry about interpreting what it saw, his eyes were free to convey every detail. Only his instinctual mind could react to those details, but that was all he needed to win.

No longer in control of his body, Iren watched as he spun around to face Rondel. She was mere feet behind him, but he was ready for her attack.

She must not have realized his new state, because she tried to run around him and stab him in the back. Iren tracked her, and when she attacked, he blocked effortlessly.

The unexpected maneuver caught Rondel unprepared. Iren saw his chance. He spun his blade off Rondel's and flicked it up.

The satisfying gush of red from Rondel's side told Iren the blow had connected. It wasn't enough to defeat her, but now Rondel would feel shaken. She had believed Iren couldn't keep up with her, but he'd proven her wrong.

Rondel's grim expression deepened into a frustrated scowl. She launched a blistering assault, her dagger a flash of light as it danced. Iren blocked each strike as he waited for an opening. It wouldn't take long. He and Rondel had equal speeds, but Iren had greater reserves of magic. Eventually Rondel would have to slow down or risk her dragon overwhelming her. When that happened, she would die.

The hag's face contorted with panic, and Iren knew he would win. Rondel made her mistake. Her foot caught on a stone. The momentary distraction halted her strikes and left her vulnerable on her left side. Iren disarmed her and sent the Liryometa flying.

In his No Mind state, Iren reacted at once to Rondel's exposed form. His katana swept toward her neck. The battle was over.

Inches away from contact, the impossible happened. Rondel, still off-balance, ducked Iren's blow. The Muryozaki cut empty air.

The attack had left Iren wide open. Rondel looked up at him with a cold smile. Her hands glowed blue. She reached up and put both of them on Iren's chest.

The shock ripped through him as strongly as the pain from breaking his magical barrier. Iren screamed, and the agony ripped him out of No Mind. He went limp. The Muryozaki fell to the ground, and a moment later Iren collapsed as well. Smoke rose from his body.

Rondel kicked away the Muryozaki. She crouched in front of Iren, and he had an odd feeling of nostalgia. The hag had done the same thing after defeating him last year in Ziorsecth.

"You used No Mind," she said. "Melwar must have taught you that."

Iren couldn't answer, so Rondel continued, "Do you think I'm that inexperienced? I know all about No Mind, including its flaw. Doing away with conscious thought isn't all Melwar claims it to be. True, it will improve your reaction time, but without higher thought, you can't plan beyond the next move. You can't analyze, so you misread signals. You saw my panicked expression, so you assumed I panicked. Your instinctual brain couldn't fathom that I might fake such an expression. The same is true of my stance. I didn't trip on that rock, and I was never off-balance. I made it look that way to trick you. I even let you disarm me. I planned it all in advance, knowing No Mind would fall for it."

Iren tried to move, to speak, to spit at her, to do anything at all, but he couldn't. He could hardly breathe.

"I have to admit I'm impressed," Rondel prattled on. "You've improved a lot. I put all the magic I could manage into that strike, and it still didn't kill you. I'd hoped that it would. It would have been cleaner."

Her patronizing incensed Iren. If Rondel wanted to kill him, she should shut up and get on with it.

Rondel seemed to read Iren's thoughts. "Well," she said, "I guess I have to make a messy end of it."

She retrieved her fallen rondel and returned to Iren. Her diminutive frame towered over him. As the blade descended, Iren promised himself he wouldn't give her the satisfaction of another scream.

CHAPTER FORTY-SIX
Shattered

Using the air current surrounding him, Balear charged, moving faster than he ever had before. As he neared the Fubuki, he leapt into the air. The wind carried him to twice the Fubuki's height. He crashed down and swung his sword at the monster's head.

The Fubuki looked startled for a second, but it recovered. It raised its hammer to block Balear's strike. The weapons clashed. Balear felt the hammer give.

His opponent must have felt it too, because the monster stepped sideways and out of the path of Balear's sword. It then let its hammer drop, causing Balear to fall to the ground.

The spear end of the Fubuki's weapon whirled toward Balear, but the beast didn't get a chance to attack. As the Auryozaki struck the earth, it threw up a cloud of snow, dirt, and rock that repelled the Ice Dragon Knight.

Sensing an opening, Balear lunged. The Fubuki roared in frustration and retreated. As it did, it created a wall of ice between it and Balear. The Auryozaki pierced the barrier and splintered it into thousands of pieces. The resistance the wall provided, though, slowed Balear's attack enough for the Fubuki to get out of range.

Balear charged again, but then he realized his predicament. He aborted his attack and leapt back as a rain of ice shards from the destroyed wall pierced the spot where he'd been standing. Other shards careened in midair and launched themselves at him, controlled by the Fubuki's magic. Balear was soon dodging for his life as hundreds of frozen blades aimed for him.

Just as he was certain the shards would find him, magic welled in him again. Balear threw his hand out to one side and called up a small tornado around his body. The blades struck it and bounced off, flung in every direction by the vortex.

The tornado took more energy than Balear had expected. When it cleared, he sank to one knee. His previous spells hadn't felt draining on their own, but in total they had pushed his body to its limits. He could use magic, but not to the degree that someone of a magical race like the Maantecs could handle.

"Stand up!" a voice roared. "Are you going to let him kill you? Keep fighting!"

Balear glanced around. The Fubuki hadn't spoken, and Balear couldn't see anyone else.

"I'm not out there," the voice said. "I'm in you, and in your sword."

Realization dawned. "Ariok?"

The dragon's presence brushed against Balear's mind. He recoiled, but Ariok said, "Wait! I want to help. When I saw you training in the forest, I knew you were preparing for an impossible task, yet you insisted on pursuing it. Your tenacity impressed me, so I sent you some memories of past Sky Dragon Knights."

"Then those weren't dreams," Balear said. "They were real events."

"That's right," Ariok replied. "I knew that if you had those experiences, your body would know how to release my magic even if your mind didn't."

"But it's not enough," Balear said with a frown. "I can't beat him, and if I can hear your voice, then that means I've used too much magic. You might take over my body, like Feng did to Amroth."

"No," Ariok said, "I have no intention of raging like Feng. Some of us dragons have more honor than that. Let me take over the battle. Become a dragon, and we'll defeat this monster together."

Balear considered a moment, but then he shook his head. "I can't agree to that. I don't know a lot about magic or dragons, but I know enough. I can't let you take control. I'll win this battle myself."

As Balear spoke, the Ice Dragon Knight attacked. Balear leapt back to avoid a hammer swing that would have pulverized him. He tried to step forward and counter, but he fell to his knees. Confused, he stood back up and attempted to take a step. His feet refused to leave the ground. When he looked down, he saw the reason. Ice encased his legs up to his knees.

Balear struggled, but he couldn't escape. The Fubuki waved its spear, and the ice spread to Balear's waist. It then extended out and trapped his arm so that he couldn't swing the Auryozaki. He swore. The monster had won.

"You never could have killed me, human," the Fubuki said as it approached. "When I fought you before, I had to use almost all my magic to maintain the cold. In the winter, with my magic free for combat, I could defeat even Hana."

Balear's jaw dropped at the name. "How do you know Hana?"

"That traitor gave me this Toryokiri," the Fubuki snarled, holding up its hammer, "and then she tried to kill me!"

"That can't be true. Why would Hana give you that weapon?"

The beast sprouted its cruel smile. "You think she's your friend," it said. Its voice dripped with mockery. "You think she helped you. But Hana serves Melwar, and he ordered her to give me this Ice Dragon Hammer last winter. They wanted my help to wipe out Lodia."

Balear swooned. It couldn't be real. Hana . . . who and what was she? Balear had trusted her. No, it was more than that. He'd loved her. Yet all the while, she'd plotted Lodia's destruction.

He wouldn't believe it. Hana wasn't the one who had butchered everyone in Veliaf. The Fubuki was lying about her.

It would suffer for that!

"Ariok!" Balear called. "You want control? Take it. Take it and kill this bastard!"

The Fubuki raised its spear to pierce Balear's chest, but a gust of wind threw the monster to the ground. The wind pulled in tight around the ice that held Balear in place. Then, with a wrenching screech, the ice exploded.

Balear screamed as Ariok clawed into his mind. His body stretched in every direction, and the pain made losing his arm seem like getting a splinter. His feet grew until they shredded their boots. His fingers and toes lengthened into sickle-shaped claws. Blue scales covered his skin as his body elongated into a serpentine shape. A pair of great, bat-like wings sprouted from his back.

His face changed last of all. His nose and mouth morphed into a square muzzle, and two long whiskers grew out from his upper lip.

Ariok roared in triumph. The dragon took flight, and as he did, he swept aside Balear's consciousness. The Lodian had no control over his body's movements, but he still had his senses. He could see the Fubuki far below him. He could feel the cold air rushing over his wings.

And he could smell. Oh, he could smell. It was as if he had been blind and had regained his sight. He could smell the snow and the ice, and he could differentiate between the two. He could smell the carcasses of the slain Fubuki, and he could smell the fear in the one that remained.

The Ice Dragon Knight fled. Balear could sense Ariok's indignation. A human, a Maantec, or a Kodama would have had the honor to stand and fight. The Fubuki, by contrast, raced for Akaku Forest. It no doubt hoped for safety among the thick trees.

Ariok shrieked. His voice shook the ground. The Fubuki stumbled, but it managed to keep going.

Flying low, Ariok passed the Fubuki and landed in front of it. The Fubuki skidded to a halt. Its blood-red eyes searched frantically for a way to escape.

The Sky Dragon didn't give them time to find one. Ariok waved his front leg, which still clutched the Auryozaki. Balear heard a bizarre sucking noise, and then the Fubuki's right arm snapped up. The beast strained to move it, but Ariok somehow held it in place.

The sucking sound grew louder, and the Fubuki's left arm snapped up too. Then its feet lifted off the ground. It floated in midair.

Balear gasped in his mind as he realized what the dragon had done. Ariok had pushed all the air away from the spaces around the Fubuki's wrists and ankles. The air wanted to return to those voids, and the resulting force gripped the Fubuki's limbs as securely as the strongest chains.

The voids wrenched on the Fubuki, and it howled in torment. Balear couldn't forgive the monster for what it had done, but all the same, he pitied it. He knew what would happen next.

With an easy motion of the Auryozaki, the Sky Dragon ordered the voids to separate. Balear wanted to close his eyes, to block his ears, but he no longer had control of his body. The Fubuki's final scream as Ariok drew and quartered it would haunt Balear the rest of his life.

"It's done," he managed to say inside his mind when the Fubuki's shout faded. "Now return me to my body."

Ariok's face appeared in his consciousness. "Return you to your body? Why would I do that?"

"Because you promised! You said you wanted to help me!"

"And I did want to help you, so you, stupid human, would free me."

"You tricked me!" Balear yelled. "You didn't want to protect Lodia. You wanted to escape. You lying, treacherous worm!"

Ariok's smile gleamed full of blade-like teeth. "So guess what happens now?" The dragon shifted his gaze from the Fubuki's tattered remnants to the village of Veliaf.

"No!" Balear cried, but Ariok thrust aside the man's mind as effortlessly as a spring breeze tosses a leaf.

With a single wingbeat the dragon was airborne. He surveyed the frozen village below him. Nothing moved within it. It was likely everyone was dead, but perhaps a few remained alive, clinging to life and hoping the ice would recede.

The dragon hovered above Veliaf and pointed the Auryozaki down. Wind from behind him rushed into the village square. There it condensed into a sphere the height of a man.

Terror gripped Balear. He'd seen a spell like this before. He recalled the flash as Iren's Dragoon magic ignited and defeated Feng. It had been an amazing yet horrifying sight.

The air continued to gather, and Balear could only watch. "Don't," he said. He repeated the word over and over until his mental self was crying.

Ariok ignored him. The Sky Dragon swung his Ryokaiten to release the magic binding the wind sphere together. Freed of its constraints, the pressure released in a hideous blast.

In less than a second, Veliaf disintegrated.

Balear wailed as the frozen town's shattered pieces settled over the countryside. "Why?" he moaned. "Why, Ariok?"

"Because mortals imprisoned us. I'll teach them to mock us and play at being gods."

The dragon faced south, and Balear's fear increased. Ariok had Balear's memories, as well as those of every knight who had ever bonded with him. He knew the locations of all the cities in Lodia, and likely many outside the country as well.

"Which one should I destroy next?" Ariok asked. "Ceere's closest, but Terkou has more people. It makes for a difficult decision."

Balear had to stop this. No one else could. There were no other Dragon Knights for hundreds of miles. He had to subdue Ariok's consciousness.

But he had no idea how. Ariok's mind had overwhelmed his own, and the dragon's strength only grew as it pulled more magic from the Auryozaki.

That gave Balear a desperate idea. During the battle with Feng, Rondel had tried to defeat the dragon by knocking the Fire Dragon Sword away from Feng's body. Without the connection to his Ryokaiten, the dragon couldn't sustain a physical form.

Balear attacked Ariok's mind. He wormed his way into the part that controlled the dragon's front leg. "Throw away the sword!" he commanded. "I won't let you destroy Lodia!"

Ariok's mind was a hammer, one stronger than the Fubuki's. It smashed against Balear's consciousness, and he knew that if he blacked out, he would never wake up. He would die, as Amroth had died.

Even so, he wouldn't give up. He'd sworn to protect Lodia. Amroth had trusted him to do it. Rondel had trusted him to do it. And for the first time, he realized his father had trusted him to do it too.

With the full strength of his will, Balear took control of Ariok's front claws. It was all he could manage, but it was enough. With a mental scream, he forced them open. The Auryozaki plummeted.

Ariok roared and shot down in pursuit of his fallen Ryokaiten. At the same time, he threw his will at Balear. The dragon picked up Balear's mental form and threw him. Balear's vision failed, and his only sensation was that of falling into a black, endless abyss.

CHAPTER FORTY-SEVEN
Ultimate Defense

Minawë's eyes flicked to Iren and Rondel. Their fight hadn't started yet; they were still circling each other. She needed to stop them, but as long as Hana was here, she couldn't.

There was no point in hesitating. Minawë drew back the Chloryoblaka, and the bow created its own arrow. The shot struck Hana between her nose and upper lip.

The arrow splintered on impact. Its remnants clattered to the ground. Hana smirked, unharmed. "Is that it?" she asked.

Minawë readied to shoot again, but then the ground rumbled. Two walls of stone rose on either side of her. She jumped back just before they slammed together. The impact shattered the blocks, and shrapnel flew in every direction. Minawë shielded her face, but she still received cuts on her arms and legs.

Rock shards struck Hana too, but the Maantec didn't flinch or even blink. The pieces bounced off her.

Minawë couldn't understand it. Hana wasn't wearing armor. She couldn't take all those hits, not to mention the arrow from earlier, without injury.

Incensed, Minawë pulled back the Chloryoblaka and loosed three arrows in quick succession. Hana remained motionless, and once again the arrows snapped when they struck her.

"How many arrows can that thing make?" Hana asked. "Why don't you shoot them all now and be done with it? I'll stand here and let you attack."

Minawë grabbed the bowstring, but then she thought better of it. Hana wanted to drag out their battle to keep Minawë from intervening with Rondel and Iren. The first four arrows hadn't worked. The rest wouldn't either.

A sinking feeling grew in Minawë's stomach. Maybe she couldn't win. After all, even Rondel had failed to wound Hana. Attacking at full strength had only resulted in her mother breaking her hand and dagger against Hana's stone armor.

In this fight, though, Hana didn't have stone wrapped around her. She just stood there, barefoot, with that arrogant smirk on her face.

Then Minawë understood. Hana was wearing armor—her skin. With her feet in contact with the ground, Hana was using magic to draw the rock's strength into her body. She'd hardened herself to the point that nothing could wound her, not even an arrow.

That defense had to have a weakness. If Hana were truly invulnerable, she would have invaded Ziorsecth and wiped out the Kodamas long ago.

Still, the armor was formidable. Worse, Minawë didn't have the magic of Ziorsecth or Aokigahara to support her.

Perhaps, though, there was more power here than appearances suggested. Grasses and shrubs filled the plain where they stood, and farther up the hills, scraggly pines and hardwoods grew. None of them had much magic, but if Minawë could combine them, she might have a chance.

"Yoo-hoo!" Hana called. "Come up with any ideas yet? Well, don't expect me to wait. I get impatient." The three pebbles floating in front of Hana lifted another foot in the air. "You shot me," she said. "It's only fair that I get to shoot you."

Faster than any arrow, the stones crossed the distance between Minawë and Hana. Minawë leapt and avoided the pebbles by inches. On instinct she shot another useless arrow, but Hana wasn't even looking at her anymore. The Maantec's eyes focused past Minawë, who had the good sense to look behind her. The stones were coming back.

She dove aside a second time, but the rocks seemed ready for her moves. They circled in midair. Minawë readied to dodge again, but as she was about to jump, pain filled her right arm. A fourth stone, trailing blood, flashed into her line of sight before starting its own return arc.

Minawë fled, zigzagging to avoid the rocks. Hana laughed and increased the number of pebbles to ten. Minawë cursed. The stone that had struck her had only landed a glancing blow. If one hit her directly, it would pierce her body even worse than an arrow would.

She had only one hope of survival, let alone victory. She dropped to her knees and placed her palm on the ground. Her magic radiated out and tapped into the nearby plants. Under her direction, they knit their roots together so they linked up like the shared roots of Ziorsecth.

Hana's pebbles converged for a final strike, but as they neared, Minawë didn't leap out of the way. Instead, she held firm and commanded the plants in their strange language, "Protect me!"

Vines sprouted around her, and from them ten leaves unfolded. Each appeared in front of a pebble so that it caught and held the stone in its grasp. The leaves twisted, bent, and pushed against the stones. At last the rocks dropped to the ground, their momentum spent.

Minawë looked at Hana and mimicked the Maantec's smirk. "I should thank you," she said. "Because of you, I figured out how to win this battle."

Still kneeling on the ground, Minawë unlaced her boots and removed them. She stood up, barefoot like Hana.

"What, you're going to throw your shoes at me?" Hana asked.

Minawë didn't bother replying. She had to concentrate for the next part of her plan. She sent magic through her feet into the soil and called to the plants she had connected. Their roots wrapped themselves around her legs.

As if lightning had struck her, a surge of energy ripped through Minawë's body. The plants' power was incredible. Even when Minawë had drawn magic from the plants in Aokigahara, it was nothing like this. Though smaller than Aokigahara's trees, these plants had a hardiness that gave them unexpected strength.

They were also far more numerous. The circle of plants Minawë had connected was wider than what she'd used against Azar. It was almost overwhelming.

Minawë looked across the expanse between her and Hana. More than a hundred feet separated them, but the distance mattered little. Minawë's circle extended well beyond Hana. She wouldn't have to get close to the Stone Dragon Knight to attack her. She wouldn't even have to move.

Minawë half-smiled. Considering the way Hana had fought up until now, Minawë's strategy had an irony to it.

She melded her magic with the energy surging through her from the plants. Rather than speak, she relayed her instructions as pictures, and the plants changed to reflect her desire.

In front of her, a knee-high shrub grew in seconds to a giant maple. It barreled toward Hana. The Maantec blinked twice in astonishment, but otherwise she remained motionless.

Then the maple smashed into her. It swung with its largest branch and caught Hana in the stomach. For the first time, the Stone Dragon Knight stepped backward.

Now Minawë understood why Hana had added another layer of stone when she'd fought Rondel. Hana's hardened skin was tough, but it wasn't invincible. A powerful strike could break it, and if that happened, Hana would have no time to recover before the blow landed.

The tree raised a second limb to strike again, but this time Hana ducked low and avoided it. She placed a hand on the ground.

Energy pulsed through Minawë's feet. It felt different from the plants, and Minawë realized it was Hana's magic.

The plants near Hana were tugged upward. She probably wanted to raise a rock shield for extra protection. Minawë put her own magic into strengthening the plants' roots. She pictured them thick and vibrant, gripping the soil and holding it in place.

For a moment her magic and Hana's clashed in the ground, invisible to anyone observing. The pair of them were motionless, yet their wills dueled against each other.

Distance determined the outcome. Hana was closer to what she was manipulating, so her magic triumphed. The plants' roots ripped apart as the rock around Hana launched itself up. It surrounded her in a stone cocoon.

Minawë put a hand to her chest. The pain was immense. It felt like her own limbs had been ripped off when the plants died. She recalled the time, shortly after she'd become the Forest Dragon Knight, when she'd sensed a cougar kill a deer. When something died that she was connected to, she felt that death as if it were her own.

Recovering, Minawë directed her efforts back to her maple tree. It swung two limbs into Hana's rock shield. The shield pushed forward at the same time. Wood and stone slammed together, and their combined might shattered both. Splinters, rock shards, and dirt erupted over the battlefield. The debris engulfed Iren and Rondel.

As it did, Iren lunged. He had taken advantage of the distraction to attack Rondel. Their battle had begun.

It wouldn't last long. With their speed, the winner could be decided any second. Minawë needed to end this fight now. She poured energy into the plants and created a tangle of vines each thicker than her calf. She would use them the same way she had against Azar. Hana's armor wouldn't survive such a crushing force.

But Hana was ready for her. Minawë felt the Stone Dragon Knight's magic through the ground again as Hana raised dozens of rocks and sent them to crush the vines. The plants retaliated by smashing the stones into dust. It all happened without either woman moving at all.

Amid the barrage, Hana counterattacked. A hailstorm of pebbles converged on Minawë from every direction.

The assault didn't worry her. Minawë had given the plants closest to her standing orders to protect her in whatever way they needed. She was momentarily surprised when a tree sprouted beside her and deflected the stones, but then she refocused on her attack.

Seconds passed, then minutes. The battle was going nowhere. Minawë gritted her teeth. She and Hana were evenly matched, each with defenses too flawless for the other to breach. Both stood as motionless as they had throughout the fight, yet all around them the ground had churned into fine sand as their magics clashed.

Then Minawë felt her heart stop. A glint of metal reflected in the sky. Rondel's dagger arced through the air and landed on the ground.

Minawë screamed. She was about to lose her mother a second time.

Rondel, however, ducked Iren's beheading strike and placed her hands on Iren's chest. Minawë couldn't tell what Rondel did, but Iren's body shook like a just-caught fish and then flopped to the ground, unmoving.

"No!" Minawë cried. She tapped into the grasses beneath Iren. She could feel him breathing. He was alive.

He wouldn't be for long. Rondel retrieved her dagger and walked back to him.

Minawë had no idea what to do. She wanted to stop them. She had to stop them. "Stop," she murmured as Rondel raised the Liryometa. "Stop," she repeated, louder as the dagger fell.

"Stop!" The ground shook with the word.

Rondel paused, her blade an inch from Iren's neck. The old Maantec retreated from her attack and glanced around in concern. Minawë shifted her gaze to Hana, thinking the vibrations were some trick of hers.

But the Stone Dragon Knight looked as surprised as Minawë. Whatever this magic was, no one on the battlefield was creating it.

Then Minawë dropped to one knee. Her strength plummeted. Her breath came in gasps. Her vision tunneled, and she threw up. She didn't understand. Magic poured out of her, but she hadn't ordered the plants to do anything.

The tremors increased. Finally, like a great beast ripping free of the earth, a swarm of vines erupted from the plain. Five ensnared Rondel, restraining each of her limbs as well as her neck. Others wrapped around Iren and covered his body in a shield of plant life.

In a flash, Minawë realized what had happened. She had given the plants an order: "Stop." Stop Rondel from killing Iren.

Now that Minawë knew the devastation was her own doing, she felt more in control. She was exhausted, but maybe, just maybe, she could last long enough to finish this battle.

She couldn't kill Hana. The Maantec's armor wasn't invincible, but it was stronger than what Minawë could throw at it.

Fortunately, she didn't have to kill Hana to get what she wanted. With a grim smile, Minawë sent all the vines not holding Iren or Rondel against the Stone Dragon Knight. Hana raised new rock walls around herself, as Minawë had expected. Instead of attacking the shields, she directed the vines to wrap around them. She then had the plants rise as high in the air as they could so that Hana, stone barrier and all, separated from the ground.

As Hana's cocoon floated higher, a long-hafted war hammer fell. It was the Maantec's Ryokaiten. Throughout the battle, she had kept it underground, her foot in contact with it at all times.

Without her connection to the Stone Dragon, Hana had only her own magical reserves to draw from. She could attack or block, but she couldn't do both. Minawë knew as much from her experience with the plants. During the fight, she had combined her magic with those of the Forest Dragon and the plants themselves. It took all of them together to maintain the constant blend of offense and defense.

Hana sensibly settled for defense. The rock attacks against Minawë stopped.

Minawë was almost out of magic. She was furious that she couldn't defeat Hana, but helping Iren and Rondel was more important. They had to escape before more Maantecs showed up.

Severing her connection with the plants' roots, Minawë threw on her shoes and ran to Iren and Rondel. When she reached them, she saw that her vines, in their mindless zeal to carry out her orders, had squeezed Rondel to the point where the old woman had lost consciousness. Fortunately, though, they had left her alive.

Minawë released the magic controlling the vines and let them settle back into the ground. Retrieving the Muryozaki, she slid it into Iren's sheath. She knelt and heaved both Iren and Rondel onto her back.

They were too heavy for her to carry as a Kodama, so Minawë transformed into a horse and galloped off the battlefield. She ran for hours, not stopping until Hana and the terrible Maantec city Hiabi were far behind.

At dusk Minawë spied a cave in the distance. She walked inside it, changed back into a Kodama, and leaned Rondel and Iren against a pair of stalagmites. Then, her strength long exhausted, she collapsed on the cold stone.

CHAPTER FORTY-EIGHT
A Reminder

Night had fallen by the time Lord Melwar saw fit to find Hana. She was still clenched in that Kodama's accursed plants. Her only window was a small opening she'd left in front of one eye too narrow for the vines to penetrate.

Lord Melwar adopted the faintest of smiles. "Let me go out on a limb here."

"That's not funny," Hana snapped. "Would you mind helping me down?"

He shrugged. The darkness around him deepened, then split into half a dozen knives. Each was as long as Rondel's Liryometa, and each was black.

Hana shuddered as they appeared. She remembered, years ago, the feel of those knives slicing through her armor like it was wet rice paper. Afterward, she'd lain in a pool of her own blood as it leached out of cuts all over her body. She would have died had Lord Melwar not kept a healer at the ready.

The knives floated in midair as they cut away the vines with ease. They also carved through the walls of earth Hana had constructed around herself. She dropped to the ground unharmed.

As she landed, though, one of the knives brushed against her sleeve. The blade sliced through her clothing and hardened skin. It left a shallow scratch on her bicep.

"Thanks," she spat. She brushed herself off even though she wasn't dirty. "What was that for?" She pointed at her arm.

"You spoke rudely just now," Lord Melwar said. "I felt you needed a reminder."

Hana's expression turned leaden. She had let her frustration get the better of her. "I remember," she murmured.

Lord Melwar half-smiled. "Yes, it is hard to forget your first and only loss. I suppose today will help with that."

A sudden anger took Hana. "Someday I'll drive you both to your knees."

"Perhaps," Lord Melwar replied. He shrugged again. "Until then, please keep in mind who owns that pretty body of yours."

Hana clenched her teeth. "That," she growled, "I promise you."

Lord Melwar put his back to her, and Hana had a flash of an idea to attack him. She could call up two stone walls and crush him before he had a chance to respond.

But his casual stance unnerved her. He knew she might attack, and he didn't care. He knew that whatever she did, he could escape it and slay her.

Instead of murdering him, then, Hana asked, "Why didn't you come with us today? We could have used your help."

"It was not my place to kill Rondel," Lord Melwar said without turning around. "I leave that task to Iren."

"Iren can't defeat her," Hana said. "He needed No Mind just to keep up with her. Even then, she won."

Lord Melwar shrugged his irritating shrug. "I warned him he was not ready to face her. He is headstrong, though, like his father. I knew he would not listen to my caution."

"Then you knew you'd sent him into a fight he couldn't win."

"True, but I also knew he would not die. That Kodama would never allow it. It was obvious that they care about each other. Only Iren could have removed Saito's curse from her."

"You ordered me to keep her from interfering. If I'd killed her, Iren would have died."

"Ah, but you did not kill her," Lord Melwar said. He smiled over his shoulder. "At best you could call your match a draw, but that would be giving you a great deal of credit."

The smooth way he said it made Hana realize what he was implying. "You sent us into battle knowing neither of us could win. You knew they'd take back Iren."

Lord Melwar shrugged again but said nothing.

His nonchalant manner infuriated her. "Why bring him here at all then?" she roared. "What was the point? How was he supposed to become the Maantec emperor and save us all if you were just going to let him go?"

"Little girl," Lord Melwar said in his most condescending voice, "do you not understand? Iren lost today. That will only increase his resolve to kill Rondel. I trained him. I taught him No Mind. I am the reason he lasted against Rondel as long as he did. That is why he will return to me. When he does, I will own him just as I own you."

Hana let that comment pass. Fighting Lord Melwar was pointless. "Iren won't come back," she said. "He found out about the Karyozaki."

For the first time since he had released her, Lord Melwar's smug expression dropped. "How did he find out about that?"

"Rondel mentioned Azar before we fought. Through that exchange, Iren learned that you reforged the Fire Dragon Sword and set the Yokai against the Kodamas."

Lord Melwar stroked his chin. His brow furrowed, and he walked twice in a tight circle.

Hana tensed. She could sense the man's frustration, and his frustration made him dangerous. Iren was vital to their plan to reunite the Maantecs and conquer Raa. If he turned away from them, all their careful maneuvering would have been wasted.

Worse, it was her fault. Not only had she been the one to reveal Lord Melwar's plan to Iren, but she'd only had to do that because she had failed to kill Rondel in Serona.

Maybe it wasn't too late. "I could retrieve him for you," Hana offered. "Rondel had to use almost all her magic to defeat Iren, and that Kodama did the same to restrain me. Neither of them will have recovered yet. I can track them down and bring back Iren. I can even kill the others."

"No," Lord Melwar said. He looked at her with a perilous glint in his eye. "We have pushed Iren as far as we can. If we force him to come back, he will be useless. Even if he became the Maantec emperor, he would never accept being my puppet. We must not concern ourselves with it. His desire for vengeance may still bring him back. If not, then he was not valuable in the first place."

Hana dug her toe into the ground. "We never should have reforged the Karyozaki," she murmured.

Lord Melwar frowned, his mouth a thin line. Hana gulped. She'd gone too far. Remaking the Karyozaki had been his idea. She felt the blood trickle from the wound on her arm. Lord Melwar wouldn't let her die quickly.

Then the annoying shrug came back. "Perhaps I was hasty," he said. "I assumed you told the truth when you said you had killed Rondel, and in my excitement to launch our war, I did not verify your claim. But the Fubuki were in position to invade Lodia, and it was logical to weaken all our foes at once. That mistake has cost me my emperor and control of Aokigahara. Still, it was one battle. We will yet win the war."

With that, Lord Melwar started walking toward Hiabi. Hana sighed in relief. Given the depth of her failures and the setbacks in their plan she'd caused, she had expected a greater punishment.

Lord Melwar had gone ten feet when he stopped and craned his neck around. "By the way," he said, "now that Iren is gone, I trust you will be spending your nights with me instead."

Hana balled her hands into fists. The gesture only made Lord Melwar smirk. So much for escaping punishment.

She hated him. He was no better than the human filth who had tried to rape her all those years ago. Hana had counted on Iren to be her savior. Had he stayed, had he become the emperor and she his empress, all the Maantecs would have united with them. They would have ruled over Raa, and together, they would have deposed and executed Lord Melwar. She would have been rid of him. She would have been free.

Hana recalled the feel of Iren's skin against her, his endearing timidity that first night they'd spent together. He'd been so innocent. She and Lord Melwar had ripped all that away.

What had they done to him?

Then a second face appeared in her memory, this time a human one. Human names weren't worth remembering, but this one came to her with ease. Balear smiled at her with an expression that promised he would protect her, even though he knew she didn't need protecting. As though it had just happened, she pictured him standing in front of the Ice Dragon Knight, blocking the Fubuki from her. He'd known he had no chance of victory, yet he'd offered up his life to save her. No one had ever done that for her.

She wished things could have turned out differently. She wished that Lord Melwar had never found her, that she had never become the Stone Dragon Knight, and that she had never handed over the Ice Dragon Hammer to that Fubuki. She wished she hadn't needed to betray Balear or make him lose an arm on her account. She wished that instead of sharing a futon with Iren or Lord Melwar, she was sharing one with him.

A twinge of pain rippled through Hana's arm. She looked at the scratch from Lord Melwar's shadow knife. "A reminder," he had called it. He was right.

Hana dropped her head and walked to the Maantec lord. Together they headed back to Hiabi.

CHAPTER FORTY-NINE
Oath

Balear was still in the abyss, but at least he'd stopped falling. He lay on his back on what felt like flat stone. Blinking his eyes made no difference. He saw only darkness either way.

A drop of water landed on his forehead. Balear started. He hadn't expected there to be rain in the afterlife.

Several feet away, other drops fell into a pool. Thirst attacked him. Balear scrambled over the stone. He cupped water in his hand and gulped it down.

Sated, Balear sat back and listened to the water drip from somewhere above him. If this was the afterlife, it was unlike any he'd ever pictured. He felt over his body. Everything seemed to be intact, except for two things. One was his missing right arm. The other was his hair. Someone had cut it short and shaved off his beard.

The change to his hair was odd enough, but he was also wearing new clothes. His outfit had ripped apart when he'd transformed into Ariok, but now he wore a woolen tunic and breeches.

Footsteps echoed nearby, though in the darkness Balear couldn't tell from where. A red light appeared in the distance, dim at first yet growing brighter in time with the steps. Balear groped for the Auryozaki, but he couldn't find it. He stood and raised his fist in preparation for a fight.

"Who's there?" he called, uncertain he wanted the answer.

The footsteps stopped. The red light wavered. "Balear?" a tentative voice asked. "Are you awake?"

Relief enveloped Balear. "Dirio!" he shouted. Then grief took him. "Does this mean we're both dead?"

The mayor's laugh echoed through wherever they were. "Not yet! You gave it a good try though."

Dirio's step quickened, and the light, which Balear could now see was from a torch in the mayor's hand, came closer. As it did, it illuminated some of the pool Balear had drunk from. It also cast a glow to the ceiling.

A memory came to Balear. He had been in this room before. "This is the cavern where the Quodivar imprisoned the people of Veliaf."

Dirio walked up to him and nodded. "Sorry to leave you down here by yourself," he said, "but the villagers were nervous about having you too close. They didn't even like the idea of having you aboveground since you'd be exposed to the sky."

Balear felt his heart—his beating, living heart—hammer in his chest. "Then you all survived!"

The mayor looked at the deep pool in the cavern's center. "Most of us," he said. Regret tinged his voice. "When the ice spread over the walls, we fought back with bows and arrows. That Fubuki Dragon Knight stopped our shots with shields of ice. I was there for some of it. I saw ice engulf my men and turn them to statues. After that, I realized we couldn't fight back. I ordered everyone to evacuate, but by then, Fubuki were pounding on the gate as well. Our only escape route was through the mine."

Balear could have hugged Dirio. The former general had forgotten all about Veliaf's mine, let alone how it connected to this cavern and ultimately to Akaku Forest.

"I'm sorry, Balear," Dirio continued, biting his lip. "I never should have thrown you out. If you hadn't shown up, those Fubuki would have killed everyone. Once they figured out we weren't in the village, they would have discovered the mine and come after us. You saved our lives."

In his mind, Balear heard Ariok's triumphant roar. He watched Veliaf shatter from the dragon's pressure wave. "No, you were right to send me away," he said. "I wasn't the one who stopped the Ice Dragon Knight. Ariok did. I let him take over my body."

Dirio grabbed Balear by the shoulder. "If you hadn't," the mayor insisted, "you would have died, and all of us would have too. There is nothing to feel guilty about."

"But Veliaf—"

"Was destroyed before you reached us. No one was in the village when Ariok cast his spell. In a way, the Sky Dragon did us a favor. We would have needed to rebuild Veliaf anyway after having everything covered in ice. He cleared the debris for us."

"But you can't rebuild," Balear said. "Without your wall, you no longer have protection. You'd be vulnerable to the Lodian cities. The civil war is still going on."

Dirio nodded solemnly. "I know. Actually, I've known Veliaf couldn't last for a long time now. Even if the Fubuki hadn't come, the first city's army that showed up at our gate would have meant our end. We're only a few hundred people. I would have surrendered to whomever showed up first."

"What will you do now?"

"The villagers decided to head for Kataile, south of Ceere along the coast. Ceere's in no shape to handle refugees, and Terkou's reputation is too rough for me. Kataile's a tourist town, or at least it was before the war. They're used to outsiders. Plus, they have access to the sea, so they should have plenty of food. We'll join up with them. I hope you'll come with us. They might not be keen to have a couple hundred more mouths to feed, but they'll take us more seriously if we offer a Dragon Knight in return."

Balear thought about it. It meant the end of Veliaf, but at least this way its people could continue living.

In the end, though, he shook his head. "I'll come with you," he said, "but I can't go as a Dragon Knight."

"Can't?" Dirio asked, cocking an eyebrow. "Or won't?"

"Both," Balear growled. "How can you say you want me to go as a Dragon Knight? Did you see what I did to Veliaf?"

"As I recall, the Fubuki froze the village, and Ariok turned it into splinters," Dirio said. "You didn't do anything to it."

"But how can you trust me? How do you know I won't destroy Kataile? Next time, you might not have a handy cavern to escape into."

"That's the risk I take," the mayor admitted, "but I'd be taking a bigger risk showing up at Kataile with nothing to help them win the war. We don't have many weapons, and we don't have any soldiers. Other than me, those few who could fight died trying to stop the Fubuki."

The thought of going to Kataile as the Sky Dragon Knight made Balear sick. Dirio could convince himself that Balear wasn't to blame for Veliaf's fall, but Balear couldn't. He knew how easily he'd given Ariok control. Worse, he knew that in a similar situation, he would do it again.

Maybe, though, there was another choice. The only reason Ariok had taken over was because Balear had used magic. If he didn't cast any spells, Ariok wouldn't have a chance to overwhelm his mind.

"All right, Dirio," he said, "I'll go to Kataile with you. I'll even come as a Dragon Knight. I owe you that much after everything you've done for me, and after all the pain I've caused Veliaf. But I have one condition. Don't ask me to cast any spells. From this moment on, I swear I will never use magic again."

Dirio rocked back on his heels. It took him a moment to recover. "I don't know how Kataile will take that," he said at last. "Still, I know by now that I can't persuade you once you've made up your mind."

Balear smiled, but his expression quickly darkened. "There's one problem with your plan," he said. "I have no idea where the Auryozaki is. You won't convince anyone in Kataile that I'm a Dragon Knight without it."

"That's no problem," Dirio said. "We carried you here after the battle and dressed you in a spare set of clothes one of the women was thoughtful enough to bring with her. The Auryozaki, though, was beyond us. Four of us tried to lift it, but we couldn't make it budge. It seems you're the only one who can carry it. It's waiting for you where Ariok dropped it. We'll head up to Akaku Forest and join the rest of the villagers. We grabbed only what we could carry on our way into the mine, so it won't take long for us to get on our way. You can retrieve the Auryozaki as we head past Veliaf on our trip to Kataile."

Dirio paused, and then he held up a finger. "Oh, that reminds me!" he said. "I have a present for you."

He guided Balear to the far end of the room and up the tunnel that led to Akaku. At one of the side chambers, Dirio gestured for Balear to enter. The mayor then stepped to the far end of the room and held up a leather harness. "I asked the blacksmith and leathersmith to team up on this," he said. "I intended it to be a reward when you came back to us."

The mayor offered the strange creation to Balear. "What is it?" the soldier asked.

"Let me show you," Dirio said with a grin. He took the harness and strapped it onto Balear's back. It hung balanced on both collarbones. Reaching back with his left hand, Balear felt a strip of metal along the top passing between his shoulder blades.

"That strip is magnetic," Dirio said. "Some of the metal in the mine is naturally that way. Used to give us all kinds of trouble, but for you it should be perfect. It occurred to me that since your sword is weightless when you have it, the magnet should hold it in place. Even with one arm, you can carry the Auryozaki with you anywhere and still have your hand free."

Balear marveled at the harness and its craftsmanship. It had clearly been designed with a one-armed man in mind. He could both take it off and put it back on with just his left hand.

Tears welled in the soldier's eyes. "This is more than I deserve," he said. "Thank you."

Dirio smiled but said only, "Let's head up now. The trip to Kataile will take a few weeks at best, likely longer with all the snow. The sooner we go, the better."

The mayor led the way as the pair followed the passage to the surface. It was after dark, but most of the villagers were awake, clustered around fires for warmth. Dirio called them together and announced his intention to leave at dawn. There were some grumblings, but everyone knew it was the only decision they had.

Of course, that didn't stop them from glaring at Balear. He flushed. Dirio might have forgiven him, but that didn't mean his people had.

After facing their angry expressions for a few minutes, Balear needed to escape. He left the survivors and headed south.

He paused in shock when he reached the border between Akaku and Lodia. The aftermath of Veliaf's destruction was more horrifying than he had dared to imagine. Where once a thriving town had stood, only a flat ring of debris remained.

Balear walked the short distance from Akaku to Veliaf. As he approached, he realized "debris" was too optimistic a term to describe what was left. The largest piece was smaller than his hand. Shards stretched for miles, and some had even embedded themselves in Akaku's trees.

He clenched his fist. This was why the dragons had been imprisoned. They might provide great power, but they were not benevolent.

Amid the rubble, Balear saw the Auryozaki spearing the ground. Even at night, it was easy to spot; it was the only object still standing in the village. Balear pulled it from the soil and held it in front of his face. "You weren't there for my oath," he told the sword, "so I'll say it again. Don't expect to escape a second time. I will never use magic again."

If Ariok could hear him, the dragon gave no sign. Balear didn't care one way or the other. Ariok no longer mattered.

Balear placed the Auryozaki against his harness's magnet. The sword stayed in place when he let it go.

He smiled. He didn't need magic. Even without it, he was still the Sky Dragon Knight.

"I promise you," he said to the ruins of Veliaf, "I'll end this war, and I won't let this happen to any more towns."

Satisfied, he returned to the villagers in Akaku.

CHAPTER FIFTY
Beneath Strange Stars

Minawë jolted awake. Something was wrong, out of place. No, someone was out of place.

Iren was gone.

She raced out of the cavern where they'd been resting. It was the middle of the night. Stars and a sliver of moon filled the sky.

Her eyes darted over the landscape. At last she spied the form of a man walking away from the cave. He must have left just a few seconds ago, because he was only a hundred feet from her.

"Iren!"

The man stopped. "I didn't want to wake you," he said without turning around.

That voice, at once familiar and foreign, took Minawë aback. She choked up as she asked, "Does this mean you're going back to Melwar?"

He didn't answer right away. Minawë's breath caught in her throat. The only reason Iren could have for not answering was if that answer were yes.

She wouldn't allow it. She couldn't allow it. She reached for the Chloryoblaka, but in her haste, she'd left it in the cavern. If she went to get it, Iren would be gone by the time she returned.

Iren looked at the sky. Minawë found herself following his gaze. The stars here were different than those she had seen from the canopy of Ziorsecth. They made her realize how far she had come since leaving her forest home.

At great length Iren lowered his eyes and, to Minawë's relief, faced her. "No," he said, "Hana admitted to Rondel's accusation about the

Karyozaki. I risked my life to seal away Feng. The world was free of him, and Melwar brought him back just to fulfill his outdated wish for Maantec dominance. I can't return to him, knowing that."

"Then that means you're coming back with us!" The words sounded desperate even to her. "You only came out here for some fresh air."

Iren shook his head. "I can't go with you. Rondel would never allow it. Right now she's helpless. I doubt she has enough magic to cast Lightning Sight, let alone hit me with a spell like what she used today. Give her a few days, though, and she'll have enough magic to challenge me again."

Minawë's heart beat faster. She could barely breathe. "Where will you go?" she asked. "We're in the middle of nowhere."

"I don't know yet. All I know is that, for the moment, I need to be alone."

"But why?" Minawë cried. "Why do you need to be alone? We're your friends, Iren! We came all the way across Raa to bring you home."

"Maybe you did," Iren said, "but Rondel didn't. You heard her today. She came knowing she would kill me. That was always the purpose of your journey. You just helped her get here. It's hard to swallow, I know, but she used you."

His cynical tone cut deeper than a sword. Minawë wanted to lash out at him, to scream, to tell him he was being a moron, but she couldn't speak. She stood frozen to the ground.

"I trusted Amroth," Iren continued, "and he used me to gain power. I trusted Rondel, and she murdered my parents. I trusted Melwar and Hana, and they planned to turn me into a puppet emperor. I've tried over and over again to trust others, and every time, I'm betrayed. That's why I'm better off alone." He put his back to her and started walking again.

Minawë's fists shook with rage. This time she found her voice. "What about me?" she demanded. "How have I betrayed you?"

Iren stopped again. "Where did you fight today?" he asked.

"The same place as you," she snapped.

"Then you should understand. When I moved to attack Rondel, you shielded her with your own body."

"Because I don't want either of you to die! Because I love you both!"

Iren whipped around. Minawë thought she'd broken through to him, but then he lowered his head and shook it. "You can't love us both," he said, "and it's pointless for you not to want one of us to die."

He looked Minawë in the eye. Even in the dark, she could see the determination on his face. "I am going to kill Rondel," he declared. "She murdered my parents. I won't forgive her for that. I wasn't strong enough today, but I'll keep training until I am."

"So you'll choose revenge?" Minawë asked. "I told you before that revenge can't make you happy. It can't make anyone happy."

"You think I care about happiness? My happiness vanished eighteen years ago when Rondel took away my parents."

"I tried to stop you today. What if I do that again?"

Iren looked her up and down. "I don't know if you'll believe me or not, but I do still care for you. That's why I'm walking away tonight. I could have killed Rondel while she was helpless. I held back on your account. But I will fight her again; that's a promise. If you get in my way when that day comes, I'll kill you as well."

Minawë felt lightheaded. She knew what she had to say next. "If that's how you feel," she told him, "then you've turned into the very person you despise so much. If you kill Rondel, you'll do to me what she did to you. Is that what you want? For me to wind up like you? I'd have to kill you then! And when I did, surely someone would mourn your loss. Balear, perhaps? He would come after me. The cycle will never stop."

"So stop it. When I kill Rondel, let me go."

"How can I do that? She's—"

"Your mother?" Iren finished. "Exactly."

Hot tears flooded Minawë's eyes. This wasn't the Iren who had rescued her from the Quodivar. This wasn't the Iren who had become the Dragoon to protect everyone from Feng. That Iren was gone.

She should kill him. It horrified her that the thought came so readily, yet she knew it was the right thing to do. If she let him live, he would become more dangerous even than Iren Saito.

Iren put his back to Minawë once more. This was her only chance. He wouldn't expect an attack. There was no way he had recovered from his fight with Rondel. Granted, Minawë wasn't in perfect condition herself, but she could manage it. She wouldn't need the Chloryoblaka. She could channel magic into the ground, make a vine sprout beneath Iren, and pierce him with poison needles before he knew what was happening.

She could do it. She should do it. Mother would have done it. Both of her mothers would have done it.

As Iren walked away, Minawë stayed where she was. She watched him shrink. Finally he vanished into the night.

Minawë fell to her knees and wept.

℁

From the cavern entrance, Rondel saw Iren disappear. She saw her daughter collapse. Her lips pursed.

Any lingering doubts she might have had were gone. Evil must be annihilated. It had escaped her this time, but next time it would not. She and Iren would fight again. When they did, Iren Saitosan would die.

ABOUT THE AUTHOR

Josh VanBrakle is a Left who is overjoyed to live in an age when authors can type their stories instead of handwriting them. He is the author of two fantasy novels, including the award-winning *The Wings of Dragons*.

When he isn't writing, Josh works as an education forester at an environmental non-profit promoting rural land conservation. Originally from Hershey, Chocolatetown USA, Josh now lives in the Catskill Mountains of upstate New York with his wife Christine and two ill-behaved cats.

Writing *The Dragoon Saga* has been Josh's dream since high school. It's his first book series, so please let him and other readers know what you thought of it by reviewing this book wherever you purchased it. Josh appreciates these reviews and uses them to grow as an author and improve future books.

To stay up to date with the latest news about upcoming titles in *The Dragoon Saga*, please visit www.joshvanbrakle.com or follow Josh on Twitter @joshvanbrakle.